THEY DANCED ON

They Danced On

a Darling Family novel

CARRE ARMSTRONG GARDNER

Tyndale House Publishers, Inc.
Carol Stream, Illinois

Visit Tyndale online at www.tyndale.com.

Visit Carre Armstrong Gardner's website at www.carregardner.com.

TYNDALE and Tyndale's quill logo are registered trademarks of Tyndale House Publishers, Inc.

They Danced On

Designed by Jennifer Ghionzoli

Edited by Sarah Mason Rische

Published in association with literary agent Blair Jacobson of D.C. Jacobson & Associates LLC, an Author Management Company. www.dcjacobson.com.

They Danced On is a work of fiction. Where real people, events, establishments, organizations, or locales appear, they are used fictitiously. All other elements of the novel are drawn from the author's imagination.

Library of Congress Cataloging-in-Publication Data

Names: Gardner, Carre Armstrong, author.
Title: They danced on : a Darling family novel / Carre Armstrong Gardner.
Description: Carol Stream, Illinois : Tyndale House Publishers, Inc., [2016]
  | Series: The Darlings
Identifiers: LCCN 2016000706 | ISBN 9781414388168 (sc)
Subjects: LCSH: Families—Maine—Fiction. | Amyotrophic Lateral Sclerosis—Fiction.
  | Recovering addicts—Fiction. | Domestic fiction. | GSAFD: Christian fiction.
Classification: LCC PS3607.A7267 T54 2016 | DDC 813/.6—dc23 LC record available
  at http://lccn.loc.gov/2016000706

Printed in the United States of America

22   21   20   19   18   17   16
 7   6   5   4   3   2   1

To my own darling mother, Wanda Jane Leigh Armstrong:
the hub around which our wheel of family turns.

CHAPTER

1

THERE WERE FEW BETTER PLEASURES in life, thought Jane Darling, than to sit on the screened side porch on a Saturday morning in June, in the white wicker chair, with her coffee and oatmeal, and listen to the day wake up around her. All her life, Jane had risen with the birds; she never used an alarm clock.

A year ago, Leander might have been joining her now, rummaging in the cupboard for his favorite mug, the white one that said *Aetna, for life*. It had come free from an insurance company, and he liked it because it was tall and thick and kept his coffee hot longer than other cups. Now, it was just Jane and the birds. She watched a male cardinal light on the crab apple tree, a small slash of scarlet against the riot of pink. From high in the branches, a white-throated sparrow unspooled its sweet-and-sour thread of song against the lightening sky.

When she had finished her oatmeal, Jane flipped the pages of her worn, pen-marked Bible until she found what she was looking for. *"Praise the Lord, my soul, and forget not all his benefits—who forgives all your sins and heals all your diseases . . ."*

One floor above her, Leander still slept. He had always been an early riser too. Sleeping late was the luxury of the very young and the very old, he said. But her husband was neither very young nor very old; he was sick. Fallen prey, at the age of sixty-two, to a nearly unpronounceable disease abbreviated to three innocuous letters: *ALS.*

It sounded so innocent. Like a committee she might have joined during her children's school years: *Academic Leadership Seminar.* Or possibly some kind of nonprofit: *American Literary Society.* But Leander had drawn no such harmless lot. His collection of letters stood for something far more malignant: *Amyotrophic Lateral Sclerosis.* Lou Gehrig's disease. And day by day, Jane stood by and watched as her husband's body wilted in the grip of this wasting illness like an uprooted plant in the hot sun.

These days, he stayed in bed until eight o'clock. Jane would listen for the thump of his feet on the floor, then head upstairs to putter about the bedroom while he washed and dressed in the attached bath. She would make the bed, and straighten the dresser tops, maybe fold a load of laundry with one ear attuned to the bathroom door, in case he should call for help.

". . . who redeems your life from the pit . . . so that your youth is renewed like the eagle's."

He could still shower by himself, although he was slow at it. In the spring, a man had come and installed bars in the bath and around the toilet. There was a seat in the shower now, too, which their daughter Sephy had helped her pick out at a medical supply store in Quahog. Jane had protested these changes, insisting they were not necessary, but her children had overridden her. Even David, who never made waves, had said, "Mom, it's time. What if he falls?"

"He's not going to fall," Jane had snapped. She never snapped at David.

"His balance is off. He stumbles all the time," Ivy pointed out.

"Amy and I are both here with him."

"But you and I can't be around every minute, especially not in the bathroom," said Amy. Her youngest was always quick enough to offer an unsolicited opinion.

Sephy, who was a nurse, added, "The bars will help him stay independent longer, Mom, that's all."

Jane had been exasperated. Where was their faith? Did not God promise, right in His Word, that He would heal those who asked Him? And it was not as though she and Leander were old and senile and needed their children making decisions for them. They were not even retirement age, and both of them fully in their right minds! But in the end, it was Leander who had agreed with the rest of the family, and she had no choice but to acquiesce. It was a hard thing, she was finding, to have your grown children veto you in matters of your own household. Behaving as though you were the child, and not the other way around.

It was only six o'clock, and Leander would sleep for a couple of hours yet. Jane said her prayers, then put her Bible aside, opened a spiral-bound notebook, and started three lists. One, she titled *Graduation Party*; the second, *Wedding Reception*. The third was for groceries. Under each of the first two headings, she wrote *potato salad*. No summer gathering would be complete without it. But since the two celebrations were happening the same weekend, she would make two different kinds.

For DeShaun's party on Friday, she would make his favorite: red bliss potatoes with bacon and just a hint of dill pickle juice in the dressing. She smiled as she wrote down the ingredients she would need. Her first grandson was graduating from high school! He had come into their lives only four years ago, but it seemed to Jane that there had always been a space in their family waiting for him to come along and fill it. The awkward, quiet boy who had once been so busy taking care of his little brother and sister that he had never given a thought to dreams of his own had blossomed into a deep-voiced, focused young man who loved to cook. He was still quiet, and still protective of the younger ones, but he knew where he was going now: he was going to culinary school. And while other boys in his class were asking for cars or laptops as graduation gifts, what DeShaun wanted was a good set of chef's knives. This, Jane knew, would be Ivy and Nick's gift to him. She and Leander had bought him a Vitamix. Even DeShaun's brother, nine-year-old Hammer, seemed to realize the importance of the occasion. He had saved his own money for fireworks, which Nick had taken him to buy the previous weekend. It would be a graduation party such as Copper Cove had never seen before; it would make up for all the parties DeShaun had missed in his life.

Red bliss potato salad for DeShaun, then. For Sephy's wedding reception, she would make her daughter's favorite, with buttermilk dressing and dill. There would be no big wedding, only a quiet ceremony before the justice of the peace on Saturday and a small picnic reception in the backyard before Sephy and Justice caught a flight for Namibia. There, they would each work in a clinic: she, vaccinating children, and he, vetting goats and cattle and any other creatures the African community might lead his way.

Cake, she wrote under each heading. Ivy would make DeShaun's cake. Sephy's had already been ordered from a bakery in Quahog. *Settlers' beans* went in DeShaun's column. For Sephy's—

A loud thump sounded from overhead. Jane froze. It was the sound of something much heavier than Leander's feet hitting the floor. *Oh, God—*

She dropped the notebook and pencil and bolted for the stairs, every nerve electrified.

Leander, in his white T-shirt and flannel pajama pants, lay on the floor beside the bed.

"Oh, honey!" She dropped to her knees. "What happened?"

"I fell."

"I can see that." Instinctively, she groped along his arms and legs. "Are you hurt?"

"I don't think so. I got up to go to the bathroom and just . . . tripped over my own feet."

"You didn't hit your head?"

"No. My arm will be black and blue, but I think that's all." With an effort, Leander shifted onto his back. Looking at the ceiling, he said, "Help me sit up, will you?"

She put an arm under his shoulders. He was all bones,

these days. "Up you go!" She heaved him to a sitting position and felt a twinge of pain between her own shoulder blades. "Can you stand from here?"

He pushed ineffectually at the floor and shook his head. "You'll have to help me."

Jane had no idea how to go about doing that. "Maybe if you put your arms around my neck, I could sort of pull you up?"

"You'll put your back out. And I don't know if I'm strong enough to hold on. Can you get Amy?"

"She left for the gym an hour ago."

"She should be back soon."

"We're not leaving you on the floor until Amy gets home. I'll call rescue."

"Don't do that. This is humiliating enough without lights and sirens and the whole neighborhood coming out to watch. Call Sephy. Maybe she can tell you how to get a hundred-sixty-pound man off the floor by yourself."

Had he lost over thirty pounds already from this wretched disease? Jane used the bedside phone to call Sephy. Her third daughter answered by saying, "What's wrong?"

"Did I wake you?"

"Of course you woke me; it's six forty in the morning. Is everything all right?"

"Your father's fallen, and I can't get him off the floor. Amy's not home, and he doesn't want me to call rescue."

"Is he hurt?"

"He says not. We did manage to sit him up."

"Should I come?"

"No, you're half an hour away. We can't leave him on the floor that long. Just tell me what to do."

"Okay. Put me on speakerphone so you have both hands free."

Jane obeyed. Following her daughter's instructions, she stood behind Leander and wrapped her arms around his chest.

"Lift with your legs, Mom, not your back!"

"I am!"

To her surprise, it worked.

"Got your balance?" Jane asked, when her husband was standing.

"Yep. I'm okay." The tremor in his voice belied his words.

"He's up," she called toward the phone.

"Should you just run over to UrgiCare, Dad? Make sure nothing's broken?"

Leander managed a smile. "Nothing's broken but my dignity. I'd rather pretend this never happened."

"If you're sure . . ."

"I'm sure. Thank you, Sephy. I hope you can go back to sleep."

"No, I'll stay up. I have packing to do. I'm glad you're okay."

When their daughter had hung up, Leander reminded Jane, "I never did make it into the bathroom."

"You feel steady enough?"

"I'm all right."

"I'll follow you, just to be sure."

In the bathroom, the ugly metal bars along the toilet and bathtub gleamed smugly at her. Jane looked away. The man who had installed them had drilled holes in the plaster and tile of her beautiful walls. He had secured the bars with huge,

heavy bolts and some kind of cement. They were a permanent part of the structure now. Even when the day came that
they were no longer needed, when Leander was better and
the man came back to take the bars away, the scars they left
would always be there. You would never get rid of holes like
those.

The morning of DeShaun's graduation dawned cool, with a
fine, drizzling rain. "It figures," Ivy said to Nick, over breakfast. "We made arrangements for an outdoor party, with no
contingency plan, and now it's going to rain all day."

"It'll clear up" was her husband's unhelpful reply from
behind his newspaper.

"It had better." Ivy, who was eating from a take-out container of leftover linguine with clam sauce, pointed the fork
at Nick. "It had just *better* clear up, or we're in trouble."

"Do you have to eat fish and garlic this early in the morning?" said Nick, over his own sensible breakfast of whole-
wheat toast and scrambled egg whites. "It stinks the whole
house up."

"Sorry," she said, twirling linguine around her fork with
great concentration. "But seriously, what are we going to do
if it doesn't stop raining?"

"It will stop."

"But if it doesn't?"

Nick sighed. "If it doesn't stop, we'll move the party in-
doors somewhere. I don't know . . . the community arts center, maybe."

"There's an idea! But Amy might say no. She might consider it nepotism to let her nephew use her arts center for a private party."

"This isn't business or politics, so does it matter? Besides, Amy doesn't own the arts center; she only directs it."

"Or the church. We could have it at the church."

"Stop worrying, Ivy. The rain will be over by graduation. The forecast says so."

Nick and the weather forecast turned out to be right, as usual. By ten o'clock, the rain had subsided, and the sun was rapidly warming the wet world to greenhouse levels of heat and humidity.

"*Wow*, it turned hot," Ivy said. She was in her bedroom, trying to tame her daughter's thick, frizzy hair into two French braids, something she was never very adept at, even when the humidity wasn't 80 percent.

"You don't know how to do black hair, that's *your* problem," she was informed by Jada, who was thirteen and thought everyone had a problem. "If you'd just let me get cornrows, you wouldn't have to go through this every day. Cornrows are amazing: you get them once and they last for *months*."

"Do you know how much cornrows cost?" Ivy finished one braid with an elastic and, moving Jada bodily a quarter turn to the right, began on the second. "Besides, where would you get them done? You're the only black girl in a thirty-mile radius. What hairdresser around here is going to know how to do cornrows?"

"We could go to Bangor."

"*Or* we could just French braid your hair every day." Ivy finished the second, very creditable braid, and gave it a tweak. "You look lovely. Now go put your dress on."

Jada rolled her eyes and sighed heavily as she went.

"And I've seen just about enough of the whites of your eyes, miss!" Ivy called after her.

DeShaun appeared in the doorway of the bedroom, wearing his blue graduation gown. "Why I gotta wear a dress shirt and pants under this thing? It's like a sauna. Can't I just wear shorts and a T-shirt?"

"And have eight inches of hairy legs showing, with your bare feet in flip-flops? I don't think so."

"I bet everybody else wears shorts under theirs."

"This is high school graduation, DeShaun. It happens once in a lifetime. You can dress up for it."

Hammer came racing down the hall and careened into his brother, knocking him forward a few inches. "Go in just your underwear, DeShaun!"

DeShaun ignored him. "Just a T-shirt at least, then."

"Underwear, underwear, DeShaun's wearing his underwear!" Hammer chanted. "I'm telling everyone!"

"Shut up, Hammer!" DeShaun cuffed his younger brother on the back of the head. Hammer punched him, hard, in the arm. DeShaun got him into a headlock and dragged him into the bedroom. "Come on, Mom," he called, above his brother's shrieks. "I could wear the pants and dress shoes with a T-shirt instead of this long-sleeved thing with a collar and necktie. It'll suffocate me."

"He has a point," said Nick, who was already beginning to look damp around the edges in his own sport coat and tie.

"Let me go!" Hammer, kicking wildly at anything within reach, caught Nick in the leg.

"Ow! DeShaun, let go of your brother."

DeShaun let go of Hammer and gave him a push backward, into the hall.

"DeShaun pushed me!"

"Come on, just let me wear the T-shirt."

Hammer let out a piercing yell of indignation.

Ivy put her fingertips to her temples. "All right. You can wear a T-shirt under your gown. But the same rule applies today as for church: no stains—"

"No holes," DeShaun finished for her. "I know." He made for his bedroom to change out of the offending dress shirt and tie, pulling Hammer into another headlock as he went, and dragging him, screaming, down the hall.

"Oh, my aching head," said Ivy to her husband.

The high school auditorium was already crowded when they arrived. Ivy's youngest sister, Amy, and her best friend, Mitch, were already there, saving a row of seats. Ivy gave a little wave to Nick's family, across the aisle, and sat down, fanning herself with the paper program. "It is *hot* in here."

"Tell me about it. Hottest day of the year, so far."

"I'm thirsty," said Hammer, pulling at Ivy's sleeve. "Can I get a drink?"

"You know where the drinking fountain is—but come right back!" she finished in the direction of her son's head, which, bobbing and weaving, disappeared at once into the crowd.

Her parents arrived, with Grammie Lydia Darling, eighty-five years old but looking fifteen years younger in a mint-green dress. "So, our boy's graduating!" She bent to kiss Ivy on the cheek. Sephy came after that, squeezing Ivy's hand as she edged past and saying, "I'm so proud of DeShaun I can't stand it!" David, the oldest, and his wife, Libby, slipped in just as the school superintendent stepped to the microphone and cleared his throat. Ivy looked down the row of her family with a great swell of fondness. Except for Laura, who lived in Phoenix, they were all here. Each of them had embraced DeShaun so wholeheartedly, when he had come into their family. . . . Every one of them was as proud to watch him graduate as they would have been if—

A silent, instinctive warning bell interrupted her thoughts. *"Nick!"* she hissed. "Where's Hammer?"

Her husband looked around. "I thought you had him."

"He went to the drinking fountain, but I told him to come right back. That was fifteen minutes ago!"

Nick closed his eyes briefly, then stood and shuffled past the row of knees to the aisle.

Ivy's mother shot her a puzzled glance.

"Hammer," Ivy mouthed, rolling her eyes.

"Ah!" Her mother flashed a better-you-than-me smile and turned her attention back to the superintendent, who was introducing the Copper Cove High School class of 2016.

Ivy stood to applaud with the rest of the crowd and put Hammer out of her mind. Nick would bring him back. But by the time the superintendent finished speaking and turned the podium over to the principal, neither of them had returned.

That was when the first burst of gunfire sounded from the hallway.

Ivy's breath left her. The auditorium erupted in screams.

"Get down!" the principal shouted into the microphone. "Everybody get *down on the floor*. Down. On. The. Floor! Close those doors!" He pointed toward the back of the auditorium, where two fathers sprang forward to obey, pulling the double doors closed on either side.

Nick. Hammer. Where are they? From her kneeling position, wedged between her own seat and the seat back in front of her, Ivy scanned the front of the auditorium, trying to catch a glimpse of black skin. *DeShaun! Where's DeShaun?* She could tell nothing. The stage was a mass of blue and white gowns: the backs of the graduates, crouched between the rows of chairs for protection.

A second spatter of shots sounded. More screams. Ivy thought her heart would choke her. Nick and Hammer were out there, somewhere.

One of the doors slammed open, and a wave of terror moved over the crowd, like wind over a wheat field. "It's okay!" a voice called. "It's not a gun! It's just some kid, setting off firecrackers in the hall."

Ivy groaned. She did not have to lift her head to see who "some kid" was. As the friends and neighbors and families of her community climbed stiffly off the floor, buzzing with adrenaline-fueled righteous indignation, Ivy crawled on her hands and knees into the aisle, got to her feet, and tried her best to be invisible as she made her way to the corridor, where she would collect her youngest son and, very probably, have to face a police report as well.

2

WHILE DESHAUN'S GRADUATION PARTY was in full swing, Sephy's bridegroom arrived on an afternoon flight from the West Coast. He was picked up by the bride-to-be at the airport in Quahog, half an hour away. Sephy and Justice had not seen each other in more than a month, and though Jane could not help but notice that it took them substantially longer than thirty minutes to make it from the airport back to the party, she nevertheless vowed not to say a word about it. As the wedding the next morning was to be a simple civil ceremony at the town hall, there was no rehearsal. Instead, at seven, the Darlings reconvened for dinner at The Lobster Pot, with their longtime neighbors the Hales.

With sixteen at dinner, the restaurant had reserved a private room for them. David Darling, as Justice Hale's best man, welcomed them all with a toast. "I know Sephy and

Justice wanted to keep this whole wedding as quick and quiet as possible, because they have bigger fish to fry: namely, a plane to catch for Africa tomorrow night, where they'll start their new life together.

"Sephy has never liked to be the center of attention, and neither has Justice, so they made me promise not to make a big deal out of either of them tonight. Still, I feel like we should have at least one speech on the eve of their wedding."

"Hear, hear!" from Amy's end of the table.

"I promise, though, that it won't be about them. Or at least not *much* about them."

Polite laughter. David cleared his throat. "The Darling and Hale families have lived next door to each other for over two decades. We've ridden the same school bus, grown up in the same church, shared backyard barbecues . . . and eventually, Justice and I each decided it would be a pretty good idea to marry the girl next door." He looked down at Libby, who was Justice's sister, and winked at her.

"It seems to me," he went on, "that there aren't many places left where that kind of thing can still happen. Statistics tell us that most Americans live in cities now, and the average family moves once every five years. Small towns, where people have the same neighbors for decades, and grow up with them, and love them, are a vanishing way of life. I think that's too bad, because the Darling family has been richer for having Tom and Abigail, Libby and Justice be part of our lives all these years. And I hope—" he turned and gave a little bow to the Hale parents—"that you might be able to say the same about the big, noisy, chaotic family that grew up directly to the left of you."

Tom and Abigail Hale both murmured their smiling assent.

"Tomorrow, Sephy and Justice will be married and on their way to the other side of the world. I think I speak for all of us when I say that although we will miss them every single day, we can't help but admire the selflessness that's taking them there—Sephy, our nurse, to care for the human population, and Justice, our veterinarian, to care for the animals that are so vital to the Namibians' way of life. Your compassion and dedication, Sephy and Justice, speak volumes about you and the parents who raised you."

Raucous applause, with much hooting and cheering, from the Darling and Hale children.

David held up his hands for silence and went on. "I count us all fortunate that, with Libby marrying me and Sephy marrying Justice, our families, who have always been friends, only get to become more closely entwined. So here's to Sephy and Justice, and their new life." He lifted his glass. "And to neighbors, family, and friends . . . and to having them all be the same people."

"To Sephy and Justice!" The rest of them raised their glasses and drank.

Out in the main dining room, a live band was playing, and as some of the party lingered over coffee and dessert, others slipped away in pairs to the small dance floor. First Nick and Ivy went, followed by Justice and Sephy, David and Libby. Amy and Mitch stayed at the table, because Mitch could not dance and flatly refused to try. He had succumbed once, six months before, to Amy's pleas that he dance with her at David and Libby's wedding. They had danced one number—if Mitch standing in one place and shuffling his feet could be called dancing—and once had been enough for him. He had declared himself exempt from that particular activity for the rest of his life, and he meant to stick by it.

Jane watched as Tom and Abigail rose to join the others for a slow number, and was surprised when Leander stood as well and held out his hand to her. "Shall we?"

She regarded him dubiously. "Do you think you're up to it?"

"Don't expect any fancy footwork, and I might have to lean on you a bit, but I think I could still work my way around the edge of a dance floor."

"In that case . . ." She took his hand and smiled. "I would be delighted."

On the small stage, a young woman was singing about having loved someone for a thousand years, and loving him for a thousand more. Leander pulled Jane into his arms and began a fox-trot. He smiled down at her. "Remember when we took dancing lessons?"

"In nearly thirty-six years of marriage, it's still one of the most romantic things we've ever done together."

"Ten lessons on waltz, fox-trot, and swing: just enough to get us through our wedding reception looking respectable. I never expected to love dancing, but darned if I didn't surprise myself."

"After those ten lessons, we just kept practicing and practicing. Remember dancing around the tiny kitchen in our first apartment?"

"And later, when David was a baby, around the living room of the house, while he watched from his playpen?"

"That was before we tore up all that old carpeting and

found the lovely hardwood floors underneath. Dancing was a lot easier after that."

"We got pretty good, didn't we?"

"*You* got pretty good, at least. You're the kind of leader who makes it easy to follow."

"And you've always had a way of setting me straight when I miss a step, without making it seem like you're doing it."

"We're not such a bad old pair, are we?"

He kissed her on the forehead. "Best dance partners in the world."

Sephy's wedding day dawned cool and clear, the sticky heat of the previous day having been relieved by a short, violent thunderstorm that arrived from New Hampshire in the night, vented its feelings for half an hour over Maine's down east coast, and blew out to sea by two o'clock in the morning, taking the humidity along with it.

The ceremony before the justice of the peace was short and sweet. As Ivy later told her mother, it seemed no time at all before the vows were said, the pair was wed, the crowd was fed, and both families were standing in the driveway of 14 Ladyslipper Lane, waving good-bye while Sephy, incandescent with joy, hung out of the car window and waved madly back. David and Libby were driving the bride and groom and their mountain of luggage to the airport.

When Sephy had hugged her good-bye, she'd said, "Don't worry about me, Mom. That's God's job."

Jane had laughed through her tears. "I'm a mom," she said. "Worrying about my kids goes with the territory." It might seem there was much to worry about. Sephy and Justice had only discovered that they loved each other at New Year's. Such a short time ago. Most of their engagement had been spent apart as they wrapped up the details of their separate lives on opposite coasts. Could a marriage begun in love's infancy survive a whole lifetime? Still, Jane reminded herself, Sephy had a good head on her shoulders. And Justice was a steady young man. They had known him all his life. If any two people could make a go of it, they could.

And now, Jane was waving good-bye to part of the bedrock of her own life: the nearness of this sweet, supportive daughter who was also a friend. Who knew when they would see each other again? Watching them go, she did not even try to stem the tears that flowed freely down her face.

Beside her, Leander put an arm around her shoulders and gave her a squeeze.

"Another one gone." She searched her pockets for a Kleenex. "First Ivy, then Laura and David, now Sephy." She blew her nose and wiped her eyes. "And twice this week, Amy's mentioned getting her own apartment."

"They were always going to grow up and move away, I suppose."

"It's just that it's all happening at once. I don't think I'm quite ready for an empty nest yet. I thought I was, but I'm not."

"I know," he said, putting his other arm around her and pulling her close. "I know just what you mean."

❧

Laura Darling woke at 4:59, as she did every morning, remembered it was Saturday and she didn't have to work, and rolled onto her back to consider the ceiling. Get up or sleep in? She felt dizzy; she'd had too much wine last night, although she hadn't meant to. Dizziness tinged with regret was never a good start to the day. Hydration was the cure for the first; distraction would fix the second. She sat up and pushed back the covers.

In the kitchen, she flipped the switch on the coffeepot and drank a glass of water as she thought about the day before her. She had a salad and dessert to make for the church picnic at the reservoir this afternoon. She noted the faint rasping of anxiety that had begun, like sandpaper beneath her skin. The prospect of being around a lot of Christians always had this effect on her. It would be fine, she told herself. They were her friends. The picnic would be fun, and by the time the fireworks started, she would be more than glad she'd gone.

Opening the fridge, she took inventory and decided a run to the store was called for. Feta cheese, dill, and kalamata olives for the salad . . . heavy cream, eggs, and coconut for the coconut cream pie bars. From the top shelf, the black box beckoned to her. *Five o'clock in the morning is five o'clock somewhere,* it seemed to say. She could appreciate the humor of this. *Just a small one, then.* Taking a coffee cup from the cupboard, she poured herself half a cup of white wine and drank it while the coffee finished brewing. The nervous rasping calmed at once. She poured a second cup, full this time, and, forgetting the coffee, headed for the shower.

∿

"A hundred and two degrees!" was Theo's greeting.

"I could have sworn it was hotter than that." Laura

opened one of the large refrigerators and found room for her salad and pie bars. The reservoir, less austere than its name suggested, was really a freshwater lake, dug into the middle of the Arizona desert, that boasted a sand beach, a playground, volleyball courts, shaded picnic areas, and an air-conditioned community building with bathrooms and a full kitchen. "Where are Evan and the boys?"

"Swimming. I told them they'd better hold off until it cools down a little, but the kids couldn't wait." Evan was the church pastor, and Theo, with her shaved head, facial piercings, and multitude of tattoos, his unconventional wife.

Laura gave Theo a one-armed hug. "Well, you're only four and six once, I suppose." She glanced discreetly around the room. All women. "Is Rob here?"

"He's at the beach too. He, ah . . . brought a new friend with him." Theo's tone was too casual. A woman friend, then.

"Oh, good! Good for him. I look forward to meeting her." Possibly the biggest lie she would tell all day. Laura bent to rummage in her beach bag while she composed her face and came up with a purple plastic water bottle that said *New Life Presbyterian Fellowship: Celebrating 25 Years* on one side and *Martin Luther is my homeboy* on the other. She raised it in Theo's direction. "Better stay hydrated."

"Good thinking." Theo picked up a matching water bottle from the counter and drank. She shuddered. "Iced tea. Evan makes it unsweetened."

"Mine's water," lied Laura. "Also unsweetened. Come on, we might as well swim too."

They stopped at Laura's car to pick up beach chairs and headed for the water. Most of the church seemed to be there:

the adults crowding into the shade beneath trees or striped cabanas, the children and teenagers shrieking and splashing in the water. They found a spot under a Palo Verde, set their bottles in the sand between them, and settled in to watch.

Behind her sunglasses, Laura scanned the crowd for Rob. She spotted him at last, in the water, carrying a teenage boy on his shoulders. They were playing chicken, the boy grappling with a girl who sat on the shoulders of a woman Laura didn't recognize. All she could make out from this distance was long, dark hair plastered to the woman's shoulders. Obviously the new friend. Laura looked away and concentrated on what Theo was saying. Other women joined their circle, and for a while, Laura was nearly able to forget about Rob. Twice, when she grew too hot, she went down to the water and plunged in. The second time, she felt someone grab her ankle, and he suddenly surfaced beside her.

"Hi." He grinned and shook wet hair out of his eyes.

"Hi there." Her stomach did a quick spiral, and she smiled back. "Nice to see you here."

"Back atcha. I'm glad you came."

"Who's the new friend?"

"Her name's Kendra. I met her on a case." Rob was a police investigator for the Phoenix police department.

"The detective falls in love with the victim? I thought that only happened on TV."

He laughed. "She works for the DA's office, actually. She's an attorney."

"Well, you'll have to bring her over and introduce her."

"I will do that."

"I'm going back to the shade now."

"Okay. See you, Laura." He swam off in the direction of Kendra's sleek, black head, bobbing above the water amid a circle of teenage girls.

Laura went back to her beach chair and, wrapping her towel around herself, picked up her water bottle. She tipped it up, expecting a soothing swallow, and nearly spit it out again. Unsweetened iced tea. She saw, with horror, that Theo was holding the matching bottle.

"Theo," she said, more sharply than she intended, "you have the wrong—" But it was too late. Her pastor's wife was already squeezing the bottle into her mouth. With dismay, Laura saw the jolt of surprise cross Theo's face. She kept her own face cool and expressionless and merely held out the bottle of tea. "Trade you."

Theo handed the purple bottle of wine back, with a thoughtful look, but said only, "All cooled off now?"

"Yes, I feel much better." Laura held her head high. She did not have to explain herself to Theo, or anyone else.

She hoped her flaming cheeks would be attributed to too much sun.

༈

Amy was just getting into bed when Mitch called. He did not bother saying hello. "I think I found a place for you."

"A place?"

"An apartment. Two bedrooms. Washer and dryer. Natural gas heat. It's half a duplex. The landlord lives in the other half, so if you need something fixed, you shouldn't have to wait."

Amy pulled a second pillow behind her and sat up against the headboard. "Is it in Copper Cove?"

"Close enough. It's about four miles south on Route 1."

"How much?"

"Six hundred a month, plus utilities."

"That's not bad at all. Better than I was hoping for. How in the world did you find it? I thought I'd looked everywhere."

"The guy who came to inspect my wiring today? The landlord's his father." Mitch, who was a contractor, was spending all his free hours renovating a vast wreck of a house he had bought the previous January. Somebody was always inspecting something for him.

"What's the catch?" Amy asked.

"There isn't one. The old tenant moved out last week. Or died, maybe. The owner just hasn't gotten around to advertising it yet."

"Do you think I could look at it tomorrow?"

"You can go right now, if you want."

"Now? I'm in bed already!"

"Come on, Granny-Pants, it's only nine o'clock. Haul yourself out of bed, get dressed, and I'll pick you up."

Amy hesitated. She was possibly the least spontaneous person on the planet, a creature of deeply ingrained habits who did not like to change her mind once she had made it up on a matter. Still, good apartments with affordable rent were thin on the ground. "I guess it *would* help to have you go with me. To look at . . . at the pipes and things."

"The pipes?" Mitch sounded amused.

"Or whatever. All that pounding on walls you do, when you're looking at a building—isn't it the pipes you're checking out?"

"Oh. Yes, of course. The pipes." She could almost hear him rolling his eyes.

"Don't patronize me!" she cried.

"No, really, I'll look at the pipes, if that's what you want. Be ready in fifteen minutes."

Amy dressed quickly and twisted her dreadlocks into a knot atop her head. In the family room, she found her parents sitting on the couch, her mother's feet propped in her father's lap as they watched TV. Amy saw at once that her mother was crying. Her heart twisted; not for the first time, she wondered if this was the wrong moment to be thinking of moving out. She was twenty-three years old, and it seemed high time she had a place of her own, yet to leave now meant her mother had to bear the increasing burden of a sick husband all by herself. Amy went to her and knelt, putting her arms around her shoulders and saying gently, "What is it, Mom?"

"Hallmark Channel," Jane choked, and blew her nose lustily into a Kleenex. She waved the tissue at the screen. "It's a little girl and her old grandfather. They've just had to put him in a nursing home—" She gave a great, wet sniffle and, locating a dry spot on the Kleenex, blew her nose again.

"Oh, brother." Amy pushed her mother away and sat back on her heels. "I've told you not to watch that tripe."

"We *like* it."

"Hmmm . . . To each his own, I suppose," she said skeptically. "Listen, Mitch thinks he may have found me an apartment. He's picking me up and we're running over to look at it."

"Oh, good!" said Leander. "I wish I could go along. Make sure the place is sound."

"You can, if you want. I'd love to have your input."

He grimaced. "I'm afraid ye olde rubber legs aren't up to the task tonight. But you're in good hands with Mitch. He'll see to it you get a fair deal."

Amy stood and kissed him on the top of the head, choking back the pressing ache in her throat.

Her father reached up and gripped her hand. "Take pictures to show us."

"I will."

She waited for Mitch in the driveway. He pulled in, and she had the passenger's door open before the truck was fully in park.

"You're almost like a grown-up, being out this late at night," Mitch said, as she swung into the seat.

"Yes, well, don't think this means you can start leading me all kinds of astray." She buckled her seat belt. "I'm still a working woman who needs her beauty sleep."

"You're doing all right on beauty sleep," Mitch assured her, backing out of the driveway.

It was one of those moments when, had things been different, they might have held hands, Amy thought. He was her best friend, and she loved him, too, in more complicated ways. But of course, they couldn't yet. Mitch was committed to pursuing a full year of sobriety before they could be anything more than what they were now. She was certain, at times, that he would have caved, given the slightest encouragement from her. Would not only have held her hand, but would also have said all the things that meant there would never be any going back, for either of them. But a year without romantic relationships was what he needed, and she loved him too much to be the reason he might fail. Saying no, she had learned, could be as much a way of loving someone as saying yes.

The duplex was small, set close to the road, with a matching driveway and small side porch on either end. In the rapidly fading light, Amy could make out half a dozen chickens pecking around the bare yard.

"Chickens!" she cried rapturously. "I could have free-range eggs!"

"Seems like it." Mitch parked in the left-hand driveway, behind an ancient blue Chevy of indeterminate lineage. "Not sure about his taste in trucks." Mitch was a Ford man on principle.

They got out, mounted the three steps to the side door, and knocked. The man who opened it was small and white-haired, with a good deal of razor stubble on his thin red cheeks.

"Mr. Pelletier?" Mitch said.

"Joe's the name. And you are . . . ?"

"Mitch Harris. And this is Amy Darling. We're here to look at the apartment. Barry told me you'd be expecting us."

"Sure, sure. Let me just get the key here. . . ." Joe lifted a grease-stained John Deere cap from a hook inside the door with one hand, while, with the other, he took several swipes at getting his plaid shirttails tucked into his green Dickies. With a motion, he indicated that they were to precede him down the steps. He unlocked the door of the apartment and waved them in. "Freshly painted and carpeted," he said, "as I'm sure you can smell."

He was right. The air was saturated with the clean, sharp

odor of fresh paint and the less pleasant chemical smell of newly installed carpeting. Off-white paint. Buff-colored Berber carpet. Faux-wood laminate flooring in the tiny kitchen. It was a spare, functional apartment devoid of personality, but in Amy's eyes, it was a blank canvas on which anything might be possible. At once, she saw the long wall entirely occupied by a Gatsby-esque mural, a potted palm in one corner, a black-and-chrome table . . .

Mitch did indeed pound on walls, examine the kitchen and bathroom plumbing, and stoop down with a flashlight to inspect the small closet that housed the water heater. All the while, Joe stood impassively at the door, his greasy hat, which he had removed the moment he'd walked inside, in his hand.

When their short tour was over, Amy said, "I'm very interested. How much are you asking?"

"Six hunnert a month, plus utilities, fer one year. First and last month's rent down, last month's refundable if you leave the place in good shape. And no roommates or sublets without permission." He leveled a narrow, accusatory stare at them.

"That won't be an issue," said Amy. Then, quickly, "I see you have chickens. Could I keep chickens as well?"

A strange expression crossed the man's face. "Them chickens was m'late wife's. I got a man comin' to take 'em away for slaughter tomorra."

"Oh, don't kill the poor things!" At Joe's raised eyebrow, she coughed. "I mean, if it's okay with you that I keep chickens, I could just take them off your hands, couldn't I? Buy them from you, of course. I wouldn't expect them for nothing."

"Chickens is dirty animals."

"I'd clean up after them."

Joe's face worked as though he were trying to spit, and his Adam's apple bobbed once, twice. "I'd want the yard raked up regular. I keep a clean place."

"I'd be glad to do that."

"Well, then." He cleared his throat. "They's a coop out back where they roost and spend the winter, and half a sack of feed still left. Come back on over to my side, and I'll get you the contract."

Joe's apartment smelled of coffee, bacon, and metallic grease. On the small kitchen table lay some kind of engine, partly disassembled, but Joe moved several pieces out of the way and pulled up chairs for them.

"Cuppa coffee?" he said gruffly.

"Oh, no thank you," Amy said, at the same time Mitch said, "I would."

Joe picked a dirty mug off the counter, dumped its contents into the sink, ran it under the cold water tap, and wiped it on a begrimed dish towel before filling it from an old-fashioned camp coffeepot on the stove. He set the mug in front of Mitch, along with a can of evaporated milk that had been sitting on the counter and a bowl full of sugar cubes.

Mitch dropped three cubes into the cup, added evaporated milk, and stirred with the cloudy-looking spoon Joe provided. As Amy stared in horror, he took a long, enthusiastic swallow and closed his eyes blissfully. "That, my friend, may be the best cup of coffee I've had in a good, long time."

Joe's guarded face relaxed a bit. "The secret is boilin' it on the stove. Ain't nobody makes coffee thataway anymore."

"My father used to, when I was a kid. We drank it just this way, with canned milk and sugar cubes. I haven't seen sugar cubes in years. I didn't know you could even buy them anymore."

"You cain't get 'em just anywhere, but they still sell 'em up to the IGA at the crossroads."

"I'll have to stop by and get a box."

"You got a percolator?"

Mitch shook his head regretfully. "Just a plain old drip coffeemaker."

"Wait a minute, I got a extra one around here you kin have, and welcome to it." Joe opened the cupboard under the sink and pulled out a box of sundry aluminum pots and pans. This he dug through before holding aloft a battered coffeepot that matched the one on his stove. "Here 'tis!"

"Are you sure you don't need it?" Mitch asked.

"Naw. Ain't got but m'self to make coffee for, nowadays." A fleeting sadness crossed his face.

"Well, thank you," said Mitch. "I'll be glad to take it. It'll be good to have the real stuff again."

"I'll getcha that contract," said Joe. He rummaged in a drawer and produced a wrinkled but official-looking sheaf of forms, which Amy and Mitch both read over before she signed. As Joe added his signature below hers, Amy sneaked a glance around. A sagging sofa held what appeared to be a pair of disassembled chain saws. A car battery sat on newspapers beside a recliner like a strange, low end table. On the coffee table, a red toolbox stood open, and Amy could see hammers, wrenches, and screwdrivers inside. Apparently, she thought, Joe's boast of keeping a clean place referred only to the outside of the building.

"How soon can I move in?" she asked him.

"First of August, it's yours."

Mitch stood. "We'll be here. Pleasure doing business with you, sir."

"And you." Joe shook both their hands with dignity. "Here's m'card." From a back pocket, he took a battered wallet, and from this, he drew a business card.

Joe Pelletier Engines

All sizes repaired

(207) 555-3013

"It's m'retirement business," he said modestly. "I used to be a auto mechanic, but when the cars all went to computers, I quit foolin' with 'em." He handed the card to Mitch. Amy recognized him as being of the ilk that was used to doing business solely with other men and did not take offense.

"Thank you," she said. "And . . . will the chickens be all right with you until I move in?"

"I'll keep 'em fed and watered."

"Thank you. How much do I owe you for them?"

He waved this away. "You kin pay me in eggs."

"Thanks for the coffeepot," said Mitch.

"Drop in for a cup anytime you're around."

"I'll do that." The two men shook hands, and Mitch and Amy left.

When they were in the truck, backing out of the driveway, Amy said, "You made a friend for life."

"He's my kind of people."

"Well . . . don't get so enthralled with him and his wonderful coffee that you forget to visit his neighbor, will you?"

"As if I could ever forget his neighbor." The look Mitch gave her made her stomach do a warm little flip.

"Thanks for finding me the apartment," she said hastily. "And for going with me to check out the pipes."

"No problem. Gotta take care of my best friend, right?"

And again, Amy wished the time was now to say all the other things that remained unsaid between them. But it wasn't. That time was still months in the future.

❧

They sat in the waiting room of Dr. Gutierrez's office and read *People* magazine together. It was one of the guilty pleasures Jane allowed herself on these grim quarterly visits. All the other magazines had titles like *Neurology Today* and *Neurology Now*, which always prompted her to wonder if the second truly had more up-to-date information than the first. She sometimes tried to picture the two presses racing against each other to get the latest issue out. Jane secretly loved *People*, especially when there were stories about the royals. She was an unashamed royal-watcher. When William and Kate had married, her friend Constance had thrown a party where they all wore hats, drank tea, and watched the wedding replayed on plasma TV. This summer, there was yet another new prince or princess expected and the pregnant Kate looked, if possible, more radiant than ever. Of course, Jane thought, most women did when they were expecting.

"Leander?" The medical assistant, whose name was

Dakota, looked younger than Amy and always sounded a little unsure of herself.

Leander shuffled to the little room with the scale.

"How has your summer been so far, Dakota? How's your brother Hawk doing?" Jane always remembered to ask about Hawk.

"Real good. He got out of prison in February—I think I told you that—and he'll be done with his time in the halfway house next month. Step right up, Leander."

Leander stepped onto the scale, and Jane watched the digital numbers shuffle, settle, change their minds, and shuffle again. At last, they stopped at 70.4 kilograms. She waited for Dakota to translate.

"The office administrator here said she might hire him to clean at night. That would be a big step for Hawk. His first real job, outside of prison. You can step down, Leander." Dakota typed the number into the iPad she carried. "That's 155.2 pounds."

On his six-foot frame.

They followed her down the hall to an exam room. "You tell Hawk that I've been praying for him," Jane said.

"I will. I will tell him. He'll appreciate that so much. It's nice of you to be so interested in him."

"Well, I have a son, and I'd hate to see him struggling like your brother has."

Dakota wrapped a blood pressure cuff around Leander's arm and clipped an oximeter to his forefinger. "I'm not saying he hasn't made bad choices," she said. "But I think he really is sorry this time. I think he could really stay out of trouble if he tries hard."

"'What is impossible with man is possible with God,'" Jane quoted. "Tell him to get himself into a good church. I'll keep praying for him."

"Your pressure's 112 over 62, Leander. Pulse ox 98 percent on room air." Dakota released him from the cuff and the clip. "I'll tell him that, Jane. Thank you for . . . for praying and everything. Most people don't seem to care all that much what happens to him, including his own mother. Dr. Gutierrez will be right in." She fluttered her fingers at them and left, closing the door behind her.

The chairs were hard and plastic, the walls a muted dove gray, the air sharp with the alcohol tinge of antibacterial hand gel. "When I was a kid," Leander said, "I used to go to a little country doctor. Dr. Plourde."

Jane knew this story, but she said nothing, only tucked her hand into his arm and laid her head on his shoulder.

"He was an old man. As far back as I can remember, he had a head of white hair and a big white mustache, like Mark Twain. And even though I saw him from the day I was born until I was eighteen and went off to college, he never seemed to get any older. His wife was the nurse and receptionist. They did that, back in those days."

"I remember."

"She'd weigh me and measure me and send me to the bathroom with a little cup to pee in, then put me in a room to wait. It seemed like I'd have to wait for hours in that room. Sometimes I got bored enough and brave enough to snoop in the cupboards. I'd take a tongue depressor or one of those long Q-tips out of the jar and play with it. They had a rack full of the plastic black cones for the thingy they look in your ears with. I'd stick one of those in my pocket; then later at home, I'd use it as a whistle."

"Leander Darling!" Jane raised her head from his shoulder. She had never heard this part before. "A thief from your earliest years!"

"Oh, my sins found me out," he assured her. "Once, I was sitting on the table, playing with a tongue depressor, when Dr. Plourde walked in. I stuffed it under my leg and thought I'd gotten away with it, but then he asked me to stand up so he could check my spine. The jig was up then. I stood, and there it was, lying on the table, larger than life. I acted like I'd never seen it before, and Dr. Plourde didn't say a word. Just kind of half-smiled. And I knew that *he* knew I'd been snooping around in his medical supplies."

Jane laughed. "Serves you right!"

"Well . . . I don't know many boys who could sit alone in a doctor's office full of strange and fascinating things and not give in to temptation."

With a peremptory knock at the door, Dr. Gutierrez blew in, peering at a manila folder. Jane liked him. He had a way of delivering bad news in a way that didn't rob you of all your hope at once.

"You got here just in time," she told the doctor. "Leander was about to start looking through your cupboards and playing with the medical supplies."

"Oh, stop it; I was not!" Her husband nudged her in the ribs with his elbow.

Dr. Gutierrez laughed. "Stealing my tongue depressors! I used to do that when I was a boy. I credit the colorful Band-

Aids in my pediatrician's office with sowing the seeds of my own interest in medicine."

He had Leander sit on the exam table and went through the familiar choreography of nerve function tests. Sniffing an alcohol swab. Sticking out his tongue. Shrugging his shoulders, and on and on. The doctor tapped elbows, wrists, knees, and ankles with a reflex hammer. He asked questions about symptoms. They told him about Leander's fall on the way to the bathroom.

In the end, the doctor sat back and folded his arms. "Well, there's no doubt you've lost function, but that's no surprise. ALS isn't something you get better from. Are you still driving?"

"I haven't officially given it up, but no, I don't drive much anymore. I don't trust my reflexes."

"Good. You shouldn't. Let Jane take you where you need to go. Also, I'm wondering if it's time for you to start using a cane. It would add greatly to your safety. Help prevent another fall."

"He doesn't need a cane!" Jane was appalled. Canes were for old men. Leander was only sixty-three.

Beside her, Leander was silent.

"You wouldn't use a cane, Leander, surely?"

"I think he's right, Janey. It might help my balance."

"Yes, it would do that. It would certainly be a crutch to lean on." She heard the rising shrillness in her voice. "But maybe if you paid attention to picking up your feet when you walk, you'd find you wouldn't trip so much."

"It's not something I can control."

"You can't just . . . just give up!"

Dr. Gutierrez spoke gently. "A cane was always going to be part of the equation, Jane. And his neuro function tests show that this really isn't something he can help. It's a matter of physical deterioration beyond his control."

With an effort, she reined herself in. "I'm sorry." She squeezed Leander's hand. "Of course you should have a cane, for the time being, if you think it will help. We'll get you the fanciest one we can find at Sam's Club."

The doctor capped his pen and stuck it in the pocket of his lab coat, signaling the end of the visit. "Fine. I'll get my nurse Heather in here to fit you for a basic one and show you how to use it. Go up and down stairs with it and all that."

The cane was hideous. Black, angled metal, with holes for adjusting the height and a great, clunky rubber tip. A foam handle. Leaning on it and tottering down the hall, her husband looked, as she'd known he would, like an old man. Heather walked him up a small flight of stairs and back down while Jane looked on.

Where is his faith? She would have to talk to him about that, but now was clearly not the time. Not with relief written so starkly on his face. As they waited at the checkout desk, Jane slipped her arm through his and forced gaiety into her voice. "It certainly lends you a dashing air, Mr. Darling. We should have gotten you one years ago."

"It's not so bad, is it?"

She wanted to weep. Instead, she fixed a smile to her face and handed the receptionist her credit card.

3

THE FLOWER BEDS had gotten ahead of her, Jane realized. In her front garden, the heavy pink heads of the peonies drooped earthward, some to the right, some to the left, like the parted Red Sea. One hard rain would flatten them for good. She should have staked them up weeks ago, but with one thing and another, she hadn't gotten around to it. For Mother's Day, the children had thrown in together to give her a truckload of mulch and an afternoon of hard labor. On that day, David and Libby, Ivy and Nick and the children, Sephy, Amy, and Mitch had all shown up after church, bearing casseroles and garden tools. They'd mulched the flower beds, but run out of mulch three-quarters of the way through the front one. Now, in the neglected quarter, sorrel, vetch, and creeping Charlie were taking over as if they owned the place. Why weeds should grow so much faster and be hardier than the wanted plants, Jane had never figured out. And it was as true in the rest of life as it was in a flower bed.

She was bent over, wresting a root from the earth, when Leander found her. He leaned on his cane. "Janey, there's an e-mail you'll want to see."

She straightened, putting a hand to her stiff lower back. "The insurance company again?"

"No, it's Ellen."

"*Ellen?*" Jane's older sister never contacted her. Never responded to the newsy e-mails or Christmas and birthday cards Jane sent. Jane had learned long ago not to bother phoning. "Why in the world is she writing *me?*"

"She says she wants you to come for a visit."

"She wants *me* to come for a visit?"

"She says she wants you to come, and asks if you could stay for a couple of nights."

"*Well!* I'd better read it." She tossed the weed to the side, glad to leave the chore for the moment, and, wiping her hands on her jeans, followed Leander back into the house.

As she read, Jane could almost hear Ellen's clipped, scornful tones piercing the miles between them like resentful arrows.

Dear Jane,

I don't suppose you could find time to make a visit to Durham and spend two nights with me? I know you're busy, but if you could manage it, I would be grateful. I'll even take you out to dinner. Would next Wednesday be convenient?

Yours,
Ellen

Jane looked wonderingly at Leander. "What in the world—?"

"Hard saying, not knowing. Will you go?"

"Well, I don't know. . . ." Jane found the idea forcefully unappealing. The scar that rived her relationship with her sister was an old one: deep, and jagged, and entirely of Jane's own making. She had spent decades nearly swamped by the remorse and regret of it. Had tried for years to smooth things over. Jane's efforts, and Ellen's relentless rejection of them, served only to rub the wound ever more raw. It had become easier simply to avoid each other. Although Jane invited herself to visit her sister every few years, purely in the interest of keeping the lines of communication open, she always took Leander or one of the children along as a buffer. Unhelped by any warmth or encouragement from Ellen, the visits always left her battling a low-level sense of despair. Now, she searched for a reason to refuse. "I wouldn't want to leave you, Leander. What if you fall again?"

"I'm not going to fall. I have this miraculous cane, guaranteed to prevent that, remember?"

"In any case, I won't let you stay alone, especially at night."

"I'll bet Ivy would lend me DeShaun for a few days. He'd be more than able to help if I need anything. And you wouldn't have to leave any meals, because he'd jump at the chance to cook for us."

"What about . . ." But she could think of no other reason to refuse. She sighed. "I suppose I'll have to say yes."

"I don't envy you. It'll be like spending a couple of nights with a porcupine."

"Don't I know it? Still, she's never invited me before. Maybe she's thawing in her old age."

Leander smirked. "Sure she is."

That evening, Jane sent her reply.

Ellen,

I'd love to come for a visit. Wednesday would work just fine. Why don't I plan to arrive sometime in the late afternoon? I'll stay until Friday, if that's convenient for you.

She thought for ten minutes about what else she might write that would sound cheerful and optimistic, and came up with nothing. So she closed with:

Looking forward to seeing you,
Jane

In the days leading up to the visit, Jane was beleaguered by a dull nausea at the prospect of spending two days in the same house as her sister. She prayed over it, repeating again and again her mainstay Scripture: *"Do not be anxious about anything, but in every situation, by prayer and petition, with thanksgiving, present your requests to God. And the peace of God, which transcends all understanding, will guard your hearts and your minds in Christ Jesus."*

Like salve applied to a wound, it always helped for the moment, but had to be often reapplied. She supposed that was the blessing of pain: it demanded that you return, and return often, to the Healer for relief.

On Wednesday afternoon, she saw DeShaun safely installed at 14 Ladyslipper Lane with Leander and kissed them both good-bye. She drove the nearly two hours to Durham, pulling into Ellen's driveway shortly before five o'clock. Turning off the car, she observed her sister's house and yard without pleasure. The clapboards were a freshly painted gray, the shutters black. Marigolds and begonias lined the gravel walk, surrounded by wide aprons of ugly red bark mulch. All annuals, Jane noted, which would be uprooted in the fall and thrown onto the compost heap. Not for her sister the lushness of a perennial bed. Flowers that came back of their own accord year after year would make someone like Ellen nervous.

On the small front stoop, Jane pressed the doorbell and waited.

Ellen came at last, opening the door and saying through the screen, "Oh, you're here."

"Weren't you expecting me?"

"Of course I was expecting you. Come in. Do you have bags?"

"Just the one." Jane nodded at her overnight case. "I packed light." She moved aside so Ellen could open the screen door and stepped into her sister's cool and spotless living room. "You have new furniture!" she said at once.

"Yes, I'd had that last set for ten years, and it was getting a bit worn, so it was time."

Jane wondered what kind of wear and tear furniture sustained in a home with no children and no spouse, no pets, and where few friends were ever mentioned. She went to the sofa and touched the heather-colored wool. "It's lovely."

"You're thinking it'll show stains."

Jane laughed. "I might be. I suppose it's an old habit. When you have a hundred children, you buy dark, and you buy patterned."

"Well, I don't have a hundred children."

Jane's laugh withered in her throat. The ticking of a brass coach clock on the mantel seemed suddenly loud.

"You know where the guest room is," Ellen said. "Go on and take your bag up, and we'll have a drink on the back deck."

Ellen's guest bedroom was furnished with a hard, high double bed and an oak dresser. Soulless prints of flowers, their Latin names inscribed beneath them, hung on the walls in brass frames. The small nightstand held a lamp and a crystal vase of silk geraniums. Jane moved the vase aside and placed her Bible and journal there. *Lord, I don't know what to say to my sister. I've never known, even before . . . even when we were young. You'll have to do it for me.* In the attached bathroom, she found that fresh towels and a bar of clear orange soap had been laid out for her. She unpacked her toiletries, washed her unmade face, and brushed her teeth. Then, feeling marginally more equipped to face the evening ahead of her, she went down to meet Ellen for the promised drink.

"Gin and tonic?" asked Ellen, whose glass, with a floating lime wedge, was a very tall one.

"That would knock me right out. I'll just have water."

"There's iced tea."

"Perfect."

When Ellen opened the refrigerator for the tea, Jane shamelessly looked. She always did this in the grocery store, with other people's shopping carts. You could tell so much about someone just by seeing what they ate or fed their families. Jane's own refrigerator—not to mention her shopping cart—was perpetually overflowing. A few times a year, she went through and got rid of jars with forgotten smears of jelly in the bottom, consolidated the pickles into one container, wiped the stickiness from the shelves, and brought all the condiments to the foreground, vowing once again not to open a new bottle of ketchup or salad dressing or barbecue sauce until all the old bottles had been used up. Jane's was the refrigerator of an abundant and hungry family. Of a woman who loved others by feeding them.

Ellen's fridge, she saw at a glance, was spare and tidy. A wedge of white cheese, a lone jar of jam. A butter dish. A salad bowl covered with Saran Wrap. A quart jug of orange juice and a bottle of tonic water. That was all Jane had time to note before the door swung shut.

Her sister handed her a glass clinking with ice cubes. "Let's go out back."

On the deck, Ellen waved Jane to an Adirondack chair and paused to deadhead a petunia in one of the railing planters before she sat down. Beyond the deck, much of the small backyard was occupied by an in-ground swimming pool and concrete patio. Half a dozen neat recliners and chairs stood around it at intervals. Jane tried to imagine Ellen hosting pool parties here, the water filled with splashing, shouting children whose parents, in colorful hats and swimsuits, looked on and laughed.

"I hope you brought your suit."

"I did, thanks."

"So, how's the family?"

"Mostly well, I think. Busy. Ivy's always on the run with

her three. Amy's still directing the arts program, and she's helping a friend renovate his house." Jane paused to take a sip of her tea. Peach-flavored, from a mix. She covered her involuntary grimace by saying, "Sephy's in Africa, working at a family clinic, while her husband vets goats and cows and I don't know what all. David and Libby seem to be happily settled. Laura's still out in Arizona."

"My, you *are* a busy crew." Ellen's mouth was a thin, hard line.

"Better busy than bored, I always say."

"And Leander? How is he doing?"

"Fair. I sometimes think I see signs of improvement. He can do most things himself, but I help him with his buttons and zips, and he has to be careful what he eats. He chokes easily. But his spirits are good. He never complains."

Ellen raised a delicate eyebrow. "I thought this wasn't a disease you got better from."

"We have faith that he will."

"Oh yes, your unquenchable faith. Let me know how that works out for you." Ellen's tone was snide.

Jane looked at her evenly. "Did you invite me down here so you could be cruel?"

After a moment, Ellen said, "Sorry. I only meant that you might be better served by . . . preparing for the worst, just in case. I forgot what a cockeyed optimist you always are." She turned her gaze to the flashing water of the swimming pool and sipped her drink. "And do you hear from Laura much?"

"Not much," Jane said. "We talk once a month or so, but I don't get a lot of news. She seems happy, I suppose."

Ellen said nothing.

"How about you, Ellen? What are you up to these days?"

Her sister swirled her glass, making the ice cubes clink. "I'm thinking of taking an early retirement, actually."

"And . . . is that a good thing? Are you happy about that?"

Ellen shrugged. "I'd always planned to retire at seventy, but L.L. Bean has offered me a very nice package if I'll do it now instead of waiting five years. It's tempting." She gazed across the patio, at the rippling blue of the swimming pool. "To tell you the truth, my own health hasn't been the best."

"What is it? Are you all right?"

Ellen did not look at her. "I have breast cancer."

Jane's hand flew to her heart. "Oh, *Ellen*! Oh, I'm so . . . Are you . . . ?"

"Stop gasping, Jane." Ellen's face was etched with disapproval. "I'm going to be fine. There's no reason to fuss. Only . . . I have to have a small surgery. A mastectomy."

Jane reminded herself not to gasp. "When?"

"Tomorrow."

Then she did gasp. *"Tomorrow!"*

"Yes. The hospital won't let me drive home by myself." She lifted her chin. "And I'd rather my coworkers not hear about this."

"But surely you'll need some kind of support system after the surgery. People to bring meals, or . . . or help with the housecleaning. That's what friends are for. . . ." Jane faltered.

Her sister's face was scornful. "I don't want people feeling sorry for me. Or getting involved in my business. If you could spare a day or two, just to help me get home and settle in, I'd be grateful."

"Is this why you wanted me to come?"

"That's why I *asked* you to come, yes."

Jane sipped the vile iced tea while she digested this news. "How advanced is it?"

Ellen made a motion as if swatting at a fly. "Not very. I'll be fine. I just have to stay one night in the hospital, and be driven home the next day."

"Are you . . . are you going to have reconstructive surgery?"

"I see no point in that. I'm not in any kind of *relationship*—" Ellen spat the word—"and I have no plans to ever be in one."

Jane blinked. What did you say to a statement like that?

"Anyway, I have to be in Portland at six o'clock tomorrow morning. My surgery is at seven thirty. I'll come home the following day. Is that convenient for you?"

"Of course."

"Thank you. Now, we'd better think about something to eat. I can't have anything after midnight, so this is the Last Supper, if you will." Her sister's voice softened. "Cheer up, Jane. Women go through this every day of the year, and they come through it just fine. Now, what do you think about having dinner at the Broad Arrow Tavern? My treat."

Jane understood that she was to ask no more questions, offer no sympathy. She took a long breath and fixed a smile to her face. "I love the Broad Arrow Tavern."

Ellen nodded at Jane's red capris and T-shirt, both well wrinkled from the drive. "I hope you brought something dressier than that to wear."

"I did."

"Good. Why don't you shower and change, and we'll leave in . . . say forty minutes?"

"All right." It was a relief to be told what to do. And a shower would be just right. She could dissolve into tears all she liked, in the shower, out of Ellen's sight and hearing. She followed her sister into the kitchen and left her unfinished tea on the counter beside the sink. "See you in forty minutes."

She was halfway up the stairs when Ellen said, "Jane."

Jane stopped. Her sister stood in the middle of the living room, squeezing her hands together, looking frail and alone. Her face had crumpled like a used napkin.

Tears rushed into Jane's eyes. "Oh, honey . . ." She leaned over the railing, stretching out a hand.

Ellen blinked and lifted her chin. "I just wanted to say . . . I just wanted to say you should put on a little makeup, while you're at it. Your age is showing." She turned her back and went into the kitchen.

∾

At the hospital's information desk, a security guard pointed them to the second floor, where a nurse in blue scrubs gave Ellen a clipboard of papers to sign. Jane and Ellen found seats in the waiting area. In one corner, a television played the Weather Channel.

"I've never understood our society's obsession with predicting the weather." Ellen was more querulous than usual this morning.

"I suppose it helps us make more reliable plans."

"Plans! What good are plans, when in the end you can't predict anything at all?" Ellen was signing her name in vicious black slashes across the bottom of each form.

"Are you nervous?"

"No, I am *not* nervous. What I am is hungry. I want this over with, so I can have something to eat."

"Would you like me to pray with you, before you go in?"

"I would not."

"Then I'll just pray *for* you."

"Do what you like." Ellen stood and carried the clipboard to the desk.

The nurse took it from her. "Good enough, Ellen. I'll take you back, and we'll get you changed into a gown and put an IV in you." She smiled at Jane. "You're welcome to come with her and stay right up until she goes into surgery."

"That's not necessary," said Ellen. "Just be here tomorrow to pick me up, Jane."

"Don't be ridiculous. I'm staying until the surgery's over. I'll see you afterward."

Ellen blew out her breath in an aggrieved gust.

"I'll be praying for you," Jane said.

"All right then," said the nurse. "Come with me, Ellen, and let's get this party started." Ellen followed her through a set of swinging doors into the white corridor beyond.

Jane sighed and turned to the receptionist. "Is there a cafeteria where I can get some breakfast?" Although she had been awake for hours already, she had not had so much as a cup of coffee, finding it easier to skip it and avoid the unspoken resentment of her sister, who was not allowed to eat or drink.

"First floor. Take a left off the elevators."

Jane sat at a corner table with her coffee and a breakfast sandwich and called home. When Leander's solid, familiar voice answered, she felt such a rush of homesickness that she nearly cried. She had called him just the night before, to put him in the picture, but already it seemed days since they had talked. She gave him the update on Ellen and tried to make a joke out of her sister's prickliness.

Leander wasn't fooled. "You're a saint, Janey. Anyone else would've left her on the front step of the hospital and told her to find her own way home."

It occurred to her, not for the first time, that penance and sainthood often looked alike. Only the penitent or the saint knew the motives that lay behind the things they did. She longed to say this to Leander, but he knew nothing of this part of her past and would not have understood. Instead, she spoke briskly. "I'm not a saint. Ellen's afraid, that's all. She'll be better once she's through the surgery."

"You still think you'll come home tomorrow?"

"I'll stay 'til Saturday, if she wants me to. But I won't be surprised if I get her home and settled in tomorrow and she orders me off the property."

"Well, let her fend for herself, then. She'll appreciate you once you're gone."

She hung up with Leander and finished her sandwich, wishing for a newspaper to read. Then, carrying her coffee with her, she went in search of the hospital's gift shop.

She found it, but it was closed. *Hours: 10 a.m.-5 p.m.* read a sign on the door. She went back to the surgery waiting room, where the receptionist gave her a Portland newspaper. Jane whiled away the time by reading everything except the sports section, which she could not bring herself to take an interest in. At 10:03, she was folding up the paper in preparation for heading back to the gift shop when a short, bespectacled woman in surgical scrubs pushed through the swinging doors and called, "Jane Darling?"

"Here." Jane stood and went to meet her.

"I'm Dr. Haskell. Ellen came through the surgery with flying colors. I'm confident we got all the cancer, although we've sent a lymph node to pathology, just to be sure. It'll be a day or two before we have the results from that."

"What does . . . results?"

"If the lymph node is clean, we'll know the cancer hasn't spread. If not, we'll have to consider how to proceed. For now, I saw Ellen in the recovery room. She's waking up and doing just fine. You can wait for her in her room, if you like. Norman here will tell you where she'll be, once she's transferred out of recovery. She'll probably be another hour or so, so no hurry." The surgeon nodded to the receptionist, then to Jane, and disappeared back through the swinging doors.

Behind the desk, Norman said, "Hang on. I'll call the floor and see where your sister's going." He consulted briefly with someone over the phone, then hung up. "She'll be in room 4015," he told Jane. "The nurse said you can go on up and wait for her there, if you want."

"Thank you." Jane made her way to the gift shop, where she bought a basket of cheerful daisies with a small, turgid Mylar balloon bearing the message *Get Well Soon!* stuck among them on a plastic lollipop stick. En route to the elevator, she found a trash can and got rid of the balloon.

On the fourth floor, a secretary pointed her toward the room that would be Ellen's. Jane found it, set the daisies on the bedside table, and went to the window to look out. Before her, the city of Portland stretched away to the water.

It had a friendly feel to it: low and old-fashioned, with a lot of brick, and not much in the way of glass or steel. An exhaustion that was not entirely physical permeated her like a chill fog. She felt as though she'd been awake for days. In one corner of the room stood a recliner, and she sat in this, wishing for a blanket to pull over herself. Outside, in the corridor, voices called, some cheerful, others clipped and efficient. Wheels swished on linoleum; distant alarms beeped in half a dozen tones. The air smelled close and artificial with cleaners and breakfasts and other nameless things that didn't bear thinking about. She closed her eyes.

Then a voice was saying, "Here she is!" Jane shook her head to clear the smog of sleep and saw two orderlies pushing a bed through the door. Against the pillows, Ellen's face was aged and colorless.

A world-weary nurse followed close behind the bed. "Why don't you wait in the visitors' lounge?" she said to Jane. It was more of an order than a suggestion. "I'll come find you once your sister's settled."

Jane obeyed and was thrilled to discover a pot of fresh coffee in one corner of the tiny waiting room. A table held several magazines. By the time the nurse came to fetch her, Jane felt quite restored. She held up a back issue of *Birds & Blooms*. "Do you suppose anyone would mind if I took this with me to read?"

"Be my guest."

In Ellen's room, Jane went straight to her. "How are you feeling?"

"Not so bad. It hurts to move my arm, but they said that's normal."

"Can I get you anything?"

"That's what the nurses are for."

Jane held up the magazine. "Something to read, maybe?"

"Don't hover, Jane. Go back to my place and get some rest. You can come back in the morning. They said I should be discharged by eleven." Ellen turned her head away and closed her eyes.

Jane knew Ellen well enough to realize that she meant what she said. It felt wrong to leave her sister alone in the hospital, yet if Jane stayed, it would be a matter of comfort to no one but herself. "Good-bye, then," she said to the back of Ellen's head. "Be sure to let me know if you need anything. You can call the house, or I have my cell."

Ellen lifted a hand in acknowledgment but did not open her eyes. Jane wondered if she would even see the basket of daisies, much less care about them.

She followed the signs through the parking garage to her car, then began the task of finding her way back to her sister's house, feeling disheartened and at odds with the world. Used to the wide and quiet streets of Copper Cove, she was cha- grined to rediscover that Portland was a warren of one-way alleys that were often half-blocked by buses pulled to the curbs. Very little of it seemed familiar from the years she had spent there as a young, single music teacher just out of college. The population—and with it, the traffic—seemed to have doubled since then. As well, there were panhandlers on every corner, and pedestrians evidently thought nothing of ambling out in front of you with no warning whatsoever. Several wrong turns and harrowing lane changes later, she finally found a sign pointing her to I-295 north and began to breathe easier.

It was a brilliant summer day. Along the highway, the waters of the Presumpscot River flashed with sun pennies. Two white egrets lifted from a marsh as she passed. With every mile she put between herself and the hospital, the tension ebbed away, and peace began to seep into her soul once more. *Thank You that Ellen came through the surgery safely.* It was the first time all day that she'd prayed for her sister without effort. She would not be pulled under by Ellen's perpetual misery, she decided. Instead, she would do what she could to serve her: she would cook some meals to see her through the days ahead. Recalling the state of her sister's refrigerator, Jane decided a shopping trip was in order.

She pulled off at a likely looking exit and found a Shaw's supermarket, where she bought bread, milk, eggs, butter, cheese, pasta, fruit, and vegetables. Disposable freezer containers. A box of whole-grain cereal. She would roast a chicken, too, she thought, and leave it for Ellen to eat however she chose.

Back at her sister's house, she threw open the kitchen windows to the glorious sunshine and set to work. A breeze blew through, carrying the scents of geranium and chlorine from the pool. Jane found herself humming as she worked. Hers was a home where people were always stopping by to eat: friends; grandchildren; David on his lunch breaks; Ivy, out doing errands; Mitch, come by to see Amy. Cooking for one person was foreign to her. Now, over and over again, she had to remind herself not to double or triple recipes. Her reward, four hours later, was a phalanx of single-serving plastic containers lined up like a small gastronomic army on the counter. Chicken parmigiana, Swedish meatballs, pasta salad, shepherd's pie. A pot of minestrone soup sat cooling in the refrigerator. A pan of brownies, she cut up and bagged individually for the freezer.

She felt better than she had all day. She had successfully returned good for evil, and by tomorrow night, or Saturday afternoon at the latest, she would be back in Copper Cove, among people who loved and wanted her. That was something Ellen, with all her acrimony, could never take away from her. She put the last clean pot back in the cupboard and went to change into her bathing suit for a well-earned swim.

When Jane got to the hospital the next morning, she found Ellen sitting in the recliner, already dressed, with her bags packed to go.

"How are you feeling today?" she ventured.

"Fine. I'll just call the nurse and get her to take this IV out of me, and we can go." Ellen pushed her call button.

The basket of daisies, Jane saw, still sat on the bedside table where she had left them. "Don't you want to take your flowers home?" she asked her sister.

"What am I going to do with flowers? They'll only die and be something to clean up after. Let the nurses have them."

Jane stifled the stab of hurt that had, no doubt, been Ellen's intention. *Bless those who curse you,* she reminded herself. Forcing a smile, she said, "I've put a few meals in the fridge and freezer for you, so you won't have to think about cooking for a while."

"Nothing with onions, I hope. I don't eat onions, you know."

She hadn't known. "Oh."

"They give me gas."

Jane refrained from confessing that she had, in fact, used a good quantity of onions in her cooking the day before. "Where can that nurse be?" she wondered aloud.

One breezed into the room at that moment, younger and more cheerful looking than the nurse of yesterday. "You probably want that IV out, don't you, Ellen?"

"I should think so. I've certainly waited long enough." Ellen thrust her hand in the direction of the young woman, whose smile, Jane noted, became a bit fixed.

Within moments, the IV was out. "Any last questions, before you go?" the nurse asked, taping a piece of gauze to Ellen's hand.

"If I had any questions, I would have asked them by now."

The nurse's smile disappeared altogether. "I'll order you a wheelchair, then, and you can be on your way." She stalked from the room.

Jane picked up the basket of daisies. "I'll just take these to the desk." She hurried after the nurse and caught up with her halfway down the corridor. "I'm so sorry about my sister," she said. "She's not usually like this." An outright lie.

The girl's face softened. "Well, she's been through a lot. Nobody's on their best behavior the morning after a mastectomy."

"We really do appreciate the care you all have given her. And please, take these for the nurses to enjoy." She held out the basket.

"Oh, how nice of you. They're lovely. I'll put them at the nurses' station."

Jane went back to Ellen's room, feeling a little better. The wheelchair arrived. They found the car, and as they pulled out of the parking garage, Jane was grateful for yesterday's practice run in navigating the city; she didn't think she could have borne her sister's contempt, had she gotten lost on the way home.

At Ellen's house, she was allowed to carry her sister's overnight bag into her bedroom for her. She had the sense to realize that Ellen would not want her hanging around for long and decided not to wait for the indignity of being asked to leave. When the patient was installed on the couch, with a stack of pillows, her laptop and cell phone, and the TV remote, Jane asked, "Can I do anything else for you before I head north?"

"No. No, I have everything I need."

Jane did not mention lunch, which was supposed to be the minestrone soup made with onions. "Well, then, I'll say good-bye."

Ellen's expression, or lack of one, let Jane know that a hug was out of the question.

"I hope you'll have a quick and uneventful recovery, Ellen. Please don't hesitate to call if you need anything. I'm not that far away."

"Yes. Well. Thank you for coming down, Jane." It was a formal little thanks, and Jane recognized how much it cost her sister.

"I was glad to do it. And I'll be praying for you." She went to the door, picked up her small suitcase waiting there, and gave an awkward wave. "Good-bye."

"Bye."

And then there was nothing to do but walk away, against

every loving and maternal instinct she possessed, leaving her sister by herself. Ellen might recover with no complications, but she was far from being healed. They were two very different things, Jane thought. They were not the same at all.

4

THE FIRST WEEK OF AUGUST, Amy moved to her new apartment. Jane spent Moving Day—and the several days before and after it—sorting through the attic and basement for boxes of dishes and odds and ends of furniture that Amy might want.

"It's mostly the dregs, I'm afraid," she told her youngest. "Your siblings picked it over before you got to it."

"I don't mind." Amy was cheerful. "Matching furniture is so mainstream." She chose four wooden ladder-back chairs of disparate designs and a drop-leaf kitchen table with a finish that had seen better days. "I'll paint it red and it'll be better than new," she declared, panting, as she and Mitch together muscled it down the stairs. She took the bed and dresser set from her bedroom, but in Quahog, she visited a furniture store where she bought an acid-green club chair and a small sofa upholstered in Persian blue. A steamer trunk that she had discovered at an antiques store served as a coffee table; yard sales yielded up lamps and other miscellany, which she had been collecting and storing since Memorial Day.

On Monday evening, a small moving crew appeared in Ladyslipper Lane: Amy's coworkers Crystal and Paul were on hand to help, and Ivy had sent DeShaun over. DeShaun had signed the papers on a small blue pickup truck of his own that very week, and he was trying hard to look casual about the whole thing as he pulled to the curb with one arm slung across the steering wheel and the other elbow resting on the open window.

Mitch leaned on his horn as he parked his own truck behind DeShaun's. "Sweet ride, for a Chevy!" he called out the window.

DeShaun grinned.

In short order, they had Amy's Escort and Paul's Vanagon packed with all her suitcases, boxes, and bags. Crystal took a load of towels, sheets, pillows, and blankets in her car, and Mitch and DeShaun brought up the rear of the caravan with the two trucks, both full of Amy's furniture. They drove to the new apartment, unloaded the vehicles, and returned to Ladyslipper Lane, where Jane had raspberry pie and ice cream waiting for them.

Tuesday, after work, Amy spent several hours at the apartment setting up her furniture with Mitch's help, then came home to stay one last night in the house where she had grown up. She slept in Sephy's old bed because her own was gone.

Jane kissed her good night and waved her off to bed, but much later, she stole into Sephy's old room, where she knelt beside the bed and watched her daughter sleep. In the story of her life, the child-rearing chapters had all been written. This night was the last page. She knew now, from her experience with David, Laura, Ivy, and Sephy, that once your children were out from under your roof, they were out from under a good deal of your influence as well. These moments were more than just a farewell to a certain living arrangement; they signaled the end of one kind of relationship with Amy and the start of a different one.

Would her daughter be all right in the days and years ahead? Would she lapse back into her old ways, spilling out all of herself for the sake of her job, until she was drained dry and sick from overwork? And if she did, what was Jane to say about it? Amy's life was her own to answer for.

Mitch was another concern. Surely, Amy would marry him someday. And though Jane loved Mitch as a son, indeed had raised him as her own for several years, she could not ignore the potential pitfalls of marriage to a recovering alcoholic. Again, if that was what her daughter chose, what could Jane do? You could not—should not—ease the consequences of other peoples' choices. No, Amy had grown up and it was hands-off time. Time to trust that she and Leander and the rest of the family had sown well into the life of their youngest. That they had done enough, and the harvest would be good.

Although Jane had said this good-bye to each of her older children, those other times had lacked this aching sorrow, this hollow sense of loss. It was not just the presence of Amy and the others she was mourning. Perhaps it was her own identity. For thirty-four years, she had been a mother with children at home. Tomorrow, what would she be? She leaned forward and rested her forehead on the quilt beside her daughter's limp hand. Jane could feel the heat radiating from her as she slept on, her breathing light and even. She prayed her favorite blessing from the Old Testament, the one she had always prayed over people to whom she was saying good-bye. *The Lord bless her and keep her; the Lord make His face shine on her, and be gracious to her. The Lord turn his face to her and give her peace. And give her peace.*

ℛ

The very next day, the farmer called.

"Good morning, Mrs. Darling. This is Stan from Windy Acres."

Jane's stomach sank. "Oh, Stan, hello."

"I'm just calling to let you know we sent the cows to the butcher this week. Your meat should be ready for you on Friday." He might have been informing her that she had won the lottery, so pleased did he sound.

She had forgotten all about the half cow she ordered every year, butchered and wrapped for the freezer. For a decade, the Darling family had been on Stan's automatic reorder list. It had never occurred to Jane to cancel her order this year. But who was supposed to eat it all? Laura was gone; David and Ivy had families of their own, and Sephy was on the other side of the world. Amy, who didn't eat meat in any case, had her own place now, and preparing beef for Leander meant dicing and pureeing small amounts of it finely enough that he wouldn't choke. Last year, Jane's half cow had netted her 282 pounds of meat for the basement deep-freeze; there was at least a third of it still left down there, she was sure.

"Any chance it was a smaller cow this year, Stan?"

He laughed. More good news. "No, you lucked out. Your half was 304 pounds."

Oh, for heaven's sake.

With nearly a hundred pounds of last year's beef still in the freezer, where in the world was she supposed to *put* it all? Well, die all, die merrily, she supposed, and asked the next question with reckless abandon. "How much do I owe you?"

"Your total is $992.60. That's $760 for the cow and $232.60 for the butcher's fee."

Jane sat down on a kitchen stool rather faintly. "Oh."

"You want us to deliver it, or would you rather come out and pick it up yourself?"

"What's your delivery fee?"

"We deliver free on orders over five hundred."

She hadn't known that. And here she'd been trucking forty miles round-trip out to the farm in David's pickup every year, schlepping home thousands of pounds of frozen meat in her Coleman coolers. "I'd appreciate a delivery, thanks."

They set up a time and date, and after hanging up, Jane went to the basement to have a look at the freezer. It wasn't as full as she'd feared, but still . . . no way would it hold another three hundred pounds of hamburger, roasts, and steaks.

She called Ivy. "Could you use some beef?" She explained her dilemma, and Ivy was delighted to take half of last year's meat off her hands. The other half, she would offer to David and Libby.

"I'll stop by and pick it up this afternoon, if you want," Ivy said.

"Sure. That'd be fine." Not to Ivy or anyone else would

Jane admit how embarrassed she was by her lapse. Her very *expensive* lapse. A mother, she had learned early on, had to be something of a businesswoman: an expert in organization, planning, budgeting, and the coordination of resources. There were small businesses that required fewer administrative skills than Jane had employed on a daily basis simply to raise her children. And for three decades, she had managed it well. Now, she felt amateurish, inept. *Nearly a thousand dollars!* For meat she didn't even need.

She had a sudden need to lie down.

Hammer would turn ten years old on the sixth of August. He wanted a party at the beach, he told his mother.

"That seems harmless enough," Ivy said to Nick. "Half a dozen fifth-grade boys at the beach for the afternoon, grilled hot dogs and hamburgers. It's actually a great idea."

"Just think: no video games." Nick was quick to grasp the hopeful straw where he could find it. "And the house will still be standing at the end of the day."

"How much trouble could they get into at the beach, right?"

"There are lifeguards."

"They can blow their whistles if things get out of hand." Ivy's tone was wistful.

"I'll get you your own whistle, if you want."

She sighed. "Hammer would be utterly deaf to any whistle blown by me."

The birthday fell on a Saturday, which Ivy conceded was both a good and a bad thing. It was good because Nick, who kept banker's hours, could not possibly cry off the party with work as an excuse. As well, she bullied Amy into coming along. "The arts center has a horde of employees and volunteers who are well able to keep it running for one day without you."

Amy, who was tied to her job like a mother to a newborn baby, tried to protest, but Ivy overrode her. "You are needed on the beach that day. Besides, you owe me one."

"That's not true! What do I owe you for? I don't remember anything about that."

"Oh, trust me." Ivy was vague and mysterious. "You don't want me to remind you."

"Hmmm . . ."

Ivy knew when her sister was beginning to crack. "While you're at it," she said, daring to drive the wedge a bit deeper, "you might ask Mitch to help. We could use another man among the chaperones."

Amy brightened at this. "If Mitch will come along, I'll do it."

Ivy smiled to herself. Mitch, she thought, would say exactly the same thing about Amy. She mentally checked *badger two more adults into helping* off her list. Done.

The downside to a beach party on an August weekend in Maine, of course, would be the crowds. Not only would every able citizen of Copper Cove be out in force with blankets, umbrellas, and picnic coolers, but the summer tourists would at least double their number.

"What's our strategy for not losing these kids?" Ivy asked Amy.

"T-shirts," Amy said promptly. "Neon green, or some

other color no one else will be wearing. Have them printed with some fun slogan, and tell the kids they have to wear them all day, even when they swim."

"They could say *Happy Birthday, Hammer.*"

Amy shook her head. "No, the kids will want to keep wearing them after the birthday. What fifth-grader named Matt or Mark is going to show up to school in a shirt that says *Happy Birthday, Hammer*?"

"I despair," said Ivy. "I've turned into one of those out-of-touch, irrelevant mothers, haven't I?"

"Yes," Amy said, "but that is why you have me to help. Here's an idea: how about making it a shark-themed party? The T-shirts can be printed with a picture of a shark and say something like *I Survived Shark Day at Piper Point Beach.*"

Ivy was horrified. "You can't have a shark-themed party for children at the *beach*!"

"They're not five-year-old girls, Ivy; they're preadolescent boys. They'll love it."

"You are an appalling person."

"I know," Amy said serenely. "But it'll be the party of the year. That's what counts."

❧

August 6 was forecast to be clear and hot, and Ivy was up before dawn, assembling supplies. Ten neon-green T-shirts printed with the Shark Day theme: six for Hammer and his guests and one each for Ivy, Nick, Amy, and Mitch. Shark-themed party favors. Hot dogs, hamburgers, buns, condiments, chips, red Hi-C that Amy had dubbed "shark's blood." Her mother would run cupcakes and ice cream cups over to the beach in the afternoon. Boogie boards, sunscreen, buckets and shovels . . . the list seemed endless.

"It would have been less work to have the party here at the house," she told Nick, when he woke two hours later and eyed askance the growing heap beside the garage door.

"But having it at the beach is cheaper than home repairs," he reminded her.

They got to the beach by ten o'clock, before the crowds arrived, and staked out a section of sand above the high-tide line, close to the bathrooms and charcoal grills. Ivy left Amy and Mitch there to supervise as the party got under way and went back to the parking lot to greet Hammer's guests. Nick acted as escort, outfitting the boys with green T-shirts and walking them from the parking lot to the sand as they were dropped off. Once they had all arrived, Ivy waved the last of the mothers off with a "See you at three o'clock!" and joined the party.

At first, it went beautifully. The boys ran, splashed, and bodysurfed in the water. Amy organized and supervised a sand sculpture contest. Nick and Mitch started the charcoal grills, while Ivy set up the picnic lunch. Jane arrived, bringing Jada and DeShaun with her, as well as dessert in an ice-filled cooler.

"Grampie doesn't feel well this afternoon, Hammer," she told him. "But he sends his love and says happy birthday."

Not until Hammer began to open his gifts did things start to unravel. Jane and Leander's gift to him was a new soccer ball. "Wow, thanks, Grammie and Grampie!" His face was alight as he set the ball aside and moved on to the next gift.

Amy, who was sometimes efficient to a fault, picked up the ball, extricated it from its cardboard packaging, and set it back on the table while she folded the cardboard flat and stuffed it into a bag for recycling.

Hammer was exclaiming over a Super Soaker he had just unwrapped when a boy named Jonah picked up the soccer ball and said, "Hey, Hammer, watch this!" He drop-kicked the ball, and Ivy looked up in time to see it soar over the heads of the beachgoers and land in the ocean, thirty feet away.

"My ball!" Hammer cried. He dropped the Super Soaker and, scrambling over the picnic table bench, took off for the water, kicking up sand behind him, oblivious to protests from the well-oiled sunbathers in his wake.

He reached the water's edge and waded in, but the ball, borne on some rogue current, floated just out of his reach. Hammer was not a good swimmer. He turned back toward shore with an anguished yell. "My ball!"

Nick and Mitch jogged down to the water. "I'll get it," Nick said, wading in. The ball bobbed maddeningly out of reach. Mitch plunged in behind him, and the two of them swam after it. As if pulled on an invisible string, the ball floated always just ahead of them. The farther out it went, the faster it was carried away, until Nick and Mitch, treading water far beyond the crowd of swimmers, looked at each other, shook their heads, and turned back for shore.

"No! Get my ball!" Against the roar of the waves and the cacophony of shrieking gulls, Hammer's voice was thin and ineffectual.

When they finally reached shore, Nick said, "I'm sorry, buddy, we just couldn't get to it." He shook wet hair from his face like a dog.

Hammer's eyes narrowed, and for a moment, he went very still. Then, wordlessly, he turned and stalked back toward the picnic tables. He walked faster. He began to run, and before Ivy realized what was happening, he had reached the huddle of boys and body-slammed Jonah into the ground.

Jonah fell with a cry of alarm, and the two of them rolled together, instantly coated in sand, until Hammer came up on top and began to pummel the other boy with both his fists. A stream of profanity such as Ivy had never heard before flowed from her son's mouth, unbroken, vivid, and edged with red fury.

She was incapable of doing anything except to stare, shocked at the scene of mayhem.

Nick dove in, with Mitch and DeShaun behind him, and together, they pulled the two boys apart. Jonah, beneath the coating of sand, was white with shock, one cheek blood-smeared. Hammer, held back by his father and brother, continued to kick and thrash like a wild thing. At times, both feet came off the ground and pedaled the air with the force of his struggle to get back to the other boy and finish the job. "I hate you!" he screamed. "I hate you!" The air around him was fractured with curses.

Everyone within earshot had stopped to listen. "Take him to the car!" Ivy cried when it was apparent that Hammer was nowhere close to calming down.

Nick and DeShaun bore the little boy bodily away. He seemed to have lost his senses; in that moment, he was more wild animal than human child.

The boys and adults watched them go, the only sound in their circle the hiccupping sobs of Jonah. Ivy went to him and knelt. "Are you okay?" She tried to keep the tremor from her voice, but did not quite succeed.

"I wanna go home."

"I know. I'm sorry Hammer did this, Jonah. Let me see where you're hurt, okay?"

He pointed, with a martyred air, to his nose, and Ivy, after brushing away the sand, saw that this was the source of the bleeding. Amy handed her a freezer pack and a wad of paper napkins, which Ivy applied to the boy's nose.

"I'm going to put this ice pack on the back of your neck, okay?"

He jerked his head away from her. "I don't want it. I want to go home."

"Okay. I can call your mother. We'd love it if you'd stay, though."

Jonah shook his head mutinously.

In her periphery, Ivy saw that Mitch and Amy were organizing the other boys into some kind of activity to lead them away from the scene, and she was grateful.

"If that's what you really want, I'll give her a call."

Jonah nodded.

She called his mother, walking a short distance away in order to give a synopsis of the events. Fortunately, Jonah's mother seemed to be practical about the subject of raising boys and did not seem inclined to make a big deal about it. "I'm sorry it didn't work out," she told Ivy, "but sometimes boys just fight. I'll be there in fifteen minutes."

Ivy wanted to believe it was simply a case of boys being boys. She hoped Jonah's mother was right, but all it took was a look at Amy's white face and the grim set of Mitch's mouth, and she was suffused again with doubt. How were you supposed to tell which behavior was normal, and which you should actually worry about? She watched as the boys, minus Jonah and Hammer, ran back to the water. The day that had been so brilliant and full of fun now felt tinged with an alkaline smog of fear and dread. Not for the first time, she realized the possibility that she could ruin these three children she'd been entrusted with. Who was she to think she could raise them? What did she know about being a mother? The answer was as plain to her as it must be to the rest of the world: nothing. She knew nothing at all.

She prayed that by some grace, her nothing would turn out to be enough.

❧

Kendra the Attorney was at church with Rob for the fourth Sunday in a row. Laura, seated several rows behind and across the aisle, scrutinized them narrowly throughout the sermon. Rob's arm was slung across the back of Kendra's seat, and he toyed idly with the sleeve of her blouse as, from the pulpit, Evan expounded on something to do with forgiveness.

Rob had, as promised, introduced Kendra at the Fourth of July picnic, and Laura had taken an instant dislike to her. She freely acknowledged that her aversion had nothing to do with Kendra herself, who seemed nice, practical, and down-to-earth; it had everything to do with exercising the preroga-tive to resent any woman who had met Rob's standards when she herself had not been able to.

Of course, Rob had been clear about *why* he would not date Laura: it boiled down to differences of faith. Rob's was the kind of conviction that informed and translated every corner of his life. Laura's relationship with God was more like the tolerant acknowledgment of a little-known grandfather whom she was required to visit once a week for the sake of staying in good graces. Where faith was concerned, Kendra the Attorney was clearly of the Rob Haskie school of thought. Laura kept a dispirited eye on them throughout the service and wished, not for the first time, that she could be one of those people who effortlessly loved Jesus. But she simply wasn't. Agency over her own decisions was a freedom she cherished and had no intention of giving up. As Rob had once pointed out to her, it would be nice if she could have it both ways, but even Laura knew better than that. Either God was in control of your life, or you were—never both at once. She had made her choice, and she was sticking by it.

But she had one claim on Rob's attention that Kendra did not: Rob was the volunteer youth pastor, and Laura directed the youth group band on Sunday nights. To be sure, Kendra had tagged along to the last few practices, but she had the grace to sit discreetly in the back row, absorbed in her phone, and leave Rob and Laura to their business.

That night, Laura dressed more carefully than usual for band rehearsal and touched up her makeup before leaving the apartment. When she pulled into the church lot, she saw Rob and Kendra shooting baskets with Cassie, who played keyboard, Drum Set Trevor, Adam, who played lead guitar, and one of the vocalists. Laura put her car in park, in time to see Kendra dribble around Trevor and make a layup. Oh, wonderful. Apparently it was not enough for Kendra to be a beautiful, educated, successful professional: she had to be athletic too. Laura got out of the car and strode toward the group.

"Hi, Laura!" Cassie called. They all stopped to wave at her.

"Come on and play. Our team's a man short," said Rob, panting, with his hands on his knees.

"I can't play basketball."

"Neither can I," said the vocalist, "but that doesn't stop me."

"Come on!"

"Yeah, come on, Laura."

They really had no idea what an astronomical fool she could make of herself with a basketball in her hands. She waved their pleas aside. "I'll stand here and be your cheerleader." To her relief, another car pulled in just then and deposited their bass player courtside. "Look, here's the other Trevor. He'll join you." Bass Trevor did join them, and Laura was off the hook.

But Laura was not through feeling inept. Later, at rehearsal, more than one girl rolled her eyes at a sharp direction she gave, and she heard Cassie mutter, "Kendra's *way* nicer." When the session ended, the boys stayed on the podium to pack up their instruments while the girls, as one body, surged toward the back of the sanctuary, where Kendra was applauding and crying, "Great practice, guys!"

Laura was intensely irritated. It had *not* been a great practice, by any stretch. The vocalists had been persistently flat, the instrumentalists halfhearted in their efforts. She picked up her purse and stalked up the aisle.

"Great practice, Laura," said Kendra.

"It's *rehearsal*, not practice." It was a matter of semantics, but Kendra didn't need to know that.

"What's the difference?"

Laura stopped. "You practice alone. You rehearse as a group."

"Oh, well, great rehearsal, then." Kendra's smile did not change. "You seem to be really good with the kids." A bald-faced lie if Laura had ever heard one.

Still, she was smart enough to know that making an enemy of this woman would get her nowhere with Rob, so she accepted the olive branch with gritted teeth, dredged up a smile, and extended one back. "Not as good as you. I don't play basketball, remember?" She escaped before she had to listen to Kendra's reply.

Despondent and humiliated, she swung by the drive-through liquor store on her way home, buying a bottle of cran-berry juice and half a gallon of cheap vodka. She had earned it.

❧

Laura opened her eyes to sunlight streaming through the cracks in the living room blinds. Her head felt cleaved in two, from scalp to jaw; the room reeled around her. She squeezed her eyes shut and groaned. The upholstery of the sofa rubbed against her cheek, nubbly and rough. Cautiously, she cracked one eye again and groped for her phone, finding it on the floor beside the couch. It read 2:14. Three new voice messages. Those had to be from work, wondering where in the world she was.

She sat up, and the room shifted again. Her last memory was of stopping at the liquor store—she did the math—eighteen hours before. Her mouth felt like a chalkboard eraser and tasted like a sewer. Pushing herself to the edge of the couch, she managed to stand, despite the spinning room, and groped her way toward the kitchen, accidentally kicking the vodka bottle under the coffee table. Halfway there, she changed tack and made it to the toilet just in time to throw up. After that, she brushed her teeth, drank two glasses of water, and felt marginally better.

Eggs! She needed protein, and a glass of wine to stave off the shakes and sweats. She made herself two scrambled eggs with cheese and drank her wine, then felt strong enough to call her manager.

It was food poisoning, she explained. She had been up all night throwing up and had slept straight until ten o'clock that morning. She had tried to call work then, but the line was busy, and she had begun throwing up again, and then had gone straight back to sleep. She did not have to fake either the exhaustion or the contrition in her tone, and her manager, Chris, was instantly sympathetic.

"If you're not better by tomorrow, don't even think of coming in," he told her. "Just concentrate on feeling well."

Laura hung up, relieved. She had never done such a thing before, and she soothed her conscience with the promise that she would never do it again. On her knees, she fished the vodka bottle out from under the coffee table. She took it to the sink and, with distaste, poured the last three inches down the drain. Normally she would have tossed the bottle into the recycling bin in her broom closet. Instead, she stuffed it deep into the trash can and pulled yesterday's garbage over it. It seemed less true that way, as if it hadn't really happened. It wasn't the quantity she had drunk that shocked and disturbed her; it was the blacking out.

Anyway, it was just a one-time thing. She wouldn't let it happen again.

CHAPTER
5

ON THE FIFTEENTH OF AUGUST, Jane did not start her morning as usual, with her coffee and Bible and the songbird choir on the side porch. Instead, at 4 a.m., as the sky outside her window was just beginning to pearl into gray along the edges, she slipped away from Leander's warmth and, leaving him still asleep, his breathing deep and even, pulled on the yoga pants and sweatshirt she'd laid out the night before. She had set the coffeepot to start an hour earlier than usual, and now she poured some into a thermal mug, added half-and-half, and sat on the ladder-back chair in the hall to pull on her sneakers.

It was a ritual she observed on this same day, every year.

She put up the automatic garage door, backed the Subaru wagon into the water-cool morning, and headed for Piper Point, sipping her coffee as she drove. She met three cars on the way. People on their way to the airport, no doubt, for early morning flights. Maybe a bakery worker or two.

The parking lot at the beach was empty. She turned off the car, pulled two paper napkins from the glove box, stuffed them into her sweatshirt pocket, and got out. The gulls had beat her here. They patrolled the hard-packed sand along the water, as cocksure and arrogant as prison guards. Humans might be stronger, faster, and possessed of weapons, but on the beach, seagulls had a way of making you feel that you were the interloper, there on sufferance alone.

She headed north, toward the jetty. Later, in the fall months, the surf would churn and pound in its waxing and waning, but this morning, the ocean merely lapped at the shore, gentle and languid, as though reluctant to surrender the ground it had only just gained at high tide.

To her right, the argent-rimmed sky bled like a water-color: vermilion and tangerine into purple, and one small patch the color of goldenrod. *"The heavens declare the glory of God; the skies proclaim the work of his hands."*

It was not until she had set a good pace against the crumbling sand that Jane allowed her mind to go to the place for which she had, all year, reserved these moments. To the things she never wanted to think about, but which she made herself remember, nonetheless, for this one day of the year.

Steven. He would be forty-four today, wherever he was. Was he called Steve? she wondered. Probably not. Most likely, his parents had renamed him. Possibly something like Stanley or Roger, if they had been fans of *The Guiding Light.* And hadn't they all been, back in the early seventies? Michael wouldn't be bad, she often thought. A lot of boys were named

Michael back then. Or Christopher. Chris for short. That was a nice name. But Steven was her favorite, and in her mind, that was how Jane always thought of him.

He had been a beautiful baby, although in those days, Jane hadn't had anything else to compare him to. She had never paid attention to babies before. When it was all over, she had been allowed to hold him for just a moment. The ward sister had whisked him away then, her mouth a grim line, but her eyes looking as though they wanted to weep.

His hair had been black and plentiful, his rough and nubbled cheeks the color of toast. For one piercing moment, he had opened his eyes and looked into Jane's. They were blue, and nearly unlashed, but they had said, *I know you. I recognize you.* Then he had closed them again, and Sister had come to lift him from her arms.

Later, another nurse had said, heartlessly, "All babies are born with blue eyes. They change to their real color after a few weeks." But Jane knew that Steven would have grown up with eyes the color of the Atlantic in summer. Deep and dark and mirroring the changing sky.

The color of his father's eyes.

At the jetty, she reached out and touched the damp stones. With their covering of barnacles and slime, they gave her no pleasure, yet she felt compelled to touch them every time. As if to say, *I was here.* As if to leave her imprint, somehow.

On the way back, the tide was lower. She prayed for Steven, wherever he might be. At forty-four, it was likely he was a father himself now. Perhaps even a grandfather. Jane examined the notion that she might, without knowing it, be a great-grandmother already. She dismissed the idea. It was easy enough to feel old with the daily proof that was offered up to her. No sense borrowing years if she didn't have to.

Make him wise, Lord. I hope he has a good life; a stable, happy family. I hope he knows You. Maybe thinks of me from time to time.

Always before, on these fifteenths of August, Jane had been content to leave it there. God knew. God saw Steven, and loved him, and would take care of him.

This time, it was different. For some reason, she was overwhelmed, as never remotely before, by a desire to find her other son, her firstborn. She and Leander knew nearly everything about each other, yet she had never told him about Steven. If Leander did die—an impossibility she rarely allowed herself to entertain—there would die with him many things that she would never know. Some, no doubt, because he had kept them from her, as many married people kept things from each other. Others, because it had never occurred to her to ask. She felt, as never before, the fragility of life. What if Steven were to die without her ever knowing him? Already, she had missed so much of his life; there was a whole universe of things she would never find out, stories she would never hear, parts of him that would never be familiar, even if they did meet. She was overcome by grief for all the undiscovered things, and a burning need to learn, before it was too late, all that it was still possible to know.

A large black dog ran at her and skidded to a stop, spraying her legs with sand.

"Oh!" she exclaimed, pulled suddenly out of her thoughts. The sun was up now, and the beach was filling with walkers, both canine and human.

The dog dropped a dirty tennis ball at her feet. His hind-quarters convulsed frantically, and he pawed at the sand.

Jane laughed. "Is that your ball? Want to chase your ball?"

"I'm sorry!" An elderly woman, barefoot and wearing a vast straw hat, called to her from the dunes. "Ignore him! He's incorrigible."

"I don't mind," Jane called back. "Can I throw it?"

"Throw at your own risk!" The woman approached. She had a face that was generous and vibrant, finely etched with lines. "He may never leave you alone."

"That's all right. I wasn't made to be left alone." Jane picked up the soggy ball gingerly and threw it as hard as she could. The delirious animal leaped after it.

The dog's owner fell in step with her. "Look around," she said, her lined face radiant in the morning sun. "We're on a beach with a dozen unleashed dogs, on a summer morning in Maine. Where else are you going to find a place with this much happy energy?"

Jane laughed. "Not many places, this side of heaven."

"Ahhhh!" The woman flung her arms wide as the sand-covered black dog barreled back toward them, and dropped the tennis ball at their feet once more. "'Earth's crammed with heaven, and every common bush afire with God; but only he who sees, takes off his shoes.' Elizabeth Barrett Browning said that." She bent to pick up the filthy ball and fling it again, this time into the ocean, where her dog plunged without hesitation.

"That's a lovely thought," said Jane. "Akin to St. Paul's advice: 'Give thanks in all circumstances; for this is God's will for you.'"

"There'd be a lot fewer people on medication if we all adopted such attitudes," observed the woman, shading her eyes to follow the progress of the black dog.

"I think I needed to hear that today."

"Oh, honey, we all need to hear it every day." They had reached a narrow path through the tall sea grasses. "This I where I turn off," the older woman said. "Here's another one for you: 'When you walk to the edge of all the light you have and take that first step into the darkness of the unknown, you must believe that one of two things will happen. There will be something solid for you to stand upon or you will be taught to fly.' Patrick Overton."

Jane had no idea who Patrick Overton might be. She smiled. "'Trust in the Lord with all your heart and lean not on your own understanding; in all your ways submit to him, and he will make your paths straight.' King Solomon."

"Two different ways of saying the same thing," the woman agreed amiably. She waved her fingers at Jane. "Nice talking to you. Come on, Steven! Home, boy!"

Jane watched her turn up the path with the sand-covered black dog trotting behind. Steven . . .

"Take that first step into the darkness of the unknown." . . . *"He will make your paths straight."* Was it a message for her? she wondered.

But she didn't really wonder. She knew.

❧

Leander was still asleep when Jane got back to the house. It was just after six; he wouldn't be up for hours. She left her sandy sneakers at the door. Her sweatshirt was tacky from the salt breeze, so she pulled it over her head and hung it on the back of a chair to air out. Then, pouring herself a fresh cup of coffee from the pot, she went through to the first-floor office and shut the door behind her.

Her husband had always been the bookkeeper of the family. Consequently, the office was much more his domain than hers. But Jane's objective this morning was not the filing cabinet, where Leander kept the bills and receipts and tax statements. She ignored this, and the oak desk, and went instead to the closet.

Like all the closets in the house, it was old-fashioned and deep, with a door of well-polished walnut veneer and a glass doorknob. It was known as "Mom's sewing closet," and it held a dressmaker's dummy, plastic totes of fabric, a sewing machine in its case, and a multitiered sewing basket filled with thread, scissors, notions, and anything else a seamstress could want. When David, Ivy, and Laura were little, Jane had made most of the girls' clothes, because she enjoyed doing it. Things got busier when Sephy came along, however, and she began to buy more of the children's things. By the time Amy was born, Jane had given up functional sewing altogether. She still made curtains from time to time: she'd made them for her own home and Sephy's apartment and David and Libby's little house. Amy, when she had moved to her own place, made her own. Where Jane was an able seamstress, Amy was a truly innovative one.

Still, she had never been able to shake a proclivity for fabric. Lovely patterns and textures beckoned to her the way books in a bookstore beguile a reader. As kitchen equipment or gourmet groceries must beg to be bought and taken home by a chef. Jane might have sewn but rarely these days, but no one would ever know it by the state of her sewing closet.

She pulled Leander's desk chair over to the closet and, standing on it, reached onto the shelf above the fabric totes. From this she pulled an ancient Thom McAn shoe box. *Women's Cut-Out Wedge Oxfords, Brown Suede, Size 7* read the faded sticker on one end. She remembered buying those shoes with her mother when she was sixteen. The shoes were long gone, but the box had survived and traveled with Jane on her many moves over the years. Decades before, when the box had housed an assortment of crayons, stickers, and scrap paper, Ivy or Laura had labeled it in large black magic-markered letters: *SSB. Stuff Shoved in a Box.* That had been during what Ivy called their "hilarious years."

When Amy had, at last, outgrown crayons and stickers, Jane had repurposed the box. Now, she stepped down from the chair and carried it to the office's small, faded love seat. Butternut wandered in and rubbed against her ankles, mewling fretfully. "Come on, kitty." She patted the cushion next to her. The cat jumped up and settled in, wedging too closely. Covering his face with one paw, he fell asleep.

Jane pulled the cover from the shoe box, releasing a lingering perfume of crayons and construction paper. Her rolled-up college diploma was there. An envelope of blue-and-red ribbons, from what, she couldn't remember. Her high school diploma. A few music awards with her name written in a delicate, lacelike script. Nobody did penmanship like that anymore. At the bottom, she found the plain white business envelope she was looking for. From this, she pulled two color photographs, each square, with a thin white border bearing the date 1972 along the side. Each pictured a small, wrinkled baby swaddled in a faded blue blanket. Feminine arms, in yellow flowered sleeves, formed the background. The baby's eyes were squeezed shut against the camera flash.

It was funny, the things you would remember and the things you wouldn't. For instance, Jane remembered well the blanket her son had been wrapped in on that day. It was a soft, deep blue, not the faded, anemic color it appeared in these snapshots. She remembered lying on the delivery table, exhausted and euphoric, listening to the sounds, like ducks calling in flight, that were her newborn son's first cries. Out of her line of vision, a nurse cleaned him. The doctor said, "Just another push or two, and we'll have the placenta."

She had been allowed to hold him after that. It was then that her aunt Sophie must have taken the pictures. Jane remembered the baby and the soft blue blanket so clearly, but she had no memory at all of having owned a yellow-flowered bed jacket. Surely the arms in the pictures must be hers, but she did not recognize them.

With a finger, she traced the little, faded face. As before, on the beach, she was overcome by the urge to find this person, her first child. When it became apparent how fleeting was the time you had on earth with the people you loved, why not grasp at all the opportunities that were left to you to love them—love them all?

Before today, Jane had never seriously considered looking for her son. She would hardly know where to start. The

Internet, she supposed, was as good a place as any. Ivy swore you could find anything on the Internet. She had taught Jane to use Google, a phenomenon Ivy referred to as "consulting the Oracle." What could Jane google? She knew the date of Steven's birth: August 15, 1972. She had been just seventeen years old.

She had arrived in Boston in the evening, the last day of eleventh grade, wearing a cotton sundress with an empire waistline that hid the rising swell of her abdomen. "Sent away," like fallen women in the old days, to Aunt Sophie, where she stayed until the baby was born. On Labor Day, she came home, her waist still thickened and her arms empty, but by homecoming weekend, in October, she was able to wear a dress with a real waistline, and no one at school was ever the wiser. Aunt Sophie, under clear directions from Jane's mother, had listed the baby's father as *unknown*. He wasn't unknown, of course, but perhaps it would have been better for all of them in the end if he had been; surely there would have been less strife and bitterness all around.

Jane tucked the two photographs back into their envelope. From now on, it would reside in her bedside table drawer, its proximity an immediate reminder of the task she had set herself. The rest—the diplomas and certificates and ribbons—she put back into the shoe box, and returned it to its place in the closet. Then, she went to the computer to consult the Oracle.

Robert Redmond, she typed in. *Calais, Maine, 1951.* Seven thousand entries, a virtual Pandora's box. Her heart gave a small leap, and she clicked on the first link.

September 9, 1998 BURLINGTON—Robert
Redmond, 47, of Calais, Maine, passed away
unexpectedly at his home on Friday. . . .

Jane closed the page and pushed the keyboard away. She
felt nothing.

CHAPTER

6

AMY PULLED HER ESCORT into her driveway one evening and, getting out, was surprised to hear the strains of classical music coming from the open windows of her landlord's side of the house. She listened, bemused. Mozart's Serenade in G Major, if she wasn't mistaken. *Joe, Joe, Joe,* she thought. *Still waters certainly run deep!* This would bear investigating. Twenty minutes later, having changed into shorts and a T-shirt and raided the chicken coop, she was knocking on his door, a bowl of fresh eggs cradled in her arms.

He answered it, wiping his hands on a greasy rag. "Oh, h'lo there, Amy. Everythin' all right over on your side?"

"Fine, Mr. Pelletier. I just wanted to bring you some eggs." She held up the bowl.

"That's very kind of you. Come in, come in." He pushed open the screen door, and she stepped inside. In spite of the open windows, the air was close, and heavy with the overpowering odors of motor oil and old bacon fat. On the kitchen table lay the parts of some disassembled machinery on a bed of newspaper pages. The source of the music, she saw, was a dust-covered phonograph beneath the window that had to date back to her grandmother's era.

"I'm workin' on a car for a buddy o' mine," the old man said, waving toward the table. "Rebuildin' the whole thing, a '65 Mustang 289. He don't let just anybody fool with it. That's the carburetor right there. The rest of it, we'll haul over to the backyard here, come spring."

Amy, at a loss for anything better to say, said, "Wow. Very cool."

"Can you set down for a cup of coffee? Place is a bit of a mess, I'm afraid."

She could tell he was hoping she would refuse. "Thanks, but I can't stay. I just got home from work and should probably see about supper." She set the bowl of eggs on the counter, pushing a stack of crusty plates out of the way to make room for it. "I didn't realize you liked classical music."

"Oh, yes, yes. M'late wife and I were allus fond of it."

She remembered that he'd said the chickens had belonged to his wife. "How long ago did you lose her?"

"Just last spring. She come down with diabeetus young in life, and her kidneys went. She was on dial'is for the last three years."

"I didn't realize it was so recently. I'm sorry."

"Well, we knew for a while it was comin'. In the end, she passed peaceful-like, in her sleep. That was a mercy, anyhow. 'Course, some days is harder 'n others." He shook his head and gazed at the rag in his hands.

"How long were you married?" she asked gently.

"Forty-seven years. That don't happen on accident, let me tell you."

"No, I've learned from my parents that marriage takes a lot of work."

"Mary made it easy, though she might not've said the same about me. No, she was a good woman. Pretty, too, right up 'til the end. Here, take a look at this." He went to the living room bookcase, which held more dusty knickknacks and picture frames than it did books, and brought back a brass-framed photograph. With the hem of his none-too-clean T-shirt, he wiped the dust from the glass and handed it to Amy with evident pride. A smiling, middle-aged woman in a blue-sequined cocktail dress and high heels stood posed with him. Joe, in a tuxedo, looked dapper and twenty years younger.

"She was beautiful," Amy said truthfully, examining the photo. "But, Mr. Pelletier, are you two *dancing* in this picture?"

"Call me Joe," he said gruffly. "That Mr. Pelletier business makes me feel old." Then, "Yep, we were quite the pair in our day. Went ballroom dancin' near ever' weekend. Oh, we had us a good time."

"*Really.* That's fascinating." She handed the picture back to him. "I never would've guessed it of you."

He smiled for the first time. "You cain't judge a book by its cover, they say."

"No, you can't." She smiled back. "Thanks for showing me the picture. I hope one day I'll be able to say I've been married forty-seven years."

"You will, most likely, if you're willin' to work at it."

"I'll remember that." She moved toward the door.

"I thank you for the eggs."

"You're welcome." She pulled the screen door shut behind her, and as she walked back to her own side, across the small yard where the chickens foraged for insects, the strains of a new waltz floated out to meet her, mingled with the summer breeze and the scents of engine oil and bacon grease.

She told Mitch about it when he came for supper. They were drying the dishes together, with the door open to let in the cool, grass-scented night. "Ballroom dancing!" she exclaimed, handing him a clean plate. "Can you just picture *Joe*?"

But Mitch missed the point entirely. "Are you sure he said a '65 Mustang?"

"I think so. Why, is that good?"

"Amy, that's an amazing car! I've never actually seen one. Do you think—would you mind if I ran over there and took a look?"

"The car's not there. It's just the engine in pieces on the kitchen table."

"Engine block would be too heavy for that table," he said, as if to himself. "It's probably the carburetor."

"Whatever."

He put the plate in the cupboard. "I'll just be a second, but I've gotta see this."

"Be my guest."

"You could come too."

"It's tempting." She rolled her eyes. "But I've already seen it once. Twice would be more excitement than I could handle."

"I'll be right back!" he called, the screen door already slamming behind him.

Ivy was rolling out pie pastry one afternoon when Jada came into the kitchen and leaned against the counter to watch.

"What kind of pies are you making?"

"Blueberry. I need to use up last year's supply from the freezer. We had so many this year there isn't room for all of them. Especially after Grammie Jane gave us all that beef." She gave the waxed paper a quarter turn and kept rolling. "What are you up to?"

"I'm bored."

"You know my cure for boredom," Ivy said cheerfully. "There are plenty of chores around here."

Jada reached for a scrap of dough and considered this. "Would you pay me?"

"That depends on the job."

"I'll clean the bathtub for five dollars."

Ivy shook her head and reached for a pie plate. "You don't get paid for your regularly scheduled chores. I do need some windows washed, though."

"How much?"

"A dollar a window, inside and out, top and bottom panes, including washing inside the frames with soap and water."

"A dollar a *window*?" Jada cried. "I'll never save a hundred dollars at that rate!"

Ivy flipped the sheet of waxed paper over one forearm and carefully peeled it away from the circle of pastry, then began to fit the circle into the pie plate. "What do you want a hundred dollars for?"

Jada kicked at the floor and muttered, "Cornrows."

Ivy looked at the droop of her daughter's shoulders and felt her heart soften like the pastry under her hands. She remembered the peculiar pain of being Jada's age and the burning need to feel that she was pretty and unique. How tempting it was, when you loved your children so much—how easy it would be—to simply hand them everything they wanted.

Instead, she said, "The window cleaner and paper towels are under the bathroom sink."

With a sigh, Jada heaved herself away from the counter and headed for the bathroom. "We need a union around here," she muttered.

"Maybe you can convince Hammer to organize with you," Ivy said cheerfully, but she felt a stab of sympathy for her daughter. Cornrows weren't cheap. It was a lot of windows to wash.

❧

When Jane had finished her Bible reading and prayers on Friday morning, she carried one last cup of coffee into the office and there discovered that most delightful of presents to unwrap: an e-mail from Sephy. In her daughter's tiny Namibian village, the World Wide Web was still little more than a distant rumor, so once or twice a week, Sephy and Justice drove an hour to Mariental to pay for computer time at an Internet café. Those few hours a week were all the opportunity they had to catch up with family and friends, pay bills back in America, read the world news, order veterinary supplies, and do a dozen other tasks for which Internet access was indispensable. The very scarcity of e-mails from her daughter made each one of them all the more precious to Jane. Now, she opened the letter with a little thrill of expectation and settled back in her chair to read.

Hi, Dad and Mom!

We've had a cool week here—only about 21 degrees in the daytime (that's 70 Fahrenheit to you—ha ha!) Last Tuesday night, I got called out to attend a birth. When I left the house, it was 8 degrees (high 40s F), and by the time I came home at around 5 in the morning, there was a skin of ice on Ted and Nana's drinking trough. I worry that it will be too cold for them, but Justice says goats are made to withstand weather like this and their body heat keeps their shed nice and warm. This is our winter, the dry season. Around January, when Copper Cove is lying dormant in cryo, we will (so they promise) be sweltering on our side of the world, with temperatures in the 30s (90s F) and humidity to match.

I'm trying to learn to think in terms of Celsius, but I'm not very good at it yet. I still have to do the conversions in my head. Same with the money. Right now, one US dollar is about 12 Namibian dollars. I'm getting very quick at mental math, though: I've learned my 12's time tables backward and forward!

I said I got called out to a birth. The native nurse, Glory, delivers almost all the babies in this village and another one about 24 kilometers (15 miles) southwest of us. I go with her as her assistant, but I learn more every day, and the idea is for me to start taking over the uncomplicated births by myself soon, with my own assistant to help. It will take a load off Glory, who teaches prenatal classes and makes home visits to new mothers as well, and is stretched about as thin as a person can be stretched without snapping right in half.

I've had some kind of weird virus for a few weeks now. It's nearly gone, although I still get aches and chills from time to time. I'd suspect malaria, except I've had all the medication. (I know: it's not foolproof.) Glory says not to worry, that all foreigners get sick a lot when they first come here. We haven't built up immunity to all their specific bugs yet. Whatever this illness is, it's not serious, but it does make it harder to get up for a birth at 2 in the morning . . . especially if it's the third night in a row! I don't know if more babies are born in the middle of the night than during the day, but some weeks it sure seems that way. It would be nice for moms and the midwives alike if they all came during bankers' hours, but do they? No. They come when they're ready, without a thought for the sleep schedules of anyone involved!

My time's almost up on this computer, and there's a line of people waiting, so I'll say good-bye. I'll write a long, newsy letter by hand and get it in the mail later this week. Give our love to everyone and thank them all for their prayers.

Love, Sephy, for both of us

PS—Stop worrying, Mom. I'm fine!

Love, S

Jane printed the e-mail for Leander to read. Later, she would add it to the growing binder in which she kept all her children's correspondence: a book of family history in the making. It was fruitless to be told not to worry. Of course she worried about her children; that's what mothers did. The trick was to channel that anxiety into prayer, where it would fall on the ears of God and accomplish some real good, instead of eating her alive inside. Like Sephy's attempts to think in terms of centigrade temperatures or Namibian dollars, learning to think in terms of prayer instead of worry did not come naturally. It was a skill that took long years of practice, and still Jane did not always do it well.

Overhead, she heard the small stirrings that told her Leander was up and ready to start the day, but Jane's mind was still on her daughter's health. *They don't* know *it's not malaria . . . or some other terrible tropical disease . . . or a parasite. That part of the world is full of parasites. . . .* With an effort, she turned the worry into prayer. *You see Sephy, Father. You know all about malaria and parasites and viruses. Please keep her safe and healthy. . . .*

Prayer was just another kind of work you did on behalf of your family. You carried children and birthed them; you bathed and fed and dressed and taught them, and when it was time to let them go, you were given a crash course in how to do that too. But praying for them was work you never had to let go of. It was a lifetime calling, a job with no retirement plan. Its power was unlimited by bounds of time or space: that belief had always been her biggest comfort.

E-mail in hand, she headed upstairs to make the bed and help her husband dress.

"How about a walk on the beach tomorrow morning?" Jane said to Leander. They were sitting up side by side in bed, reading. It was the way they had ended almost every day of their life together. "We haven't done that in ages, and summer will be over in a few weeks."

"Now that sounds like a plan. I could use the fresh air and exercise."

"Good. The tide should still be out at nine o'clock. How about shooting for that?"

"It's a date."

She felt as happy as a child at the prospect.

In the morning, when Leander had finished his toast and coffee, Jane helped him put on a pair of sturdy sneakers and tied them for him. They were in the middle of a heat wave, and already the thermometer on the back porch railing read 80 degrees. Well, so much the better, Jane thought. Her husband was always cold these days. She took a Windbreaker from the closet for him, in case it should be breezy by the water, and helped him into the passenger side of the car. The seat belt buckle proved too much for him, and she had to fasten it for him. Some days were like that. Others, he seemed to manage perfectly fine.

They drove the short distance to Piper Point. There were only three other cars, but it was promising to be a gorgeous beach day. An hour or two from now, the lot would be full, she knew. She herself had spent nearly every summer day here with the children, when they were young. At ten o'clock every morning, they would begin to pack a picnic lunch, Ivy manning the sandwich assembly line, with Sephy tracking down cookies, fruit, and chips. Amy would fill the two-quart thermos jugs with ice water and count out Tupperware cups. David and Laura would round up towels, sunscreen, and Frisbees and pack them into the canvas tote bags. As the children grew and were able to drive or bike to the beach by themselves, Jane had been freed up to spend the early afternoons at home, working at those household tasks that never seemed to end: laundry, grocery shopping, and cooking enough food to feed an entire branch of the armed forces. Still, she had often managed to make it to the beach for an hour or two in the afternoons, where she would sit in a chair alongside her friends Abigail and Constance and Rita and watch the children chase the ebbing and flowing surf while the shadows grew long across the sand.

Those golden days had seemed to last forever while she was living them, yet somehow the years had sifted away like sand through her fingers, gone and never to be reclaimed. Remembering, she felt oppressed by a faint, lingering grief she could not shake off. She helped Leander out of the car, handed him his cane, and waited while he got his balance. "Want your Windbreaker?"

"No, I'll be all right."

The sand, when they reached it, was dry and soft, and deep. Jane matched her steps to her husband's. Alone, she would have taken the beach in long, burning strides, letting the clean salt air scour her lungs to their depths. But now Leander took her arm, clinging to her like a child. "My legs are a little wobbly, I'm afraid."

"That's all right. Give yourself time to get used to it. It's been a while since you walked on sand." It had, in fact, been just about a year—the previous Labor Day. He had negotiated the beach with no hint of unsteadiness then.

He took three steps and stumbled. She grabbed for his arm and kept him from falling.

"It's just so uneven." His voice was full of apology. Five more painstaking steps. The sweat was standing out on his forehead. "I can't. It's not firm enough. It's like trying to walk in one of those bouncy houses at the fair. I'm afraid I'm going to fall."

You're not going to fall! Ahead of them, the long, lovely sweep of the ocean beckoned. The water was calm today, lapping at the shore in a laconic, disinterested way, inviting them to run barefoot through it.

"I'll never make it to the water."

She wanted to weep with frustration. *Just try, Leander! Where is your faith?*

"I'm sorry, Jane."

She looked over her shoulder at the pavement of the parking lot, fewer than ten steps behind them. "Can you make it back to the car?"

"I think so."

She put her arm around him, over bones that projected thin and sharp beneath his T-shirt. "Come on." She steered, and Leander, leaning heavily on her with every step, managed to get turned around. With excruciating slowness, they gained the blacktop.

"Terra firma." His voice was shaky.

"Terra firma."

She felt she had been forced to abandon something precious there on the sand. The days of walking the beach with her husband were over. *For now,* she thought guiltily. *Don't forget that part. God can still heal him.*

Some days, it was harder to remember than others.

They made their way back over the pavement to the car, Leander steadier now with the help of his cane. Jane did not look back.

❧

On the last Sunday of August, Theo made her way over to Laura after church. "A little bird told me you have a birthday on Friday."

"Ah! And would that little bird have a name?"

"Actually, it was on the visitor's card you filled out when you first came here."

"You still have that?"

"The church secretary keeps a list. Anyway, Wendy and I want to take you out for dinner."

Wendy, a woman about ten years older than Laura, joined them. "Did you ask her?"

"I did, but she hasn't said yes yet."

"You don't have to take me out to dinner," Laura protested. In truth, she was delighted that they would think of it.

"We want to. And you can name the place."

They agreed on an Italian restaurant in Chandler, and on Friday night, they met there after work. When the server arrived to take their drink orders, Laura and Wendy both ordered wine, and Theo asked for a Pellegrino.

"You're not one of those Christians who thinks drinking's a sin, are you?" Laura asked her when the server had brought their drinks and gone.

"No, I just don't do it anymore."

"Why not?"

Theo appeared to give this some thought. Then said, "'We admitted we were powerless over alcohol—that our lives had become unmanageable.'"

"What?" said Wendy blankly.

But Laura recognized it from her own attempts at rehab. "It's the first of the Twelve Steps." She put her wineglass down.

"What?" Wendy repeated.

"Alcoholics Anonymous."

"You mean you're—?" Wendy put her glass down as well.

"—a recovering alcoholic, yes," Theo finished for her. She smiled. "And you don't have to stop drinking your wine. I'm fine with it, really."

"Oh." Laura remembered, with a guilty flash, how Theo had accidentally drunk from her bottle at the reservoir. She felt her face flush.

"It's okay, really." Theo sounded amused.

Laura picked up her glass again. "Are you sure?"

"I'm sure. I've been sober eight years. Back then, I couldn't have been around people who were drinking without wanting a drink myself, but it's easier now."

Relieved, Laura took a sip of wine. "So you go to meetings and . . . everything?"

"About three times a week. I have a sponsor, and I sponsor other women."

Briefly, Laura debated telling them about her own stints in rehab, but decided against it. Theo knew she had been drinking wine from her water bottle at the Fourth of July picnic. As the kind of alcoholic who had gotten sober through AA, she would not understand that Laura could be a onetime pill addict who now drank in moderation. AA did not believe in that kind of thing. It was all propaganda, of course, but if it helped people like Theo, who was Laura to protest? She found herself intensely curious about this new side of her friend. She tried to picture happy, confident Theo lying on the couch, slack-faced, with a bottle dangling from her hand, and found she could not. "Would you mind telling us your story?" she said.

"Not at all." Theo shrugged. "I grew up in a great family, where my parents only drank the occasional glass of wine with friends. My mom was a professor of classical languages at a university. My dad was a commercial pilot. We went to church, and all of us kids were good students. I had a happy life.

"I started drinking my freshman year in college, the way kids do. At first, it was just on weekends, at parties. I always bounced back on Monday morning, ready to hit my eight o'clock class, no problem. But by the second semester, I was drinking on weeknights too. I still thought it was no big deal. I was more or less keeping my grades up, and still working part-time." She paused to squeeze a lemon wedge into her Pellegrino and stirred it slowly.

"That summer, I started hanging around with a different crowd at home and discovered pot. I thought I was being smart by staying away from harder drugs. I'd drink in the mornings, before work, smoke pot on my lunch break, and get wasted in the evenings. I told myself I was just being a normal college kid."

"Did your parents know?" Wendy asked.

"They knew I was using, but had no idea of the extent of it."

"So what happened?"

"By Christmas of my second year at college, I was drinking all day, every day. In the spring, I passed my classes by the skin of my teeth and the grace of my professors, and dropped out of school. I moved back home and got a job waitressing. I started dating the bartender just for the free booze. My parents were pretty clued in by then, but what could they do? They didn't want me at home, but they didn't want to kick me out, because they were afraid of where I'd end up."

"Did you realize you had a problem?" Wendy asked.

Theo shrugged. "Sure. But I didn't care. The first step of AA has two parts: 'We admitted we were powerless over alcohol' and 'our lives had become unmanageable.' I understood that I was powerless over alcohol, but I didn't care because my life was still manageable. In my opinion, I was just having fun, and as long as my drinking wasn't hurting anyone else, why not?"

The server appeared with their appetizers. Theo waited until he'd gone before picking up her story.

"The thing about alcohol, for an addict, is that at first it's just fun. Then it becomes fun plus problems. And eventually, it becomes just problems without the fun. My problems started that summer. I lost two different jobs for showing up drunk, or not at all. I hocked all my jewelry and cashed in my savings bonds to pay for booze. I sold a little pot on the side. I got a job at a toy store, stocking shelves after closing, which was something I could do while I was drunk, since I didn't have to interact with the public. That was all I really wanted in a job. I stayed there for a year. But I began to have blackouts. Sometimes I'd get home after work with no memory of anything that had happened after one or two o'clock in the morning.

"Somehow, I still believed I was managing my life. My poor parents were frantic. I might have gone on like that for years, except that alcohol finally just . . . stopped working for me. That's the short version of the story; obviously there were a lot of painful lessons in there that I won't bother going into. But by the time I was twenty-one, it took a crazy amount of alcohol to even get me drunk anymore. And being drunk at that point just meant being filled with a kind of blind despair. I'd fall into these terrible, black depressions and begin to think about all the ways the world would be better off without me. It scared me to death. I knew it was the chemicals talking, and that I had to stop, but I couldn't."

She paused to eat some calamari.

"Don't stop now!" Wendy said. "What happened?"

"I kept drinking and blacking out. And one night, I suddenly came to and found myself standing on top of a bridge, all alone, in the middle of winter. I had no idea how I'd gotten up there, or what time of night it was, or even *what* night it was. I've never been so terrified in my life. Somehow, I got down from the bridge and started walking. My phone and purse were gone, and I had no coat. I was crying, I had frozen tears and snot all over my face, and I just kept saying, 'Please, God, get me home and I'll never drink again.'

"Then a police car came along. I know God sent it: I was pretty desperate at that point, but I still don't think I would have gotten into a car with a stranger, unless he was a police officer. The cop took me to the hospital, where they looked me over and called my parents. The next day, I checked into a thirty-day rehab, and . . . that was it."

"It was that easy?" Laura asked doubtfully. "I mean, you never looked back?"

"There was nothing easy about it. To this day, it was the hardest thing I've ever done. But I had grown up in church, so the concept of a higher power clicked right into place for me. For the first time in my life, my faith became a matter of survival. It was no longer just a life view that my parents foisted on me; it became really, organically my own. I went to meetings and worked the steps, and before I knew it, I was back home. I found new friends in AA and the church who didn't drink. Then I was celebrating my first year of sobriety. It got easier. I met a woman in my home group named Cynthia, and she became my sponsor. On my second anniversary, she introduced me to her son."

"Who was her son?"

"Evan. I married him six months later."

Wendy put down her fork. "Wait a minute. This woman knew you were an alcoholic, and she actually set you up with her son?"

Theo laughed. "Cynthia is an unusual and wonderful woman. Plus, she watched me for almost two years, as my life completely changed. She knew it was the real thing."

Laura finished her Caesar salad and pushed her bowl away. "That's a great story. I'm really happy for you." In spite of the noisy restaurant, her voice seemed unusually loud.

Theo smiled. "I think it's a great story too."

Their meals came then, and the subject changed. Laura was just as glad. She hoped Theo wasn't passing judgment on her, trying to send her veiled messages about the state of her soul. Theo's story was inspiring, but it had nothing to do with Laura. Midway through the evening, she ordered more wine and enjoyed it thoroughly, guilt-free.

It was late when she got home, and she kicked off her shoes and went to put on her pajamas. She pulled out her phone, which she had left in her purse during dinner, and saw that she had missed calls from her parents, Ivy, Amy, David, and an unrecognizable number that she would bet was somehow connected to Sephy, in Africa. All of them calling, no doubt, with birthday wishes. Even as she felt a surge of gratitude toward her family, the thought of engaging with any of them at this time of night was exhausting. Besides, she remembered, it was already much later on the East Coast. She would call everyone back tomorrow, including her twin, whom she still had not wished a happy birthday.

For now, she curled up on the corner of the couch with a bottle of Malbec on the end table beside her, found Jimmy Fallon on TV, and prepared to end a satisfactory evening in her favorite way of all.

※

On Saturday afternoon, Ivy called her mother. "Have you talked to Laura? She didn't answer her phone all day Friday, and she's not answering today."

"She hasn't called me back either. Maybe she's away?"

"I don't think so. Friends were supposed to be taking her out to dinner for her birthday last night."

"Well, you know Laura. She'll get around to us when she gets around to us," said Jane.

"I suppose so."

On Sunday, at church, Amy said to Ivy, "Where's Laura? I've been calling and texting her since Friday, and she hasn't answered me."

"No idea. I haven't talked to her either."

"She hasn't called to wish you a happy birthday yet?"

"No, but it's only 9 a.m. in Arizona. She's probably at church."

"Hmmmmm . . ." Amy looked thoughtful. "Well, anyway, happy belated birthday from Mitch and me." She handed Ivy a large paper shopping bag, folded over and stapled shut.

"What is it?"

"A dozen fresh eggs."

Ivy raised her eyebrows. "Gee, thanks." She hefted the bag. "They're awfully heavy eggs."

"I have healthy chickens," Amy said loftily. "I have to run, but we'll see you over at Mom and Dad's for cake tonight. And be careful with those eggs: they're breakable," she called over her shoulder as she went.

At home, Ivy opened the bag and found that Amy's humble dozen eggs were nested inside a hand-thrown bowl exactly the same shade of blue as the September sky, and painted all around with cheerful yellow daisies. "A dozen eggs!" she said to Nick. "That sister of mine is a keeper."

"I agree." Nick had a particular soft spot for Amy.

Ivy looked at her phone once more. "Still nothing from Laura. Not even a text."

"*That* sister, on the other hand, has a lot of room for improvement."

"Nick!" Ivy tried to sound reproving, but it was a half-hearted effort. *Where could Laura be?*

❧

Laura emerged from sleep as though from a gradually clearing mist, and groaned. Her head again. She really needed to stop drinking like this before bed. She groped for the bottle of Advil on the bedside table and washed the pills down with half a glass of wine that had sat there overnight and begun to turn vinegary. Pushing herself to a sitting position, she squinted at the clock. *Not again!* It said 9:19, and if she had her calculations right, it was Tuesday morning after the holiday weekend. Scrambling for her phone, she called Chris at the grocery store's warehouse headquarters. As it rang, she pictured her disheveled boss in his crowded corner office, shuffling around the stacks of files on his desk, searching for his phone. She hoped he wouldn't find it, and she could just leave a voice mail. The drive to work would give her time to invent the right story. Unfortunately, he answered.

"My neighbors had a fire in their kitchen at eight o'clock this morning," she invented wildly. "It wasn't bad, but everyone had to clear the building, and of course I'd left my phone inside. The fire department just now let us back in. I am so sorry! I'll be there as soon as I can."

"No problem, Laura," her manager said. "Thank goodness it wasn't *your* apartment. We'll see you whenever you can get here."

"I haven't showered yet."

"That's okay; take your time. Drive safely."

She rushed and got there at five minutes past ten. "I'll work until six to make up the time," she assured Chris.

"Are you okay? Your eyes are bloodshot, and look—your hands are trembling."

"There was a lot of smoke," she managed. "The whole thing was quite a shock."

"What about your neighbors—are they going to be okay? Did they lose anything?"

"It was just smoke damage, I think. They have renters' insurance. Hey, I should get started on September's billing today."

He was watching her closely, his kind blue eyes filled with concern. "Sit down and let me bring you a cup of . . . whatever it is you drink. Tea, coffee?"

She rarely drank tea, but at the moment, it sounded just right. "I'd love a cup of tea."

He went to the break room to fetch it, and Laura, watching him go, felt withered and ashamed. She did not deserve for anyone to be this nice to her.

CHAPTER

7

ON THE FIRST DAY OF SCHOOL, Jane drove Leander to work and dropped him at the front doors. "Don't let your cane get away from you," she said. She had at last resigned herself to the cane she had once despised. Today she was glad he had it with him.

"I won't."

"Dean Street is still planning to bring you home at the end of the day?"

"Yes."

"Call if it's too much, and I'll come get you."

"It won't be. Relax, Janey."

But she could not relax. Back home, she changed the sheets on their bed and threw in a load of laundry. She tried to settle down to read her e-mail, but found it impossible to sit still. She found herself jumping up to put the kettle on for a cup of tea she did not want. She searched the bookshelves for a book she did not have in mind. She opened the refrigerator with no idea of what she was looking for. This was no good; she could not go on all day like this. She needed something to keep her mind occupied. Cleaning the attic would do the trick, she decided. It was a gargantuan chore, one she had last tackled nearly four years before, when Laura had been in that car accident and landed in drug-and-alcohol rehab. Heavy cleaning was a wonderful antidote to overthinking. Gathering her vacuum cleaner, bucket, and rags, she headed for the third floor.

The music rooms at the high school, she reminded herself as she shifted heavy boxes away from the back wall, were all on the ground floor. Leander would not need to go up or down stairs. Still, there were any number of other obstacles for him to navigate. Tangles of folding chairs and electrical cords he might trip over, heavy instrument cases and amplifiers that would need to be hoisted around. *Stop it, Jane!* she commanded herself. *"Do not be anxious about anything, but in every situation, by prayer and petition . . ."* She drowned her thoughts in the roar of the vacuum cleaner and slashed viciously at a corner full of cobwebs.

It was just that he tired so easily these days. The previous spring semester had been nearly too much for him. *". . . in every situation, by prayer and petition, with thanksgiving . . ."* She brought her mind back to her flagship verse. Gratitude: that was the ticket! *Thank You that he can still do the job he loves.* She repeated it like a mantra as she wiped dust from rows of books and scrubbed at the shelves with Murphy's Oil Soap.

". . . present your requests to God. . . ." Washing windows that nobody ever looked through, she presented them. *Heal*

him, Lord . . . You are the Great Physician; You are the doer of miracles. You can heal my husband.

She stood on a chair to take down the light fixture and empty it of the crisp, dead flies that lay in the bottom like cargo in the hold of a miniature ship. *". . . And the peace of God, which transcends all understanding, will guard your hearts and your minds in Christ Jesus. . . ."* By the time the school day was over, her back ached and the attic shone. Wringing out her mop for the last time, Jane assessed the results of her day with mixed feelings: Butter-colored sunlight spilled across the weathered pine floor, and the air smelled as fresh as springtime, but her heart still knew nothing of peace.

She was emptying her bucket into the kitchen sink when she heard Leander at the door. She went to meet him, searching his face for a clue to how the day had gone. His mouth was framed with vertical lines of fatigue. "How was it?"

"Fine, fine. Looks to be a good group in concert band this year. Choir starts tomorrow, so I don't know about them yet." His voice was strangely slurred.

"How do you feel?"

"Tired, but I expected that. I'll get back into the swing of things before long."

"Come and have some coffee, and tell me about it."

He yawned. "I think I'll lie down first."

"Of course."

❧

DeShaun stood behind his station at the long steel table. The white chef's jacket with his name embroidered above the right pocket, the apron smeared with cake batter, and the white toque on his head filled him with a sense of purpose and authority he had never imagined possible. This was only the first week of culinary school, yet he already felt he had been here all his life. The grinding hum of mixers, the smells of cinnamon and burnt chocolate sponge, the grit of spilled sugar on the red tile floor beneath the soles of his black nonskid shoes . . . all of it was as familiar to him as his own attic bedroom back in Copper Cove.

He liked this place. Chef Andrews, who was in charge of the whole culinary arts program, was cool, and smart, and already knew each of their names. He had a way of making even the weekly ServSafe classes fun and interesting. Harder to describe was the . . . he searched for the right word for it . . . the *joy* that everyone around him seemed to find in cooking. It was the same feeling that had come over him the very first time he had cooked something by himself. A grilled cream cheese and grape jelly sandwich on raisin bread, it had been. He had made one for Jada, too, and had been overcome then with a sense of wonder that he could create something that tasted so good and made someone else so happy. That thrill had never left him.

Not only that, but there were kids of all colors here. Not like Copper Cove, where everybody stared at him because he was the only black kid in town, besides his brother and sister. It was a relief, sometimes, to feel invisible. DeShaun looked around him at the other fifteen students in their own white toques and aprons. For the first time in his life, he really belonged somewhere.

Leander didn't get back into the swing of things, not really. Three weeks into the school year, he was perpetually exhausted. Everywhere he walked, he seemed to trip over his own feet and his voice had developed a lazy drag that never went away. One Saturday afternoon, toward the end of September, Jane went looking for him and discovered him missing. Perhaps he was taking a nap. She put her head around the bedroom door. "Leander?" The quilt on the bed was smooth and unruffled, just as she had left it that morning. The door of the attached bath stood open; he was not there either. She went through the rooms of the house, calling. "Leander?" Not in any of the other bedrooms, nor in the family room, nor anywhere else on the first floor.

She found him in the little attached workshop where he had for so long made a second income by cleaning and repairing musical instruments. He was sitting on the high stool at his workbench, absently running the smooth metal of a roller cone over the palm of one hand.

"There you are! You crazy man, you had me worried. What are you doing?"

He held up the roller cone. "Many's the dent I've removed from the bell of a French horn or trombone with this little tool."

"I remember when your mother got you that set for Christmas. What was it, ten, twelve years ago?"

"Something like that." He fitted the roller cone back into its place on the storage board. "It's been well used."

Jane looked around the shop, at the tools hung neatly on their pegboards, the shelves of cleaners, and the hooks that held Leander's aprons. The air smelled of metal, of valve oil and brass polish. It was a warm and familiar world—her husband's own corner of the universe. On the workbench lay a disassembled tuba. She picked up one curved brass piece and ran a hand over it. "What are you mulling over, out here all by yourself?"

"I'm going to sell it."

"*Sell* it?" For some reason, she thought he meant the tuba.

"All of it." He swept his arm to take in the whole room. "I can't repair instruments, Jane. I don't have the dexterity or the strength or—frankly—the heart for it anymore."

"But, Leander, one day you will again!"

He shook his head.

"Yes, you will! God promises! His Word says He heals people, if only they have enough faith. Don't you believe what the Bible says?"

"You know I do. Of course I do."

"Then why don't you believe it when it says God can heal you?"

"Of course I believe God *can* heal me. But you've heard Dr. Gutierrez—"

Fury rose in her like soup in a boiling pot. "It's *God* I'm listening to, not some human doctor!"

"Not every disease is curable."

"Then how do you explain Scripture? Verses like, 'I will do whatever you ask in my name'? Jesus healed people all the time and . . . and He told them, 'Your faith has made you well.' Are you saying the Bible's not true?" She could not help the shrillness in her voice. She needed him to understand what she was saying. His life—their life together—depended on it.

He sighed. "I don't know. I don't know why, so often, the Bible seems to say one thing when our experience tells us something else."

"Lack of faith."

"Oh, Jane."

"Don't *Oh, Jane* me! Does or does not the Bible say that God will heal people?"

He was silent for a long time. At last, he said, "Maybe it's like math. Just like mathematic principles say that one plus one equals two, the Bible also tells us that if you have enough faith, you can be healed."

"See?" She felt a triumphant relief.

"But you don't really grasp the truth and depth and beauty of math until you begin to understand calculus."

"What is that supposed to mean?"

"Jane, who is it that learns the formula 'one plus one equals two'?"

"That's a ridiculous question."

"It's schoolchildren, that's who. First-graders. But who is it that learns the deeper truths of calculus?"

"You're clouding the point."

"Mature students. Calculus is for people who are growing up."

"I'm going back in the house."

"When we camp on one plus one equaling two, we know so much less about the world. I'm just saying that when the numbers don't seem to add up, maybe it's an invitation out of first grade and into Calculus 101."

She was trembling with rage. "You're just looking for an excuse to give in."

He shook his head.

"I never took you for a coward, Leander Darling." Jane turned her back on him and went to the kitchen. There, she pulled a bunch of celery and a bell pepper from the refrigerator and began to chop them with savage intent.

Halfway through the second celery stalk, her anger began to subside to remorse. Leander might lack faith, but he was not a coward. Of all things, he was not that. She should never have said such a thing. She laid down the knife and stared out the window. She would just have to be patient with her husband until God revealed the truth to him. *Lord, show him that I'm right. That Your Word is right when it says You can heal him.* Wiping her hands on a dish towel, she went back to the workshop.

He was still sitting on the stool, his head in his hands.

"I'm sorry, Leander. You're not a coward. You're facing this ordeal with courage and humor and . . ." She could not say *faith*, because that was not true. Not yet. She pulled up a stool next to him and sat.

He said, "I may as well be completely honest. I'm thinking of hanging up my teacher's hat after Christmas. I don't have the stamina to stand up and teach for six hours a day anymore."

Jane knew without question that this was a mistake. She could not let him talk about such a thing; to leave teaching would be the beginning of the end for him. She said the first thing that came to mind. "Let's get out of the house. We could call Tom and Abigail, or Ken and Constance, and see if they want to go to Quahog for dinner."

He hesitated. Then, with a resigned smile, "All right. What should we have? Italian? Seafood?"

"Your call."

"Ivy and Nick mentioned some little Irish pub they like. Give them a call and ask where it is."

She felt relief in her very bones. "Better yet, why don't we ask them to go with us? It'll be nice to see the children. DeShaun's home for the weekend."

"Now you're talking."

She got up and went to call Ivy. She would *make* him listen to her, and to God. It would just take time.

Ivy received the invitation with enthusiasm and gave her mother directions to Paddy O'Leary's in Quahog. "Meet you there at six?"

"Six is fine."

"Nick will probably go straight from work and meet us there," Ivy said. "What's the occasion, anyhow?"

"Your father needs a pick-me-up. He's talking about selling his repair equipment and giving up teaching."

"Oh, my."

"Yes. He says he doesn't have the dexterity or strength to repair instruments, nor the stamina to stand on his feet all day."

"I'm so sorry."

"I know. Let's try to cheer him up tonight, shall we? Be tactful and don't mention it."

"I'm always tactful."

This was far from the truth, but Jane only said, "See you at six, love."

"See you at six."

❧

Ivy and the kids were waiting at Paddy O'Leary's when Jane and Leander got there. Nick arrived just as they'd ordered their drinks. Leander tended to choke on steak, no matter how small Jane cut the pieces, so she helped him choose a lobster macaroni and cheese made with Irish cheddar instead.

When the server had collected their menus and left them, Ivy turned to her father. "Mom says you're selling the repair business, Dad."

Jane was irritated. "Ivy!"

Leander put a hand on her arm. "It's okay, Jane. We might as well talk about it. Yes, I'm going to sell my equipment. It's time."

"And what's this about giving up work?"

"Call it an early retirement."

"Isn't that a little premature? I mean, you could still teach if you didn't have to stand on your feet all day. Have you thought about a wheelchair?"

"*Ivy!*" It came out sharper than Jane intended.

"What? It seems like the obvious solution. School buildings are already handicap accessible. They have ramps and the right bathrooms and things. Why shouldn't Dad take advantage of them?"

Jane did not like the look on Leander's face. As though he had caught a glimpse through an open door into a new and wonderful world. "Your father is not going to need a wheelchair."

Jada spoke up. "There's a girl at school, in fourth grade, who has one. It's electric. She controls it from the armrests or something."

"It's a great idea, Leander," put in Nick. "You could try it, at least, and if it's still too much, maybe the school would let you work half days."

"Yeah, Grampie." This from DeShaun. "Everyone there

thinks you're really cool. They'd be bummed if you didn't come back."

"That's enough of that kind of talk!" Jane cried. She stifled a childish urge to clap her hands over her ears. "He does not—*not*—need a wheelchair, do you hear me?" In the sudden silence, she looked around the table into each face, so that no one would miss her message. "It would be like giving up. And we are *not* ready to give up."

DeShaun, Jada, and Hammer, always uneasy in the presence of raised voices, began to shoot one another apprehensive glances.

Ivy cleared her throat. "It would be like giving up *what*, exactly, Mom?"

"Hope." Jane gestured futilely. "Faith. Once he's in a wheelchair, there'll be no going back."

"There was never going to be any going back." Leander's voice was gentle. "This disease moves only forward. You know that, Jane."

Tears rose in her eyes and began to slip down her face.

Ivy said, "It seems like the real giving up would be in quitting teaching, which is what Dad loves to do."

"It will wear him out. He'll—" The words choked her, and she could not finish.

Leander took her hand. "I'll what?"

"You need rest. You can't heal if you're exhausted all the time."

"I'd rather drop in the harness than standing in the stall, Jane. I've always said that."

Across the restaurant, Jane noticed two servers heading their way, laden with trays of what could only be their meal orders. She sat up straight and wiped her eyes with a napkin. "Well. We don't have to think about it now; there's no hurry. Let's see how you get along this fall and decide then."

A busboy hurried ahead of the servers to set up a pair of tray stands beside their table.

"Hope everyone's hungry!" called their server, in her shiny waitress tone.

"Oh, we are." From the corner of her eye, Jane saw Ivy exchange a look with Nick. "Now," she went on brightly. "Fish and chips belong to Jada and Hammer—yes, there, and there. And what did you have, DeShaun, the Guinness stew? Oh, that smells wonderful! Lobster mac and cheese right here, and who ordered that delicious-looking burger . . . ?"

By the time their plates had been disbursed, everyone seemed willing enough to let the subject lie. It was easy then to turn the topic to the children's busy lives. The whole point of this dinner was to cheer Leander up, Jane thought. There was no need to go talking about things that were only going to upset everybody.

8

THE SUNDAY CHURCH SERVICE WAS OVER, and Laura's pilgrimage from her seat to the front door of the church had begun. It was never as easy as walking from point A to point B. The Presbyterians of Phoenix were a friendly lot, and a journey of twenty feet could easily take her twenty minutes. Laura didn't mind. In fact, talking with people after church was one of her favorite parts of the week. The first to waylay her that morning was old Milton waiting in the aisle, leaning on his cane, smiling toothlessly and holding out a gold-wrapped Werther's caramel.

"Hi there, Milton." She accepted the candy, holding her breath, because poor Milton always smelled like he hadn't bathed or washed his clothes in about four years. "How are you this week?"

"Finer'n frog hair, Laura. On Tuesd'y, I won twenty-five

dollars on a scratch ticket." His gummy smile could have wrapped around the room.

"You did? Wow, I've never won anything on a scratch ticket!" The fact that she had never bought a scratch ticket was beside the point.

He leaned in close. "Want to know what I did with the money?"

Laura leaned back. "Mmmm . . . bought more scratch tickets?"

"Yessir!" Milton slapped his leg and laughed, exuding a noxious cloud of breath into her face. "And by gum if I didn't win me another thirty-five dollars!"

Laura coughed. "So, how much of the first twenty-five did you have to spend before you won the thirty-five?"

"All of it. I got me five five-dollar tickets, and 'twasn't but the last one that won anything. I spent five on the first one, then twenty-five on the next ones, but I come out five dollars ahead, didn't I?"

"I can't argue with math like that. Congratulations, Milton."

"Thank you. And have another candy, here. I got two bags this week." Laura took the second Werther's and moved on. Behind her, she heard him telling the news to someone else: "On Tuesd'y, I won twenty-five dollars on a scratch ticket!"

An unexpected wave of something sweet and painful rushed through Laura. In his simple life, Milton had probably forgotten more about happiness than she had ever learned. He was old and poor, likely uneducated, probably lonely. Yet he got more joy out of winning twenty-five dollars on a scratch ticket than Laura got out of her whole paycheck.

The next morning, she made a phone call and spoke to the semiretired grandmother who ran the church office.

"Dora, when is Milton's birthday?"

It was in November, apparently. Laura hung up, satisfied, made a note to herself on her phone calendar, and went back to work.

David opened the front door of his parents' house and stepped inside. From the kitchen, he could hear the faint chugging of the dishwasher, but otherwise all was silent. "Hello?" he called.

"Up here!" His mother's voice floated down from the recesses of the second floor. A second later she appeared at the top of the stairs with a white sneaker in one hand. "I'm just helping your father dress his feet. He'll be right down."

"I'll wait in the kitchen."

The pot still held an inch or so of coffee. In the cupboard, he found a mug that said *Aetna, for life*, and poured himself a cup. The mug had been in that cupboard for as long as David could remember. No doubt it had come as a freebie from an insurance company and, in a contrary twist of the universe, had survived intact long after mugs with more sentimental value had broken and been thrown away. On the kitchen bar lay the Saturday morning paper. He found the sports section and sat on a stool to read while he waited. The Red Sox had beat the Phillies. The Pirates had beat the Reds. The Patriots' coach was moving on. An Eagles tight end was being investigated for anabolic steroid use. Halfway through the second page, he heard his parents coming down. David folded the paper loosely on the counter and went to meet them.

He stood at the bottom of the stairs and watched his father's slow progress. With his right hand, Leander clutched the wall railing. With his left, he leaned on his cane. Jane stood just behind him, ready to grab him if he should stumble.

"Hey, Dad."

"Good morning, David." He wore a plaid flannel shirt a size too big and jeans cinched tightly at the waist. The pants hung away from each thin leg like loose sails luffing around a mast. With his too-large clothes and new white sneakers, chosen for traction rather than style, his father looked like a child dressed up for the first day of school.

David forced back a sudden ache in his throat and took the stairs two at a time. "I'll take you from here, Dad."

"Are you sure?" His mother sounded tired.

"Sure."

David waited as his father moved his cane down a step, followed by his left foot, then his right.

"Maybe just grab his jacket from the front closet before you go," Jane said.

"I will."

"Give me a kiss, then," she said to Leander. He tipped his head back so she could drop a kiss on his lips. "Have a good time. I'll be here when you get home." Jane retreated to the second floor, leaving David alone on the stairs with his father.

"Bye, Mom." To his father, he said, "Ready to do some serious damage to a plate of corned beef hash?"

Cane down. Left foot. Right foot. Rest. His father smiled.

"Poached eggs may be more my speed. I'm afraid corned beef hash would do me in."

"I'll eat enough of it for both of us, then." Cane. Left foot. Right foot. Rest. They reached the bottom at last. "Want to sit down and catch your breath a minute?" David asked.

"No, no. Once I'm up, it's easier to stay up. Just get my jacket, if you wouldn't mind, and we can be on our way."

They went to the Silver Star Diner, the only restaurant in Copper Cove that served breakfast. When they had ordered and their coffee had been poured, Leander leaned forward. "David, what am I going to do about your mother?"

"What do you mean?"

"This expectation she has that somehow I'm going to be healed." He made an irritated gesture. "She insists on clinging to it, and she blames me because it's not happening."

"Blames you?"

"She says it's my lack of faith."

"Don't take that to heart, Dad. She's in denial."

"That's what Ivy and Amy say."

"They're right. She's convinced herself that refusing to accept your disease is an act of faith."

His father sipped his coffee. "Your mother has never liked to face unpleasant truths."

"None of us do, I guess."

"Well, she's going to have to face it sooner or later, and I'd rather it be sooner." Leander rubbed his forehead with one hand. "She has no idea the difference it would make to have her in my corner right now."

He hated to see his father helpless. "What can I do, Dad? Want me to talk to her?"

Leander gave a halfhearted shrug. "You can try, but I don't think it will help. Until the scales fall from her eyes and she's able to admit that I have a terminal disease, nothing anyone says will change her attitude. And I . . ." His voice faltered. "I just don't have it in me to stand up to her. I know it sounds stupid and . . . and weak, but some days it's all I can do to put one foot in front of the other. To keep my own head above water, so to speak. I don't have energy left over to take on a fight with someone as determinedly committed to her own point of view as your mother is on this."

David felt a surge of anger. Why couldn't his mother put her own need for comfort aside for the sake of giving real, material help to her seriously ill husband? But the anger was gone as quickly as it had come. His mother was one of the kindest, most loving people he knew. It was just that people couldn't help their blind spots. "If you and Mom were entirely on the same page with this thing . . . ," David asked. "That is, if you were really facing this illness head-on as a team, what would be the next step for you?"

"The next step?"

"The next . . . I don't know, action. What would you do on your own behalf?"

"A walker. I'd get a walker."

"It's time to graduate from the cane, then?"

"It's not enough support anymore. But your mother will have a conniption if I mention it. She'll say I'm moving backward, not forward, and where is my faith, and on and on."

"With a walker, you'd have enough support to . . . what, feel safer? Move around more freely?"

"Yes. For now, anyway."

"Then consider it done."

His father frowned.

"The girls and I will take care of it."

"But your mother—"

"Leave Mom to us. She's no match for the combined forces of Ivy and Amy."

"Poor woman."

"She'll thank us in the end. She wants what's best for you, Dad; she really does. She's just . . . a little mixed up about what that is. She'll get there. Meanwhile, the rest of us will see to it that you have what you need."

"Thank you, David." The relief and gratitude on his father's face brought sudden tears to David's eyes. Hastily, he picked up a bottle of hot sauce and examined the label.

There was silence for several moments; then his father cleared his throat. "Well," he said briskly. "Looks like the Patriots will be getting a new coach."

David looked up from the hot sauce and grinned. "Yeah, looks like it. And it's about time too."

∿

After church on Sunday, David caught up with Amy at the front of the sanctuary, where she was coiling microphone cords. "Listen." He glanced around to be sure their mother was nowhere in earshot. "I think Dad should have a walker."

Amy did not seem surprised. "I think so too, but you know Mom. She'll say it's not necessary."

"Meanwhile, it's Dad who suffers. I've talked to him, and he doesn't think a cane alone is enough for him anymore."

"Well . . . I'm open to suggestions."

"What if we just *got* him a walker and dropped it off at the house one day? Bypass her and give it straight to him."

Amy thought about this. "All right. There's that medical supply place in Quahog. But isn't it supposed to go through their insurance company first?"

He waved this away. "They can always submit the bill later. Want to run over there with me right now and pick one out?"

"Might as well. Mom's not going to be very happy with us, though."

"This is about Dad, not Mom. Besides, I thought your motto was 'It's easier to get forgiveness than permission.'"

Amy smiled demurely. "Well, yes. And one must live up to one's mottoes, after all."

❧

DeShaun stood at his station, hands clasped behind his back, attention fixed on Chef Couteau, a small man with an enormous walrus mustache who spoke jovially in a French accent. The topic of the class was knife skills. On the board before each of them lay a pile of carrots, a bowl of green peppers, several onions, and a bunch of herbs.

"Ve-ge-tab-les," Chef pronounced, "can be *vairy* witty things. For eenstance, does anybody know how should you keel a salad?"

DeShaun looked around. He hoped he wasn't the only one in the class who had no idea what it meant to "keel a salad."

With his knife, Chef Couteau feigned a slicing motion across his throat. "How to keel a salad, anybody? *Non?*"

Was he saying "*kill* a salad"?

"Well? Nobody? I'll tell you zen: to keel a salad, you go for the carrot-id artery!" Picking up the carrot from his own board, Chef waved it in the air as he beamed around at them all.

The class stared at him blankly.

Chef was undaunted. He exchanged the carrot for a pepper and brandished it at them. "A bell peppair!" he cried, in his French burr. "Where does a bell peppair go, to have a few dreenks after work?"

More blank stares.

"She goes to ze salad bar!" he shouted.

DeShaun was as uncertain as the rest of his classmates.

Picking up the onion: "What can you make wiz ze beans and *les oignons?*" Chef looked around in the silence, nearly bursting with a sense of his own hilarity. "Tear gas!" he gasped.

In the silence, DeShaun's face began to burn with that peculiar embarrassment that comes from watching somebody else make a fool of himself.

But Chef Couteau did not seem to realize that no one thought him funny. "Why should you be cairful to tend to your herb garden?" he cried. "Why? Uzzerwize, you will have a bad thyme! Get it? *Bad thyme!*"

The class stared at him, baffled, except for one student. After a beat of silence, the girl at the station next to DeShaun's released a snort of laughter. Then, with her hand over her mouth, she began to giggle.

DeShaun shot her a sideways glance. Her shoulders were shaking with silent mirth. DeShaun looked at Chef again: had he noticed?

Chef had, and was smiling and nodding around the room

like a performer who had just received a standing ovation. "A bad thyme!" he repeated triumphantly.

DeShaun wasn't sure what to do. Around him, the rest of his classmates seemed to be waking up to the joke, although only the girl beside him actually seemed to think it was funny enough to laugh at. Her stifled giggles escaped in a snort, and then a whoop, and then she was laughing freely, as though from her very depths, while around the room, her classmates shifted uneasy *What's her problem?* glances at each other and half-smiled in pity.

"It's not that funny," DeShaun muttered to her.

The girl pulled a tissue from the pocket of her chef's jacket, wiped her eyes with it, and put the tissue away. "Sorry!" she called to the instructor. "Sorry about that. I've got myself under control now."

Chef Couteau began to show them how to slice their carrots, but DeShaun was only half-listening. The other half of him was watching this girl with the long, shiny dark hair pulled into a ponytail and the eyes shaped like a cat's. When Chef instructed them to pick up their knives and follow along with him, DeShaun took one side step closer to the girl.

He held his carrot down with one hand and concentrated on copying Chef's movements. "What was so funny?" he said.

She smiled down at her own carrot. "You couldn't hear it?"

"Well . . . I heard the jokes, but they were pretty lame."

"It wasn't the jokes; it was . . . He's not really French."

DeShaun looked at the rotund man in the jaunty chef's toque. "He's not?"

"You can't tell?"

"How would I know? He sounds French."

She made a noise of contempt. "No, he doesn't. I grew up in France, and he doesn't sound anything like a real French person."

"You mean he's faking it?"

"Bet you anything."

DeShaun shook his head and, smiling, began to julienne another carrot.

When the girl spoke again, it startled him. "What's your name?"

"Me? DeShaun."

"Nice to meet you, DeShaun. I'm Penelope. I'm going to be a pastry chef. How about you?"

"Ah . . . maybe a caterer, I'm not sure. Hey, that must've been cool, living in France."

"It was. I'll tell you about it sometime, if you want."

"Sure. Maybe we could have dinner together." His knife slipped, and he nearly cut his hand. He couldn't believe he'd said that: it had just come out. DeShaun hadn't always appreciated having skin the color of dark cocoa, but he was grateful for it now; maybe she wouldn't notice his neck turning red.

Her knife moved through her carrots faster and surer than his. "Tonight? Five o'clock at the dining hall?" She flashed him a quick smile. "We can critique the food together."

"Okay. Good. That sounds good."

"A leettle less talking in ze back, *s'il vous plait*!" called Chef, from the front of the room.

There went Penelope's shoulders again, shaking with laughter. Five o'clock seemed a long time away.

When Jada had come to live with Ivy and Nick, at the age of nine, she had often spent nights at Jane and Leander's house. She and Jane had cooked together, sung songs, and read stories. They had been the best of friends. But as Jada grew, they had done this less often, until one day, Jane realized that it had been nearly a year since their last sleepover, and she was missing her granddaughter. Well. That would have to be remedied. Midweek, she called and invited Jada for Friday night. They would make pizzas, they decided over the phone, and deep-fried doughnuts—Jada was an avid fan of the deep-fryer—and afterward, they would paint each other's toenails and watch *Pitch Perfect*.

Friday evening found them in the kitchen together, while Leander watched the evening news in the family room. Jada was shredding cheese for the pizzas, but her mind was clearly on other things. "Did girls have cornrows when you were a teenager, Grammie Jane?"

"Oh, I suppose some girls had them, in places like Boston or Providence, but it wasn't really the style for white girls, and there weren't any black girls where I grew up. In any case, I think Afros were more popular back then."

Jada regarded her grandmother's gray head with interest. "What was *your* hair like?"

"Long and straight was the name of the game." Jane, slicing mushrooms, smiled at the memory. "Back then, we didn't have the flatirons girls use today, so we'd flip our hair over the ironing board and iron it with the same iron we used on our clothes."

"That seems like it would be really bad for your hair."

"I'm sure it was. We were always conditioning it with mayonnaise or rinsing it with things like eggs and beer to make it shiny. In the summer, I'd rinse it with lemon juice and lie out in the sun to bleach it blonde."

"Did it work?"

"Not really. I was a redhead, so it turned more brassy than anything else, but I didn't mind. I thought I was very glamorous. The things we did for the sake of beauty!" She added wryly, "The things women *still* do."

Jada, who loved a story, said, "What? What else did you do?"

"Well . . . let me think. We wore our pants very tight back then—the tighter the better. If you had a date in the evening, you'd start getting ready for it that morning by putting on your smallest jeans—usually, they were so tight you'd have to lie flat on your back to get them zipped up. Then, with the jeans on, you'd sit in a bathtub of warm water until they were soaked through, and all day long, as those jeans dried, they'd get tighter and tighter."

Jada was listening with her mouth open.

"And if you felt like having your hair wavy instead of straight one day, you'd roll it up on tomato soup cans before you went to bed and sleep in them."

"Ow!"

"Ow is right. You'd roll up a pillow under your neck, so that the back of your head stayed off the bed, and you'd sleep on your back all night like that. There was a certain knack to it."

Jada finished with the cheese, reached for a stick of pepperoni, and began to slice it. "Mom says if I want cornrows, I have to earn the money for them myself."

"That's not a bad thing, you know. If you really want them, you'll do it."

"Why can't she just pay for them? I'd pay her back, when I earned the money."

Jane had to laugh. "I'm sure you would. But it sounds like she's already said no to that particular plan."

"She says I have to learn to take no for an answer."

"That's true. We all have to learn to take no for an answer in life. It's part of being an adult. Try to do it with good grace, honey."

Jada was concentrating on her pepperoni. "Like . . . how you ask God to heal Grampie and He tells you no."

Jane stared at her granddaughter, feeling oddly as though the air had been sucked out of the room. She opened her mouth. "I . . ." She had no idea what she had started to say, and closed it again.

"You have to accept His answer with good grace, right?"

That's different! she wanted to protest. *It's God's will to heal people!* But all it once, it seemed so complicated and sad and hard to understand. She did not want to think, tonight, about why Leander did not seem to be getting better. She wanted to enjoy her granddaughter and forget the weight of the world for a few hours. So she said only, "That's right, Jada. Sometimes, I have to take no for an answer too." And in the next breath, she said, "How about we sing some duets while the pizzas cook?"

"Ooh, can we do the whole score from *West Side Story*, like we did for the arts program grand opening?"

Jane, breathing a prayer of thanks for the distractibility of thirteen, agreed.

For a full week, Jane had lain in bed until nearly eight o'clock every morning. She still woke by instinct, as the darkness beyond her curtains silvered into dawn and the last birds of September wove their scant songs through the pale light. But, whereas for decades this time of day had been Jane's cue to push back the quilt, pull on her robe and old shearling slippers, and make her way downstairs to the coffeepot, now she wanted only to pull the covers over her head and go back to sleep.

All week, Leander had washed and dressed without her help, had made his own precarious way downstairs and fixed his own breakfast, then gone off to school with Dean. Every day, he had peered into her face, concerned, and asked if she was all right, if there was anything he could do for her, and every time she said no, she was just being lazy, and hoped he wouldn't mind making his own toast again this morning. Listening as he made his hesitant, thumping way down the stairs, she prayed that he wouldn't fall, and despised her own inability to get up and help him. Now, having heard the front door close at last, Jane rolled onto her back and stared at the old crack that ran horizontally across the ceiling. Leander had vowed for years to patch and paint it, something he had never gotten around to.

It was the comment Jada had made, of course. About having to take no for an answer where Leander's life was concerned. That was when this lassitude had set in, this crushing fatigue. She was sensible enough to recognize it as a warning flag of depression, yet she felt incapable of taking action. What was she supposed to do: go to the doctor and get a pill? She felt in her bones that she wanted a different solution. Something that would get to the root of the problem and not simply manage it, but actually heal it. Hers was, she was certain, a spiritual problem, and as such should have a spiritual cure. She let her mind drift, casting about for comfort she never found. *Where are you, God? Help me!* It was more a cry of the heart than a fully articulated thought. Day after day, no answer was visited on her. No help came.

Eventually, she forced herself out of bed. The coffeepot, on its automatic cycle, had brewed the coffee, kept it hot for two hours, and shut itself off. In the daylit kitchen, Jane poured herself a tepid cup, put it in the microwave for two minutes, and carried it to the front porch. The Bible, when she picked it up from the wicker side table, felt burdensome and unfamiliar. Like an obedient, preprogrammed robot, she leafed through to the day's reading.

Praise the LORD, my soul;
    all my inmost being, praise his holy name.
Praise the LORD, my soul,
    and forget not all his benefits—
who forgives all your sins
    and heals all your diseases,
who redeems your life from the pit
    and crowns you with love and compassion,
who satisfies your desires with good things
    so that your youth is renewed like the eagle's.

Really, God? she thought. *"Who heals all your diseases," really?* Was it just an empty promise? That same God, who was supposed to be able to heal all your diseases, in the same sentence claimed the ability to forgive all your sins. Why should she believe one and not the other? It didn't make even the most basic of intellectual sense.

She snapped her Bible shut and, burying her face in her hands, tried to will away the numbness that had seeped like a sour fog into her every cell. Was everything she'd based her life on a lie? Had she invested her soul in a snake-oil God: attractive, promising, but ultimately powerless? There was no answer. There was only emptiness and a profound fatigue. Feeling as fragile and spent as a November seedpod, she laid her Bible back on the end table, got to her feet, and shuffled to the refrigerator, where she found a carton of eggs. More for something to do than because she had any real plan for them, she began to crack them, one by one, into a bowl.

Shortly before lunch, Ivy called. "Mom, I'm worried about you."

"That's sweet, Ivy, but we're fine."

"No, not *you* plural—*you* singular. I'm worried about *you*."

"Whatever for?" Jane, who had been sitting at the kitchen counter, trying to summon the energy to go face the laundry, felt as though she were speaking in some kind of dream.

"You seem . . . frazzled. Overwhelmed. Listen, is there anything I can do to help? With Dad, I mean. Please tell me if there is. You know Nick and I want to do whatever we can."

The real problem, Jane knew, was not Leander and his

needs. The real problem was her own lack of peace and reso-
lution, and that was not something Ivy or anyone could help
with. "That's good of you," she said, "but we're doing just fine
right now. I'll let you know the minute we need anything."

"Well . . . How about if we have family supper at my
house this week? Just to give you a rest, I mean. Not forever
or anything."

Jane felt her hackles raise. "I'm not an invalid. I am perfectly capable of hosting family supper here, just as I've always done."

"I know you are, Mom. Of course you're capable. I just
thought maybe you'd welcome a break from having to do
everything yourself."

"I don't do everything myself." Her words came out as
tightly wound as violin strings. "You kids always bring something to contribute."

"Right. I'm just saying I would be glad to host it for a
week or two, if it would help."

"Not necessary, but thank you. I'll see you on Thursday
night, as usual." Jane hung up, anger like a cold band around
her heart. In these days, when she had little enough to hold
on to, why would Ivy try to take this away from her too?

9

On Thursday morning, Jane awoke with a headache. Leander had been up twice in the night to use the bathroom, and fearful that he would trip, even with the new walker the children had brought him, she had walked him there and back. The second time, she had lain awake until nearly four thirty, then drifted into a half doze, only to jerk awake again and again. At seven thirty she got up at last, irritated with herself for already having wasted half the morning. Her Bible reading was wooden; to pray was to hammer against a brass sky. At ten o'clock, she lay down on the couch and fell asleep. Her dreams were vivid and unsettling, and when at last she awoke, the clock on the mantel said 1:34 in the afternoon.

She still had not given a moment's thought to family supper. It was Jane's turn to provide the entrée tonight, and they would all be arriving in a few hours. Mentally, she catalogued the contents of the refrigerator and freezer. Not enough chicken to feed everyone. Not enough time to thaw and cook a roast. Amy would bring a salad, and Ivy was on dessert. Libby would bring a side dish.

Spaghetti? She had enough pasta, and there was plenty of ground beef in the freezer. Heaving herself to a sitting position, she rubbed her face. Cooking seemed a gargantuan task, a veritable Everest looming before her, demanding to be scaled by five o'clock. She shuffled to the kitchen and opened the refrigerator, feeling uninspired. Parmesan cheese.

She opened a cupboard. No canned tomatoes. Closing it again, she turned to the coffeepot, poured herself a cold cup, and took a long, shuddering swallow. There. That should do the trick. She followed this with a glass of water and began to feel more awake. *What to make for supper?*

Jane took her light jacket and purse from their hook by the door, and found her clogs. She scribbled a note for Leander, in case she should still be gone when he got home from school. *Ran to the store.* Leaving it on the counter, she went out.

Price Mart, two blocks down, was a small and shabby grocery store of 1970s vintage. Jane hardly ever shopped there, preferring the bigger and cheaper Hannaford supermarket across town. Today, however, she could not summon the energy for that kind of trek. She pulled into Price Mart's tiny parking lot and went in. It was like walking back in time, with yellow hand-lettered signs announcing the sales. The two cash registers at the front still rang when they opened.

In the thickly frosted freezer section, she discovered bags of Michelina's meatballs and, shamefaced, bought four of them. She added premade spaghetti sauce to her cart, a thing she had never bought in her life. It would have to do, she thought dully. It was all she could manage.

At home, she emptied the sauce into a large pot, added the frozen meatballs, and buried the empty jars deep in the recycling bin. She set it to simmer on low, then went to lie down on the couch again. Leander still was not home. Within minutes, she had slipped back into the relief of semi-sleep.

At four, she woke with a start and remembered she had forgotten to put some meatless sauce aside for Amy.

"Hello, Sleeping Beauty," Leander said from the recliner, where he was reading a magazine.

"A nap." Jane sat up, befogged and disoriented. "I was just taking a nap." She shuffled back into the kitchen and considered the bubbling, heaving morass under the pot lid. It needed something. She added thyme, oregano, and a dash of red wine, and set it again to simmer. But first, she ladled out a small pot, minus the meatballs, and set it aside. Not exactly vegetarian, perhaps, but what Amy didn't know wouldn't hurt her. She began to count out the plates and silverware for the table.

By the time the family began to arrive, she was fighting a migraine.

Ivy saw it at once. Setting her salad bowl on the counter, she took Jane's face between her hands. "Mom, what's wrong?"

Jane only shook her head, afraid she would disintegrate if she tried to speak.

"You're exhausted," her daughter said. "Enough is enough. I'm hosting dinner after this, no discussion."

She opened her mouth to protest, but Ivy spoke over her. "This is *family* dinner, not the Jane Darling show. Everyone gets a vote about where we'll meet, and if I have to speak to the rest of them about siding with me, believe me, I will. We love you, Mom; you're a wonderful hostess and the very hub of our family, but for right now, you need a break. Week after next, family dinner will be at my house. All you have to do is show up."

Mutely, Jane nodded, a little afraid at the overwhelming relief that washed over her. She felt that she was surrendering forever something that was precious on many levels, and moreover, that she was glad to do it. "Thank you," she managed.

Ivy kissed her on the forehead and released her face. "You're welcome."

✒

"What makes a waltz different from other dances is that it's a three-count, instead of a four- or eight-count," Joe explained.

Mitch looked at him blankly. At least two nights a week now found him at Joe's place. Amy thought he was helping Joe rebuild the Mustang, but that was just smoke and mirrors, an excuse for all the time he was spending on the landlord's side of the building.

From the moment Amy had told him about Joe and his ballroom dancing, Mitch had known he would ask the old man to teach him. The thought had sprung fully formed into his mind. Never had he so much as considered such an idea before. Until that moment, Mitch Harris had never been a dancer, and did not care to ever learn, thank you very much. In fact, so foreign was the very notion, and so shocked and surprised was he when the idea entered his head—yet at once so certain—that he figured God Himself must have planted it there. It was something that happened to him from time to time, hearing God's voice this way. It came most often when he was faced with a tricky problem on a job.

The first time, he had been fresh out of prison, working with a contractor who had dared to take a chance on him, and desperate to do a good job so the contractor would keep him on. They were siding a house, and the man had handed him a circular saw and told him to change the blade. Mitch had never even held a saw before but, too proud to ask, had determined to figure it out himself. He'd wrestled with the thing for a few minutes, then, in desperation, had done something he'd seen the Darling family do in the years he'd lived with them. He'd said, "God, please help me figure this thing out." And just like that, he'd seen what he needed to do. He changed the blade and took the saw back to his boss, limp with pride and relief. It seemed like such a small thing now, but it had been a big deal at the time. He knew God had shown him how to change that blade. He wasn't stupid, though: after that, if he didn't know how to do something, he asked his boss. When his boss wasn't around, he asked God, and God usually answered. Mitch figured that had something to do with why he had built such a good professional reputation. He and God didn't carry on what you might call minute-by-minute conversations throughout the day, but they were partners in the building trade; there was no doubt about that.

So one evening, Mitch had worked up his nerve, made his appearance in Joe's living room, and muttered his request.

"I . . . ah . . . was wondering if you might teach me . . . ah . . . you know . . . how to dance. As a surprise for Amy, sort of." His face burning, he'd added, "I'd pay you, of course."

A smile broke across the old man's leathered face, and he slapped his leg. "I'll be danged. You're a romantic, Mitch!"

He was no such thing, and he tried to protest, but Joe would not hear it. "Nothin' wrong with bein' a romantic, son. In fact, it'll get you from zero to sixty with yer girl faster'n a Corvette Stingray." He winked broadly.

If a person could spontaneously combust from embarrassment, Mitch was about to do it. He cleared his throat, a pitiful sound, and stared at a corner of the ceiling.

"Let's get 'er done, then!" Joe's enthusiasm for the job was high. He shuffled over to an old-fashioned phonograph under the window, and dropped the needle onto a record. Music filled the room.

A flash of panic went through Mitch. "Wait—here? Now? I thought I'd make an appointment with you next week, or something."

"No time like the present!" Joe was having a marvelous time already. He came and stood before Mitch, and held out his arms.

Mitch had learned a simple box step that night. Now, they were moving on to the waltz.

"You count 'one-two-three-one-two-three . . .' like that." Joe cocked his head toward the phonograph speakers. "This one's Strauss," he said. "One-two-three-one-two-three-one-two-three, see?"

"I think so."

"Good. Now, you're the fella, so your right hand goes on her back, just below her left shoulder blade, like so."

Mitch obeyed, putting his palm flat against the old man's grimy T-shirt.

"Elbow up, higher'n your wrist. And you want to hold her right hand about shoulder height. Not too tight, now, but not too loose neither."

Mitch took Joe's hand. "I feel stupid." He always said this.

"Ain't nothin' stupid about dancin' with the woman you love," Joe said firmly, as usual. "And you gotta learn somehow. Might's well do it in the privacy of my livin' room. Now, on *one*, you step forward with your left foot, and she steps back with her right, see?"

"She knows to do that?"

"You said she knows how to dance."

"Right. She does."

"So, you step forward—no, left foot. The man always leads with the left foot. Good. And on *two* . . ."

No matter how much they practiced, it didn't get any less embarrassing. Mitch, his face aflame with self-conscious heat, sincerely hoped this was all going to be worth it.

Thursday night family dinner would be the first at Ivy's house. The early weeks of autumn had not been friendly to the coast of Maine this year, shooing summer out with a stretch of dismal, rainy days and raw temperatures. This was one of the last evenings they would be able to eat outside.

"We probably shouldn't try it," said Nick. "It's too cold. There'll be frost by morning."

"Let's have a bonfire, then," Ivy said. "We'll have hot food in Crock-Pots, and we can roast marshmallows for dessert."

"Yes, a bonfire!" cried Hammer. "Can I build it?"

Nick amended this suggestion: "How about you and Jada and I all build it together?"

"Mom, can I invite Dillon?" asked Jada.

"Who in the world is Dillon?"

"My boyfriend."

Ivy and Nick looked at each other.

"Your *boyfriend*?"

"Yeah."

"Since when do you have a boyfriend?"

Jada looked away. "Since, like, a while."

"And who is this boyfriend, exactly?"

"I told you: Dillon. He's the hottest guy in eighth grade."

"Jada has a boyfriend!" Hammer singsonged.

"*And* the coolest," Jada added.

"How about if we try to describe our fellow human beings in non-temperature-related words, okay?" said Ivy.

"And no animals either!" put in Hammer. "Mom says you can't call girls foxes, chicks, or dogs."

"He's not a *girl*, and I didn't call him any of those things. Besides, nobody asked you," said Jada. "So, can I invite him, Mom?"

"Jada has a boyfriend!" Hammer made loud kissing noises in his sister's direction.

Jada rolled her eyes. "Shut up, Hammer."

"Don't tell your brother to shut up. And you're too young for a boyfriend."

"I'm thirteen!"

"Which is too young."

Her daughter was outraged. "I should have known you'd say that. I should never have told you!"

More kissing sounds from Hammer's quarter.

"Hammer, take that noise to your room. Jada, if you're ready to sit down and talk, then we can all discuss what might be the appropriate age for having a boyfriend." Ivy's voice was rising. "Hammer, *please*! Stop the kissing or get out of here!"

With a cackling laugh, Hammer ran from the room. Jada fixed her parents with a mutinous glare.

"Dad and I are going to need some time to talk about this," Ivy told her.

Jada gave a disgusted flip of her braids and stormed off in the direction of her own bedroom.

"And don't you roll your eyes at me!" Ivy called to her daughter's rigid back. To Nick, she said, "I'm right, aren't I? Thirteen's too young for a boyfriend named Dillon, who is both the hottest and the coolest boy in eighth grade?"

Nick was unequivocal. "As far as I'm concerned, she'll never be old enough for that."

"Correct answer. But how in the world are we supposed to enforce it when they're at school?"

"I don't have a clue."

"I wish kids came with an instruction manual."

"They don't," he said heartlessly.

"I know," said Ivy. "But they should."

Thursday evening was chilly, but Jane helped set up a buffet of hot foods in Ivy's kitchen.

"The problem with a bonfire," Amy pointed out as they carried their plates to the backyard, where the men tended the fire, "is that one side of you blisters while the other side freezes."

"Ah, the charms of autumn in Maine!" said Ivy.

Jada had been tagging Amy closely all evening. Now, she asked her aunt, "If you're in love with Mitch, how come you guys never hold hands or kiss or anything?"

Ivy shot an alarmed glance toward the other side of the fire, where Mitch was talking with her father. He appeared not to have heard.

Amy cleared her throat. "It's, ah . . . complicated."

"I have a boyfriend."

"You do?"

"His name is Dillon, and he is *so* hot. And so cool." Jada avoided her mother's eyes.

"Oh. And . . . um . . . what do your parents think about that?"

Jada made a noise of disgust. "Please. They don't remember what it's like to be in love."

Ivy spoke up. "It might surprise you to hear that I actually *do* know what it's like to be in love. Right at this very moment, in fact."

"Jada—" Amy began, but interrupted herself with, "Ivy, is your toolshed *on fire?*"

Ivy turned to look. There were, indeed, flames licking from one window of the little outbuilding at the edge of the lawn. "Nick!" she cried. "The shed!"

Nick looked up, frozen for one shocked second before he sprang into action. "Get the hose!"

Heart racing, Ivy ran toward the side of the house, where the hose hung, neatly coiled beneath a spigot. "Take the hose to Nick," she called to Libby, who was nearest. Libby obeyed, and Ivy turned the tap as far as it would go. The flames were shooting out of one side of the roof now, and in their eerie light, the fir trees behind the shed loomed black and menacing. Ivy's heart leaped high and raced ahead with that sickening dread she always felt when she saw a house fire. *Oh, God, don't let it spread. . . .*

Nick pulled the hose from Libby's hands and trained it toward the roof. The spray was wide, and the shed small. In minutes, the flames were out. Still carrying the hose, Nick kicked open the door, releasing a cloud of smoke and steam. With Mitch and David close behind him, he stepped inside. Seconds later, he was back, this time marching a terrified Hammer before him by the collar of his soaking-wet jacket.

"Look what was inside," he said grimly.

"Oh, Hammer!" cried Ivy. "What have you done now?" The rest of the family, lured away from the bonfire, gathered around them.

"I was just making a fire with some of that old scrap wood."

"You could have burned yourself alive!"

"No, I couldn't. I had a bucket of water."

"You can't play with fire like that!"

David and Mitch rejoined them. "It looks like it's all out," said David. Mitch went to the side of the house, turned off the water, and coiled the hose, hanging it back on its hook.

"Come on," said Jane. "Let's go back where it's warm."

While the rest of the family filtered back to the bonfire's

circle of light and heat, Ivy and Nick took Hammer into the house.

"Go change your clothes. We'll talk about this when you come down," Nick told him.

Three minutes later, Hammer was back, dressed in dry sweatpants and a flannel shirt that belonged to DeShaun.

"Did you leave your wet clothes on your bedroom floor?" Ivy asked.

"Yeah."

She raised her eyebrows until he flung himself around and sloped back up the stairs to get them. He reappeared with them in his arms.

"Take them to the laundry room, please."

He obeyed sullenly. When he returned, Nick said, "Why were you trying to burn the scrap wood?"

Hammer shrugged. "I just wanted to see if I could."

"But why?"

He looked at the floor. "You said I could start the bonfire, but then you went ahead and did it yourself."

Ivy looked at Nick.

Comprehension dawned on Nick's face. "Oh . . . I guess I did, didn't I? I didn't do it on purpose, Hammer, I really didn't. I just forgot you'd asked. I'm sorry."

"'S okay." Hammer scuffed one bare foot on the tiles.

Ivy sighed and put her arm around her youngest son. "What are we going to do with you, Hammer?"

"Well, first," said Nick, "he and I are going to build another fire tomorrow, which he can start himself, as promised. After that, he's going to help me repair the toolshed some weekend this fall. And he can do extra chores for two hours every Saturday until he earns the money to pay for the materials."

Hammer said nothing, but Ivy, looking down at him, did not miss his infinitesimal expression of satisfaction.

"It should only take you until about Christmas," Nick added.

Hammer's small smile evaporated like a spark in the darkness.

10

Ivy usually gave up on a new idea the way a dog gives up on a bone, so Jane was a bit surprised that her daughter had said nothing more about a wheelchair since the night it had been mentioned at the restaurant. Jane should have known that the other shoe was yet to drop. It came one afternoon, when Ivy stopped by on her way home from work at the bookstore.

"Look, I found all kinds of information about wheelchairs for you," she said, holding out an orange folder.

With poor grace did Jane take it from her hand. "You shouldn't have gone to all that trouble. Your father doesn't need one."

"A wheelchair would let him stay working longer. He wouldn't get as tired out—"

"I know. I know all your reasons." Jane laid the folder on

the counter, unopened. "But he'll never gain any strength back if he doesn't use his legs. No, Ivy, I feel strongly that a wheelchair would be very bad for him at this point."

"I think you're in denial about this, Mom."

"That's *enough* now. I'm not going to discuss it any further."

Later in the week, David dropped by unannounced. He sat at the kitchen bar with both his parents, hammering down on a piece of the rhubarb pie Jane had made that morning. "I hear there's talk of a wheelchair for you, Dad."

Rarely did Jane lose patience with her children, but now she was really angry. "Ivy's been speaking out of turn. I've already told her your father won't be getting a wheelchair, and I have heard about all I'm prepared to hear on the subject."

David looked at his father. "How do *you* feel about it, Dad?"

"I'm partial to the idea. I think it would be a great help to me, especially for teaching."

Jane stared at him, mouth agape. "Leander Darling, where did that come from?"

He passed a tired hand over his face. "I've been trying to say it to you all along, Janey. You've just not been hearing me."

"You think I'm in denial, like Ivy does."

"The bottom line, Jane, is I would like to look into getting a wheelchair."

"*Well.* Well, then, I guess there's nothing more for me to say." Ivy's orange folder lay in the phone basket, where Jane had tossed it two days earlier. Now she reached for it and shoved it in Leander's direction. "Be my guest."

Her husband opened the folder and addressed David.

"Actually, I've been looking at them since Ivy brought this over." He shuffled through the papers in the folder. "I like . . . this one." He pointed to one on the third page, and he and David put their heads together to read the description.

Watching them, Jane felt a mild panic. Was it possible she was wrong? She had thought it such a great act of faith to believe that Leander would be healed, yet this once clear and certain faith now seemed to be slipping from her grasp like wet soap. How much longer could she hold on to it? She no longer knew if she should try. Just where was the line between faith and denial? She stood up from the counter and went to fill the teakettle.

"I've already talked to the health insurance company," she heard Leander say. "They'll cover 80 percent. We'll have to have a ramp built up to the door, of course."

"With Mitch's help, we can knock that out in a weekend."

"The real expense is going to be a wheelchair van. I haven't looked into that yet."

"I can start asking around. Ralph Cloutier from church is a car dealer; maybe he can point us in the right direction."

Jane listened to them, feeling only half-present. The kettle boiled and began to shriek. She turned the gas flame off. She didn't feel like tea after all. Leaving her family to enthuse over wheelchair models together, she slipped up to her bedroom, lay down on the bed, and waited for the soothing anesthetic of sleep to wash over her.

❧

Tuesday was Leander's day for regularly scheduled maintenance with Dr. Gutierrez. "It seems like we're always running to Bangor," Jane sighed, backing the car out of the driveway. She felt peevish and out of sorts. A headache the night before had left her with a lingering residue. As well, she was still beleaguered by the low-key, nameless dread that was so apt, these days, to creep up on her, seep into her very bones, and settle like a dirty smog, robbing her of joy.

Midway along Route 1A, a strange banging noise began to issue from beneath the hood of the car. "That doesn't sound good."

"Pull over and I'll take a look."

Their cold and sullen September had subsided to a dazzling October, and traffic was heavy with leaf-peepers out to take full advantage of the clear, brilliant day. Jane slowed and searched for a wide swath of shoulder to pull over on. She found one, at the mouth of an unmarked side road, and stopped the car. Leander wrestled his walker out of the car door and unfolded it, then heaved himself out of the seat and shuffled around to the front.

"Pop the hood!"

Jane groped for the latch. She could never remember where it was. No, that one went to the gas tank. "Sorry!" she called. "Just a second!" She found it at last and pulled.

Leander lifted the hood and disappeared behind it. Moments later, he was back, leaving the hood still raised. "It's the serpentine belt."

"Is that bad?"

"We can't drive without it. We'll have to call Triple-A. Got your cell phone?"

"Don't you have yours?"

He shook his head sheepishly. "Forgot it."

She reached into the backseat and retrieved her purse,

which she dug through until she found the little phone the kids insisted she carry for just such emergencies. She squinted at the screen.

Leander looked on with her. *"Searching for signal?"*

They watched the little blinking cursor make a complete circle of the screen, then another. At last, it stopped. *No signal detected.*

Leander sighed. "I guess we're not calling Triple-A."

"What'll we do?"

"Keep the hood up, for one. Then stand by the car and hope someone sees two harmless, middle-aged people in distress and stops."

They got out. "I feel pathetic," she said.

"*You* feel pathetic? You're not the one leaning on a walker." He put an arm around her and squeezed her shoulders. "We'd better start praying."

It was the kind of autumn day that belongs only to New England. On every side, scarlet maples and golden beeches glowed lambent with the stored light of a hundred summers; the air was as cool and crisp as a winesap. From the sun-warmed earth rose the faint, mapled scent of leaves subsiding sweetly to decay.

"It's a nice day to break down, anyway," said Leander as a car thundered past, close enough to dust them with a fine spray of road grit.

"Thank heaven it's not raining." Several more cars blew by. None so much as slowed. "We're going to miss your appointment."

"Ah, well. What's he going to tell me that I don't already know?"

She smiled weakly. "He'll say you're not walking so well."

"He'll remind me to use my walker for stability."

"He'll say eat soft foods so you don't choke."

"Get plenty of rest."

"Take your meds."

"And for all that news, what do you suppose he'll charge our insurance company?"

"I shudder to think."

"We're better off where we are." Leander leaned against the car. "I know: let's count cars! What color do you want?"

She didn't want to count cars. "White, I guess."

"I'll take blue. First one to ten wins. Someone will have stopped by then."

"Do trucks count?" She strove to keep the discouragement from telling in her voice.

"Pickups, but no semis or delivery trucks." A blue SUV whipped past. "Readysetgo!" he called. "That's one for me!"

"Leander Darling, you cheater!" she cried. But the next vehicle to pass was a white Beetle, and they were tied.

Thirty-two minutes later, Jane claimed her fifth white car, and still no one had stopped. "I'm thirsty."

"Me too. I don't suppose you brought any water along?"

"No. All those years of traveling with children, you'd think I'd know better."

Several more cars, both blue and white, passed, but neither of them bothered to count. Jane checked her phone again. "Still no signal."

"We're probably in a dead zone."

That figured. Jane looked around. "What about this road behind us? Maybe someone lives on it."

"What if we walk down it, and meanwhile, someone stops?"

"Good point. Maybe I should go look for a house, while you stay here with the car, just in case."

"All right."

"You sure you're all right to stay on your own?"

"Jane," he said, with a touch of exasperation. "I'm a grown man. Of course I'm all right to stay on my own. Get going!"

She set out on the road that was little more than a dirt track, hardly wide enough to accommodate a car. It did not look well-traveled, and she did not feel hopeful. Her thirst was becoming insistent and hard to ignore. *I could use a drink, Lord.*

No sooner had she formulated this prayer than she rounded a bend and heard the chuckling sound of water running over rocks. A little stream had emerged from the woods around it to travel merrily along beside her path for a few yards, before disappearing among the trees again. Oddly, the sight made her angry. Why was it that God would provide a small thing, like water, as soon as she asked, but would not hear her pleas for her husband's life? Keeping an eye out for poison ivy, she stepped down to the water and, crouching at the edge, cupped her hands and drank. It was too bad she had no way to take some back to Leander.

Her thirst taken care of, she made her way back up the short embankment to the dirt path and continued her exploration. The nagging dispiritedness hung about her like a tangible weight. *What is it, Jane?* Was it loneliness? She dug deep. No, it was not quite loneliness, but close. It was more like . . . like the *fear* of being lonely.

At the very thought, a wash of anxiety went through her. Did not studies show that being alone was everyone's greatest fear? One son was already lost to her; her other children were increasingly scattered to the four winds, and even those nearby had busy lives that often did not include her. And Leander . . . Automatically, her mind veered hard in the opposite direction, groping for anything else to engage it. Around her the woods, though not silent, were steeped in quietude. Squirrels leaped from limb to limb in the treetops. Far back among the trees, the brook still laughed faintly to itself. The forest floor rustled with the soft patter of dropping acorns and leaves. There was the feeling, as some saint or other had once said, that "All shall be well, and all shall be well and all manner of thing shall be well."

Stopping beneath an oak, Jane leaned her back against the knobbled bark.

What are you so afraid of?

She forced her mind to finally put words to it.

She was afraid that God, who had always provided everything she needed, would not be enough this time. That He could not see her through the certain, terrible loneliness of losing her husband. She *was* going to lose him; she knew that now. Maybe, on some level, she always had. But unable to look the truth fully in the face, she had looked away and called it something else, something nobler than fear.

"*But my God shall supply all your need according to his riches in glory by Christ Jesus.*" She had memorized that verse as a child, in the King James Version, which hardly anybody used anymore. God *had* supplied everything she had ever needed, and much of what she merely wanted, to boot. But this . . . this was going to be different. This, when it came, was going to be gutting, wrenching desolation like she had never known before. Without Leander by her side, she might find herself shipwrecked with loneliness, adrift in an empty ocean, clinging on for the survival of her very soul.

Maybe, came the still, small voice. *Maybe so. And then what? Then what?*

The very worst. Think it through to its end.

The tree against her back was warm and rough. Cautiously, she probed at the thought, as she might probe an aching tooth, afraid the pain of it would be too much.

One day, Leander would be gone. Her best friend and soul mate . . . They would not grow old together. *"If two people love each other there can be no happy end to it."* Hemingway had said that. The tears came then, shuddering out of her, taking her violently by surprise. Wrapping her arms around herself, she crouched at the base of the tree, turned inward, fetal, and rocked like a child. In great, animal sounds of grief, she sobbed. *Alone.* He was going to die and leave her all alone.

They had worked hard at their marriage. It had not been easy, but they had purposed, early on, to always be good to one another, to cultivate their friendship, even when they didn't feel friendly. Jane had never understood people who reserved their best behavior for strangers and outsiders, yet treated their own family members with shoddy disregard. The best of you, she and Leander had always agreed, should be given to those you love the most. And it had worked. In a week, they would celebrate their thirty-sixth anniversary. Thirty-six years in, and they were completely safe with each other. They were part of one another's skin. It was so unfair of God to set two people up for a lifetime of happiness, then snatch it away from them in this cruel and painful way. *Unfair! This is not how I expected life to turn out.*

But as Jane crouched there, sucking in ragged gasps of air, the grief and rage began to ebb and with them, the racking sobs. Was there, after all, such a word as *unfair*, in God's economy? In truth, if God were absolutely fair, Jane would have nothing. She might, like much of the rest of the world, be living in poverty, victim to war or hunger or preventable disease. If God were fair, He would treat her sins as they deserved; she would have long ago been lost, cast out, her soul abandoned to darkness.

Instead, there was daily grace. She had been given more than three decades of a wonderful marriage—was that not grace enough, right there? And Leander had not been snatched from her without warning, like Sue Henderson's husband from church, who had had a massive heart attack last year and died instantly in his sleep. No, Jane was being given time to say good-bye to her husband. To end well with him.

And that was the conclusion of the matter. When the very worst happened, there would still be grace. She would continue, as she always had, to walk hand in hand with God. She would trust Him to be enough, and more. This was not first-grade math; this was calculus.

She wiped her eyes on the hem of her shirt and got stiffly to her feet, wishing for a handkerchief. She felt washed-out, spent, but immeasurably cleaner. Groping in the pockets of her jeans, she found a crumpled tissue and gave her nose a hearty blowing. A breeze rustled the branches of the oak above her. Lighter, she walked on. The smog of despair was gone, burned away by a good cry and the consciousness of God's enormous grace. In its place was peace.

Minutes later, the road petered out to a footpath barred by a metal arm. She read the sign on it.

No Motor Vehicles beyond This Point
No Snowmobiles, No ATVs
No Live Bait Fishing

Clearly there was going to be no house with a phone—or, as was increasingly becoming a concern, a bathroom—at the end of this road. Fortunately, Jane was a country girl, and she did not hesitate to avail herself of the surrounding woods and some obliging, broad-leaved ferns before she started back in the direction of the car.

What happens when you realize that life isn't going to turn out like you expected? But alongside the question, the sense of peace remained, unshaken. As the old saint had said, all would be well. Not easy, but well. She knew it as clearly as if she had seen God's hand write it across the blue and cloudless sky.

She emerged from the woods to see a battered red pickup truck pulled to the side of the road in front of their car and a man bent over with Leander, looking into the mysterious inner workings beneath their hood. She stepped alongside them. Her husband, she saw, was holding two bottles of Poland Spring water. Of course: another need met. "What's the verdict?" she asked.

"This is Butch," Leander told her. "He called Triple-A

for us. And he happened to have a couple of extra bottles of water in his truck." He handed her the second bottle. "Butch, my wife, Jane."

"Pleased to meet you, Butch. Thanks for stopping."

Butch, burly in a grease-stained white T-shirt, gave her a two-fingered salute.

She opened the water and took a long, grateful swallow before saying, "I thought there was no phone signal here?"

"I got 4G," Butch said, around a wad of chewing tobacco.

"Oh. Well . . . we appreciate it more than we can say."

Butch said, "They got a guy out now, openin' up a locked car in Win'erport. Should be here in a minnit or so. Yep, here 'e is now." As he spoke, a white tow truck with the AAA logo on the hood was slowing and pulling in behind them. "Welp." Butch sent a jet of tobacco-stained spit into the grass on the berm, pulled a wad of greasy shop toweling from his back pocket, and wiped his hands on it. "I'll be on m'way, then. All the best to you folks." He gave them the two-fingered salute again, revealing dark yellow stains under his arms, and headed back to his truck.

Jane watched him swing up into the cab. "Thank you!" she called. She fumbled her water bottle to the other hand and waved, dropping the cap on the ground. As she bent to pick it up, she heard the door of Butch's truck slam shut with a loud report. When she straightened again, holding the bottle cap, the truck was simply . . . gone. She blinked. It had not driven away; it was nowhere on the straight stretch of road before them. There had not been time for it to round the bend far in the distance. It had literally just disappeared. A chill broke over her scalp and ran down her neck and arms.

"Leander! Did you see that?" But her husband had his back to her, talking to the AAA man, and had noticed nothing.

Jane looked back at the place where, seconds ago, Butch's truck had stood. All at once, she wanted to laugh. Why shouldn't an angel appear in a sweat-stained T-shirt, with 4G and extra bottles of water in his truck? How like God to provide—now and always—exactly what they needed. She shaded her eyes and squinted down the road, in the direction Butch's truck should have taken. Not only had God provided, but He had allowed her a glimpse of a small miracle as well.

Thank You, she prayed, *for taking care of us now and in the future.* She turned back toward her husband, her heart brimming over with joy.

CHAPTER

11

IT HAD BEEN A MISTAKE, Jane realized, to tell Ivy about the car breakdown. What she had intended to be a lighthearted story had turned into occasion for an all-out lecture. Ivy completely missed the point about her mother's encounter with an angel and railed on and on about the necessity of Jane getting an iPhone.

To compound matters, Amy called later that day, clearly clued in by her sister, to voice her own opinion that Apple products were not the only game in town, and say that her mother should definitely look into an Android. Jane had always believed it one of the privileges of life in a sleepy, rural village that she should not feel compelled to keep up with the latest and greatest in ever-changing technology. She had never enjoyed that kind of thing, and she had no intention of struggling through the learning curve of a new phone now, just to mollify her daughters. Nevertheless, she made the proper reassuring noises into the phone and hung up. *Over my dead body,* she thought, and went to watch the evening news with Leander.

One day early in November, Laura made two stops on her way to work. The first was at a pharmacy, where she picked out a birthday card. The second was at a gas station, where she bought two scratch tickets. At work, she sat at her desk and wrote:

> *Dear Milton,*
>   *Thank you for always bringing a smile to my face on Sunday mornings. Have the happiest of birthdays.*
>   *Laura*

She slipped the scratch tickets into the card, addressed her envelope, added a stamp, and put it in the outgoing mail tray.

The following Sunday, Milton was at her side almost the minute the service was over.

"I thank you for the card, Laura. It was an awful nice thing to do." He took a much-used blue handkerchief from his back pocket and mopped at his rheumy eyes. "When you get to be my age, you don't hardly get birthday cards n'more."

Laura patted him on the shoulder. "I meant what I said. You're the kind of person who makes the world a happier place, Milton."

"Well, the good Lord didn't make me none too smart, I guess, but He made me good-natured, and I don't know but what that's better, sometimes." The old man folded the handkerchief carefully and put it back in his pocket. "Guess what?"

"What?"

"One of them scratch tickets was a winner!"

"You're kidding! How much?"

"Two dollars. And guess what I did with it?"

"Bought two more tickets?"

"That's right!" He slapped his leg and cackled, showing his gums, and in that instant, a flash of joy pierced Laura, as sharp and bright as a lightning shaft. She could not have felt happier if she herself had won the entire lottery. She slapped her own leg and cackled right along with him.

❧

The wheelchair was not as bad as Jane had feared. It looked quite comfortable, actually, and when she sat in it to try it out, the day it was delivered, she found it to be so. There was a headrest with a brace, to keep Leander's head from dropping forward or to the side, and an electric knob on the right armrest so he could control it. A similar knob was in the back, in case he needed to be steered from behind. Hammer, who was magnetized to anything with a motor, was allowed to drive the chair up and down the driveway a few times; then Nick told him firmly that that would be the end of it.

Mitch, David, and Nick spent a Saturday building a ramp to the front door according to the code Mitch had researched. They had to dig up one end of Jane's tulip bed to do it, but she did not mind too much. Tulips were expendable. Leander's safety and freedom were not.

The wheelchair van was next. It was David, not Jane,

who had taken Leander to shop for one, and what arrived in their driveway, midway through November, was not the great, square, clunky thing Jane had envisioned. Instead, it simply looked like a minivan, and a classy one at that. The color was called Champagne Gold, and the van had a heated driver's seat and a little camera screen so you could back up without looking behind you. The wheelchair sat in place of the passenger's seat. When it was time to get out of the car, Leander simply backed his chair up a couple of feet onto the lift. Jane opened the door with a remote control, and the van graciously lowered itself a few inches toward the ground.

"Makes the incline less steep," David explained.

"I can't get over it," Jane kept marveling. "It's so *easy*." She had been picturing herself folding up an old-fashioned wheelchair and stuffing it into the trunk every time they went anywhere. Hauling it out and setting it back up again at every destination. But this was a pleasant surprise. In spite of herself, she liked it very much.

❧

One Friday morning, Chris stopped by Laura's desk. "Come see me in my office." He was not smiling.

Laura minimized the screen with the spreadsheet she'd been working on and, with a surreal sense of dread, followed her boss to his office.

"Have a seat." He moved a stack of file folders from a chair, and Laura sat.

Chris pulled his desk chair over and sat beside her, so close their knees were almost touching. He scrutinized her face until Laura felt it burn with self-conscious heat.

"What is it?"

"Laura, have you been drinking at work?"

"What?" Her best shocked stare. *"Drinking?"*

"Someone in the office said they've smelled it on you more than once, including yesterday."

She was outraged. *"Who?* Who said that about me?"

"That's not important. Just answer my question. Have you been drinking at work?"

"No! That's ridiculous! You know me, Chris, I'm a good employee. I get my work done, and I do it well." *Linda. It had to be Linda from purchasing who ratted me out.*

"That's true, you are, and you do. But I have to ask. Someone said they smelled vodka on you yesterday."

Oh, please! Vodka doesn't have a smell. She pulled up a thoughtful, earnest expression. "I spilled a bottle of whiteboard cleaner at my desk yesterday, and I used half a box of tissues to clean it up. Do you think that could be what they smelled?"

Her boss's face cleared. He was a nice guy, the kind of man who wanted to think the best of everyone. "Oh, I didn't realize that. Yes, I could see how someone might mistake the smell of whiteboard cleaner for . . . ah . . . something else." Chris was a Mormon and didn't drink. What did he know?

"That has to be it." Laura shook her head in bafflement. "Still . . . I'm disappointed that this person didn't come to me first. It feels a little juvenile for someone to be going behind my back, making accusations like that."

He patted her on the knee. "Well, she was just trying to do the right thing."

It was *Linda!*

"I can appreciate that. But I promise you, Chris, I would never drink at work. I'm a glass-a-day kind of gal in the evenings, and that's my limit." She laughed. "Anything more would put me flat on my back."

He smiled widely now, relieved that it was all a big mistake. "In that case, please accept my apology. You understand I had to follow up on her concerns. Now, go on back out there, and continue to do the great work you always have."

She stood and saluted him. "Aye, aye, Cap'n." She turned for the door.

"And Laura?"

"Mmm?"

"You really are a pleasure to have around the office."

"It's a pleasure to work here."

Back at her desk, Laura shot a narrow glance at Linda, whose desk was on the other side of the office. The older woman was examining a sheaf of papers in her hand with too much concentration. Laura took her shoulder bag from the back of her chair and stalked to the bathroom, right past Linda's chair. Linda did not look up.

In the bathroom stall, Laura pulled the water bottle that did not contain water from her shoulder bag and took three long swallows. At once, calmness spread through her neck and shoulders, better than a warm shower. She took another three swallows and felt the familiar loosening of her joints, the safety of detachment from the harsh world around her. Capping the bottle, she stuffed it deep into her bag and pulled out a stick of cinnamon Dentyne. Let Linda sniff *that*.

She took the long way back to her desk. Across the room, Linda still had not looked up.

On the way home, Laura made two stops—the liquor store and a Chinese restaurant—and went home to hibernate. But a pupu platter and half a box of wine later, she found herself wide awake, with nothing good to watch on TV. She settled for the Hallmark Channel, because she was unaccountably homesick, and the movie that was showing happened to be set in New England.

"I miss Maine in the fall," she said aloud, to no one. A tear leaked out of each eye. Here she was, practically alone in Phoenix. Her so-called friends had not called or texted in days, and her coworkers had it in for her. No one cared about Laura Darling.

A dog food commercial came on, and she watched the black Lab helping his master: a young boy with an artificial leg. She began to cry in earnest then. "I need a dog," she said to the empty room. Why were dog food commercials so sad anyway? She felt a burning need to talk to someone about this and decided that the only person in the world—the whole world—who could possibly understand the pathos of Hallmark Channel commercials was Ivy. She found her phone and punched in the number.

"Laura!" The cheerful welcome in her twin's voice was just what she'd been needing.

"I need a dog," Laura sniffed.

"What?"

"I need to get a dog. For companionship and . . . and to help me."

"Help you with what? Laura, don't even think of getting

a dog. You live in the city and work full-time. When do you have time to take care of a pet?"

"There's this dog food commercial, and the little boy only has one leg, and the dog *helps* him."

Ivy was silent. Then, a resigned "Laura, have you been drinking?"

Rage boiled up in her like a volcano. How like Ivy to assume that. To accuse her, at the first sign of emotion, of being drunk. She called her sister a filthy name, hung up on her, and sank her face into a couch cushion. The tears came then, unchecked, flowing over all the tragedy of life: lost lovers and accusing coworkers, handicapped children and the dogs who helped them, family who didn't love you. . . . She would write a poem. She *should* write a poem about this!

She sat up and made her way to the kitchen, where she blew her nose on a paper napkin and dug a pencil and a small notebook out of her junk drawer. Back on the couch, she poured another glass of wine, giggling when she slopped a bit of it onto the couch cushion. Then, she settled down to write her poem.

Twenty minutes later, her poem was still unfinished, but her mind felt cleansed, her soul expurgated. All would be well, she felt. She would quit that hypocritical church and find a new job, one she really loved. The world was a good place. Her poem was a good poem. Filled with such expansive emotion, she decided she could even forgive Ivy her accusations. Tomorrow, she would call and tell her sister that she loved her.

She fell asleep on the couch, her face pillowed on her notebook, an unfinished glass of wine on the floor beside her.

Laura awoke late Saturday morning, only half-surprised to find herself on the couch again. The night before was a dim fog. She thought she had called someone but couldn't remember who. Maybe she had only dreamed it. She had fallen asleep with her face on a notebook. Now she sat up and examined it. A series of unintelligible scribbles, except for a word that emerged here and there: *Dog. Pain. Rain.* It came back to her then, the profligate sentiment she had felt over the dog food commercial. The outrage at Ivy for guessing the truth. Her cheeks burned with shame, and although there was no one there to see her, she cringed against the couch cushions, sinking into herself. She was such an idiot. She had made a complete fool of herself. Tearing the page of scribbles from the notebook, she carried it to the trash and shoved it down deep, then tossed in the remains of last night's duck sauce, a few slivers of sweet and sour pork, and two sticky chicken wings. The half-empty glass of wine, she started to dump down the drain, but changed her mind and drank it instead. No sense letting it go to waste.

A shower helped her feel better, and she resolved, while rinsing the conditioner from her hair, to call Ivy and set things straight. She did this as soon as she had brushed her teeth.

"I'm sorry I was a jerk last night," she said, when her twin answered. "I had a bad day at work yesterday, and yes, you were right: I'd had one glass too many with friends, before I got home."

Ivy said only, "Don't think another thing about it. We all have those days."

But Laura knew her sister well. The lack of emotion in Ivy's voice, her utter neutrality in discussing the issue, meant bad news. Ivy had her number, and no two ways about it. Laura said a carefully cordial good-bye and hung up the phone, wishing her twin were a little stupider. Hating her just the tiniest bit for not being so.

In the afternoon, Theo called, but Laura, curled up on her bed for a nap, rejected the call. She was fairly sure she had mentioned getting together with Theo today, but at the moment, she just didn't have the energy for it. Later, maybe. Half an hour later, Wendy called. Laura let it go to voice mail. Right now, she needed to be alone.

At three thirty, she got up and poured herself some wine. Three thirty in the afternoon was five o'clock somewhere. Theo called again, but she did not answer. She found a channel that was showing a *Dawson's Creek* marathon and settled in to watch. She dismissed three more calls from Theo and one from Wendy. Tomorrow was Sunday. Going to church and facing them all seemed more than she could bear. At half past nine, having exhausted the box of wine, she went to bed, wondering how she was ever going to get through the next thirty-six hours until she would be back at work and able to concentrate on anything except how dissatisfying her life had become.

The Tuesday before Thanksgiving, Jane dropped Leander off at school. She got out and, with the remote, opened the sliding side door while Leander backed his chair into place on the lift. As he was rolling down the ramp, a group of students trotted over. It happened nearly every day—today, it was two girls and a boy she recognized from the choir.

"We'll take him for you, Mrs. D!" called the boy. Ethan, she thought his name was.

"Thank you." She handed her husband over to the kids, kissed him, and waved as Ethan took hold of the back joystick and wheeled him away. Leander had his own joystick on the armrest, but the kids liked to drive, so he let them. The wheelchair had been a good idea after all; Jane saw this clearly now. Because of it, Leander was much less tired at the end of a school day. It was not a weakness—it was a tool, a wonderful tool that was making it possible for him to continue doing the work he loved. *Thank You for wheelchairs,* she prayed, and marveled once again at how much her heart had changed on this matter in just a few weeks.

This was the day she had earmarked to give the house a thorough cleaning before the onset of the holidays. Back home, she collected her bucket, rags, Lysol, and Toilet Duck, and determined to get the worst over with first. When you'd chosen to spend most of your life as a homemaker, people assumed you had some special affinity for housework. This, Jane thought, as she sloshed cleaner into her bucket and let the hot water run in, could not be further from the truth. She had always intensely disliked cleaning. She did it faithfully because what she *did* like was having a clean house. As with so many things in life, one might not like doing the necessary work, but there was undeniable satisfaction in having done it well. She turned off the water, lugged the bucket out of the bathtub, and pushed up her sleeves.

As she wiped down the bathroom sink, scrubbing around the base of the faucet with a small toothbrush, she reflected on the part of being a housewife that she had loved most of all: raising children. Oh, she had often despaired of the endless messes, the bottomless laundry pile; had wondered if she would ever again have a minute to call her own. But never had she seriously felt that her children were a nuisance, nor longed for the days when they would be grown up and gone. She had not been one to bemoan Christmas or summer vacation like her friends had, and wish for school to start again so she could get the kids off her hands. Now, she prayed for them each as she cleaned sink, tub, and toilet. She included their spouses, and Ivy's children, and Mitch, who, since the years he had lived with the Darlings as a teenager, was as good as family. He and Amy would probably, one of these years, be making it official.

Only when she had prayed through all of them and their families did she allow her mind to turn to Steven. She prayed for him and for any family he might have and then—hesitantly—added, *I would love to meet him, Lord. Just to see how he turned out. To know once and for all whether I did the right thing.*

But then, what if she didn't like what she learned? What if he had turned out to be a criminal or a sociopath? What if, meeting him, she were to discover that she had in fact *not* done the right thing in giving him up? That very decision might have ruined his life. Then she reminded herself that there had been no decision, really. No one had asked her; they had *told* her, *This is where you will go, and this is what will happen after the baby comes.* She didn't recall even having signed a paper. The baby had been born, and she was allowed to hold him briefly, and then he was gone. She had spent two nights in the hospital before going back to Aunt Sophie's, where she had lain, curled in a fetal ball on the guest room bed for another two days, and cried until her soul was squeezed dry of every last drop of emotion.

She had discovered she was pregnant right after Thanksgiving, the year she was sixteen. It had begun as a nagging carsick feeling, three days in a row, with no other symptoms. She wasn't stupid; she had heard other girls talking in the locker room after gym class. She had looked in her pocket calendar then, and counted backward. Two weeks late. Not days—*weeks*. The calendar slipped from her hands, and all the world ground into slow motion as the words *two weeks* ricocheted inside her head, slow as astronauts inside the space shuttle, in zero gravity.

Abortion was illegal. People were always talking about it on the evening news, and maybe someday it would be an option, but for now, it wasn't. Besides, she was Catholic—abortion was a mortal sin. If she killed this baby, she would be excommunicated from the church. She would spend eternity in purgatory, if not hell, and there would not be enough prayers in all of heaven and earth to save her. She did not dwell long on what she might have done if she had been given a choice. It was impossible to think of this baby inside her as a real person. She felt that she ought to be flooded with soft, maternal instincts, or at least compassion for the tiny heart growing beneath hers, but every better emotion was swamped by paralyzing terror. She would have done anything at that point—anything at all—to avoid the shame and recrimination that was coming. She was ashamed of herself for this, for what it revealed about the kind of person she was. But she could not help it. In the end, she was glad the choice was not hers to make.

She did not know whom to tell, or whom not to tell. She considered her options, lying on her bed, heart pounding, staring at the stretch of bare potato fields beyond her window. Her mother? Her mother would kill her, and if not, then her father certainly would. Ellen? No way. Because the baby's father, the one who had gotten her into this condition in the first place, was Ellen's boyfriend, Robert.

He was Ellen's first boyfriend. She had met him in college, at Farmington, and brought him home for a weekend in October, the year Jane was fifteen. He was given a discreet bedroom at the opposite end of the house from Ellen's, was polite and charming to her parents, and when he and Ellen went back to college on Sunday afternoon, he had a standing invitation to visit anytime.

They came every few weeks, and by the end of Christmas break, the whole family was besotted by the thoughtful, handsome Robert. He brought in wood for the woodstove, shoveled the front walk, fetched and carried for their mother. Jane was in awe.

One Saturday evening in March, when Robert and Ellen were visiting and a snowstorm had confined them all to home, the three of them played Parcheesi at the dining room table. Ellen had gone to the kitchen for a tray of popcorn and cocoa, and Robert said, "So who's *your* boyfriend, Jane?"

"Me? I don't have a boyfriend."

"Why not? You're so pretty."

Her face flushed hot. "No, I'm not."

"You are." He reached out to tuck a strand of hair behind her ear, letting his finger graze her cheek. "If I was still in high school, I wouldn't be able to keep my eyes off you, pretty Jane."

A stab of heat went through her so violent and sudden that it took her breath away. She stared at him and heard her own breathing, loud in the silent dining room.

He leaned close to her. "In fact, if I was in high school, I would want to kiss you. I'd think about it all the time."

Ellen's voice came floating in from the kitchen. "No, I've got it, Mum, thanks." And then she was there, setting her laden tray on the table.

Jane's whole body felt electric. She could not look at Ellen, so certain was she that Robert's words were etched on every inch of her face. Ellen would take one look at the pair of them and know exactly what he had said.

But Robert was taking cups of cocoa from the tray, saying, "Hey, outta sight, Ellen! You think of everything." He passed a cup to Jane. His fingers brushed hers, and she jerked back, spilling hot cocoa over her hand and the Parcheesi board.

"Jane! You are so clumsy!" Ellen was exasperated. "Look at you: you've ruined the game!"

"I'll clean it up." She jumped up, knocking her chair over backward, and fled to the kitchen.

Her mother was washing dishes at the sink. "What do you need, honey?"

"I spilled cocoa."

"Oh, Jane! Here." Her mother wrung out a dishcloth and handed it to her. "Make sure you get any that splashed on the table legs or spilled on the floor. It'll be sticky for weeks.

Wait—better take another one." Jane took the second dish-cloth and returned to the dining room, as robotic as one of the Daleks from *Doctor Who*. She began to mop up the spilled cocoa.

"Here, it's my fault. Let me do that." Robert took the cloth from her hand. Again, his fingers touching hers. Once more, her face flaming hot.

She let go of the dishcloth and backed away. "Thank you. I just . . . I think I'll watch TV with Dad. You two go ahead and play without me."

As she left, she heard Ellen's exaggerated sigh. "She is *so* moody sometimes."

She thought about it for weeks after Robert and Ellen had gone back to school. Lying on her back, on her bed, staring up at the ceiling, she would play over and over in her mind the words he had said. *"I would want to kiss you. I'd think about it all the time."*

Had he really said it, or had she just dreamed it? She counted the days until his next visit.

The telephone extension in her bedroom rang, jerking Jane back to the present moment. Dropping her cleaning rag into the bucket, she stood, with one hand to her aching lower back. This was old ground, scars that, though not for-gotten, had nonetheless faded. The sharpest of the shame had long gone from them, though there were times when they ached worse than others. Every August, the month Steven was born; every Thanksgiving, the time she had first known of his existence. And of course, there was still every guilt-ridden encounter with Ellen. Jane wondered, as she did each year, where her bitter, solitary sister was spending the holiday, and her heart ached all the more. So many mistakes made, and so little she could do about any of it now.

Leaving the bathroom, and her thoughts for the moment, she went to her bedroom to answer the phone.

CHAPTER

12

NEXT TO NEW YEAR'S EVE, Thanksgiving was Jane's favorite holiday. It was a day that included all the best things in life—family, friends, and food—with none of the pressure and expense that was so much a part of Christmas. She loved the way the world, or at least her corner of it, stopped for one Thursday a year and devoted the day to gratitude.

On Thanksgiving morning she woke at four thirty and, with a full heart, went to the kitchen to take stock and start the coffeepot. There was a lot to cook by two o'clock and the oven was only so big. The turkey would take up most of the space from nine o'clock on, so when it came to getting the rest of the meal hot on time, there was a good deal of planning and shuffling involved. Fortunately, in addition to a large oven, she had six burners and a warming drawer to work with. The night before, she had peeled ten pounds of potatoes and left them sitting in a pot of cold water. The butternut squash was similarly prepped; the bread for the stuffing had been cubed before bed and set out on baking sheets to dry. Satisfied that she had made a good start, Jane took her coffee and Bible into the living room to start her day.

Her mother-in-law arrived at ten o'clock, with the rolls, and Jane was delighted to see her. From the moment Leander had introduced them all those years ago, Lydia Darling had embraced Jane as a daughter. Much later, she would confess that her acceptance had not been entirely motivated by affection. "Oh, I thought you were just the sweetest thing," Lydia assured her, "but there was a bit of politics in it too. When it comes down to a choice between his mother and his wife, a wise man will choose his wife every time. I thought that if I wanted to stay in Leander's good graces and have full access to my grandchildren, I'd better make friends with you as quick as possible." She'd said this with heartfelt warmth and laughter, yet Jane had not a doubt that it was true. The love between herself and her mother-in-law was made up equally of natural affection and the *resolve* to be loving. So much of any kind of love boiled down to choice.

"Just find a place for the rolls on the counter there, Mom, and have a seat. Here, let me bring in the captain's chair from the dining room. How've you been?"

"Oh, ticking along, just like an old Timex watch. My, it must be quiet around here these days," said Lydia, helping herself to a cup of coffee from the pot on the counter. "The children seem to be scattered to the winds." She settled herself in the chair and watched her daughter-in-law measure herbs into the enormous stainless-steel bowl of dried bread cubes.

"You're not wrong about that," said Jane. "Laura's in Phoenix; Sephy's in Africa; Amy, Ivy, and David all have their own homes. . . . Life was so chaotic for so long around here. Remember those years?"

"I remember."

"All the laughing and bickering, and enormous meals going on, and someone always playing the piano . . . friends running in and out, the phone never free when I wanted to make a call. Somebody always needing a ride somewhere. It was a wonderful, controlled chaos of course, but chaos all the same. Now it's as quiet as a museum, and I don't know what to do with myself."

"It seems to me you have your hands full anyway, what with taking care of Leander and playing piano for the church and the arts program. And Ivy's children certainly keep you hopping. You never miss one of Hammer's games or Jada's recitals."

Jane paused with a tablespoon of sage in midair. "Sometimes it doesn't feel like enough."

"Mercy! How much busier do you want to *be*?"

"I mean the things I'm doing these days don't seem as . . . I don't know, as compelling as raising children, I guess. As engaging. I miss the good old days."

"Nonsense, Jane!" Lydia said with spirit. "There is no such thing as 'the good old days.' You ought to know that by now."

Jane looked at her in surprise. "What do you mean?"

"I mean that those times in life when we can't even hear ourselves think, all we want is a little peace and quiet. And when peace and quiet finally come, what do we do? We look back on the busy days and think of all the excitement we're missing. It's human nature."

"I guess that's true."

"The 'good old days' are always now, Jane. Remember that. We make our own contentment wherever we are."

"It's just that I've never liked change."

"Well," said Lydia philosophically, "who does? But if there's one thing I've learned, it's that change is going to happen. You can't avoid it. It's almost always uncomfortable—sometimes downright painful—but that doesn't mean it can't be good too."

"I know," said Jane. "It's just—" But she stopped. *Just what?* What her mother-in-law had said was true; she couldn't qualify or improve on it in any way. So she said again, "I know," and left it at that.

Lydia set aside her empty coffee cup. "Now, what can I do to help with dinner?"

Jane looked around the kitchen, mentally crossing off her to-do list. "How about cooking the celery and the onions for the stuffing?"

"Glad to." From her handbag, Lydia dug out a cheerful yellow apron and tied it around her waist.

Jane pulled her big red pan from the cupboard and set it on the front burner, then found the container of onions and celery she had chopped the night before. She handed this to her mother-in-law, along with a stick of butter and a wooden spoon.

Lydia bent to fiddle with the control knob on the stove. "There's something I wanted to mention, and I know this is probably none of my business . . ."

Jane watched the gas burner spring into life and braced herself for whatever was coming. When people started out by saying, "It's probably none of my business," they were invariably right.

Lydia went on. "You know we lost Leander's father when he was just fifty-five."

Jane did know this. It had happened before she met Leander, and she had never gotten to meet her father-in-law, but she had heard the story many times. James had gone into the hospital for triple bypass surgery, and sailed through it. Then suddenly, two weeks after surgery, he had died in his sleep at home.

Lydia went on. "In our family, James was the one who paid all the bills. He got the car in for repairs, fixed the plumbing, put gas in the lawn mower, and I don't know what all. Usually, there's some division of labor like that in a marriage, whether it's the husband or the wife who does it."

Jane saw where this was headed. "Leander pays the bills and does most of the banking," she admitted.

"When James died, I had to figure out how to do all those things on my own. Where did we send our mortgage check? When was the electric bill due? Who should I call if the sump pump went out in the middle of the night? I ought to have asked him to teach me before he ever got sick. It would have been so much easier in the long run." Lydia adjusted the flame under the pan and stirred the vegetables into the melted butter. "But like I say, whatever arrangement you and Leander have is none of my business."

"No," Jane said thoughtfully. "You have a point. Sooner or later I'm going to have to take over those things. Might as well be sooner."

"And it's not a bad thing for a woman to know how to fix

a leaky faucet. I still do it from time to time. Saves me quite a bit of money on plumbers."

Jane smiled. "Remember two winters ago, when Sephy stopped by to visit and caught you up on your roof, installing heat tape all by yourself?"

"I still haven't lived that one down."

"Well, you shouldn't have tried it. You have a strapping grandson and grandson-in-law who would have been only too happy to do it for you."

"I don't like to be a bother."

Jane stooped to kiss her mother-in-law's lined cheek. "I can't imagine you being a bother."

To Jane's surprise, Lydia reached for her hand and gripped it urgently. Her mouth trembled; the bright blue eyes brimmed with tears. For a moment, the spunky, sharp, capable woman Jane admired so much looked like nothing so much as a lost and baffled child. Jane understood. She slipped her arms around Lydia's tiny frame and pulled her close, answering tears welling in her own eyes. How easy it was to forget, in the midst of her own pain, that she was not the only one who would someday say good-bye to Leander. For a parent to outlive a child must surely be one of the greatest tragedies a human being could bear. Lydia had no other children; she had already lost her only husband. One day, there would be no one left to share her reminiscences over the early years of her family, the precious years when it had been just James and Leander and herself. There would be no more, "Remember that old blue car we had?" or "Remember that Christmas when Dad and I—?"

Against Jane's shoulder, she spoke, her tone plaintive.

"We'll get through this, won't we?" It struck at the mother's heart in Jane with a force that took her breath away.

"We will. When the time comes, we'll get through it together. You and me, and the children and grandchildren."

"How? How will we?"

Jane closed her eyes and rocked her mother-in-law as she had once rocked her own children. "Grace alone, Mom. When we reach out for it, the grace we need will be there."

For the third year in a row, Laura was helping her church team serve Thanksgiving dinner at the homeless shelter. This year, she was on desserts. Each of the clients was supposed to come through the line and pick up a piece of pie, either pumpkin or apple. Laura's job was to replenish the supply by opening a stack of prepackaged frozen pies, cutting them into eighths, putting each slice onto a plastic plate, and adding a squirt of whipped cream from an aerosol can. As in other years, Laura could not help comparing this to the kind of Thanksgiving dessert experience she had always known growing up. Apple pie, not semi-frozen from a box but hot from the oven, served with really good cheddar cheese or with vanilla ice cream melting on the side; vast wedges of pumpkin pie with her mother's rum-spiked whipped cream and candied walnuts; cheesecake and rhubarb pie and pecan . . . For days after Thanksgiving, everyone in the Darling family ate pie morning, noon, and night until it was finally gone. Still . . . She pulled herself back to reality. No one here was complaining about dessert. In fact, she had become used to the eagerness and gratitude of the men, women, and children who came through the line. Who knew the kinds of

Thankgivings any of them remembered? But she gave them all twice as much whipped cream as she was supposed to, and when a tiny black kid called Big Mike couldn't make up his mind between pumpkin and apple, she winked at him and slid a piece of each onto his tray.

Afterward, she found herself washing pots in the big sink at the back, physically spent but emotionally invigorated and thinking of the evening ahead, when the whole team would go to Evan and Theo's house for their own Thanksgiving celebration.

Tracy, the shelter's volunteer coordinator, joined her at the sink, dish towel in hand. "How do you like working here, Laura?" she asked. Brandishing her towel, she picked up a clean pot and began to dry it.

"Very much. It feels good to know you're being of material help to someone. And you know, I really like the clients. Some of them are amazingly intelligent, and nearly all of them have a great sense of humor. And they're always polite and respectful, which I didn't expect when I first started."

Tracy laughed. "A lot of them were 'raised right,' as they say. I can tell you like them."

"Really?"

"Yeah. You laugh and joke with them; you remember their kids' names. You treat them with dignity. It's a quality we look for in our volunteers."

"Well, like I said, I enjoy them."

"If you're ever looking for more volunteer work, we'd love to have you."

Laura raised her eyebrows. "You mean not just on Thanksgiving?"

"Why not? We serve three meals a day, 365 days a year. It takes a lot of volunteer staff."

"How often did you have in mind?"

"Whatever you think you can commit to. One or two days a month is what most of our volunteers give us."

Laura looked around her at the warm, brightly lit kitchen with its smells of turkey and stuffing and industrial detergent. Across the room, the dishwasher churned. Cutlery and glassware clinked as Lance and Evan loaded more trays with dirty dishes, speculating about football while they worked. From the dining room came the hum of conversation and laughter, the cry of a baby. The sounds of homeless people having a homelike experience. "I would like that," she told Tracy. "I think I could do a couple of days a month."

"That'd be great! Let's put these pots away and we'll get you written into the schedule."

She signed up to help serve dinner every other Wednesday. On those days, she would plan to get to work an hour early and leave by four o'clock. She didn't think Chris would have a problem with it.

"If you know of anyone else who'd be interested, send them my way, won't you?" said Tracy. "We're always hurting for volunteers."

An idea occurred to Laura. "How about our church's youth group? I'm sure we could get half a dozen of them in here once a month or so."

"Oh, that would be fantastic."

"The youth leader is a friend of mine; let me talk to him and get back to you."

In the church van, Laura told the rest of them her idea.

"Rob will love it," Theo said at once. "The kids, though . . . You'll have to try not to scare them off, Laura." She winked as she said it. It was no secret that Laura, who was sometimes efficient to the point of brusqueness, was not exactly popular with the youth group. She had taken over the direction of the church's ragtag young musicians the year before, and although she had quickly whipped them into shape as a stellar band, she had made few friends among the teenagers in the process. Most of them were slightly terrified of her.

But Laura was warming to her idea. "Maybe it should be a required part of youth band. If you want to play, you have to serve at the homeless shelter . . . let's say twice a year."

Evan glanced at her in the rearview mirror. "I'm not sure the kids are going to like that."

"They'll love it," Laura said with a wave of her hand. "They just don't know it yet."

The days after Thanksgiving were given over, as they were every year, to addressing invitations for the New Year's Eve party. Jane liked to get them out by the first of December. It was always best, if you could, to give everyone a good month to make their plans.

The guest list was rarely difficult, as Jane saved every list and menu she'd ever made in thirty-five years of hosting New Year's Eve parties. She simply revised them from year to year, crossing off, with regret, those who had moved away or become too ill or died. Other names were added, as the great current continued to flow, shifting and changing the river of loved ones who moved through their lives. One thing was certain: the parties never got smaller. The first year—their second as a married couple—six of them had celebrated together: she and Leander, another couple from church, and two single women, fellow teachers of Jane's. According to her notes, that year they had eaten seven-layer dip with Fritos, sloppy joes, and a Carvel ice cream cake. Last year, Amy had made seventeen different five-star appetizers and desserts, and Jane had counted eighty-six champagne glasses when she was cleaning up.

She spent Saturday filling out invitations and addressing the envelopes and got her Christmas cards done while she was at it. She had a package of address labels that was supposed to go into the printer, and Libby had helped her set up her addresses in the computer, but still she preferred to use her old address book, stuffed with scraps of paper, old return labels, and loose pages, and held together with a rubber band. It seemed important that she hand-address the envelopes. Each one meant thirty seconds or a minute to think about the person she was inviting. Sometimes to pray for that person, or simply to dwell on a memory they had shared. In a world that was far too busy, she often thought, these were the little, human things that got irretrievably lost.

As always, she addressed both an invitation and a Christmas card to Ellen. Her sister would ignore both, as she did every year, but at least Jane would try.

❧

Amy opened her eyes and was at once fully awake. Without looking at the clock, she knew it was earlier than she usually got up, and she lay in her narrow bed, gazing into the darkness with a feeling that was half dread and half excitement. She was acutely aware of her own skin. Her heartbeat seemed unsteady, the very air hyper-oxygenated as it passed through her lungs. Today was the fourth of December: Mitch had completed a year of sobriety. It was the day their relationship could change from "just friends" to something better. She sat up with a vitality she seldom felt on Sundays—her only real day off—and headed for the shower.

He was picking her up for church as he always did. She showered and dressed in her long, black brocaded skirt and black satin jacket, wondering what their first official date would be. Lunch this afternoon? Dinner out, somewhere nice? A movie? Twice, she changed clothes, settling at last on the black skirt and a fitted green velvet top of 1960s vintage, which Crystal had found at a flea market. Still, she was ready for church half an hour early. Her stomach simmered with the same apprehension she always felt on an opening night. What if things didn't work out between them? It might be a disaster. What if they were one of those couples who discovered they were great together as friends, but terrible in a romantic relationship? They had always been so careful not to touch each other in anything more than a friendly way. . . . How awkward would it be the first time they kissed? At this, she said aloud, "Stop it, Amy!" Jumping up from the couch, she went into her tiny kitchen, where she dampened a sponge and began to scrub industriously at counters that were already clean.

With her ears trained to the sound of his horn from the driveway, she was startled when, instead, her doorbell rang. Her face was suddenly hot, her mouth dry. This was it: there was no going back now. Blowing out a slow breath to calm herself, she put on her coat, picked up her tote bag, and opened the door.

Mitch was wearing a wide, idiotic grin. "Hey."

Her own smile was just as wide and foolish. "Hey yourself."

"Wanna go to church with me?"

"You bet."

He took her bag while she locked the door, then walked her to the truck, where he opened the passenger's door and helped her in. He got in on his own side and turned to face her. All trace of his smile was gone. "I have something to confess."

"Uh-oh."

"Uh-oh is right." His face was red. "A couple of months ago, I was . . . not thinking about today being my one-year anniversary and . . . um . . . being able to ask you out and all that—" He cleared his throat. "And I . . . ah . . . bought a ticket for a trade fair in Boston this afternoon. A two-hundred-dollar ticket."

She blinked. "A trade fair?"

"A building fair. At the convention center. They have all kinds of tools and equipment and demonstra—"

"I know what a building fair is." Disappointment dropped into her stomach like a plumb line. A *building* fair! She took half a beat to compose herself. This was an important day for Mitch; she could not make it all about herself. Digging deep for a smile, she said, "Hey, congratulations on your year of sobriety. Happy anniversary. That's a really, really great thing."

"Thank you."

"I got you something."

"You did?"

From her bag, she pulled a small, wrapped box.

"Awww, Amy . . ."

"Open it."

He tore off the paper like an eager child to reveal the jeweler's box beneath. It held a bronze key chain bearing the Alcoholics Anonymous emblem, a circle and triangle, with the number one inside.

"Wow, that's awesome!"

"Look." She turned it over in his hand. "On the back."

He read aloud, with a break in his voice, the words that closed every AA meeting. "'God, grant me the serenity to accept the things I cannot change, courage to change the things I can, and the wisdom to know the difference.'" With one rough palm, he swiped at his eyes.

"And," she lied bravely, "I think that taking yourself to a building fair in Boston is an excellent way to celebrate."

"No, really, I'll skip it. Let's do something together."

"No, you'll *go*. You've been looking forward to this. Besides, you can't waste a two-hundred-dollar ticket."

He turned the key chain over in his hands. "Look, why don't you go with me? I mean, it's kind of a lame first date, but we could drive down after church, spend a few hours looking at saws and routers, maybe catch a welding workshop, and go out to dinner afterward."

She would rather grind broken glass into her eyeballs than sit through a welding workshop on their first date, but she did not tell him this. A year ago, she might have said it without hesitation, but she was twelve months older and wiser now. "Oh, Mitch, I don't know. . . ."

"Come on, Amy! At least we can spend the day together. I'll make it up to you; I promise."

She sighed. She truly hoped he would not turn out to be one of those boyfriends who was always going to be disappointing her and promising to make it up later. Still, she was the one who was encouraging him to go. It seemed that if she wanted to be with him today, it was the building fair or nothing. "Okay," she said, "but only because it's your anniversary."

His broad grin turned his plain face, for a moment, incandescently beautiful. "You're the best!"

"I know."

"Is it okay if we leave right after church? Better to get there as early as we can, so we can find decent parking."

"Sure," she said, without enthusiasm. Something else occurred to her. "I don't have a ticket, though."

He backed out of the driveway. "There's always someone scalping them outside," he said happily. "We'll pick you up one when we get there." He headed in the direction of the church, whistling under his breath as he drove.

She looked out the window at the bare fields of colorless hay stubble. The sky, which should have glowed blue on this long-awaited day, was flat and heavy, the color of steel. Across the field, barren oak trees clawed the air with crabbed and wasted fingers. She'd thought today would be the start of love. Instead, it was going to end up just like every other day she'd spent with her good buddy Mitch.

But ninety minutes of church was usually good for the soul, and Amy had never been one to sulk for long. By the time they got through the hymns, she felt much more equal to the afternoon ahead of her, welding workshop or no. The important thing, she reminded herself during the opening prayer, was that Mitch was one year sober and they could move ahead, even if the first step didn't look exactly as she'd hoped. Didn't they have all the time in the world? As the announcements ended, she was even able to see a glimmer of humor in the situation. Or if not humor then at least irony, which usually amounted to the same thing. And when the sermon began and Mitch reached over and took her hand firmly in his, a flush of warmth went through her from the inside out, and the last shred of disappointment evaporated.

She thought, a little deliriously, that she didn't care where she spent the rest of the day, as long as she could hold his hand while she was there.

They left after church, stopping only long enough for lunch at The Lucky Panda. The hours spent in the truck between Copper Cove and Portland vanished like smoke on a clear blue day, as time always did when they were together. They talked about plans for the house and the arts program's upcoming Holiday Extravaganza. She read him the e-mail they'd all gotten from Sephy the night before, telling about a virus that was running through the goat herds of the surrounding villages, keeping Justice on the road sometimes eighteen hours at a time.

*We've hardly seen each other in the last five days; he
sleeps at the clinic, so I won't be woken up if the herders
need him in the middle of the night. When I do catch
a glimpse of him, he's hardly recognizable beneath the
razor stubble and the hair that should have been cut*

weeks ago. He loves it, though, and knows this is where
he belongs.

Sephy herself was busy teaching prenatal classes and being
trained by an obstetrician.

> *Dr. Marta, the local OB, is so overworked that*
> *she leaves the straightforward deliveries to me and the*
> *native nurse Glory. It's being thrown in at the deep end:*
> *I pray for wisdom a lot, and so far, God's helped me out*
> *of some potentially dangerous situations.*

"She sounds happy," Mitch observed.

"I think so too. But then, Sephy would be content if she
lived at the bottom of a well. Some people are born happy."

". . . some achieve happiness, and some have happiness
thrust upon them," Mitch paraphrased, taking her hand with
a meaningful look.

Just after three thirty, he pulled off the highway in
Portland. "Let's get gas and stretch our legs."

"You're probably not going to find a gas station in this
direction—it looks like we're headed straight into town."

He muttered something about city driving and merged
into traffic.

"Mitch, we're going to get tangled up in this place, and
it'll take us forever to find our way back to the highway."

"Actually—" he shot her a sideways glance—"I was thinking the building fair didn't sound all that much fun anyway.
Would you be disappointed if we skipped it?"

"*Skipped* it? Your ticket cost two hundred dollars!"

"Yeah, but I'm not really in the mood anymore. Would you mind changing plans?"

"Ah . . . I guess not."

"I mean, I could tell you were really looking forward to learning all about welding. I saw it in your eyes as soon as I mentioned it."

She swatted him on the arm. "Was I that obvious?"

"Yes. Always."

"Seriously, I'm happy to go to the fair. I'm just glad to be with you."

"You wouldn't rather do something else instead?"

"Like what?"

"Like . . . go see the Moscow Ballet perform *Coppélia* at Merrill Auditorium?"

"Today? Now?"

"Well, at four thirty, but close enough."

"Mitch! You got tickets?"

"I got tickets. I had to ask your mother how to pronounce it, but she promised you'd love it. Of course, if you'd rather go to the welding workshop, I can turn around and get back on the highway."

"Don't you dare!"

"A two-hundred-dollar ticket!" He smirked. "I can't believe you fell for it. Who'd pay that for a trade show?"

"Well, how was I supposed to know?" she cried indignantly. Something else occurred to her. "You planned this all along?"

"You didn't really think I'd forget about a day I've waited all year for?"

"But . . . the *ballet*! Won't it be painful for you to sit

and watch people in leotards leap around the stage for two hours?"

"I won't be watching that. What I'll be watching is you being happy for two hours. That's worth the price of the ticket, right there."

Her insides were pure, molten sunlight. "You're dazzling." She meant it with all her heart.

He smiled at her. "So are you."

CHAPTER

13

Ivy worked two and a half days a week at Parchments, the only store in Copper Cove where you could buy a book that wasn't used. It wasn't a particularly challenging job, and she could have made more money as a waitress, but as she often asked Nick rhetorically, who could resist the lure of working among books all day? She got to borrow new novels as soon as they came out, which, she pointed out, saved the family hundreds of dollars a year right there. And that didn't even take into account her employee discount on stationery supplies. She reminded him of this on Wednesday evening, when he came home from work and noticed yet another large paper bag with the Parchments logo sitting on the kitchen table.

"You bring home enough journals, hand-made cards, and gift wrap from that place to open your own stationery store," he said, going to the sink to wash his hands.

"They make great presents!" Ivy was defensive. "And it's all 30 percent off. It's like they're *paying* me to shop!"

Nick, who wanted only to take the newspaper into the living room and read it in peace, said mildly, "Hey, I don't have a dog in this fight. You work because you want to, not because your husband is driving you out with a cord of whips every day, telling you to go earn a living. If you want to spend half your paycheck on Moleskine books and designer pens, be my guest."

She came to wrap her arms around him. "I know. But I do feel guilty sometimes, when you're the one slaving away full-time to pay the bills."

"I'm happy to slave away."

She kissed his chin.

He kissed her forehead.

The house phone rang. Disentangling herself from her husband, Ivy answered it.

"Hello, this is Alexandra Kelly from the Copper Cove Elementary School. Am I speaking with Mrs. Darling-Mason?"

Ivy sighed. The school never got her name right. "Just Ms. Darling. My husband is the Mason part."

"Oh, yes, I see. And your children are all Darling-Mason."

"You got it. But please, call me Ivy."

"Do you have a moment to talk, Ivy?"

What did you say to a question like that from the school principal— *"Not really, could you call back later"*? "Of course."

"It's about Hammer, I'm afraid."

"Oh, dear."

"Yes. Has he said anything to you about the incident at school today?"

"I haven't seen him yet. He's been at basketball practice."

He should be home any minute, though; a friend's mother is dropping him off. What happened?"

"The custodian caught him lighting fires in the boys' room toilets."

It was probably a ridiculous thing to ask, but she could not help herself. "How on earth do you light a fire in a toilet?"

"He was squirting lighter fluid into the toilet and dropping lit toilet paper into it."

"But . . . why?"

"I have no idea. He wouldn't say." The principal's voice carried the merest hint of impatience. "The point is he could have caused a serious fire. We don't allow our students to have matches or lighters—and lighter fluid itself should go without saying—on school grounds. I'm afraid we're going to have to suspend him."

Ivy sighed and rubbed the back of her neck. "I'm sorry he's causing problems. We'll talk to him and try to find out what he was thinking."

"Very good. Let's say he'll be suspended Thursday, Friday, and Monday. He can return next Tuesday."

"That sounds reasonable. And my husband and I will come up with some fitting consequences on our end as well."

"This will go on his permanent record, Ivy. I just wanted you to be aware of that."

Whatever that meant, in the world of a ten-year-old. "Well . . . thank you for letting us know. Again, I'm sorry."

"It's not your fault."

"I know, but I'm still very sorry about it."

"You have a good night, Ivy."

"You too, Mrs. Kelly."

"Alexandra."

"Alexandra." Well, why not be on a first-name basis with the principal? Ivy had an unpleasant notion that they were going to be talking to each other quite a lot more before Hammer was through with school.

She was telling Nick about the conversation, at the kitchen table, when the front door opened and Hammer blew in, heaving a loaded backpack and looking grubby from basketball practice.

"Hello, sir," she said. "Why aren't you wearing your coat?"

"Too hot."

"It's twelve degrees outside."

Hammer shrugged and came into the kitchen, where he dropped his backpack onto the floor.

Ivy looked pointedly at it. "Is that where that goes?"

"No?"

"Put it away and hang up your coat, please; then come tell Dad and me about your day."

The previous year, Nick had installed a set of cubbies and coat hooks in the short hallway between the kitchen and the garage. Hammer shuffled off toward these, kicking his backpack along the floor before him like a soccer ball. Ivy and Nick watched as he stuffed both backpack and coat into his cubby.

"Hang the coat up, please."

He sighed and hung his coat on a hook, then came back into the kitchen and opened the refrigerator.

"Anything interesting happen in school?" Nick asked.

"No." Hammer found the milk, poured himself a glass, then reached for the chocolate syrup.

"No chocolate," said Ivy. "It's almost suppertime."

With another sigh, he let the refrigerator door swing shut.

"Is that where the milk goes?"

Hammer looked at the milk jug on the counter as though he had never seen it before. "No?"

"That's right."

Hammer returned it to the refrigerator.

"Have a seat." Nick pushed an empty chair back from the table.

Their son brought his milk to the table and sat, looking suddenly wary.

"So . . . nothing interesting happened in school today?"

"Nope."

"You didn't spend any time in Mrs. Kelly's office?"

"Oh, that."

"Yes, that. Why don't you tell us what happened?"

Hammer shrugged and kicked at the table leg. "I don' know."

"How about you make a good guess."

"I got in trouble for messing around in the bathroom."

"Doing . . . ?"

"I was playing in the toilets."

"Playing in the *toilets*."

Ivy had a sudden, unholy urge to laugh. With an effort, she kept a straight face, glad that Nick was doing the talking.

"According to Mrs. Kelly," Nick went on, "you were lighting fires in the toilets."

Hammer shrugged. "Yeah. I guess."

"You *guess*?"

"Yeah. That's what I was doing."

Ivy spoke up. "Why? Why would you do that?"

He shrugged again. "I don' know."

"Where did you get the lighter fluid?" Nick asked.

"From the shed."

Ivy looked at her husband. "We didn't get rid of that, after he set fire to the place?"

"Apparently not. Hammer, you're not going to tell us why you did this?"

He shrugged again and continued to kick at the table leg.

"Well, the school is suspending you for three days."

Hammer's face brightened.

"Of course, there will be no basketball practice on the days you're out of school, and you won't be allowed to go to Saturday's game."

"Whaa—*no!*" Hammer sat up straight and let out an anguished yell. "That's not fair!"

"Sure it is. Besides, those are the school's rules, not ours."

His face was mutinous.

"And of course—" Ivy did not hesitate to twist the knife— "we'll be grounding you as well. I'd say . . . no screen time— that's Xbox or TV—from now until Tuesday, when you go back to school."

"That's not fair!" he cried again.

"If we get news like this again, you'll be off the basketball team for good, understand?" Nick said.

Hammer crossed his arms and slumped in his chair, his face stormy.

"Do you understand?"

Reluctantly, he gave the smallest possible nod.

"Good. Now, go shower before supper. We're eating in half an hour."

Hammer slung himself out of the chair and started for his room.

"Hammer."

He stopped, but did not turn around.

"Is that where your glass goes?"

Without a word, their son turned, swept the glass off the table, and hurled it savagely across the room into the sink, where it shattered.

Ivy stared, paralyzed by shock. It was then that one of her strongly held convictions was reinforced—that parenting was a two-person job—because Nick had the presence of mind to say calmly, "Clean it up."

Hammer hesitated a fraction of a moment, then, "No." He turned and ran from the kitchen.

Ivy and Nick looked at each other. "Should we go after him?" she asked.

"I don't know."

"I nagged him too much. I should have left him alone about his backpack and coat."

"I don't know that either. I'm feeling my way as blindly as you here."

It was not the first time they had glimpsed such rage from him. Ivy wanted to think these were isolated incidents, that it would not happen again. But the truth was their children had a past that they knew very little about. Who knew how deep this anger ran? She reached for Nick's hand. "What do we do?"

He shook his head. He had no answer for her.

❧

A week later, winter moved into Copper Cove and took up residence in Amy's favorite way: At 3 a.m., she got up for a glass of water and saw by the porch light that fat, wet flakes were beginning to pelt her small yard. By seven, only the tips of the dry winter grass showed through. The damp day promised more snow for hours to come; the forecast was calling for twelve to fourteen inches. Pulling on her Wellingtons, she went to check on the chickens.

The single lightbulb, along with the birds' own body heat, was enough to warm the coop even on the coldest day. As Amy strewed feed across the dirt floor, the birds crowded around her. Joe had told her that his wife had been genuinely fond of the hens, picking up and cuddling each of them regularly from the time they hatched. The result was a clutch of sociable birds that rushed to meet Amy every day, greeting her with gentle and affectionate pecking at her boots. Now, they kept up a steady dialogue, she with words, and they with their guttural chicken-speak.

"What's better than a nice, snug coop in the middle of a snowstorm, right?"

The chickens agreed.

"I know you'll miss your summer bugs, but this isn't so bad. And look, Joe sent bread crusts for you!"

The chickens thanked her.

"The roads won't be cleared for hours yet. I think I'll work from home today. What do you girls think of that?"

The girls thought it was a marvelous idea.

She changed their water and collected the warm eggs

from the laying boxes, then went back to the house to call her staff and tell them to take the day off.

A flurry of midmorning texts among the Darling women ended in the consensus that family dinner should proceed as usual, in spite of the storm.

It's only snow, not ice, Libby pointed out. And the roads should be plowed by then.

The storm continued in force as they gathered at Ivy's house, but by the time supper was over and the table cleared, they could see by the back porch light that it had begun to abate.

Nick took a yardstick from behind the kitchen door and went out to measure. "Sixteen and a half inches," he announced, coming back inside and kicking off his boots.

"I wanna make a snow fort!" cried Hammer. "Mitch, make a snow fort with me!"

"I don't think your snow pants have dried out from this afternoon yet," said Ivy, going to check on the pants, which were drying on a rack in front of the radiator. With school closed because of the storm, Hammer and Jada had spent a good part of the day building a family of five snowmen in the front yard. But the snow pants were only slightly damp, and as Hammer pulled them on, he said again, "Come on, Mitch!"

"You too, Aunt Amy!" added Jada, searching the mitten basket for a dry pair that matched.

Amy looked at Mitch. "Want to?"

"If you do."

"Let's go!"

For an hour, they piled snow high in the backyard with

shovels, then tunneled through it with their mittened hands, under Mitch's direction. The result was a fortress with a door on either end and a ceiling so high that Hammer could stand up inside.

"We've cleaned the yard nearly down to the grass, but it was worth it," said Amy, leaning on her shovel and gazing at the mountain of snow before them.

"I'll throw a little water over the outside, so it'll freeze up and last awhile," Mitch said.

"I'm going to sleep in it!" Hammer announced.

"No, you're not. Mom won't let you," said Jada. "But I bet she'll let us eat breakfast out here tomorrow if we want. Hey, let's make a snow table and benches inside!"

At once, she and Hammer dropped to their stomachs, shimmied through the low door, and disappeared inside.

The night was suddenly silent. The snow had stopped falling while they built, and now the last of the storm clouds drifted away like indolent partygoers in search of the next place to congregate. Above them glittered the entire Milky Way. An eyelash moon smiled crookedly.

"It's very useful to have a builder in the family," Amy said. "Are you cold?"

"My legs are numb, but the rest of me is fine. You?"

Mitch did not answer. Taking her shovel from her hand and throwing it to one side, he pulled her close against him and kissed her. The first.

It was soaring on a high air current; it was coming home. Against her nose, his face was cold, but his mouth on hers was warm. He smelled like snow. Rising up on her toes, she put her arms around his neck and pulled him closer. When at last they broke apart, they stood with arms around each other and foreheads touching.

Mitch said, "That was a long time coming."

"It sure was."

"I love you, you know."

"I think I've loved you since I was a little girl."

He cupped her cold cheeks in his warm hands and bent his head again.

"Gross!" A sudden shriek rent the stillness. Hammer, crawling out the door of the fort, had seen them. "They're *kissing*!" he called back to Jada. Making retching sounds, he scooted backward and disappeared inside again.

In the close and silent darkness, Amy looked into Mitch's eyes. "Gross," she whispered.

"Gross," he agreed, and kissed her again.

CHAPTER

14

❧

"LAURA!" Theo stopped her on her way out of church one Sunday morning. "Hey, are you going to be around for Christmas?"

"I'm not sure. I might go back to Maine. I need to check with my boss."

"Really, this close to the holiday, and he hasn't told you whether or not you have to work? Isn't that cutting it kind of close for a plane ticket?"

The truth was Laura had avoided thinking about her Christmas plans. She felt apathetic about the whole holiday, entrenched in a kind of inertia she was helpless to change. *Tomorrow,* she vowed silently. *I'll make a decision first thing in the morning.* She shrugged. "It's my fault for not nailing him down earlier. I'll talk to him tomorrow."

"Okay. Well, if you find yourself here in Arizona, please

consider spending Christmas with Evan and the boys and me. We'd love to have you."

She spotted Rob near the door, talking to a couple of teenage boys. Kendra was not with him this morning, and something like hope sprang up in her. "Thanks, Theo," she said hastily. "I'll give you a call." She made her way to the door and touched him on the arm. "Hi, Rob."

"Hey, Laura." He waved a hand good-bye to the boys, and turned to face her. "How've you been? All ready for Christmas?"

"Nearly. How about you?"

"All my shopping's done, thanks to the Internet. What are your plans: staying here, or going back to Maine?"

"Still deciding. How about you—are you going to your mother's this year?"

"Yeah, for Christmas Eve. I'm going to take Kendra with me. Introduce her to my family."

Hope deflated like a pricked balloon. "Oh. Wow. Nice. Where, ah . . . is Kendra this morning?"

"Sick." Rob's broad, friendly face creased with concern. "I think it's the flu. She doesn't believe in getting flu shots."

"I'm sorry to hear that. I hope she'll be better soon." *Or she could just die of the flu. That would be fine too.*

"I'll tell her you said so. I'm headed over there now, with some soup and magazines. Things like that."

She felt a stab of irritation. Rob had once brought *her* soup when she'd been sick. What a one-trick pony. "Well . . . if I don't see you, then have a merry Christmas."

"You too, Laura."

Outside, the day was overcast and balmy, with a pensive

feel as though it should storm, but could not quite make up its mind to. She got into her Saab, backed up, and put it in drive, but before she could pull out of the parking lot, Wendy stepped in front of her, waving her arms.

Laura rolled down her window. "Hey, you."

"Listen, I won't keep you, but Lance and I wanted to know if you had plans for Christmas Eve."

"Oh, I'm . . . I'm not sure yet. I might go back to Maine."

"Well, if you don't, we'd love to have you come for dinner. I don't cook anymore, so it's just Chinese food, but you're more than welcome."

"Thank you. I might take you up on that. I'll let you know."

"And we're serving lunch at the shelter on Christmas Day, if you're around."

She waved good-bye to her friend and drove away. Why was it, she wondered, that she could be surrounded by such kind and generous friends, and still want nothing more than to be left alone?

The Copper Cove Community Arts Center's second annual Holiday Extravaganza was only a week away, and Amy was counting on her accompanist to come through. With this in mind, Jane applied herself rigorously to polishing up the pieces Amy and her staff had chosen. This included a comic rendition of "The Dreidel Song"—although since DeShaun's friend Milo had converted back to Catholicism, Jane couldn't think of a single Jewish person she knew in the whole town. Also, there was a rather daunting rendition of "The Twelve

Days of Christmas," arranged by Leander. This last one, the evening's finale, was to include a string quartet, a full brass ensemble, an electric guitar, a good quantity of live fowl, and Amy herself playing the drums.

Her youngest was nothing if not ambitious.

The blessing and the curse of being an accompanist, Jane had often noted over the years, was that it gave you so much time to think. There was the need, of course, to learn the music, but after a bit, you got to the point where you could disengage yourself from having to concentrate so much. The fingers practiced and learned, while the mind was left free to wander.

Increasingly, as she practiced Schubert's "Ave Maria," she found her mind straying to thoughts of her firstborn son. The need to find him pressed on her ever more insistently.

It was grief, of course, and the prospect of certain loss. Within a couple of years, or three or four, Leander would be gone. Life, as she had always known it, planned for it, would be no more.

She had once read a *Reader's Digest* article about the five stages of grief. At that time, when she was relatively removed from sadness, the stages had seemed so orderly, so comforting. They made it seem like you would know what to expect when the wrecking ball of tragedy swung through your life and knocked out the very foundations. First, you would deny that this terrible thing was happening. Then you would feel angry. Next, you would enter a stage of bargaining with God about it, asking Him to change His mind. When God failed to comply, depression would set in, but then would come the final stage: like emerging from a dark but linear tunnel, you would burst into the glorious sunrise of acceptance, and life would become beautiful again. But Jane knew now that grief had no such pattern. There was nothing at all orderly or linear about having the guts ripped out of you while you were still alive and fully sentient.

Ave Maria, gratia plena, she played. "Hail Mary, full of grace." The angel's greeting to a young, unwed teenage mother. *Ave, ave dominus. Dominus tecum.* "The Lord is with thee."

Her first memory of the ocean was a trip she had taken to Popham Beach with her aunt Kay and her cousins Jacob and Danny. Jane had been perhaps five or six years old. Surely she had been to the ocean before, but this was the first clear memory she had of it. She had waded into the water up to her shins and turned to face the shore. Danny had found a jellyfish, she remembered, and was wearing it on his head like a strange, gelatinous hat, and Jane was laughing at him. And just like that, midlaugh, a rogue wave, as high as a six-year-old girl, had sideswiped her. Had swamped and buried her in the water before she even had time to catch a breath. Below the surface, the waves had pulled her in one direction while the undertow pulled her the other way. She was rolled and trapped like a fly in a spider's web. The weight of not breathing crushed her chest. She was suffocating, panicking. And then, in the brief ebb between waves, she found her footing and broke the surface, gasping in huge, burning lungfuls of air.

That, Jane thought, more than fifty years later, was exactly what grief felt like.

One moment, you were laughing, and the next, with no warning at all, you were bowled over by a massive wave of despair that rolled and suffocated you until you thought you would die from the weight of it. Then suddenly it released you, and you could breathe again. Even laugh again. Until the next time. Maybe that was the worst of it: the unpredictability. There was no way of knowing when it would strike, or when it would release you to happiness. It was a cruel and arbitrary thing. No, there was nothing linear about grief at all.

And this, she realized, was at the crux of her need to find her son after all these years. When you were faced with losing the most precious things in life, was it not right that you would grasp at all you still had, with the hope of holding it closer? Would you not reach, even, for those things you had lost, and might have a chance of regaining?

Benedicta tu in mulieribus. "Blessed art thou among women." *Et benedictus, et benedictus fructus ventris, ventris tui* . . . "And blessed, blessed is the fruit of thy womb . . ."

Jane turned a page in the music, and played on.

❧

Two days before Christmas, Laura woke up to realize she had finished all her vodka the night before. The box of white wine in the refrigerator yielded only half a cup before it too gave up the ghost. That left half a bottle of cheap merlot that she had bought for a recipe the week before. Still, it would see her through her workday. She poured it into a thermal cup, tossed the empty into the recycling bin, and made a mental note to stop at the liquor store on the way home.

At work, she opened an e-mail from Chris.

> *Christmas party today at 3 p.m.! Let's dig out the decorations and get this place looking festive.*

It would be a nice change of pace from her usual work-day, Laura thought. She found a website that was streaming Christmas music and turned the volume on her computer up. Humming under her breath, she headed toward the storage room where the boxes of holiday decorations were kept. "Okay, everybody," she called. "Computers away. This morning, we're decorating for Christmas!"

This was met with general murmurs of appreciation. Roger, one of the accountants, said, "I'll call the warehouse and ask them to send over a ladder."

Adrian, from quality assurance, said, "I'll help you bring out the decorations."

Linda put on a fresh pot of coffee. Chris appeared from his office to help and was soon up the ladder, stringing tinsel around the window frames and door casings.

Outside, the day was damp and overcast, but inside, all was warm and cheerful and festive. "Look what I found in the break room!" Linda crowed. She held up a squashed box of Danish. "It's left over from November's sale. The expiration date is only yesterday."

They cheered as though she'd found a gourmet cheesecake from a five-star bakery.

Laura was untangling a string of lights when Roger groaned, "Not this song!"

"What?" She hadn't been paying attention.

"It's that George Michael one: the worst earworm in the world. It'll be in my head all day."

Last Christmas I gave you my heart
But the very next day you gave it away . . .

"I can't stand it either," said Linda. "Can you change the station, Laura?"

"Sure." She went to her desk and shuffled a pile of papers away from her mouse. "Let's see . . ." Her hand brushed against the thermal cup and she saw it tip, as if in slow motion, and fall over, onto its side. She grabbed for it, but succeeded only in knocking it to the floor, where it hit once and bounced. The cover cracked and flew in one direction; red wine flew everywhere else, spilling across the linoleum tiles, splashing onto chairs and desks, and soaking the front of Laura's pant legs with a spreading, lilac-colored stain. It seemed only an instant before the room was permeated with the yeasty, berried scent of it.

"Grape juice!" Laura gasped, even as a flash of fear went straight through her. No one could possibly think it was anything but what it was.

They stared.

"Grape juice," she repeated, in the silence.

"It doesn't smell like grape juice," said Linda.

Adrian looked shocked, Roger anguished. In the silence, Chris climbed down from the ladder, and Laura watched him approach, as if in slow motion. At her desk, he stooped down, put his finger into the small lake of wine that was spreading across the floor, and tasted it. He straightened, his face unreadable. "Come with me."

She followed him into his office, sifting her mind desperately for a plausible explanation.

Chris closed the door and turned to her. "Well?"

She said nothing. There was nothing to say.

"When I asked you before if you'd been drinking at work, had you?"

"*No.* This is the first time, honestly. I just . . . I had some really bad news from home, and—"

He cut her off. "It doesn't matter how sympathetic I may be to your situation, Laura. The company's rules are clear. Drinking on the property during work hours is grounds for immediate dismissal."

She stared at the floor, numb and disembodied. Strangely, all she could think was, *I wish I'd gotten to drink more of it before it spilled.*

"Do you need help?" Chris's voice had softened.

"No, it's not like that! It was just this one time, I promise. I got bad news from my parents. My . . . my father has a disease. ALS. He's going to die." Any shame she might have felt in exploiting her father's long-known diagnosis for this moment was quelled ruthlessly by her greater instinct for survival.

"I'm sorry to hear that, Laura. That's really tough news to get, especially at the holidays."

She did not have to fake the tears that filled her eyes. "I don't usually drink in the morning. Not ever, in fact. It's just been a bad couple of days." She drew a shaky breath and wiped her eyes.

"Here, sit down."

She sat, clasping her hands in her lap, willing them to stop trembling.

He was silent for a long while; then at last, he said, "I have a brother who's a recovering alcoholic. I may not know much, but I do know some symptoms of the disease. And Laura, people who have a healthy relationship with alcohol don't drink it in the morning, at work, even to cope with the worst kind of news."

At once her defenses were up, like a fence of iron palings. "I'm not an alcoholic."

"The company has funds to help send employees to inpatient rehab when it's needed. It's a thirty-day program. We've done it before, and we'd be glad to do it for you too."

"I appreciate that, Chris, but I don't need rehab. I don't have a drinking problem. This was truly, sincerely a one-time thing."

"Are you sure? Think about it carefully, Laura. Because my only options here are to send you to rehab for a month, or to fire you. The company doesn't offer me another choice."

She said nothing.

"We'd hate to lose you."

Rehab again. Thirty days of not drinking. An admission to the world, no matter how untrue, that she was an alcoholic. But . . . was it worth going through the motions, if it meant she could keep her job?

"Laura?"

In the end, it was no choice at all. "I'll clean out my desk."

Fifteen minutes later, she carried her small box of belongings to her car and looked up at the corrugated face of the warehouse where she'd worked for the better part of three years. She felt neither regret nor elation at the thought of leaving. Her own lack of emotion disturbed her. It seemed that if a place had occupied so many hours of your life for so long, you ought to feel *something* about leaving. Not for the first time did Laura wonder if something was wrong with her. Surely this inability to connect, to really *care*, was not normal?

She put the car in gear, determined to call her friends and tell them she would be joining them for Christmas Eve and

Christmas Day. But neither Wendy nor Theo answered her phone, and for some reason she could not put words to, Laura did not leave either of them a message. Instead, she went back to her apartment, changed into her pajamas at eleven forty in the morning, turned off her phone, locked her door, and settled in with the remote control and the box of wine she had picked up on the way home. She would just unwind a little, from the stress of losing her job, and then she would call them back, she thought. Tomorrow was Christmas Eve. After that, she would find a new job and start moving forward again. Today, she was going to watch Christmas movies and have some time to herself. She deserved it.

❧

On Christmas Day, Jane opened a solid, rectangular package and felt her heart sink the smallest bit. It was too much to hope that it might contain a calculator.

"Ah," said Leander, pulling it from its box. "I believe this is the promised iPhone."

She gazed at the thing in dismay but, looking around the living room at her delighted family, did her best to inject some enthusiasm into her voice. "You got me an iPhone."

"It's from all of us," said David.

"*Well,*" she said.

"Well what?"

"Well . . . I guess this means Ivy won, then."

DeShaun, Jada, and Hammer, it turned out, knew all there was to know about an iPhone. By the time Christmas dinner had been consumed and cleared away, Jane was able not only to make and answer a call, but to check her voice mail, which Jada kindly set up for her, and most importantly, to take a picture. If her cheap little track phone had a camera, Jane had never bothered to learn about it.

"That alone is worth the price of the phone right there!" she kept saying, to anyone who would listen.

"Stop it, Mom," said Amy. "Stop taking candids of everyone. Here, give me that, and I'll program all our numbers in for you."

Reluctantly, Jane surrendered the phone. "Hurry up then," she said. "I'm missing some good shots."

"Take all afternoon, Amy!" called Ivy from across the room.

"I plan to," Amy muttered.

"Oh no you don't!" Jane pounced on her youngest and took it back. "You can program the numbers in later." She aimed the phone at Amy's exasperated face. "Say cheese!" The shutter clicked.

"We've created a monster," Amy groaned.

❧

It was the insistence of her bladder that finally woke Laura up. She stumbled to the bathroom, and as she took care of business, it occurred to her that she was still fairly drunk. She'd have to get that flushed out of her system before she went to Lance and Wendy's for Christmas Eve dinner, she thought fuzzily. Then, remembering that she hadn't called them to confirm yet, she found her way back to her bedroom and the phone on her bedside table.

At first, Laura was sure she was reading it wrong. 2:04 a.m. *December 26*? A shock wave of disbelief washed over her. *No, no, no, no, no.* She weaved her way into the living room, snatched up the remote control, and flipped to the first twenty-four-hour news station she could find. *December 26, 2:05 a.m.* said the tiny box in the bottom corner. She sank onto the couch in horror. How was it possible? She had come home after work on the twenty-third and had a drink or two . . .

How could she have completely missed both Christmas Eve and Christmas?

She looked at her phone again. Voice message and text notices were stacked up like planes over Atlanta. It was as though for—she counted—over sixty hours, she had completely flown the planet. Once or twice before, she had blacked out, but never like this—never for so long. Terror swept over her. Getting up from the couch, she began a feverish exploration of her apartment, looking for clues. Not one but two wine boxes stood empty beside her trash can. She remembered only the one she'd brought home after work. She must have left at some point and gone out for the second. It meant she had, in all likelihood, driven drunk, and also consumed what amounted to eight bottles of wine in less than two and a half days.

Two and a half days that didn't exist in her memory at all.

It took six more hours for the shakes to start. Laura lay on her bed throughout that night, alone, sweating and shaking the poison out of her system, with no person on earth she could call and explain herself to. She wept with despair and, far into the morning hours, wondered if, truly, the world might be a better place without someone like her in it.

15

WITHOUT A DOUBT, Jane's favorite place in the calendar was the week between Christmas and the first of January. The year's work, with its culmination in the hectic blur of December, was done, and if you were fortunate, you could say it was done well. It was a week of limbo, when nothing much was expected of anyone. When the children had been young, with a father who was a teacher, it was a time for the whole family to be together. To spend the days skiing, to stay up late at night watching movies, and to give the whole place a good cleaning in anticipation of the coming New Year's Eve party.

She always gave herself one day off after Christmas, to lie on the couch in her pajamas and slippers and read a book, before switching focus. After that, she turned her attention to the list of tasks before her as one might face a box of the best chocolates: her only dilemma was which to choose and savor first. There were the white table linens to be brought out of storage, aired, and ironed. Folding chairs and tables to be carted over from the church. Cases of champagne flutes to be washed, dried, polished, and arranged on trays in the front porch to await the last minutes of the old year. With the help of Leander and her children, she would finalize the menu and shop for groceries. Then the fun of cooking would begin.

The evening of the twenty-seventh found Ivy, Amy, and Libby sitting around the dining room table at 14 Ladyslipper Lane, along with Jada and DeShaun, who had been invited to join the planning session for the first time.

"This is a grave responsibility, kids." Amy pointed her fork at her niece and nephew, but not before licking it clean of pumpkin pie. "The whole community will talk, for all of the coming year, about what the Darlings served at their New Year's Eve party."

Jada's eyes grew wide.

"Oh, stop," protested Jane, who could not bear for anyone to be teased. "It's not as big as all that. It's just that it's our one time of the year to really . . ." She searched for the right word.

"Splash out," Ivy supplied. "Cook everything you never get to cook during the rest of the year."

"Have everyone you love best around you at once," added Amy.

"Like a wedding every year!" said Libby, whose own wedding of a year earlier was still fresh in her mind. "But isn't it really expensive? I mean, the champagne alone . . ."

Jane patted her hand. "We have a fund we put into every week, all year long. We've done it since, oh, about the fifth or six year; I'd have to check. About the time it started to get really big, and yes, expensive. We budget for this more carefully than we do Christmas!" She realized she was a bit embarrassed by this truth.

"Can I invite Dillon?" Jada asked. "Mom, I can invite Dillon, right? He would think this is the sickest party."

Jane shot a puzzled glance at Ivy, who seemed perfectly capable of interpreting this prediction.

"We'll talk about it, honey."

Ah, that essential phrase of postponement, beloved of parents everywhere! Jane smiled at Ivy, who smiled back.

"I think we should have those choux pastries with crème fraîche and caviar that we did last year," said Ivy. "They were a huge hit."

"So was the roast beef with horseradish cream," put in DeShaun.

"Mikhaila's mother made those little hot dogs in barbecue sauce for her birthday," Jada said. "Ohmigaw—" a look at her mother's face, then, "Oh my goodness, they were so *yum!*"

"Hmmm," said Ivy, not writing down this suggestion. "We'll think about that one. What else?"

"How about little shot glasses of lobster bisque?" DeShaun's culinary class was currently covering soups. "It could be mostly bisque, with a sliver of lobster meat and a tarragon leaf on top."

"I beg you, do not forsake the vegetarians among us," put in Amy.

"Oh, please." Ivy rolled her eyes. "If Crystal comes, that'll make a whole two of you. And neither of you will eat more than a couple of crackers and a smear of dip."

"Foul!" Amy cried, outraged. "I demand we be fairly represented! Not everyone likes meat and seafood, you know."

Ivy was unruffled. "Fine. Suggestions?"

Amy glared at her. "Yes, as a matter of fact. Tartlets of fig, walnut, and bleu cheese; spinach mini quiches; tortilla chips with pico de gallo, guacamole, and hummus; a cheese platter; a vegetable platter; and one of fruit."

"Is all that okay with you, Mom?"

"Sounds wonderful."

Ivy wrote it down.

"We did an onion tart in class," DeShaun offered. "With Gruyère and a little thyme."

"Ooh, now you're talking!" Ivy added it to the list.

"English muffin pizzas!" Jada said. "And tater tots with ranch dip—no, *chipotle* ranch dip!"

"Mmmm . . ." Ivy managed to sound both encouraging and noncommittal. Then, quickly, "Crab-stuffed mushroom caps?"

"Yes! They disappeared in a heartbeat last year," said Jane. "Your father couldn't get enough of them."

There was a beat of silence in which no one pointed out that Leander would be able to eat very few of the appetizers this year.

DeShaun cleared his throat. "I liked the chicken liver pâté on crostini. I think a lot of people did."

"We went out for dinner last week," Libby ventured, "and David had some kind of lamb meatballs he really liked.

Could you do those small, like appetizer-sized, and I don't know . . . serve them on toothpicks or something?"

"Brilliant, all of you. Keep 'em coming."

"What about dessert?" Jane asked.

They looked at one another.

"I feel like our usual mini éclairs and cheesecake are a bit . . . tired," said Amy.

There was silence around the table while they all considered this.

"How about a croquembouche?" DeShaun said.

They looked at him blankly.

"It's a bunch of cream puffs built up into a tower, like a Christmas tree, and covered with spun sugar."

"I know what a croquembouche is," Ivy said at last. "But I can't think where we'd order one big enough to serve nearly a hundred people."

DeShaun shrugged. "I'll do it. It's not that big a deal. Honey, lemon, and lavender, I was thinking. Actually—" his voice assumed an elaborate casualness—"I have a friend from school who wants to be a pastry chef. Maybe she could come up the day of the party and give me a hand."

Around the table, the eyebrows of his female relations shot skyward. DeShaun, intent on examining a pen he had picked up, missed the rabidly curious glances that ricocheted among them.

He tapped the pen against the tabletop and waited.

"Oh!" Ivy recovered herself first. "Yes, by all means, invite . . . her . . . over for the day to help."

"'Kay." He stood, tossed the pen back onto the table, and left the room.

Further discussion, it appeared, was out of the question for the moment.

⸎

At ten o'clock on the day before the party, David and Mitch pulled into the driveway, the Chevy pickup behind the Ford, their beds loaded with fifty folding chairs and three long tables from the church.

"Bring them in quick," said Jane, "and don't leave me holding the door open. Can you believe how *cold* it's turned?" The fashionably named "polar vortex" was apparently on the move, bringing temperatures of negative three Fahrenheit, although with the wind chill factor, it was supposed to officially feel like twenty-three below zero.

"Freezes the snot in your nose." David grinned as he sidled past her with both hands full of chairs. "Where d'you want these, Mom?"

"Put them in the living room, against the bookshelves, for now."

"It's so cold the lawyers have their hands in their own pockets," Mitch said, following David with a load of his own.

David passed Jane on his way out again. "It's so cold we had to open the refrigerator this morning, just to heat the house."

"It's so cold the fire department is advising people to set their own houses on fire."

"Oh stop, you two!" Jane, shivering by the door in her sweater and wool clogs, could not help laughing.

"It's so cold," David said, on his second trip in, "that Libby's and my words froze in midair this morning, over breakfast. We had to put them in a frying pan to hear what we were saying."

Mitch added, "I heard on the news that the police told a robber to freeze last night, and he did."

The chairs and tables were in at last, but Jane insisted that everyone have a cup of coffee before attempting to set them up where they belonged. "Let them thaw a bit," she said placidly, slicing a lemon-glazed gingerbread. When they had finished and she had sufficiently caught up on the news of the daughter and daughter-in-law she hadn't seen for at least twenty-four hours, she released the men to the living room to set up tables and chairs under Leander's direction. She followed with the crisp white tablecloths that would act as stages for the exquisite buffet they had finally agreed upon.

When it was all finished, Leander took his cane and walked out with the boys to wave them off. From her desk, Jane took the schematics she had drawn of the buffet. She was squinting at them against the tables, preparing everything in her mind, when it occurred to her that she had not heard Leander come back in. It could not have been more than fifteen minutes since David and Mitch had gone, but still—

An instinctive terror gripped her. *No*— She dropped her notes and lurched toward the front door.

Leander lay, fetal, on the walkway. He was wearing only a flannel shirt and a pair of jeans; even from the doorway, she could see his body racked with shudders.

"Oh!" It was an inarticulate sound, wrenched from the core of her. Swiftly, she pulled her long wool coat from the closet, then took from the hanger the large down parka that

Leander had last worn two years ago, before it had gotten too big for him.

Jane burst out of the door with a gasp. "Leander!" The down parka was over him in an instant. "What happened?" she panted, not even listening for an answer. "What *happened*?"

His teeth were chattering so badly he could not speak.

"Okay. Okay," she gabbled, unthinking. "Let's get you up and inside." She had no idea how she might go about this. *Oh, heavenly Father* . . . There wasn't time to call 911. It was so cold, and he had been out here so long . . . Already, his lips were purple.

She thought back to the day last summer when she had gotten him off the bedroom floor. She had done it from behind. Hooked onto his arms and pushed him up.

"Hold on, sweetheart. I'm going to get you inside," she panted. She got behind him, slipping on the ice a bit, and hooked her hands under his armpits. It was clear his legs were too numb to help, so she dragged him. She kept up a one-way conversation. "It's okay. I've got you. Just a few more feet and then . . . See, we're there! We're at the steps. Can you just, maybe with your arms, reach back and . . ."

But he could not. He seemed incapable of movement, or even sound. Prodded by desperation, Jane adjusted her grip beneath his arms and said, "*Up* we go!" With a superhuman strength that she later could not account for, she got his right hip onto the first step. "*Up!*" she cried again and heaved until his left hip was up as well.

The wind was a fine whip against her cheeks. Her exposed hands had gone painfully numb. "One more, Leander!" Then they were at the top, at the small landing where the stairs and the wheelchair ramp met. She opened the front door and sat on the floor of the front hall. Bracing her heels against the doorway, she gave a protracted heave and pulled her husband over the threshold. Victory! The relief was physical. "Wait!" she commanded, as though he were about to jump up and head for someplace better. "Hang on!" She squeezed around him, to his legs, still resting on the step. Gathering them like an armful of kindling, she pushed with all her might. Leander slid, taking the bristly welcome mat with him along the polished floor. After that, it was easy enough to slide him along the wood and close the door firmly behind them.

Warm. It was warm in here. "Oh, Leander, you could have frozen to death!" Jane sat in the hall, with her husband's shocked, benumbed face in her hands and, feeling as weak as skim milk, began to cry.

On the morning of the party, Amy and Libby arrived together at number 14 to help cook and were greeted at the door by Ivy.

"DeShaun's friend is here," Ivy hissed as they hung up their coats. "Her name is Penelope. She came up from Portland last night and is staying with us until Monday."

"Staying . . . ?"

"In Jada's room. They're working on the croquembouche in the kitchen, right now."

"What's she like?" Libby whispered.

"Cute as a button, and very sweet. She grew up as a missionary kid in France, apparently."

"Is she really *just a friend*?"

"No idea. DeShaun won't say a word about it."

"Let me at her!" cried Amy in a low voice. "I'll find out."

"If you do or say a single thing to embarrass DeShaun, I will draw and quarter you myself with his meat cleaver."

"You underestimate me." Amy's tone was injured.

"Wrong: I know you all too well."

Her sister tried, and failed, to look offended.

"Just behave yourself. Or else."

It had been the best New Year's party yet, Jane reflected, two days later, when the chairs and tables had been carted back to the church and the cleanup had at last been finished. She sat at the breakfast bar in her robe, drinking a third cup of coffee and scrolling through the photos on her iPhone. The buffets had been beautiful; the towering centerpiece of DeShaun's croquembouche, listing only slightly to one side, was admired by everyone. His friend, the tall, cheerful Penelope, fit into the family as seamlessly as though she'd been born to it.

She had gotten several pictures of Leander. Talking intently to Libby, her chair pulled close to his wheelchair, leaning in close to hear each other. With Jada, far too tall to be sitting on her grandfather's lap, but doing it anyway. Posing with David, in matching party hats. How would next year's pictures be different? She ran her hand lightly over the phone. Life was steeped in the unknown, she reminded herself, but all in all, it was a good start to the year ahead.

CHAPTER

16

FOR THIRTY YEARS, Leander's morning routine had been to wake up, go downstairs for breakfast and coffee, then return to the second floor for his shower. But the episode just before New Year's, when he had lain outside in subzero temperatures for more than fifteen minutes, had taken a noticeable toll on his strength. The stairs had become an enormous effort. Now, they agreed, the routine would have to change: it would be shower first, breakfast second. The easiest thing was to get all of the upstairs tasks done and out of the way before heading down to the first floor.

On the third day of this, Jane helped him into the shower, settled him on the seat, and left him to it while she went to make the bed. She was midway through a hospital corner when he called to her. Heart lurching, she rushed back into the bathroom. "What is it?" Leander was slumped on the chair under the warm spray, looking defeated. *Oh, God, thank You that he didn't fall.*

"I can't wash my hair. I can't get my arms up that far, or hold them up long enough."

As though for the first time, Jane really looked at him. His once-muscled arms were wasted and flaccid, the arms of an old man. His collarbones protruded so far that the water pooled behind them, twin lakes at the base of his throat. How, until this moment, had she avoided seeing what was happening to her husband? The answer, of course, was that she had not wanted to see it. Now, she sank to her knees at the side of the bathtub and reached out to touch one of his knees. Beneath the skin, the outline of each bone was clear and sharp. Leaning forward, she rested her forehead on it, lost in a swell of sadness. "Oh, Leander—"

She felt a heaviness on her hair. His hand. For a long time, they sat like that, silent, as the warm water rained down over her own head and seeped into the neck and sleeves of her sweatshirt. At last, as though coming out of a dream, she sat back on her heels. Her sweatshirt and jeans were half-soaked. Leander would be getting cold, and her floor would soon be ruined. Taking his hand in hers, she kissed his palm. "You must be freezing."

"I'm fine."

She roused herself to practicality. "Well, I'll have to wash your hair for you, but I'm not sure quite how to go about it without getting even wetter."

"Why don't you strip down and get right in here with me?"

She smiled. "Opportunist."

"It's been too long since we took a shower together anyway."

Jane did as he said, standing behind him to wash his hair, and then his back, and then all of him. She took her time, memorizing with her hands the bones of his head, his shoulders, his back. Her tears, when they came, were no longer of sorrow, but were the tears that come from finding oneself in the presence of something sacred. As they fell, they mingled with the shower spray, running down and baptizing them both with something she had no name for.

Later that morning, with Leander at work and the house quiet, Jane made several phone calls. The first was to Dr. Gutierrez's office, where Heather set all the right wheels in motion. A home care nurse would be out tomorrow, she promised Jane. She would assess Leander, and after that, an aide would be in three or four days a week to help him shower.

The second call was to David. "What do you know about those chairs that go up and down the stairs on a rail?"

"Is Dad ready for that, then?"

"Yes. He can hardly manage them, and there's no shower on the first floor." She told him about the home care aide who would be coming to help, but left out any mention of the morning's shower incident.

"Let me call Mitch. I think he'd know more about it than I would." David hesitated. "If you don't mind my asking, Mom, what happened? I mean, the cane, the walker, the wheelchair . . . This is the first time we haven't had to talk you into a new step like this."

She herself could not explain it. Something had happened

to her in the shower. She had stepped into it passive, as much a victim of this disease as Leander himself. She had stepped out like the man born blind in the Bible, with her eyes washed clean, able to see clearly what her job was. Her mission, perhaps the best thing she had been put on this earth for, was to do whatever it took to help Leander reach the end in the best, most dignified way possible. But she did not say any of this to David. To him, she only said briskly, "Call it perspective. And you're at work; *I'll* call Mitch."

Mitch said he knew a guy. Mitch always seemed to know a guy when it was needed. "He owes me one. I think he'd sell you the equipment at cost and let us install it ourselves," he said. "David, Nick, and I can do it in an afternoon. It'll save you thousands."

Not for the first time, nor for the same reasons, did Jane thank God for sending Mitch Harris into their lives all those years ago.

Ivy was dusting the living room when she heard the school bus at the end of the driveway. She stopped at the window and watched as Jada came down the steps, purple backpack on her back and green coat wide open to the wind. At the end of the driveway, her daughter turned and waved madly to some unseen person inside the bus, and Ivy was overcome with a rush of love and gratitude. There was nothing, after all, like seeing your children whole and happy in this life.

As the bus pulled away, Jada began to blow kisses toward it. Jumping up and down, she made the *I love you* sign with both hands, until it was out of sight. Ivy's warm feelings dissolved in a rush of irritation. *Dillon.* Well, it would have to be dealt with. Setting her dust rag and lemon oil on an end table, she went to open the door.

Jada blew in, already talking. "Mom, can I go to the mall with Dillon tonight? Please, please, *please*? His mom can pick me up and bring me home and everything. You won't have to go anywhere!"

"Come sit down and let's talk about it."

Jada's face instantly shuttered. "I knew you'd say no. You never let me do *anything*!" She stormed ahead of her mother to the kitchen, where she wrenched off her backpack and thrust it savagely into her cubby. Her coat came off no more gently, and she hung it on its hook by one arm, then came to slump in a chair at the table, with her chin on her arms.

"You look tragic," Ivy observed, pulling a bottle of grape juice from the refrigerator. "Piece of cake?"

Jada hesitated fractionally, then nodded, avoiding her mother's eyes.

Ivy put the cake on a plate and set it, along with the juice bottle and a glass, on the table and came to sit across from her daughter. "I haven't said no yet," she pointed out.

"But you're going to."

"Yes. But we could at least talk about it."

"*Every*body goes to the mall on Friday night!"

"I'm sure they do. But, Jada, your dad and I have told you already that you're too young to date. Sixteen is what we said, and even then, we'd need to meet the boy and his family and decide on a case-by-case basis."

"That's not fair! Everybody else I know gets to date when they're almost fourteen!"

Though Ivy was certain this was not true, she admired her own restraint in not saying so. Instead, she said, "We're not going to budge on this, sweetie. You'll just have to trust us that in this case, we know what's best for you."

Jada glared at her. "Well, he's still my boyfriend. You can't stop me from having a boyfriend at school."

"I wish you trusted and respected us enough so that it wasn't an issue."

Jada stared at the table. "That's not it."

"What do you mean?"

"I do. Respect you, I mean. And love you. But Dillon really *likes* me, Mom. And he is *so* cool!"

"And you really like him?"

Jada shrugged. "Yeah."

"Yeah? Not 'oh my goodness yes yes yes, I like him sooooo much, Mom! I'm crazy about him! I love him'?"

Jada allowed herself a small smile. Still staring at the table, she said, "Well, he *is* a soccer player."

"Ah! A soccer player! What else?"

"He's really cute."

"I know. I saw his picture on your dresser. What about his hopes and dreams?"

Jada looked at her mother as though she had asked for Dillon's social security number.

"What does he want to do in life?" Ivy elaborated.

"How should I know? He wants to be a soccer player, I guess. Professional. Probably."

"A noble goal. And . . . ah . . . what does he think about *your* hopes and dreams?"

"I don't know. We don't really talk about that. I mean, not a lot."

"Does he know what your hopes and dreams *are*?"

"I don't know."

"So . . . you don't talk all that much about the important things, but at least he's really cute, and a soccer player."

Jada regarded her narrowly.

"I'm just trying to put all the pieces together. Here, eat your cake." Ivy pushed the plate toward her, and Jada, with only a weak attempt at reluctance, picked up her fork. "Jada, you know how Aunt Amy and Mitch are best friends?"

"Yeah," with her mouth full.

"They're in love, but they were best friends first, right?"

"Yeah." Jada poured herself some grape juice.

"And Mitch isn't particularly cool, and he doesn't play soccer, and he's not . . . well, would you say he's really cute?"

"Eeew! Mom, he's *old*!"

"Well . . . he's not too old for Aunt Amy. My point is, Aunt Amy is in love with him not because he's cute and cool and all that, but because he's her best friend. He knows all her hopes and dreams, and she knows all his. That's the best way to have a boyfriend."

Jada brightened.

"After you're sixteen," Ivy added.

"So . . . I can't go to the mall with Dillon?"

Ah, well! She should know by now that parenting in real life rarely looked like it did in TV commercials for peanut butter or family cars. "No, you can't," she said. "But Dad and I were thinking: your birthday's coming up soon, so how about tomorrow, you and I go to Bangor to do some clothes shopping? We'll get you a couple of new outfits, go out to lunch wherever you want, and celebrate together, just the two of us."

Jada picked morosely at the crumbs of cake on her plate. "We wouldn't have to bring Hammer, would we?"

"No, he can stay home with Dad."

"Okay, I guess."

"I mean, don't knock yourself out or anything. We can just as easily stay home and do chores, if you want. I have plenty to keep us busy around here."

"No, I mean, I guess we could go shopping."

"All right, then. What if we left here around eight and planned to get there when the mall opens?"

"Can we eat at Friars' Bakehouse?"

"Of course, if you want."

"I'm getting a whoopie pie for dessert."

"I should hope so. Now, you might as well text Dillon and tell him your mean old mom won't let you go with him tonight."

Jada gave her, if not exactly a smile, at least a less-hostile grimace. "Okay."

"Good. Now, if you'll excuse me, I have to finish dusting the living room." Ivy left her daughter at the table, texting Dillon. As she went, she prayed. *I wouldn't be thirteen years old again, Lord, not for anything. Give her grace to navigate these years with wisdom.*

Not a bad prayer for any stage of life, actually, she thought, and picked up her dust rag to tackle the bookcase next.

The next morning, Ivy left Nick and Hammer watching a movie together, and headed to Bangor with her daughter. Jada had gotten over her sulk of the night before and, cheered by the thought of new clothes and lunch out at her favorite restaurant, was positively sunny. They passed the time in the car singing together. Ivy was often grateful that God had seen fit to give her a musical child. He didn't have to, of course, but it was nice to be able to share this part of her life with at least one of her tribe. Of the two of them, Jada was by far the more gifted musician, but Ivy had grown up singing harmony in her own family ensemble and was able to hold her own.

The mall yielded three new tops and two pairs of jeans for Jada before they broke for an early lunch. Over soup and sandwiches at Friars', Jada said, "Can I get my nose pierced for my birthday?"

Was there no reprieve? "Maybe next year," Ivy said, "when you're fifteen. But finish up, and let's get your whoopie pie. We still have to get your birthday gift from Dad and me."

"But my birthday's not 'til Monday."

"Well . . . we might as well pick it up while we're out shopping."

"Is it a puppy?"

"Of course it's not a puppy!"

"What is it?"

Ivy made a zipping motion across her lips.

"Come on, tell me!"

"I'll show you when you're done with your lunch."

Jada pushed her plate away. "I'm done!"

"What about dessert?"

"I'm too full."

"Let's bring some whoopie pies home for Dad and Hammer, then, and we'll have them for dessert tonight." Ivy signaled the server and asked for four whoopie pies to go, along with the check.

Back in the car, she turned off Central Street and parked in front of a small hair salon.

Jada looked at her. "Why are we here?"

"I thought . . . maybe cornrows for your birthday?"

Jada's eyes grew wide, and unsnapping her seat belt, she flung herself across the seat at her mother and enveloped her in a rather painful hug. "You are the *best*! The best mother ever!"

Ivy smiled and refrained from reminding her that not twenty-four hours before, she had been the mother who never let her daughter do *anything*. Instead, she said, "Yes, I am, aren't I? And you have a twelve-thirty appointment, so we'd better get in there."

As the young African hairdresser inside took her glowing daughter in hand and led her to a chair, Ivy thought that her capitulation had been worth it. And maybe—just maybe—by this time next year, she'd be adjusted to the idea of a nose piercing, and the year after that, a boyfriend. Beyond that, who knew? She was glad she only had to take this growing-up business one step at a time.

❧

"I think it's time I took over paying the bills," Jane said. They were sitting up in bed, reading.

Leander looked at her over the tops of his glasses. "Don't

say you suspect me of skimming off the top of the retirement fund."

She swatted his arm with the *Reader's Digest*. "Ridiculous man. Actually, at Thanksgiving, your mother was telling me about how she had to figure all of that out on her own after your father died. She's right: I should know how to do it myself."

"All right, then. What say we sit down together soon, and I'll show you the ropes?"

"When?"

He thought about this. "Martin Luther King Jr. Day is coming up. School holiday."

"It's a date."

On the appointed morning, they brought their coffee into the office, and he walked her through his files, explaining which day of the month each bill was due and how each was paid. Automatic withdrawal, credit card, personal check . . . Jane took avid notes on a yellow legal pad, and by early afternoon, she felt confident that she could take care of all of it by herself. She could log on to the school's website and scrutinize Leander's paycheck; she knew how much they had in their retirement and bank accounts and had noted on the calendar when the car was due for inspection and an oil change.

"Let's take a break for lunch," she said.

"That sounds good. And after that—" he rummaged through a file folder and came up with a stack of forms, which he slapped onto the desk—"we tackle income taxes."

"Income taxes!" She tried to sound as though she'd been looking forward to this all along. In reality, she felt faint at the very idea.

"I'm a little embarrassed to be just learning all this at my age," she confessed, when they were eating. "But I've never liked to think about the financial end of things."

"Well, I've never liked to do the cooking," he pointed out. "It doesn't mean I *couldn't*, if I had to, but I've always been happy to let you take care of it. That's one of the benefits of marriage: you don't have to do it all yourself."

"I suppose that would sound terribly old-fashioned to other people."

"Who cares what other people think? It's worked well enough for us all these years."

"My parents fought about money all the time," she said.

"Did they?"

"Oh yes. I'd lie in bed at night and listen to them yelling at each other. Dad was always saying he needed some new piece of farm equipment or other, and Mother would want to know how on earth she was supposed to feed a family of four on what was left over. She'd shout that we'd all be lining up for food stamps next, and wouldn't he be proud of himself when the neighbors caught wind of that?" She smiled, though there was little humor in the memory. "I know that's why the subject of money has always made me uncomfortable."

"Well, you're rising to the occasion magnificently. What do you think: are you ready to face these taxes and get them over with?"

"I'd rather take a nap."

He grimaced. "I always dread doing taxes, myself."

"We don't have to do them today, surely? It's only January."

"We should be responsible. Tackle them early!" But she could sense his resolve weakening.

"We're both still worn out from the holidays. . . ."

"It *was* a busy Christmas and New Year's."

"Don't forget Thanksgiving." They looked at each other and grinned. "Should we act like naughty senior citizens, just this once?" she said.

"Let's go for it!"

They left the tax forms on the desk and, hand in hand, with a conspiratorial sense of having gotten away with something, went to the living room, where they lay head-to-toe on the couch together, pulled an afghan over themselves, and fell asleep.

17

MORE AND MORE DID JANE'S THOUGHTS DRIFT, as though borne on an irresistible current, to the son she had never known. Most often, she tried to quell such thoughts, reasoning that they could do nobody any good. But the Saturday that David, Nick, and Mitch came to install the chair lift on the stairs, she found herself watching them, trying to insert a fourth man into the picture. He would be older than the rest of them, and tall, like his father had been, with hair that was bound to be more gray than black now.

"Don't worry about all this, Mom," David said, misinterpreting her pensive silence as she watched. "This is going to be a good thing for Dad, just like the wheelchair. Think of all the freedom it'll give him."

She had not been thinking of the chair at all, but she said, "You're right, of course. It's an invention to be thankful for."

She took herself off to the kitchen then, to sit alone with a cup of tea. As she drank it, she gave her thoughts passive permission to take the direction they wanted.

She had kissed her sister's boyfriend for the first time in the spring. Robert and Ellen were visiting from college for the weekend, again, and the whole family had gone to their bedrooms to dress for Saturday night Mass. Jane happened to leave her room, just as Robert left his, and found herself alone in the hallway with him.

"You look pretty," he said. Her heart throbbed so loudly she was sure he must be able to hear it. "I was wondering," he went on, "if I could look at the view out your bedroom window? Ellen says you can see clear to the ocean from up here, but my window looks out the wrong way."

Her voice might have been taken over by a stranger. "Oh. Um, yes, she's right. But you can see it best from the attic."

He raised his eyebrows. "Would you show me?"

"Ellen could show you."

"Ellen has a headache. She's lying down before Mass."

Wordlessly, Jane turned and he followed her through the door at the end of the hallway that led to the attic stairs. So many nights she had lain awake, imagining what it would be like to be alone with Robert, that now, climbing one creaking step after another, with him right behind her, she wondered if this was part of another daydream.

The attic held two minuscule, finished rooms and a great deal of storage space. She led him to the east room and gestured out the window. "There it is."

"Beautiful," he said, but he was not looking at the window.

Her mouth was dry. "Robert—"

"I think about you all the time."

"Stop it! Ellen—"

"Ellen," he said in a strange, rasping voice, "is the kind of girl you marry. Not the kind of girl you kiss in attics."

Kiss? She formed the word with her mouth, but no sound came out.

He pulled her toward him and kissed her. She had never kissed a boy before, and for one panicked moment she had no idea what to do. And then there was no more time to think. His hands were cradling her face, and he whispered, "Like this." And again, "Like this." And then it was as though she had been doing it all her life.

When she finally pulled back, her lips felt raw and swollen, the very skin of them burned by the searing heat of his mouth. "We can't do this."

"Yes, we can." He pulled her close and kissed her again. It was febrile and electric, and she wanted it never to end, but she knew they would be missed. And if her parents—or worse, Ellen—discovered them in the attic together . . .

"Stop it," she hissed. "Just . . . stop!"

He let go of her. "I'll stop, but I'm warning you: I can't stay away. You're too big a temptation." He smiled at her, and the possessiveness of it both thrilled and terrified her. "We'll finish this later, Jane. You can count on that."

"Janey?" Leander was calling her.

She gave her head a shake. "In the kitchen."

He appeared in the doorway, with his walker. "Mitch says to come watch the maiden voyage of this thing. Nick brought along a miniature bottle of champagne from Ivy. She says we're to break it across the bow before it leaves the dock."

"Ah, a ceremony!" Jane stood and carried her mug to the sink, putting her thoughts firmly away with it. Resting her hand on her husband's shoulder, she let him lead her to the stairway. Today was not a day for regrets; there was a new chair lift to christen. In spite of every wish she might have to turn back the years and do things differently, life was a thing that kept moving forward. There was nothing to do but make the best of what was.

But on Monday, when Leander was at work, Jane took the phone with her into the office and booted up her computer. Consulting the Oracle, she found the phone number for Catholic Charities of Boston. She called the number and asked to be put in touch with someone in adoption services.

Eighteen minutes later, she hung the phone up, hollow with disappointment. The section of the building containing adoption files from 1970 to 1973 had been destroyed in a fire three decades ago. No records for those years still existed.

She had the desperate sense that she was running out of time. But . . . time for what?

❦

The home care aide was a tall, brisk young woman named Alisha, who arrived in yoga pants the first day and announced that she was there to help Leander with his shower.

"I'm not sure how I feel about this," Leander muttered as Alisha was unpacking her things. "You can't be any older than my youngest daughter."

"Nonsense," said Alisha. "It's all just body parts to me. Might as well be knees and elbows I'm washing as anything else. Hop into your chair, now, and let's get you upstairs."

Jane knew her husband well. He wanted to die of mortification. "Maybe I should come up with you, just this first time?" she suggested.

"That would be great." Leander's relief was palpable.

"Whatever," said Alisha cheerfully. "But let's get a move on. I have four other calls to make today, and the next one's in Bucksport."

❧

Laura sat on her couch and scrolled listlessly through another page of job listings. Jobs in Phoenix, jobs in Maine. She didn't know which direction to turn. There was no real hurry. Parson's, the restaurant where she'd once worked part-time as a waitress, had given her back her old job. She was working Friday, Saturday, and Sunday nights, and the tips were good. Between that and her savings, she could get through another two months. Three, if she was careful. She was still volunteering every other Wednesday at the homeless shelter, but otherwise, there was little to distinguish one of her days from another.

Her phone rang: Theo.

Dismiss. She'd call her back tomorrow. She'd find a job tomorrow. Laura got up, wandered into the kitchen, and poured herself a glass of wine. Thank goodness for tomorrow.

❧

One afternoon, the week before Valentine's Day, Amy dropped by to see Ivy.

"This is a treat," said Ivy. "Can you stay for a cup of tea?"

"What kind do you have?"

Ivy opened a cupboard and began to rummage. "Peppermint, Sleepytime, chamomile . . . and here's an orphan bag with no tag on it." She sniffed it. "Cinnamon, I think."

"I'll take the cinnamon."

Ivy boiled the kettle, and, taking their mugs to the living room, they settled in on opposite ends of the sofa.

"What brings you here in the middle of a workday?" Ivy asked.

"I need advice."

"Ooh, I love to give advice!"

"What in the world am I going to get Mitch for Valentine's Day? I've sieved my brain for every ounce of creativity, and I can't come up with a single idea that's not either trite or ridiculous."

Ivy was instantly sympathetic. "Men are impossible to buy for. I never know what to get Nick either."

"Mitch doesn't *need* anything, and if there's something he wants, he just goes out and buys it for himself."

"Men do that. How about a tool of some kind?"

"I'm clueless about tools. I'd buy the wrong thing."

"A new pair of Carhartts?"

"Unromantic."

"A sweater?"

"Oh, please." Amy rolled her eyes. "Dig deep here, Ivy. This is our first Valentine's Day together. I don't want to mess it up."

"Why don't you cook for him?"

"Cook what, miso soup? Right."

"No, cook something *he* likes. Steak and lobster."

Amy was horrified. "I don't touch either one of those things, let alone *cook* them."

"The sacrifice is what makes it a gift. Trust me; it'll be worth it."

"Hmmm . . ."

"And watch *Die Hard* together."

"This just gets worse and worse."

"Suck it up and do it anyway," Ivy said heartlessly. "The gesture won't be lost on him. In fact, come over later this week and I'll even teach you how to cook it all."

"You don't think he'll bring me red roses, do you? Red roses are so mainstream."

"Mitch knows you better than that, Amy."

The cooking lesson, held on Saturday morning when Mitch was working on the house, went beautifully. Amy was already adept in the kitchen, although this was her first attempt at either meat or seafood. She had settled on New York strip and seared sea scallops, declaring that there was *no way* she was plunging a live lobster to its death in a pot of boiling water, not even for Mitch.

The night before Valentine's Day, she baked and glazed a lemon pound cake. "It's one that's better the second day," Ivy had assured her. And on Valentine's Day itself, she left work at three o'clock and shopped for the rest of the meal before coming home to set the table and tackle the meat. By the time Mitch arrived, the French bread was baked, the salad and dressing made, and the steak and scallops ready to go into the pan.

When the doorbell rang, she took one last glance around, to make sure everything was in place, smoothed her apron over her green velvet skirt, said a quick prayer, and went to answer the door.

Mitch stood there with both hands behind his back. "Happy Valentine's Day," he said.

The smile she was never able to contain around him broke free. "Come in."

As he stepped inside, he brought one hand in front of him. A lovely, simple bouquet of mixed summer flowers.

Red roses, indeed! She should have known better. She took them from him and buried her nose in a sweet pea. "They're beautiful."

"So are you."

There went her insides again, dissolving into liquid light.

"Aaaand . . ." He brought out the other hand. A flat of seedlings, their delicate double leaves no more than an inch above the soil. "Basil. I planted it a month ago."

Amy laughed with delight. "You are so cool."

"I know. Now put them down so I can kiss you."

She obeyed, and he pulled her into his arms with a kiss that fairly took her breath away.

"Wow," she said at last, a bit dizzily. "Happy Valentine's Day to you too."

She led him into the kitchen and set a high stool by the stove for him, then turned on the gas flame under the pan.

He eyed the raw steak and scallops waiting on their plates. "You're cooking meat? And seafood?"

"Only for you would I even consider such a thing."

Ivy had been right: the gesture was not lost on him. He put his arms around her from behind and kissed the top of her head. "I love you."

"I love you too."

He sat on the stool and watched her cook while he told her about his progress on the house. In the oven, the potatoes were baking. The honey-glazed carrots waited, warming in their pot. On the back burner simmered the tofu curry she had made for herself.

Afterward, Mitch leaned back in his chair and closed his eyes blissfully. "That was the best steak I've ever had."

"Really?" Amy was as pleased as a child.

"Really. And the scallops . . . ? Perfect. I have no words to describe them."

Ivy was right again: it had been worth it. "It wasn't such a bad experience," Amy said thoughtfully. "Maybe I'll do it again for you."

His eyes flew open, bright with hope.

"I mean, from time to time," she said hastily. "I've been a vegetarian for almost ten years. No sense trying to boil the ocean, right?"

He pushed back his chair. "I have one more thing for you." Going to the coat rack, he pulled a CD case from his jacket pocket. From the table, she watched as he slipped the disc into her player, and the strains of a Strauss waltz rose into the room. Mitch adjusted the volume, then came to stand beside her. "Miss Darling, may I have this dance?"

She felt her mouth fall open. *What?*

"I would like to dance with you."

"But . . . you can't dance!"

"On the contrary, I dance very well." Reaching for her hand, he pulled her to her feet and led her to the tiny living room. He put one hand on her back—in exactly the right place, she noted. Automatically, she rested hers on his shoulder. Her other hand, he took in his, and then they were waltzing.

"I'm astonished!" she said. "Where in the world did you learn to do this?"

But his face was tense with concentration, and he shook his head. "Shush!" he ground out. "I still can't talk and count at the same time."

Following his lead, Amy allowed herself a happy sigh. She had cooked a steak for him; he had learned to dance for her. What was better than love?

When it was over, Mitch said, "Why don't we take a piece of cake over to Joe and say Happy Valentine's Day to him?"

She agreed at once. It was the finishing touch on an evening that was already perfect: it meant they weren't going to have to watch *Die Hard* after all.

❦

The desk was littered with the flotsam of a year's finances: tax forms, receipts, bank statements . . . a small tornado might have swept through her filing cabinet and left all this in its wake. Just that week, Jane had successfully navigated the gauntlet of bill-paying by herself for the first time. She was proud to say that the electricity had not been turned off, the credit cards had accumulated no interest, and the oil company had showed up right on schedule to fill their tank. But she and Leander had never gotten around to sitting back down to the taxes, and somehow, now that she had taken on the rest of it, it did not seem fair to foist this unpleasant chore back on him. Surely she could figure it out on her own. How hard could it be?

She picked up a form and squinted at it, sighed, and put it back down. It was hard to know where to begin. She put on her reading glasses and tapped her pen against the desktop. At this rate, she'd never get it done.

All right, at the top then. Leander's and her names, addresses, and social security numbers. That was easy enough. She filled them in. Then, the baffling question of Filing Status. Were they *Married filing jointly*, or *Married filing separately*? Jointly. At least, she thought so. But then, what was this *Head of household (with a qualifying person)* option? *(See Instructions)*, she read, and shuffled through the papers on the desk until she found the instructions booklet. Five minutes later, she was reasonably sure that they were, indeed, *Married filing jointly*, and with a twinge of apprehension, she checked off the box.

Next, exemptions. Herself and Leander. What about Amy? Their daughter had lived with them most of the year, but not all of it. Did she count?

Jane's head had begun to ache. She took off her glasses and rubbed the bridge of her nose. She could always ask her children, she supposed. Nick, who took care of the taxes for Ivy's family, would gladly help her. So would Libby or David. And Amy—no, not Amy. Jane shuddered to think what her fiercely independent daughter would have to say about a grown woman who couldn't fill out her own tax forms.

She would call one or the other of them later, she decided. There was no need to bother them with her problems right now. It was only February, after all; there were ages to go before April 15.

At Thursday night family dinner, Ivy came into the kitchen in time to hear Amy ask Jada, "So what did you get your boyfriend for Valentine's Day?"

Ivy felt a flash of irritation at Amy, who was supposed to be supporting her sister by pretending Jada's boyfriend didn't exist. Unseen by either of them, she stopped in the doorway and shamelessly eavesdropped.

"Who, Dillon?" Jada blew out a disgusted breath. "I got rid of him weeks ago."

"Really! Why?"

"I asked him what his hopes and dreams were, and you know what he said?"

"What?"

"He said, 'Who are you, my guidance counselor?'" Jada caught sight of her mother in the doorway just then, and rolled her eyes. "*Not* cool," she said. "He is not cool at all."

Later, Ivy watched David carry his loaded plate into the living room and sit on the end of the couch, by their father. "So you have a home care aide now, huh?" her brother asked.

"Oh yes," said their father. "A nice girl. Tall. She comes three times a week."

"And she, what, gives you a shower and washes your hair?"

"Yes. And takes my blood pressure."

"Ah. And . . . how's that going?"

Leander squinted knowingly at his son. "It's no different from washing elbows and knees, my boy. It's all just elbows and knees in our world."

CHAPTER

18

MARCH CAME IN LIKE A LION, for a change. Even as a three-day storm moved in to scour the rooftops and windows of the homes in Copper Cove, a cautious optimism prevailed. In like a lion, out like a lamb: surely this portended an early spring? The *Farmers' Almanac* seemed to bear this out, but still . . . the *Farmers' Almanac* had been wrong before.

Jane, carrying a basket of clean laundry through the living room on a Thursday afternoon when school was closed yet again from the storm, saw that Leander had fallen asleep in his recliner. He napped like a baby these days, sometimes dozing off for five or ten minutes only to awaken abruptly at the slightest sound, sometimes falling into a profound and unshakable slumber that would last for hours. At those times, she could run the vacuum cleaner in the same room and it would not disturb him. She took the basket upstairs, put the sheets and towels in the linen closet, and went back down to check on him. From the way he was breathing, it looked like this was going to be one of his long naps.

She wandered into the kitchen and stood there, at a loss. It was only three in the afternoon. She supposed she could start supper. She opened the refrigerator. Last night's ziti looked back at her, only one small scoop missing from a corner. On the shelf below it sat a shepherd's pie that Sue Henderson had dropped off earlier in the week. "I was making it anyway, and it's so hard to cook for just one person," Sue had explained. "I'm afraid I still haven't gotten the hang of it." Sue's husband, Ron, had died eighteen months before, and she had sounded apologetic as she thrust the casserole into Jane's hands, as though ashamed of having only herself to cook for. Well, that was supper taken care of, then. For about a week. She closed the refrigerator.

There was nothing to *do*, Jane thought. Not just at this moment, but more and more often. The tax forms still sat on her desk, gathering dust, but she refused to dwell on those. The house was clean, there was no need to cook, and as Amy had chosen *The Importance of Being Earnest* for the arts center's spring production, there was not even any music for her to practice. It was frightening, this increasingly empty space in her life. Like any vacuum, it had the power to suck her in; she felt the threat of being swallowed up by self-pity and inertia. What did people fill their lives with, once their children had grown and gone? They took classes, she supposed, or developed new hobbies. They read and joined travel clubs and learned to cook vegetarian food.

She missed having a houseful. She missed her children,

and felt the urgent need to call one of them, to reach out by way of the telephone and just hear a voice and reassure herself that they were all still connected to her. David and Amy, she knew, were at work and would not appreciate being disturbed just because their mother happened to be feeling lonely. Laura would not answer her phone, no matter what she was doing, and it was too late, in Africa, to call Sephy. She went to the phone and dialed Ivy's number. Voice mail. "It's Mom," Jane said, trying hard to sound cheerful. "Just calling to say hi and see what you're all up to. Talk to you later."

More for something to do than any other reason, she measured coffee grounds into the basket and started a pot of coffee. She'd pay for it tonight when she couldn't sleep, but she stood at the counter anyway watching it brew, and when it was ready, she poured a cup and took it back to the living room, where she sipped at it while she perused the bookshelves.

Far from the Madding Crowd . . . No, not Hardy. One had to be in a certain mood for Hardy. *Olive Kitteridge* . . . She'd read it only the year before: too soon for a reread. *One Hundred Years of Solitude* . . . That was one of Amy's favorites, but Jane had started it three times and had never been able to get into it. *A Short History of Nearly Everything* . . . Ah, yes! She'd been meaning to read Bill Bryson one of these years. She took it from the shelf and settled onto the end of the couch, kicking off her wool clogs and tucking her feet up under her. In the recliner, Leander snored gently.

She opened to the first page. *"Welcome. And congratulations. I am delighted that you could make it. Getting here wasn't easy, I know. In fact, I suspect it was a little tougher than you realize."*

Outside, a gust of wind rattled the windows. Holding her place in the book with a finger, Jane got up, took an afghan from the back of the couch, and carried it to Leander. He slept on, his mouth slack, and did not stir when she settled the blanket over him and tucked it in around the edges. Returning to the couch, she opened the book once more. The second paragraph was wordy and took a bit of untangling. She counted sixteen—or was it seventeen?—words of three syllables or more. She thought of Ernest Hemingway, who was known for rarely using a word with more than two.

Sighing, Jane closed the book. It was no use. Without children at home, she was at loose ends. The future years, when she would not have Leander to take care of either, sometimes seemed to rush before her like a dark and formidable river. Rarely did she let her mind dip into it. On the occasions when she did, she found it too frightening, and retreated back to the safe bank of the present. *Now* was the time she needed a purpose. If she could not occupy herself now, what would she do then? *Father, isn't there something I can* do? *Surely the best of life isn't supposed to be over once your children are gone. Please, give me a task! Something interesting and meaningful and . . . and useful to someone.*

As was often the case with prayer, she felt only silence in response. But Jane had been at this prayer business all her life, and she knew the answer was on its way. *"Ask and you will receive,"* the Bible said. Now it was time to wait and watch for it. She only hoped it wouldn't take too long; much more of life at this pace, and she'd be climbing the walls.

By mid-March, Laura faced the fact that she had to find a full-time job soon, and preferably one here in Arizona. She didn't want to go back to Maine and face the Darling family, who did not know the meaning of "live and let live," and would feel entitled to stage an inquisition of every corner of her life. In any case, her bank balance was looking increasingly meager and would not absorb the expense of another cross-country move. She had begun to cringe silently each time she swiped her credit card at the grocery store.

She interviewed for personal assistant positions at two companies, neither of which got back to her. She applied for store manager listings at both Costco and a wholesale electronics company and for office manager jobs at five medical practices. Her résumé was listed on three websites, but no one was calling. At last, she resigned herself to the inevitability of waitressing. It was exhausting work with bad hours and no health care or retirement plan, but money was money. She found a job at IHOP, working the breakfast shift, and picked up more hours at Parson's, the bar where she still worked in the evenings. All in all, she could have done worse for herself. She would keep looking for a job with more of a future, she decided, but meanwhile, she would save and put some thought into what she wanted that future to look like.

It turned out that both jobs were more fun than the grocery store chain had ever been. She lost five pounds, just from being on her feet all day. At IHOP, she worked with college kids and single mothers; at Parson's, with a pair of hilarious, cynical grandmothers named Doris and Eva and a bartender named

Luke, whose tattoos, in number, far exceeded his vocabulary. She worked Sundays, because that was the day for the best breakfast tips, so she wasn't able to get to church. She usually made her twice-monthly commitment at the homeless shelter, and she still texted Theo and Wendy from time to time and made it to Sunday night band rehearsals with the youth group. But her life had become busy again and was taken up with coworkers who were becoming almost like friends as well. Things were finally looking up for Laura Darling.

Leander came home from school one afternoon to find his wife at the kitchen counter, reading something intently. "What's so interesting?" he asked.

Jane got up from her stool and came to help him off with his coat, hat, gloves, and scarf. "It's the adult ed catalog," she said without enthusiasm. Kissing his cheek, she carried the coat to the hall closet. "I'm thinking of taking a class," she called.

They sat at the bar and pored over the catalog together, while he drank a cup of coffee. "Look," he said. "Photography for Beginners."

She considered this. "I guess I'm not really interested in photography." She sounded apologetic about it. "Maybe poetry?"

"Do you write poetry?"

"I made a stab or two at it in my idealistic youth, but it was never very good."

"Here's one: Turbo Tax for Dummies." He leveled his best stern teacher stare at her over the tops of his glasses.

She pretended not to hear or see. "Zumba?"

"What's that?"

"A skill I'm not really interested in learning." With a sigh, she closed the catalog and tossed it into the phone basket. "I don't want to take a class just for something to do. If I could think of something I was interested in, that would be a different story. I just feel at loose ends. Like I'm not really *needed* anywhere."

He opened his mouth to protest, but she stopped him. "Oh, I know what you're going to say: you need me; the children and grandchildren need me. The arts program and the church need me. You're right, and I'm grateful for the responsibilities I do have." She smiled ruefully. "I don't mean to complain. I suppose I'm just still trying to adjust to this newer, slower pace of life. Sooner or later, I'll learn to take it easy."

But the slump of her shoulders told Leander otherwise, and it worried him. His wife had never been meant to take life easy. Since Amy had moved out, some spark seemed to have been extinguished inside Jane. His wife needed someone to take care of, to shepherd and watch over. Someone besides an invalid husband. One day in the not-too-distant future, he would also be gone, and the empty space in Jane's life would only widen. He wished he had an answer for her, a way to help her fill the void, but he did not. It was just one more form of helplessness he had to make peace with.

Meanwhile, he prayed for her.

❧

Ivy was in the break room at Parchments, drinking a latte and reading a Sophie Kinsella novel, when her phone rang. With a sinking heart, she recognized the school's number.

"Hello?" She tried not to put a sigh into that one word, but it came out anyway.

A man's voice: "Could I speak with Mrs. Darling-Mason, please?"

Then she did sigh. "This is Ivy Darling."

"Oh, I see; sorry about that. This is Joe Colucci, the assistant principal at the school. I'm afraid I'm calling about Hammer."

"Hi Mr. . . . ah, Joe. What's he done this time?"

"Threatened another student and vandalized a locker."

Ivy closed her eyes against a wave of sick disbelief. "Should I come in?"

"If you could, please. He's in Mrs. Kelly's office right now."

"Give me a few minutes to make arrangements with my boss. I'll be there as soon as I can."

She told Esme why she needed to leave. The two of them had worked together nearly six years, and her manager had always been privy to even the basest details of what she called "the epic saga of Ivy Darling's life."

"You're not a parent yourself," Ivy often said to her, "so I don't worry that you'll judge me by how my kids are turning out."

"Do other parents really do that?"

"All the time, unfortunately."

Now, true to form, Esme made sympathetic noises and shooed her out the door. "It's a slow day," she assured her friend. "The new girl, Callie, comes in at two o'clock, and I can manage alone until then."

On the way to the school, Ivy called Nick and told him what she knew.

"I have a meeting this afternoon," he said grimly, "but I'll cancel it."

"Thanks. I kind of dreaded facing this alone."

"Hey, he's my son too."

Hammer was in Mrs. Kelly's office when they arrived, staring at his knees and scuffing his shoes against the carpet. He looked up when they came in, his face stubborn and defiant.

Mrs. Kelly arranged chairs for them on either side of their son and sat across from them, at her desk. "Now, Hammer," she said pleasantly. "Why don't you start by telling Mom and Dad what happened between you and Henry at soccer practice yesterday."

Hammer shrugged and resumed staring at his knees.

This time when Mrs. Kelly spoke, there was a thread of iron running through the friendly tone. "They're going to hear the story one way or another. I'm giving you a chance to tell it from your own perspective."

Hammer shook his head.

"All right then." She looked at Ivy and Nick. "Yesterday, at soccer practice, one of the other boys apparently called Hammer's grandfather a 'cripple' because he uses a wheelchair. Hammer, do you want to tell your parents what you said to Henry, or shall I?"

Hammer muttered something that Ivy did not hear.

"What?"

Louder this time: "I said I was gonna mess him up."

"You were going to *mess him up*?" Ivy repeated. "What does that mean, exactly?"

"I don' know."

"I assume it means—what that phrase *usually* means—is that you were going to hurt him. Is that what you meant, Hammer?" All trace of pleasantness was now gone from Mrs. Kelly's voice.

"Yeah," Hammer muttered.

"Excuse me?"

He looked up. "Yeah, that's what I meant."

"When one student threatens another, we take that very seriously around here."

"How come *Henry's* not in trouble?" Hammer protested. "He said—"

"—and we are dealing with him separately. What he said about your grandfather was wrong, but in no way does it justify what you said and did to him in retaliation." The principal waited, and when Hammer made no response, she turned to address Nick and Ivy.

"This morning, Henry arrived at school to find a filthy name written on his locker in permanent marker. The locker door had been broken open, and similar words were written all over his school books and on a sweatshirt he had left there overnight."

"Hammer, did you do that?" Nick's voice was dismayed.

Hammer shook his head.

Mrs. Kelly fixed him with a steely gaze. "There's no question that you did it, Hammer. Henry's locker is near one of the school exit doors. We caught you on security camera."

Apparently Hammer had not yet been told this part. He looked up sharply and his expression was stricken. Trapped. Ivy had the brief impression of a live butterfly that has just discovered it is pinned to a mounting board.

"Do you want to tell your parents what you wrote on Henry's locker and books, or shall I?"

He shook his head mutely.

She told them, and Ivy's stomach lurched in disgust. Where was such violence coming from?

"What happens next?" Nick asked. He sounded contrite, as though he had been the wrongdoer, and Ivy felt a surge of rage toward Hammer to think that she and Nick, who had never done anything but love him, had to be humiliated in this way.

"He'll have to pay for the damages to the books and locker and replace Henry's sweatshirt. And he may well be expelled for this, since it wasn't just the vandalism but the threat against another student as well. That's a matter for the school board to decide. They meet next Thursday and will discuss it then. In the meantime, he's suspended indefinitely."

Expelled! Ivy felt her heart deflate like a leaking balloon.

"And now, Hammer, I'd like to have a word with your parents in private. Go have a seat in the attendance office, please. We'll only be a few minutes." When he had dragged out of the room and pulled the door shut behind him, Mrs. Kelly spoke again. "If I can offer a suggestion . . . ,"

"Yes. Please do."

"I think the school board is apt to look on Hammer's case more kindly if you can show that he's getting some kind of help for his anger issues. Counseling, or therapy, I mean. Your family doctor could probably recommend somebody. And the school board's decision aside, it's clear that he could benefit from professional help anyway."

Ivy and Nick looked at each other, and Nick said, "Up to

this point, we haven't been sure. We thought—we hoped, I guess—that his anger problem was confined to a few isolated episodes. It's pretty obvious now that that's not the case. We'll look into getting help."

They took Hammer to his locker, which fortunately was not in the same hallway as the locker he had destroyed. Ivy did not think she could have borne it if she'd had to actually look at what he had done. They collected his books and his soccer gear—that he was off the team seemed to go without saying—and put him in the car with Nick for the ride home.

Ivy followed in the minivan. On the way, she reflected on the pattern they were seeing in their son. She sensed the struggle that was going on inside him on a spiritual level. "I know You did not create this boy with the intent that he should be violent and tormented by anger all his life," she prayed aloud, desperation lending urgency to her words. "Show us how to help him. Heal whatever ugly wound it is that keeps rearing its head like this. Replace it with peace."

After that, she called Bailey. Her cousin, who worked for Child Protective Services, had helped Ivy and Nick become foster parents to the neglected children next door nearly five years earlier, and later to adopt them. Fortunately, Bailey was free to talk, and Ivy filled her in.

When she finished, she heard her cousin sigh. "Things like this can happen with foster kids," she said. "They can be cruising along, doing just fine, then—bam!—suddenly they're out of control. Sometimes you have no idea what it was that set them off."

"We had a few problems with DeShaun early on, but they

got ironed out pretty quickly. And we thought things were going well with Hammer until this year." Ivy sighed. "We're completely baffled."

"It's all the issues from his old life surfacing. Who knows what kind of baggage he's carrying around? Hammer probably doesn't even know himself. But it's all bound to rear its head sooner or later. The school's right: he needs professional help."

"Can you recommend a good . . . I don't know, psychologist or counselor or something?"

"Of course. We have a whole network of great professionals that we use. Let me e-mail you a few names. If you have trouble getting in to see anyone, let me know and I'll make some calls."

Ivy pulled into her driveway and turned the car off. Ahead of her, Nick had backed his own car into the garage, and she watched as Hammer hopped out of the passenger's side, slammed the door, and stalked into the house. "We've never had any problems to speak of with Jada yet," she said to Bailey. "Now I'm wondering what sort of horrors might be ahead with her."

"It's probably not a bad idea to get them all into therapy sooner rather than later," Bailey said. "They were foster children, so there are ways the state can help you with the cost of it. I'll send you some information."

"Thanks, Bailey. You're a gold mine."

"Not at all. It's my job, and in this case, it's also my family. I have a vested interest in these kids."

"Let's get together for coffee one of these weekends, and we can talk about you for a change."

"I'll take you up on that. I can tell you all about my wedding plans."

Ivy gave a small shriek. "Wedding plans! You're *engaged*? Who is it?"

Bailey laughed. "Remember Kevin? You met him at David's wedding."

Ivy thought of the date her cousin had brought to the wedding: a nice guy who was a full head shorter than Bailey. "Well . . . I never!" was all she could think to say.

Bailey laughed again. "I never either. But I have. At any rate, that's a conversation for another day. You have other things on your mind right now. Go take care of your family, and I'll e-mail you that information I promised."

They made kissing noises into the phone. Then, grimly, Ivy headed inside to join Nick in forming a game plan to deal with one very wounded and angry boy.

❧

March had come and gone, and there was no more putting off the taxes. Jane sat at her desk, a file folder open before her, and tried to organize her thoughts. The phone, which she had brought into the office with her, rang. She answered it absently. "Hello?"

"Mom? It's Laura."

"Laura!" She smiled at the wall. "How are you, my dear?"

"Oh, not so bad. A little homesick, I guess."

Glad for a reason to turn her back on the desk, Jane carried the phone into the living room, where she settled onto the corner of the couch. "You've called the right place, then. What's new in Arizona?"

"Not much. I'm still waitressing. Still looking for something better."

Not for the first time did Jane wonder what was really behind her daughter's leaving her job. The fact that she had done so before she had other work was worrisome. It did not take a genius to deduce that Laura had probably been fired. But why? Jane's mind could not help going to those two awful times when Laura had wound up in rehab: once for alcohol poisoning, and once for hitting a tree while driving under the influence. Could this be the same old problems? One would have to be naive not to consider it. But Laura would not confide in her, of that she was certain. So Jane silently breathed the prayer that had become her mantra for Laura: *Lord, do whatever it takes to help her overcome this malignant addiction . . .*

Aloud, she said, "Something will turn up. It always does."

"I know," said Laura. "I just wish it would happen sooner than later. How about you? What's going on in Copper Cove?"

"Dad's at work, and I'm sitting here trying to wrestle our taxes into submission."

Laura laughed. "Taxes! That's always a good time."

"It's a bit overwhelming."

"Why? It's just a matter of plugging in the numbers."

"I suppose so."

"Look, you have your bank statements, right? Accounts, stocks, CDs, or wherever it is you keep your money?"

"Yes."

"And anything tax-deductible—you have all those receipts? And Dad's W-2?"

"Well . . . that's the trouble. I have piles of papers, but I'm not really sure what to do with it all."

"Can't Dad help you?"

"Sure he can. But he's so tired after work, and . . . well, I suppose I want to prove that I can conquer this myself."

"There's no shame in asking for a little help if you need it."

How ironic, coming from Laura, who never asked anyone for help. But Jane only said, "I was thinking of asking Nick or Libby—"

"I could try to give you a hand."

"Here? Now? I mean, on the phone?"

"Why not? I have a few hours before my next shift. Do you have everything there in front of you?"

"It's in a file folder in the office."

"Let's get started, then."

Hope, like a shaft of sunlight, broke over Jane's horizon. "Okay. Let's do it!"

For the next two hours and twenty-three minutes, Jane read receipts, bills, and statements aloud, and Laura instructed her as to the category each should go in. And when it was done, Laura was right: it was simply a matter of tallying them up and plugging the totals into the right places.

"Oh, look at that!" Jane cried. "It says we should get a federal *and* a state refund!"

"That's the prize at the bottom of the cereal box," said Laura, and Jane heard the smile in her daughter's voice. "Good for you, Mom."

"Is that it, then? That's what all the fuss over taxes is about?"

"That's it."

"That wasn't so hard."

"No, it's really not. There are computer programs that

could make it even easier for you, next year. Listen, I'd better get going. I need to get ready for work."

"I can't thank you enough for your help."

"It was nothing. And I don't feel homesick anymore. I feel like I've been sitting right there in the office with you, so it was a help for me too."

"I love you, my dear. Have a good day at work."

"I will. Love you too, Mom."

They made kissing noises and hung up. Jane felt light with relief. Another hurdle successfully navigated. One more monumental task faced and conquered. And Laura had called her! That alone was enough to make this a red-letter day.

Jane had gathered her coat and purse for a quick run to Hannaford one morning when the phone rang. She glared across the kitchen at it, exasperated. Always! Always just as you were headed out the door. She had half a mind to let it go to voice mail, but thought better of it; it might be one of the children. Dropping her things onto a stool, she crossed to the phone and looked at it. *Peter LaRoche*, said the caller ID. For an instant she was puzzled, before she realized who it was. Jessie LaRoche from the community choir, eighty-five if she was a day, still listed her phone under her late husband's name, convinced it kept at bay predatory salespeople who might be tempted to take advantage of an elderly widow.

Jane answered the phone. "Hello, Jessie!"

"Oh, this darned caller ID," was Jessie's affable reply. "I liked it better in the days when you answered the phone and were surprised by who was on the other end."

"But caller ID lets you avoid people you don't want to talk to," Jane pointed out.

"Then I'm flattered you picked up."

"It's always a treat to talk to you. What's new in your neck of the woods?" Jessie lived two blocks away.

"Nothing new; everything's getting older, including my aching bones."

"Oh, that's too bad. Are you not feeling well?"

"Nothing that a brand-new body wouldn't cure. It's just my arthritis, same as always. How about you, Jane? How's Leander?"

Jane gave her stock answer: "His spirits are always good, and that's the main thing."

They spent a few minutes catching up on community news before Jessie said, "I'm hanging up my hat as a piano teacher, Jane. My fingers have got too stiff to play, and if I sit on that hard bench for more than five minutes, my hips let me know about it all night."

"I'm sorry to hear that." Jessie had cornered the market on local piano lessons long before Jane Darling had ever moved to town. "How long have you been teaching now?"

"Fifty-six years. I've got two students now whose grand-mothers I taught back in the year aughty-aught."

"Copper Cove will be sorry to lose you."

"My students will be looking for another teacher."

"Ah!" Jane was suddenly illuminated. "I suppose they will."

"I'd hate to send 'em across the bridge to a stranger in Quahog."

"It certainly wouldn't be as convenient for them."

"That's why I'm calling. Now, I know you're busier than a one-armed paper-hanger, Jane—"

Why was everybody convinced she was so busy?

"—but I thought I might as well ask. Would you be interested in taking on a few piano students?"

Interested! A burst of warmth broke over her like a summer sunbeam, and she smiled into the phone. "How many is 'a few'?"

"Twenty-three."

Jane gasped. "That's practically a full-time job!"

"It certainly feels like it sometimes. What do you think?"

"I think I'd like to do it very much."

"Are you sure you have the time?"

"I am. In fact, I've been praying for something like this to come along."

Jessie, who apparently did not believe in the power of prayer, cleared her throat diplomatically. "Well. Call it whatever you want. Can I give my students your name and number, then?"

"Please do."

"They all buy their own books. When one is ready to move on, I take care of ordering what they need, and they give me a check."

"All right. How much do you charge for lessons?"

"Twenty-five dollars for a half hour."

Was that what people paid for piano lessons these days? Fifty years ago, when Jane had been learning her scales, the going rate had been two dollars an hour.

"'Course, some of my older students have an hour lesson,

and I only charge them forty. This isn't Portland or Boston, you know."

"Of course not."

"And I gen'lly give a recital every spring, at the Episcopal church. They let us use the sanctuary for nothing, and they've got a real good piano. A Yamaha baby grand. They keep it tuned."

"That sounds lovely."

"And four of them compete in the fall, down in Hartford. Jennifer Greenlaw took second place in her age category last year. Chopin's Nocturne, opus nine, number one in B-flat minor."

"That's quite a piece."

"There's an association you have to join first. They don't let just anyone enter students."

Jane felt she was getting rather more information than she could process at once. "I wonder, Jessie, should you and I sit down together sometime and go over this face-to-face?"

It was exactly the right thing to say. "What's wrong with right now?" Jessie's voice was warm with approval. "I'm home. You're home. Why don't you buzz on over and we'll talk about it over a cup of coffee."

Hannaford could wait. "I'll be there in five minutes," said Jane. She hung up, radiant with happiness. *"Ask and you will receive."* Twenty-three students! Recitals! Competitions! *You will receive, and then some,* she thought.

This time, they really *were* working on the Mustang. Mitch still had a dancing lesson with Joe from time to time, but now that his secret was out of the bag, he was allowed to use Amy as a partner instead. "You're much nicer to hold on to," he'd told her one evening, when they were practicing a fox-trot in the small circle Joe had cleared in his living room.

"I heard that!" Joe had called from the sofa that he shared with a chain saw motor and an industrial-size box of screws. "And it's *slow, slow, quick-quick,* not t'other way round. Say it out loud, now, 'til you get it down."

But winter had lost its grip on the land, and as the snow-banks rapidly shrank from the roadsides and the sodden, colorless grass emerged on lawns and hillsides, Mitch and Joe began to spend more of their free hours working on the car, which they had hauled over from Joe's friend's house one night and put up on blocks in the backyard. One Sunday when they were under the hood, tinkering with the engine in the fading light of evening, Joe said, "So'r you gonna marry Amy or what?"

"I'd like to, once the house is finished."

"I cain't help but notice you two ain't livin' together."

"No, sir, we've decided not to do things that way."

"Well." Joe gave a nod of approval. "I never held with that idea anyhow. My son Barry's lived with three different women in three years, and no sign of settlin' down with a one of 'em yet. Why buy the cow when the milk is free, is what I say."

Mitch wondered how Amy would take to being compared with a cow and suppressed a smile. "Yes, sir."

"You got her a ring yet?"

"Not yet."

"She wants a big diamond, prob'ly."

"Not Amy. She won't wear diamonds."

"Why not?"

Mitch thought about this. "Political conscience, I guess you'd call it. Plus, I don't know if you've noticed it, but Amy doesn't like to do things the way other people do them. If the rest of the world's wearing diamond engagement rings, Amy'll have to have one made of . . . I don't know, wood or stone or something like that."

Joe held up an O-ring. "This?"

"Well . . ." Mitch laughed. "Maybe not quite."

"Now, hang on a second. You wait right here. I've got somethin' you might be innerested in." Wiping his hands on a greasy rag, Joe disappeared into the house. He was back a moment later, and when he reached the car, he held out a begrimed fist toward Mitch. Slowly, he opened it. "Think she'd like this?"

Mitch stared at the ring that lay on the grease-lined palm.

Joe cleared his throat. "It belonged to my Mary. Well, go on, take a look at it."

Mitch picked up the ring reverently. A milky-colored stone set in a delicate lacework of silver, the thin band worn, but still sturdy. "I've never seen anything like it."

"It's what they call a moonstone. If you think Amy'd wear it, then it's yours."

Hastily, Mitch pushed the ring back at the old man. "I couldn't take this. It was your wife's."

But Joe refused to take it. "Listen, Mitch. You been awful good to me, you and Amy. Better'n my own son, to tell you the truth. I want you to have it, and . . . and we never had a daughter. Mary would be proud to have a girl like Amy wearin' her ring. I know she would."

Mitch recognized the gesture for what it was worth and closed his hand around the ring. "All right, then. I'd be honored to have it, and I know Amy will too, when . . . when the time comes. Thank you, sir." He stuck out a hand, to shake with Joe, but changed his mind and pulled him into a hug instead.

"Don't lose it, now," said Joe, his voice not quite steady.

"No, sir, I won't."

When Mitch let him go, there were tears in the old man's eyes.

✌

Parson's tended to empty out early on Sunday nights, as the usual crowd headed home in anticipation of making a good start on the workweek. One Sunday in early April, when Laura had hung up her apron and was cashing out her tips, Luke the bartender called to her from the bar. "Come and have a drink before you go."

She looked up in surprise. She had never heard that many words in a row from him before. He was a burly man, with a shaved head and a quiet demeanor. And now that she came to think of it, he wasn't too hard on the eyes either. "Okay," she said, "I will. Just let me finish up here."

When she sat at the bar, which was empty save for one middle-aged couple at the far end, he said, "What'll it be?"

"White wine."

"Aw, that's boring. Wait, I'll make you one of my specialties." He turned his back to her and got busy with bottles, shakers, crushed ice, and tongs.

"What is it?"

"Wait and see." With a flourish, he set it before her in a tall, frosted glass garnished with sugared grapes and a straw. "I call it the Refresher. Refreshes you like anything after a long day on your feet."

At the other end of the bar, the couple signaled for their tab.

"Be right back," Luke said and left her to her drink.

Laura, who was not a fan of sweet drinks, took a cautious sip. It was delicious: tart, cool, tasting of cucumber and grapefruit, and as Luke had promised, refreshing. By the time he waved his other customers off and came back to her, she had finished the whole thing.

"That was amazing," she told him. "Was there even alcohol in it?"

"A little," he said, with a small smile. "How about another one?"

She pushed her empty glass his way and smiled back.

It was midway through her third drink that it hit her, hard. By that time, Luke was sitting on the barstool next to her, with his hand on her leg, listening to her talk about her sisters. "Wow," she said suddenly. "That last one was strong." She stumbled over the syllables, and they both laughed.

"Another," Luke announced and, getting up, went around behind the bar again.

"Wait," Laura pronounced, raising a finger in the air. "Bathroom first."

When she came back, he had another drink ready. "Come on," he said, pushing it toward her, "see how fast you can drink it. I'll time you."

She settled herself on the barstool and narrowed her eyes at him. "Are you trying to get me drunk?"

"Oh, I think that ship has already sailed."

She found this hilarious and began to giggle.

"Come on, drink up."

"Okay. Got your watch? Ready . . . set . . . go!" Laura sucked the drink down as fast as she could and slammed the empty glass on the counter with a deep, gasping breath. All at once, the room tilted. She slid off her stool and landed on her back, on the floor.

"Ouch," she said, although she was not really hurt.

At once, Luke was around the bar, helping her to her feet. "Listen, I . . . I might have made those last couple a little too strong. Maybe you've had enough."

"Mebbee."

"Let me drive you home."

She pushed him away, indignant. It was clear now what he'd been intending all along. "I have my car. I can drive myself."

"You can't drive yourself, Laura; you've had too much to drink."

"Thanks to you."

"I was only trying to have some fun."

"Where's my purse?" She squinted at the waitress station, across the room. Over there. Her purse was over there. "Lemmee get my purse," she muttered, tacking her way over, clutching at the backs of chairs to keep herself steady. Her stomach had become a roiling mass of grapefruit and cucumber. She needed to get home so she could throw up and go to bed.

"I'm not letting you drive in this condition. If you don't want me to drive you, at least let me call you a cab."

"That'll cost me twenty-five bucks. I'll drive myself." She fished around in her purse until she came up with her car keys.

"Laura!" His tone was faintly desperate. "You can't. I'll . . . I'll call the cops!"

"And tell them what? That you overserved me, after the bar was closed?" She knew, from his expression, that she had him. Holding her keys high, and her head higher, she stalked past him, out the front door.

The fresh air helped clear her head a bit. She looked around until she remembered that the lot to the right of the restaurant was where employees parked their cars. It was empty, save for her own car and a Ford F-250 that had to belong to Luke. She unlocked her Saab, got in, and started it up.

◦⥈

Ivy hung up the phone with a sigh. Voice mail again. Laura couldn't possibly be away from her phone at five o'clock in the morning; obviously she was mad at her twin about something and avoiding her calls. Well, Ivy would just have to wait it out. She was used to doing this with Laura. She'd certainly had enough practice.

19

LIGHT WAS STABBING THROUGH HER EYELIDS, as fine and
sharp as needles. Laura groaned and turned her head away.
At the motion, a searing pain knifed through her neck. She
cried out and opened her eyes to the full light of day.

She was in her car, and directly in front of her—on top
of her hood, in fact, and lying across her windshield—was a
great deal of twisted web-wire cattle fencing. Her head, when
she moved it to the left, was fine, but when she moved it to
the right, that pain shot from her shoulder to her temple
again. Her mouth was like a dehydrated sponge, and a quick
appraisal of the car's interior told her that she had thrown up
all over the dash and passenger's seat. She groaned again and
closed her eyes.

After a bit, it dawned on her that she was alone here—
wherever here was—and nobody seemed to know that she

had wrecked a good section of some rancher's fence, and probably the front end of her Saab as well. But . . . she wasn't dead, or even really hurt all that badly, except for the pain in her neck when she moved the wrong way. She wondered if her car was still drivable.

The ignition, she discovered, was turned off. Which meant she must have been conscious when she crashed and turned it off herself. No memory of any of this suggested itself to her. She turned the key and was surprised when the car started as smoothly as it ever had. Cautiously, anticipating aches and pains that never materialized, she got out and walked around the front. One very huge dent in the right front quarter, with a fair amount of the paint scraped off, and several smaller ones peppered over the hood. A crack ran from northeast to southwest in the windshield, but she had glass insurance to cover that. With some consternation, she noticed that a large brown cow was standing a good distance down the road, on the wrong side of the wrecked fence. It might be smart, then, to get out of here as soon as possible. She got back in the car, reversed, and found herself on the road again.

The problem was, she had no idea where she was, or how she had gotten there, or how to get home again. Her purse, on the floor between the seats, seemed to have been spared the worst of her stomach contents. When she had put some distance between herself and the ruined section of fencing, she pulled to the side of the road. Using her phone's navigator app, she discovered that she was on Route 60, outside the city of Tempe. She was utterly bewildered. How had she come to be there, and why? Shaking her head to clear it, she was assaulted again by the pain in her neck and the beginnings of a sick headache. She needed hydration and Advil and a bathroom. What she needed was a gas station. She pulled back onto the road, pointing the Saab west, and started driving.

Less than three miles up the road, she found a Shell station. Parking to the side of the store, in the corner near the Dumpster, to minimize the chances of anyone noticing the damage to her car, she went inside. A quick trip to the bathroom revealed a puffy, red-eyed face. "Oh," she said with disgust to the woman in the mirror. "What a loser you are."

In the store, she chose a liter of water from the refrigerator case, a bacon-egg-and-cheese breakfast sandwich, and a large coffee. As she stood in line, waiting for her turn to pay, she idly watched the wide-screen TV mounted in one corner.

"And in local news," said a smartly styled blonde reporter, "a hit-and-run accident outside Tempe in the early hours of this morning has left one child dead and his mother in critical condition."

Laura nearly dropped the things she was carrying. She felt the blood drain from her head and was afraid she would faint. Stepping out of line, she set the sandwich and cardboard cup on the coffee station and gripped the metal edge of the counter. *Breathe!* she commanded herself.

"Thirty-one-year-old Veronica May was driving her four-year-old son to day care this morning," the news anchor went on relentlessly, "when police say they were slammed into by a vehicle moving at high speed along Route 60 in the opposite direction." A picture of a generic-looking rural road, bordered by web-wire fencing. "After hitting May, the driver of the other vehicle drove off. There were no eyewitnesses to the crash, although police say paint streaks on the side of the victim's car suggest the vehicle that hit her was light-colored and of medium size."

"Excuse me, ma'am, are you in line?" It was a young man in a plaid shirt. His face tilted strangely before Laura's eyes.

"Forensic specialists are analyzing the paint further," said the voice from the TV. "Meanwhile, police ask that anyone with any information about the accident call the hotline number on your screen."

"Ma'am, are you all right?"

Whatever she did, she could not afford to faint right then. "I'm fine," she managed. "And no, I'm not in line. Actually, I need to get something from my car." Leaving her things on the coffee station, she strode to the door and burst out into the humid, oily air of the gas station parking lot. She all but ran to the Saab, wrenched open the scratched and dented door, and slammed the car into reverse. Even as she roared across the parking lot and onto the roadway beyond, she imagined that her damaged front end was lit up in neon, that every person pumping gas or buying coffee in the store was staring at her, realizing exactly who she was.

She began to sob in ragged, gasping sounds of horror. She had killed a child! She was a hopeless, drunken murderer of innocence.

Unmanageable! Her wheels sang it against the miles of pavement they ate up. *Our lives had become unmanageable.*

She flipped on the radio and searched for a station that was reporting the news. Maybe she had only dreamed it. Nightmared it, if such a word existed.

". . . a child dead and his mother in critical condition." It was a different voice, a man's this time.

Oh, God! "We admitted we were powerless over alcohol . . . *that our lives had become unmanageable.*" The words, long ago memorized in rehab, played a loop in her head.

". . . on Route 60, in Tempe, this morning . . . Police are looking for a light-colored car . . ."

"We admitted we were powerless over alcohol—that our lives had become unmanageable."

"Once more, a four-year-old child has died . . ."

"Came to believe that a power greater than ourselves could restore us to sanity." It was the second step of the program.

Her city block.

My life has become unmanageable.

Her apartment complex.

Unmanageable.

She pulled around back, alongside an area of scrub brush, where her car would be virtually unnoticed, and parked. She leaned her pounding head against the steering wheel.

". . . came to believe that a power greater than ourselves could restore us to sanity."

"Restore me to sanity," she whispered. "Oh, God, somehow restore me to sanity."

Inside her apartment, Laura locked the door and called Theo. "Can you come over?" she tried to say, but it came out only as a sob.

It didn't matter. "Are you at home?" Theo said.

"Yes."

"I'm on my way."

While she waited, Laura brushed her teeth and downed

a quart of water, then paced the floor, her head spinning and aching, her stomach like concrete. When she heard Theo's knock at last, she unlocked the door, pulled her friend inside by the arm, and shut and locked the door behind her.

"Laura, what in the world—?"

She opened her mouth to speak, but what came out instead was an inarticulate wail.

"Oh . . . oh no. Come on, sit down." Theo led her to the couch and waited in silence beside her while Laura rocked back and forth and wept in great, keening, racking sobs.

When at last they slowed to hiccupping gasps, Theo got up and came back with a roll of toilet paper from the bathroom. "Here, blow."

Laura blew her nose and wiped her face.

"Now, tell me about it."

"I killed someone."

"What?"

The sobs began again, but this time Theo stopped her. "Pull yourself together," she said sharply, "and tell me what you're talking about."

"Did you hear the news this morning, about the hit-and-run accident in Tempe? A little boy was killed, and his mother is in critical condition." Her voice dwindled to a whisper. "I think that was me."

She told Theo about waking up in her damaged car, in the middle of nowhere, with no memory of how she had gotten there. She left out nothing: the pattern of drinking she had developed, the blackouts, the drinks with Luke at the bar the night before. "And now, I've killed someone—" She ended on another sob, and would have broken down again, but Theo took her hands.

"Let's think this through, one step at a time. First, can you find the story?" She picked up Laura's phone from the coffee table and held it out to her.

Laura shook her head. "You," she whispered.

Theo did a quick search and came up with a video clip of a pair of newscasters sitting behind a desk. Together, they listened to yet another iteration of the terrible story. Nothing in essence had changed. A dead child, a mother hardly better off, a statewide search for the driver who had fled the scene.

When the sorrowful-looking reporters had frozen in the final video frame, Theo put the phone down. "Laura, we need to go to the police."

She was choking, suffocating under the strain of it. All she could do was nod.

The ride to the station was marked by a pervasive nausea that had more to do with her soul than her stomach. She wanted nothing more than to crawl into a hole somewhere and die herself.

In the lobby of the police station, Theo led her to an opaque glass window with a speaker panel set into it. "We'd like to speak with someone about an accident," she said, leaning forward to speak through the mouse hole–size opening at the window's bottom.

"Have a seat, and an officer will be with you shortly," came a bored, muffled voice from beyond.

The lobby was bare and functional, the floors and walls scarred with years' worth of scuff marks from the plastic chairs around the perimeter. They were alone, and for this, Laura was profoundly grateful. She did not think, at that moment, that she could have borne the curious eyes of strangers on her. When they sat, Theo reached over and held her hand. On the wall opposite them hung a clock. One twenty-four. The red second hand seemed to jerk backward with every tick. At one thirty-three and twenty seconds, a side door opened and a uniformed young officer with a military hair-cut said, "Come with me."

They followed him through the door to a small side room furnished only with a filing cabinet, a table, and four chairs. On one wall was a large mirror, and Laura, who had seen as many cop shows as anyone else, felt physically sick all over again at the idea of someone watching her from behind that glass.

From the filing cabinet, Officer Stuckey, as his name tag identified him, produced a sheaf of paper and several pens. "Have a seat." He sat at the table across from them. "Name?"

"Laura Darling."

He wrote it down. "Address?"

She told him this, and all her other information, which he wrote on a form. He was left-handed, she noticed.

"Now, what can I do for you?"

Laura opened her mouth and closed it again. Under the table, Theo squeezed her hand. It was enough to give her courage, and when her voice did come out, it was clear and firm. "I had a car accident this morning, although I don't remember it. I woke up after the fact. But I . . . I heard the story on the news about the hit-and-run accident outside of Tempe, the one where the child was killed, and—" She cleared her throat. "I think I might have done it."

Officer Stuckey's face was inscrutable. "What makes you think that?"

She told him, leaving out nothing that she could remember. She told him of the drinking, and of waking up under the ruined wire fence. As she talked, the weight of guilt began to drop away, bit by bit, like the shedding of a heavy skin. When she was done, the relief was so physical that she began to cry again, silently this time, the tears slipping down her face in a hot and steady flow.

Officer Stuckey tipped his chair back and plucked a box of tissues from the top of the filing cabinet. This, he slid across the table, and Laura helped herself.

"Well, I'm not sure what to tell you," he said, "except that you're not the one who hit that car."

Her heart leaped.

"They picked up the guy earlier this morning in Guadalupe. Illegal immigrant driving without a license. He confessed right away. Didn't realize he'd actually killed someone." He looked from Laura to Theo. "'Course, Forensics is still analyzing the paint on the vehicles, to make sure it matches, but it's mostly a formality. I'll take a statement from you, Miz Darling, just in case, but I don't think you need to worry."

The officer had her write out her statement and sign it, then stood up, tapping the edges of the forms against the table to square them. He cleared his throat. "You may want to give some serious thought to driving under the influence again. Just because you didn't kill anyone this time doesn't mean you won't, someday."

Laura closed her eyes and nodded.

"You're free to go. If we need to talk to you further, we know where to find you."

They drove back to Laura's apartment in silence, and Theo followed her inside.

"Sit down," Theo said, "and I'll get you some aspirin."

"There's a bottle in the medicine cabinet."

Her friend brought her two aspirin and a glass of cold water, then sat beside her on the couch. "It's time to talk about your drinking," she said.

Laura waited for the anger that had always followed someone's suggestion that perhaps she drank too much, but it did not come. Instead, what she felt was the lifting of a burden that had become too much for her to bear alone. "I know," she said. "Will you help me?"

"Of course I will. You know that community center a couple of blocks away from here?"

Laura knew it.

"There's a Twelve Step meeting there every afternoon at five. I'll go with you, if you want."

Laura nodded and, again, began to cry.

Theo put her arms around Laura, and together, they rocked. "This can be the first day of the rest of your life."

Laura leaned into her friend's shoulder, feeling as fragile as tissue paper. "Okay," she whispered. "Okay."

CHAPTER

20

LAURA SAT ON THE METAL FOLDING CHAIR and crossed her legs, pulling her cardigan tightly around her. She clutched a Styrofoam cup of black coffee that she neither wanted nor needed, but had taken anyway because it gave her something to do with her hands. She had been to a meeting every day for two weeks, and in all that time, she had not taken a single drink. The meetings had taken on a familiarity by now. It didn't matter whether it was the 2 p.m. at the Congregational church on Mondays, the 3 o'clock at the Catholic church on Tuesdays, the 6 p.m. at the rescue mission on Wednesdays, or the Saturday morning women's group at the elementary school: they were all more or less the same. The same liturgies were read, the same prayers chanted in unison. It was all part of The Program, as members euphemistically called it. And although Laura heard the same words day after day, they were still fresh every time; to her, they felt like the very words of life. They told her that countless people before her had been right where she was now and had found a solution. They spoke of the help and hope she so desperately needed to believe was here.

She was still bemused by how *normal* everyone seemed. In Laura's past experiences with rehab, most of the others had been like herself: young people there under duress, jumping through law-mandated hoops in order to avoid jail. Biding their time until they could get out and find another drink or drug. Others had been inpatients of the hospital, in varying states of psychiatric crisis. Pallid and hopeless-looking in their beige hospital gowns, staring from hollow eyes and speaking in flat voices, they had not been the best advertisements for sobriety.

But the people at her meetings now were nothing like the drunks from her rehab groups: they were professionals and graduate students, mothers with young children, and blue-collar workers. It shocked her how many teenagers showed up, tattooed and pierced, or clean-cut and looking straight out of prep school, each of them serene and smiling as they introduced themselves by saying, "My name is Ashley (or Chris or Jason), and I'm an alcoholic." At her first meeting, sitting beside Theo, Laura had been taken completely by surprise to discover that people were actually having fun. The speakers were hilarious, and in spite of her bone-deep anguish of that day, Laura had found herself laughing along with everyone else at some of the things they said. In fact, as time went on, she realized that never in her life had she met a group of people who liked to laugh and celebrate as much as these recovering alcoholics did. For this, she was deeply grateful. To her, it was proof that someday she too might be able to look back on the despair and wreckage of her life with a sense of victory and hope.

The first time she had said the words aloud—"I'm Laura, and I'm an alcoholic"—she had wept. In fact, she still cried through nearly every meeting. No matter how good she might be feeling as she pulled into the parking lot, the moment she stepped foot into a church basement or hall filled with laughing, chattering people, the tears would spring up and begin to spill over. They were tears of mingled shame and relief that seemed to come from a well with no bottom.

This was normal, people assured her. It would get better, they promised. Keep coming back, they said. And inch by inch, day by day, it did get better. The compulsion to drink was still there, but she was developing some coping strategies. Theo advised her to do "ninety in ninety"—attend ninety meetings in ninety days. "You have to begin to structure your life around recovery," Laura heard often, and she paid attention.

Tonight's meeting was in a basement room of the hospital. She recognized some of the faces from other groups around town: A businessman in a suit and tie stopping off on his way home from work. A nurse in scrubs, who would slip out five minutes early to start her night shift. A young man in a priest's collar. A middle-aged woman who ran a honey stall at the farmers' market, wearing baggy jeans and drinking green tea from a mason jar. Sometimes Laura would try to imagine these sane and smiling people drunk and sloppy and abusive, but she couldn't picture it. You would never pick any of them out in a crowd; they looked just like anybody else in the world.

An elderly woman sat down heavily in the empty chair beside her. "Hi, Laura. Good to see you here."

She looked vaguely familiar, but . . . "I'm sorry," Laura confessed. "I don't remember your name."

The woman waved this away. "Don't worry about it. I'm Sadie. We met at the Tuesday three o'clock—"

"—at Saint Dom's," Laura finished for her, and said again, "I'm sorry. It's just that I've met so many people . . ."

"No problem." Sadie settled a vast tapestry handbag on her lap. "How are you doing?"

Laura opened her mouth to say, "Fine," but there went the tears again. She gestured fruitlessly and tried to smile, but her face felt distorted and twisted instead. How embarrassing. Now her nose was starting to run. She reached under her chair for her purse and opened it to search for a pack of tissues. "I'm really okay," she managed, half-laughing through the tears. "It's just that I can't seem to stop *crying* all the time. I don't know what's wrong with me."

The older woman put an arm around her shoulders, and then Laura was completely undone. Sadie said, "Oh, honey! It's all right. You're just *feeling*, for the first time in a long time." She patted Laura's shoulder and waited until she had gotten herself under control.

"Everyone's so nice to me," Laura said at last, wiping her eyes. The tissue came away black with mascara. "So generous. Women who don't even know me offer me their phone numbers and rides to meetings. They listen to me and give me advice . . . and I have nothing to give back. I feel so useless."

"That's okay. The day will come when you'll have plenty to give back. God is going to use this, honey, but first you have to get well. Concentrate on that right now, and the rest of it will follow."

Laura hiccupped and sighed. "I hope you're right."

"You just take one day at a time, and it will all work itself out."

She managed a watery smile. "Is that a promise?"

Sadie gave her shoulders a squeeze. "It's a promise."

On Mother's Day, Jane took her coffee to the backyard to welcome the morning. The day was clear and cold and filled with the scent of damp earth. She watched the mist rise from the nascent flower beds and knew it was going to be her favorite kind of day. These were the few, fleeting weeks of the year in which two seasons existed together in friendly harmony, the sharp cold edge of departing winter blunted by the incipient warmth of spring. Perfect weather for yard work. Nearby, a robin pulled a worm from the ground beneath the mountain laurel and flew to a branch of the crab apple tree. She waited, listening, and a moment later, was rewarded by the frantic shrilling of the chicks. She smiled. The family was celebrating with lunch at Ivy's after church, and she still had deviled eggs to make. *Better get a move on,* she thought, but still she lingered. They had waited so long for spring; why not stay and enjoy it for a few more minutes?

At church, the family sat together, filling a pew and a half. Most Sundays, Ivy and Nick's family sat on the other side of the sanctuary, and Amy sat in back with Mitch, who was never going to be a front-pew kind of man. But on Mother's Day, Father's Day, Christmas, and Easter, the family always ended up together. They never discussed or planned it that way; it just seemed to happen. Nick's parents and sisters and their families filled the other half of the pew, and the one behind it. *All those people coming from just two sets of parents!* Jane marveled. One would think they'd taken God's original injunction to be fruitful and multiply and replenish the earth as their own personal mission.

And apparently, the multiplying and replenishing was not finished yet. Later that afternoon, when lunch was over, Nick brought out the croquet set and began to set up the wickets on the back lawn. Jane waved away the mallet Ivy held out to her. "I'll sit here with Dad and watch," she said, settling into a lawn chair beside Leander. David and Libby came to join them, hand in hand, and Jane, who hadn't really taken a good look at either of them until this moment, saw and comprehended the good news that glowed from both their faces before either of them said a word.

She cried anyway when Libby said it: "We're having a baby. It won't be for a while yet—probably mid-January. We just found out for sure this morning."

David added, "Our plan was to wait a couple of years, but . . . well, we changed our minds. None of us knows how this disease of yours is going to progress, Dad, and we wanted you to be able to enjoy your grandchild while you can still hold it and play with it."

Jane took Leander's hand. There were tears in his eyes as well. With her other hand, Jane reached for Libby's. "What wonderful news for you on Mother's Day! And what a gift for us too. Thank you." It was simple gratitude for such a magnanimous gesture, but she saw that David and Libby did not need anything more. This young couple actually thought nothing of altering their whole future in this way, just to give their father more time with a grandchild. Had anyone ever been blessed with children such as these? But then, thought Jane as she smiled through her tears at her family, that was love for you.

❧

The whole week of finals, DeShaun couldn't seem to drag himself out of the dumps. The exams themselves weren't that hard. He aced his practical, which consisted of two desserts: a molded coconut Bavarian cream with a fresh raspberry coulis, topped by a crisp ginger tuile, and a three-layer genoise with grapefruit sugar and blood-orange sorbet. On the written exam, he missed only two questions. He should have been thrilled, but instead he felt only a sense of despair.

"It's gonna be the longest summer in history," he told Penelope on the last afternoon. They had walked out on the causeway to the lighthouse at the end of the campus while he waited for his parents to get there and take him back home. Together they leaned over the iron railing, looking out across Portland Harbor. Everywhere, the water was flecked with white sailboats; a lobster boat drifted by, stopping at all the green and orange buoys to haul up traps. The ocean was the same deep blue as Penelope's eyes, DeShaun noticed, and he kicked moodily at an iron post.

She smiled. "Cheer up! It'll be over before you know it.

You can come visit me, and I'll come visit you. Besides, you have that great job waiting for you, right? That'll be fun."

Prep cook at the Silver Star Diner. It had sounded great two months ago, when he'd been hired; now it just seemed . . . far away. He told her this.

They watched the boats in silence for a while.

Penelope spoke first. "Would it help if I gave you a good-bye kiss?"

He looked at her, startled. "Here? Now?" He had never kissed anyone before. Well . . . except for nasty old Daniqua Holmes, back in sixth grade, in Detroit, and that was only because she'd paid him five dollars to do it.

"Right here. Now."

He couldn't hold back the grin that took over his face. "Yeah," he said. "That would probably help a lot."

One of Jane's chief delights in her family was that having four girls meant no one ever suffered a shortage of sisters. She herself had always wished for more than one. Sisters, she felt, ought to be a panacea against life's hardships. In the best of worlds, they were fonts of friendship, advice, and borrowable clothing. She had only Ellen, of course, and they had never been much more than companions who tolerated one another. Perhaps that was why Jane had attached so strongly to Sharon DeMille in her freshman year of college. They had been roommates that year and every year thereafter until graduation. Theirs was truly the closest thing to an ideal sisterly relationship that Jane had ever experienced.

But there were some things you shared only with a real

sister: Your genes, for instance. Your family history. Certain secrets. And one Thursday evening at family supper, as Jane listened to Ivy and Amy reminisce about something that had happened in their childhoods, it occurred to her that perhaps her own sister was the key to finding Steven.

Jane had all but given up on the prospect of finding her son, but as she thought about it in the days that followed, she became convinced that Ellen might know something. With her parents and Aunt Sophie long dead, she and Ellen were the only people left in the world who knew Jane's secret.

Jane was no fool. Tangling with her sister was just asking for punishment. She would likely be ridiculed, lashed out at, even refused altogether. Still, she was compelled to reach out.

On Saturday morning, Leander was to attend a high school vocal music festival in Millinocket. Dean Street picked him up at nine o'clock and Jane waved them off, already rehearsing Ellen's phone number in her head.

Her sister picked up on the third ring. "Hello, Jane."

"Hi. How are you? How's your health been?"

"As well as can be expected." Her tone told Jane in no uncertain terms that she was not to pursue this line of questioning. After a beat of silence that was too long, Ellen asked, "And how are you?"

Jane sighed. At times like this, small talk seemed a form of dishonesty. "I'm distressed, Ellen."

"I didn't think you'd be calling just to shoot the breeze."

"Do you have time to talk?"

"If I didn't have time to talk, I wouldn't have answered the phone."

"It's about the baby."

"What baby?"

"The baby I had when I was seventeen."

Silence. It went on so long that Jane wondered if her sister had hung up.

"Ellen?"

"I'm here. Why would you want to talk to me about that?"

She was as frail as a baby herself. "I want to find him."

Ellen sighed. "Don't go down that road, Jane."

"I feel like I have no choice."

"That's ridiculous. Everyone always has a choice. About everything."

"I just mean . . . I feel compelled to do this. I don't know why. It has something to do with the certainty of losing Leander, I think."

"Why is any of this my business?"

"I don't know. I just thought there might be something you'd remember, something you'd know about everything that happened back then."

"You're the one it happened to, not me."

"But it's all such a blur. I had the baby. I held him for two minutes; then he was gone, and I was shuffled back to Aunt Sophie's house, then home, and nobody ever mentioned it again."

"Oh, they did, though. They talked about it sometimes. Mom and Aunt Sophie. Mom and Grammie Thibodeau. On the phone, or over coffee, always in whispers. I remember it."

"I don't. They must have talked when I wasn't around. Can you remember anything they *said*?"

Silence. Then, "No."

Jane knew she was lying. "Please, Ellen. Anything you can remember would help me. Anything at all."

"Don't try to find him, Jane. You'll regret it. These stories rarely end well."

She wanted to reach across the miles, take her sister by the shoulders, and shake her until her teeth rattled. "Just tell me what you remember."

"I don't remember anything. Just what you said. You went off to Boston in June, pregnant, and came home in September, not pregnant anymore. And like I said, a lot of whispered conversations. I listened in the pantry sometimes. That's all."

"You really won't help me?"

"I have no help to offer."

"I think you do."

"You think wrongly then."

If Jane's desperation was the fuel, Ellen's indifference was like a match laid to it. Blind, white fury shot through her like a sheet of flame. "Why would you want to torment me like this? What do you want from me, Ellen? You want me to fall on my knees and beg you? Tear my hair out? Humiliate myself?"

"A simple apology would be nice."

"A . . . *what*?"

"An apology. For sleeping with my boyfriend. And having his baby."

Her breath left her. "It wasn't like that. It was *him*. He came after *me*."

"Really, Jane?" The bitter green edge of sarcasm that Ellen did better than anyone. "He raped you, really?"

"Well, no, but . . ."

317

"But nothing. It was your fault, every bit as much as it was his."

Jane could not speak.

"You could have stopped it, but you didn't."

She opened her mouth and closed it again.

"Don't ask me about this again, Jane."

Then, dead air on the line. The room telescoped before Jane's eyes. She had to drop the phone and lean against the table to keep from losing her balance. She sat on a barstool, laid her head on her arms, and closed her eyes until the room stopped spinning.

Ellen was absolutely, one hundred percent right. Jane *had* had a choice. It was true that Robert had been persuasive, but what she had done she had done willingly, with no thought of anyone but herself. Now, if the one person who might be able to help her find her son refused to help, perhaps it served her right. *Are You telling me no, Lord? Is that what You're saying?*

Sometimes, a closed door was just a closed door. She would have to make peace with that, and let it go.

⁓

In the interest of staying busy, Laura had taken on extra volunteer work at the homeless shelter. Since Thanksgiving, she had been helping to serve dinner every second week, but now she was there every Wednesday evening and some Saturday mornings as well.

"Their poverty is so hard to see," she said to Tracy one night as they finished mopping the kitchen floor together. "I realize that for some of them, it's a choice, and for others, it's a result of their choices, and for some, it's just plain bad luck. But it's hard all the same."

"And their material poverty isn't the worst of it," Tracy said.

"What do you mean?"

Tracy rinsed her mop in the bucket and wrung it out. "I mean their poverty of spirit. Have you noticed it yet?"

"I don't know. There's something there that I can't put my finger on. Maybe that's it."

"It's hard to maintain a sense of dignity when everything you get in life is a handout."

Laura, who had always taken pride in her own independence, said, "I suppose it must be. But what's the answer?"

"Well, I've been putting some thought into that. You know the shelter has the Christmas gift program for the kids, right? People in the community pick a tag off a Christmas tree at the bank or the hospital, and they buy whatever's on it: a boy's coat size five, or a pair of girls' sneakers size seven, or whatever, and they wrap them and drop them off here; then the shelter gives them out to the kids at the Christmas party."

"It's only June, and you're thinking about Christmas already?"

"I'm always thinking about the whole calendar. That's my job."

"Oh. Okay, I know the program you're talking about. I've bought gifts for it myself."

"Well . . . what if we did it differently?"

"How?"

"Like . . . what if instead, we took those donated items and put price tags on them. Nothing expensive: two dollars for a new pair of sneakers, say . . . like that. Something the parents could afford if they planned ahead. And the week before Christmas, we could open up a little store here at the shelter. The parents could come in and buy the gifts for their kids, at token prices, and then they would be from the *parents* instead of from the shelter. Wouldn't it give them a sense of dignity if they were the ones actually able to provide Christmas gifts for their children?"

"Not to be a pessimist here, but wouldn't some of the parents buy a pair of new sneakers for two dollars, then turn around and sell them on the street for drug money?"

"We could help the parents wrap and label the gifts here and say they have to leave them at the shelter until the Christmas party."

"I like the idea. A lot."

"I can't take credit for it, really. There's a shift going on in a lot of cities about the way we do charity. Some places are trying things like this and having great success with it." Tracy picked up the mop bucket and began to lug it to the sink at the back of the kitchen. "Of course, the board would have to approve the idea first."

"Do you think they would?"

"Probably." Tracy eyed her shrewdly. "If some enthusiastic, visionary person were to present the idea at the next board meeting and agree to coordinate the whole thing."

Laura eyed her back. "We could probably dig up a person like that, if we looked hard enough."

"Good. The board meets next Tuesday at seven o'clock." Tracy put an arm around her and gave her a squeeze. "They're going to love you."

One June morning, during her break at IHOP, Laura checked her voice messages and discovered that the urology practice she had applied to had called and wanted to interview her. She called back, set up an appointment, and then, queasy with anxiety, called Theo.

After her first week of AA meetings, Laura had asked Theo to be her sponsor, and Theo had agreed. "You're going to want to take out a restraining order on me," Laura warned, only half-joking.

Theo assured her that this was not the case, but it was true that Laura sometimes called her as many as three or four times a day.

"Try lavender oil," Theo might advise. "Studies show it's as effective as Ativan in calming anxiety." Or, "Go for a walk, and leave your money behind." Sometimes it was, "Let's meet for a walk." Sometimes she just listened as Laura talked her way through whatever stressor was before her at the moment. Always, Theo asked, "Have you gone to a meeting today?" Ninety meetings in ninety days: that was the goal. The day Laura got the phone call from the urologist's office was day fifty-one.

"I'm terrified," she confessed, when Theo had answered the phone.

"Why? You're more than competent."

"I don't know why. I haven't done this kind of thing— faced a new job, new people, a new challenge—without a drink in a long, long time. What if I fail?"

"What does *fail* mean?"

"Like . . . what if I can't do it?"

"Can't do . . . ?"

"What they expect of me."

"Such as . . . ?"

"I don't know. Medical billing. Coding. Insurance claims."

"Don't they have a billing office for that kind of thing?"

"I don't *know*!" Laura wailed at her.

"Laura, stop borrowing trouble. You have been an office manager before, and you did a fantastic job. Your last boss said so."

"That's true, he did. Before he fired me for drinking on the job."

"Have you been to a meeting today?"

Laura sighed. "Not yet. There's one at four o'clock, at the Catholic church on Mesa Street."

"And you're going?"

"Yes. I finish my shift here at two. I'll be there."

"Good."

"I might need to call you while I'm driving. You know, just through that section with the supermarket and the drive-through liquor store."

"I'll be here."

"I know. Thank you." Laura hung up, pulled a bottle of lavender oil from her apron pocket, and rubbed a drop into each temple. AA had a slogan—"One day at a time"—but they had it wrong, she thought. In reality, sobriety was about one *hour* at a time—sometimes one phone call, one *minute* at a time. She breathed deeply and, for this one minute, without a drink, straightened her shoulders and went back to work.

Laura was interviewed by not one but three urologists: a Sabrina Begay; an Alistair Gordon, who spoke with a Scottish accent; and a John White. Either they did not notice the strong scent of lavender about her or they were too polite to comment on it. In any case, when the interview was over, the three doctors exchanged discreet glances with one another, and then Dr. White said, "We'd be pleased to offer you the job, Laura, if it's what you want."

"You don't have to answer now," Dr. Begay put in. "Take the weekend to think it over, if you like."

"Oh no, I don't need to think it over," Laura said, unable to contain her smile. "I'd love to work here."

She had quit Parson's after the accident, on the advice of Theo, who pointed out that working at a place with a ready bar and a bartender willing to ply her with free drinks might not be in her best interests. At the moment, IHOP was her only job. She and the doctors agreed on a starting date that would allow her to give two weeks' notice at the restaurant, and Laura left the office feeling buoyant with hope and relief and, perversely, wishing for a glass of wine to celebrate with.

She called Theo. "Just need you to chatter in my ear as I drive by the grocery and liquor stores," she said. "I got the job, by the way."

"Of *course* you got the job. Congratulations. Good for you! Now . . ." Theo's voice became businesslike. "While you're driving, how about reminding yourself of some of the reasons you're choosing sobriety?"

"My life was unmanageable," Laura recited.

"And now?"

She thought about it. "It's nice to not hate myself when I wake up in the morning."

"Why don't you hate yourself in the morning anymore?"

"Because I haven't just consumed two thousand liquid calories. Because I still remember where I was the night before. Because I haven't destroyed any relationships by way of drunken phone calls or e-mails. Because I haven't killed anyone."

"All very, very good reasons."

"And guess what? I'm past the stores now and pulling up to my apartment. I think I'm safe."

"Excellent. Want me to stay on the line until you get inside?"

"No thanks, I'm good."

"Okay. Bye, Laura. And congratulations on your new job."

"Thank you."

"Go to that meeting."

"I will. I'm going." Laura hung up. Another hour safely navigated. It was enough.

21

THE NEW JOB FREED UP HER WEEKENDS, and Laura was surprised to find how eager she was to get back to church. Two months in AA, with its focus on "a higher power" and "God as we understood Him," had ignited her interest in the God that, she had to confess, she did not understand at all.

Her first week back, Theo met her in the parking lot. "I have to warn you about something."

Laura looked at her friend's concerned face, and knew. "Rob and Kendra are engaged, aren't they?"

"Yes. I'm sorry."

Deliberately, she allowed the regret to roll over her, letting herself experience it, not stanching or deflecting it as she had always done with deep emotion. "It's my own fault."

Theo searched her face. "Is it?"

"Yes, I think so. There was a time when Rob was interested

in me, but I was simply more interested in drinking. And in myself. Now, it's too late." It was painful to admit, yet there was a certain freedom to it, all the same.

"God is never late."

"No. No, I don't suppose He is."

"Come on in. A little worship is good for the soul." Theo linked her arm with Laura's, and together, they headed for the front doors. "Are you going to be okay?"

"I am. I really think I am." And she meant it. Later, she was able to hug both Rob and Kendra, admire the ring, and congratulate them with sincerity. It might have been nice to be standing in Kendra's place, she thought, but the timing had not been right. She let herself feel the pain of loss, and it did not overwhelm her. For now, she would count on the truth of which Theo had reminded her: *God is never late.* She would cling to this, because all the other options were unthinkable.

For Mitch and Amy, the return of warm weather and longer days meant it was time to redouble their efforts on renovating the house. Most evenings now, Amy left work at five o'clock, picked up supper for both of them at Amato's or the Hannaford deli counter, stopped home for a quick change of clothes, and met Mitch at the house by six. He had other contracting jobs to work during the daytime hours. "It would be nice if building your own house paid the bills," he often said ruefully, "but it doesn't." Inevitably, by the time he and Amy met, he was already coated in a fine layer of sawdust and tired out from a full day's work.

One June evening, as they settled themselves on the dusty floor to eat, he said, "Another month or two of this, and we should be done."

"Can you believe it?" Amy was rummaging in the paper bags she had brought. "It seems like you were just showing it to me for the first time. Here . . . Italian with oil on the side for you, and veggie with provolone on whole wheat for me. Napkins . . . water . . . large coffee for you." She finished setting out the food and went on. "It was such a huge, rotting mess when you bought it. I could hardly believe you'd ever make something of it, even though I'd already seen the magic you worked on the opera house." She paused. "You want to pray?"

"Go ahead."

They bowed their heads. "Thank You for this food, Lord, and the health and strength to do the work that's needed here. Amen. Anyway," she said, opening a bottle of water for each of them, "you've done just as beautiful a job here as you did there. You never cease to amaze me, Mitch."

"You really mean that?"

"Of course."

"Then . . . how about being amazed by me for the rest of your life?"

"I'm sure I will be." She took a long swallow of water.

"No, I mean like . . . 'til death do us part."

She lowered the water bottle. *"What?"*

"Marry me, Amy. If you will, I promise to keep amazing you for the rest of our lives."

For once in her life, Amy was speechless.

It was not as though she'd never considered it, she

thought, dazed. But they'd only been dating a few months. She'd thought that they would discuss the idea of marriage first, and shop for a ring together, and then eventually he'd propose. Never mind that she'd always found such a prospect anticlimactic. Wasn't it the way everybody seemed to do things? She looked around her, at the grimy floor and the wrappers from their sandwiches. It was Wednesday afternoon. Who got proposed to like *that*?

Yet . . . since the day she had realized she was in love with Mitch, a year and a half ago, there had never been any question in her mind that this was the man she was going to marry. She wanted to marry him. She couldn't *wait* to marry him! All at once, she was filled with a joy that bubbled up and out of her, of its own accord, in a laugh of pure delight.

"I *will* marry you, yes!" Shunting her food to one side, Amy rose to her knees and wrapped her arms around his neck. "Yes, yes, yes, yes, *yes!*"

He took her face between his hands and kissed her long and thoroughly. When at last he released her, he whispered, "I love you."

"I love you too."

"Wait—" He was digging for something in his front shirt pocket, and Amy let go of his neck to watch. It was a ring. An exquisite, milky-blue ring like nothing she had ever seen before.

"Oh—it's *beautiful!*"

"It belonged to Joe's wife. He wanted you to have it." Mitch slipped the ring onto her finger. It was too big. "We'll have to get it resized," he said apologetically.

"I don't care." She held out her hand and admired it from all angles. "It's absolutely perfect in every other way." She clasped both hands in front of her heart and said again, "I love you. And, Mitch—no. Never mind."

"What?"

"Nothing."

"No really, tell me."

"Just . . . thank you for not getting down on one knee. I was so afraid you would."

"Isn't the man supposed to get down on one knee?"

She waved dismissively. "That's what everybody does. It would have been too mainstream for words."

He pulled her close again. "I wouldn't dream of being too mainstream for words."

Coming up with meals that were soft enough for Leander to swallow without choking, but still palatable and high in protein, sometimes felt like a full-time job. They ate a lot of thick soups, because thin liquids could be as hazardous as solids. Tonight, Jane had made a beef stew and pulsed Leander's portion lightly in the blender.

"Here you go." She set the bowl down in front of him and tied a bib around his neck. "Puree of beef and root vegetables."

"My favorite."

She settled on the barstool beside him and took his hand. They bowed their heads.

"Father," Leander said, "thank You for providing so much for us, when there are people in the world who have so little. Thank You for the gifts of life and health. Teach us daily how to make the most of them, to gratefully accept what You have ordained for us without demanding more. Let us continually rediscover that You are enough and more than enough for our every need."

"Amen." Jane picked up her spoon.

Leander took a mouthful of stew. She watched him from the corner of her eye. One bite down.

"Amy and Mitch want DeShaun to cater the wedding."

"No kidding! Do you think he'll be up to it? I mean, how big a wedding are we talking about?"

"Not big, I wouldn't think. A hundred people? Fewer, probably. You know Amy: she doesn't want anything 'mainstream.'" She made quote marks in the air with her fingers.

"Will they get married at the church?"

"Who knows? They may decide to get married under a new moon in a forest clearing, with their hands clasped over running water, or some such thing. I'm asking no questions, just awaiting my marching orders."

"And the reception? DeShaun will need a kitchen to—" He choked, suddenly and violently. Beef stew spewed from his mouth, spraying the bar and the wall by the telephone.

"Leander!" Jane jumped up and pounded him between the shoulder blades with the heel of her hand.

His eyes watered and he dragged in his breath with a sound like the opening of a rusty gate.

"Throw your arms up over your head!"

He looked at her helplessly, gasping.

She managed to get one arm up and hold it over his head with one hand while she pounded his back with the other.

And then it was over. He slumped on his elbows, drooling, his shoulders heaving.

"Are you okay?"

"Shouldn't have tried to talk and swallow at the same time."

"Good advice for anyone."

He managed a shaky laugh.

Jane took a clean dishcloth from the drawer and wet it under the faucet. "Hold still."

He tipped up his face and let her wipe his mouth and his clammy forehead. "That feeding tube Dr. Gutierrez mentioned is starting to sound better and better."

She sat down on her stool, shaken, the cloth still in her hand. "How can you be so fearless about it all?"

His laugh was devoid of mirth. "I'm not fearless. I'm very afraid."

"Of what?"

"Helplessness. Dependency. Of one day not being able to breathe. It might be easier if I knew the end was going to be quick and painless. But it's not. Death is advancing on me in slow motion, and I don't get to miss a single step of its arrival. I'm afraid of that."

"But you face it with such courage."

Leander shook his head and stared down at the table. At last, he said, "What is courage, after all, but being afraid of what's in front of you and doing it anyway?"

Putting her palms on either side of his thin face, Jane gave him a long and lingering kiss.

"Well," he said, when she had finished. "It's not like I have any choice in the matter, but if that's the way you're going to be about it, I'll pretend otherwise."

In the second week of July, Laura attended the last of her ninety meetings in ninety days. Walking out of the ninetieth, she truly felt like a different person from the woman who had woken up on that deserted stretch of road three months ago, under a mess of tangled cattle fencing, and become convinced that her drinking had ended the life of a child.

She still had to go to meetings as often as possible, Theo reminded her. Together, they were working the steps. Daily, Laura acknowledged that she was powerless over alcohol. Over and over again, she surrendered her will to the care of God as the third step suggested, and was watching Him restore her to sanity. She had conducted what Theo called "the dreaded SFMI": the "searching and fearless moral inventory" described by AA's fourth step. She had gone through it all. Now, she was stuck on step nine.

It was time, Theo reminded her often. Time to make amends to the people she had hurt with her drinking. In theory, Laura could do this. In practice, it was more difficult, not least of all because she had not acknowledged to her family that she was an alcoholic. More than once, she rehearsed with her sponsor the list of people to whom she owed amends.

Ivy, whom she had unfairly blamed for her addiction problems.

Ivy's children, themselves products of an addicted mother, who had cringed in the face of Laura's drunken rantings.

Her parents, whom she had continually disappointed, worried, and neglected simply by virtue of being too drunk, too often, to show up.

Sephy, whose college graduation and wedding she had missed for no other reason that that she'd been too self-absorbed to bother.

She had missed David's wedding for the same reason, and after having committed to play in the band, had left all her siblings scrambling to replace her.

Then there were Max, her long-ago boss with whom she'd had an affair, and his wife, Carol. In her selfishness, Laura had thought nothing of stepping into their marriage and taking what she wanted for herself. This, perhaps, was not a situation where she could make direct amends. In fact, the ninth step specified making direct amends to those wronged "wherever possible, except when to do so would injure them or others." No, she and Theo agreed, best to leave Max and Carol out of it.

But there was still the farmer whose cattle fence she had ruined. There was Chris, her former boss, whom she had lied to—and therefore stolen sick time from—when she had been, in fact, too impaired to come to work. . . . The list went on.

"Who's the most difficult on that list?" Theo asked.

Unequivocally, it was her family.

Theo recommended she start with the easiest ones first.

A trip to the town hall in Tempe yielded land ordinance maps that gave Laura the name of the farmer whose fence she had destroyed. The next part was not so simple. She was reluctant to simply show up on this man's doorstep, admit wrongdoing, and perhaps put herself in a position to be sued and hounded for years to come.

Theo's husband, Evan, pointed her in the right direction. "Old Milton, who hands out the candies in church?

I'm almost sure he has a grandson who sells farm insurance. Why don't you talk to him about what kind of damages you might be looking at?"

Milton was delighted to help. She asked him on Sunday, and the following week, he came back with his grandson's name and phone number carefully inscribed on a piece of scrap paper.

"Thank you, Milton," she said, taking the paper from him.

"Not at all. I'm happy to help."

As she folded the scrap of paper, the printing on the back of it caught her attention.

AMVETS Post 5
3805 South 16th Str—

Three months ago, she wouldn't have thought twice about the idea that Milton was a person with a past, and probably an interesting past at that. Now, she said, "Milton, are you a veteran?"

"Oh yes." He leaned on his cane and smiled at her, a pink, fetid smile that still, somehow, brightened the room. "Screamin' Eagles, Hunnert-and-First Airborne. We parachuted into France on D-day, back in forty-four, west of Omaha Beach. Kept the Jerries at bay 'til the Fourth Infantry could get there by sea."

She blinked at him, her eyes suddenly full of tears. "You were a hero. I didn't know that."

"Well . . ." He patted her arm. "There's a lot we all don't know about each other."

Ain't that the truth, she thought.

"Have a candy." He thrust a gold-wrapped Werther's into her hand and tottered away, nodding and smiling at everyone.

According to Milton's grandson's best estimate, the sixty or so feet of fencing Laura thought she had damaged should cost about two hundred dollars to replace. Insurance had no doubt already paid for the repairs, but, as Theo reminded her, that was not the point of making amends. The next day, she went to the bank and withdrew the money in cash, wrote a brief, anonymous note, and left it in the farmer's mailbox.

Chris, her former boss, was a different matter. You didn't simply write an anonymous note saying, *I stole sick time from the company,* and leave it in someone's mailbox. Instead, mustering her courage, she called him one day and asked him to meet her for lunch.

They met at a vegetarian café that Laura had chosen for its proximity to his office.

"This looks dodgy," he said when they met. "No meat on the menu?"

She laughed. "There's a Chick-fil-A across the street if you'd rather."

His relief was palpable. "I could go for a Spicy Chicken Deluxe and some waffle fries."

"Let's do it."

She took his arm, and laughing, they escaped the vegetarian café and crossed the street to the Chick-fil-A.

"Ah, heaven!" Chris closed his eyes and took great, blissful gulps of the air.

They carried their trays to a corner booth, and Laura did not delay in bringing up her reason for calling. She told him of her journey since April, and finished by saying, "I want to confess that I lied to you a few times. First, when I told you I had food poisoning, and the second time, when I said I was late because there'd been a fire in my neighbor's apartment. The truth is, both times I was passed out and woke up too late for work."

His surprise was evident. "I never would have guessed that of you."

"I suppose I hid it well."

He chewed thoughtfully and swallowed. "Well . . . thanks for telling me."

"And . . . of course, I lied the first time you asked if I'd been drinking at work. And the second time, when I spilled wine all over the place."

"All right."

"That's it? I mean, can't the company require me to pay back the sick time I took?"

"I doubt it. In any case, I wouldn't pursue it, Laura. I'm just glad you're on the right road."

Grace. Everywhere she turned these days, there was grace. The tears that seemed so ready at all times sprang up again and filled her eyes. "Thank you. You're a far better boss than I ever deserved."

Chris caught her up on office news then, and asked about her new job, and when they finally said good-bye, he hugged her. "Good luck, Laura. I wish you the very best of success."

"Thank you, Chris. The same to you."

Far more difficult than parting with two hundred dollars

or making confessions to her former boss was the prospect of facing her own family. Three times that summer, Laura tried calling Ivy. Three times, she hung up before anyone could answer.

Her parents were even more difficult. She talked with them twice a month during July, August, and September, and was never able to broach the subject she had actually called to talk about. Making amends, it turned out, was the hardest step so far. She would have given anything to simply skip ahead to step ten, but Theo said no, she had to do it.

With that task before her, she bought a ticket back to Maine for Thanksgiving, and arranged the time off from work. To her surprise, Theo advised her not to tell her family she was coming.

"But why not? They'll be thrilled," Laura protested. "I haven't been home for the holidays in years."

"Hmmm. And how many times in those years did you promise your family you were coming home for a visit?"

"Oh." Thinking back on her history of showing up—or to be more precise, of *not* showing up—Laura felt her face flush. "Yeah. Okay, I get it."

"What do you get?"

"That I've done a lot of promising, but not a lot of de-livering."

"As alcoholics, we've often soothed our consciences by making grandiose promises, and later minimized the fact that we didn't follow through. We hurt people when we raise their expectations, then let them down."

"So this time, I won't promise; I'll just deliver?"

"I think that's a good idea."

Relieved, Laura put the subject of amends to her family out of her mind for the time being. In the slightly modified words of Scarlett O'Hara, she wouldn't think about it today. She'd think about it in November.

22

SINCE THE PHONE CALL WITH ELLEN, Jane had been faced squarely with an inexorable truth. She owed Ellen a real apology. She had to ask her sister's forgiveness, and that was something that should be done face-to-face. If it was in Jane's power to right the wrongs she had committed more than four decades before, then she would do it. Ellen might not forgive her. Even if she did, it might be too late for real healing between them. Maybe her sister would never help her find Steven. But none of that was the point.

She chose a rare Saturday when there was nothing on the calendar except three piano lessons. These, she rescheduled, and on the Thursday evening before, when the family was gathered at Ivy's for lasagna, Jane cornered David in the living room. "Could you come and stay with your father on Saturday? I have some errands that will take me all day."

"Definitely. No problem. I'll bring Libby along and we can watch the game with Dad on the big screen."

"What game?"

"Red Sox and Rays."

"Oh. Could you be there early? Say, seven o'clock?"

"Sure."

"And I might not be back until five or so." The best-case scenario was that Ellen would give Jane five or six hours of her time so they could really talk things over. Not that it was likely, but it was best to be prepared.

"Fine. If it's a nice day, maybe we can get some yard work done. Dad can sit outside and supervise."

"I'll leave a pot of chili for lunch." For some reason, she felt she might cry. It was this business of bearing secret burdens, she realized; they made you so fragile.

David squinted at her. "You okay, Mom?"

"Of course." She smiled. "I want to run down to Freeport and check on your aunt Ellen that day. You know she's had her own health problems, and she's more or less all alone."

"Oh. Well, give Aunt Ellen my—I mean, tell her I said hi. And I hope she's better, and all that."

How sad, Jane thought, that David could not say *Give Aunt Ellen my love.* Was there a person left in the whole world who loved Ellen? Jane was not certain she herself could say it with complete honesty anymore. Perhaps her love for her sister, gone unnourished for so many years, had simply starved away. "I will," she told David with a heavy heart. "I'll tell her you hope she's better."

On Saturday, she awoke to the first hard frost of the season. The grass on the lawns glittered as though strewn with diamond dust, and when she went out for the paper, the air was pierced with autumn, as sharp and clean as glass.

She used the time in the car to prepare what she would say. *I'm sorry about what happened all those years ago, Ellen.*

No, that would not do. It had not just *happened*; she had been fully complicit. Willing. Eager, even.

I should never have done what I did with Robert.

Too vague. Had she not always taught her children that a true apology must contain a confession not only of the hurtful action, but also of the motives behind it?

God, help me to find the right words. Help me to find the courage. But it was not just courage to ask Ellen's forgiveness that she needed. It was courage to face the fact itself of what she had done, and why.

She had blocked it out for so long. When it came to avoiding unpleasant truths, was there ever a greater champion than Jane Darling? Ahead, she saw a tiny clam shack, closed for the season. She pulled into the empty lot and put her car in park.

What is courage but being afraid of what's in front of you and doing it anyway?

The first time it had happened was on a sweltering August night. Ellen was home for the summer, and Robert had been invited for the weekend. Her parents had gone to bed, but Jane stayed up with Ellen and Robert to watch Johnny Carson. She kept her eye on them as they sat on the couch, holding hands. Curled in her father's recliner, Jane seethed with jealousy, her short nightie pulled as high up over her knees as she dared without risking a reprimand from her sister.

When *The Tonight Show* was over, Ellen said, "Isn't it time you were in bed, Jane?" Unable to think of a way to refuse,

Jane dragged reluctantly off upstairs. It was too hot to sleep. She lay awake on top of her covers, restless and resentful, trying to get cool and thinking of Robert. They had not had more than a minute or two alone that day, and she was fraught with the need to be kissed by him.

And then, as though her thoughts had summoned him, she heard a soft tap. In the pale wash of moonlight that streamed through her open window, she watched the door open a crack, and Robert slipped through.

Jane sprang up like a jack-in-the-box. "What are you doing?" she hissed. "You can't come in here!"

"I can't help myself." He came to her and took her in his arms. "I can't stop thinking about you, Jane." He kissed her in a way he never had before. It was a deep, intentional kiss, and she flamed into life.

It was a kiss that told her this time they would not stop until they finished.

After that, each weekend that Robert visited was marked by nightly visits to her bedroom. From time to time, Jane wondered if Ellen was doing this with him too. But it was never more than a passing, idle thought. Ellen would never. Prim, boring, sanctimonious Ellen was not that kind of girl. Which was why Robert visited *her* room instead.

And then came that day, between Thanksgiving and Christmas, when she discovered she was pregnant. She waited until May, when it became too difficult to hide the evidence of her burgeoning stomach any longer. She had not even told Robert yet, but she confessed everything to her mother because she thought they would make Robert marry her. She knew that he did not love her. Once, she had gotten up the nerve to say it aloud to him, when they were alone in her bedroom. *I love you.* He had gone completely still and silent, then had pushed her roughly away and left the room. After that, she knew that as long as she never said it again he would come back, would keep on visiting her. And he did. Foolishly, she believed that once they were married, he would come to love her. But her parents did not make him marry her: no one even suggested such a thing. Instead, Robert was banished from their lives forever. Ellen shrieked unspeakable names at her and took to her room, where she threw herself across her bed and sobbed violently for days. On the final day of eleventh grade, Jane was packed up and sent to Aunt Sophie, in Boston. She came back at summer's end, no longer pregnant, and no mention was ever made of it again. At least, not in her hearing.

Regret, Jane thought now, sitting in her car, in the parking lot of the clam shack, was surely the heaviest burden a person could bear in this lifetime. Confession and forgiveness, the only hope of relieving it.

I'm sorry, Ellen. I took what I wanted when it wasn't mine to take, and I hurt you in the process. It was the worst thing I've ever done. Can you forgive me?

She was nauseated with dread, but there was no way around what was ahead. Courage was being afraid, but doing it anyway. She put the car in drive, pulled back onto the road, and kept moving forward.

∿

Ellen's begonia and marigold borders were brilliant in the morning light. The frost had not reached this far south, and the leaves of the sugar maple on Ellen's front lawn were only beginning to be touched with pink at the edges. Somewhere in the branches, a chickadee called.

If Ellen was surprised to find her sister on her doorstep, she did not show it, beyond a raising of her eyebrows and a sardonic, "Well, if this isn't a nice surprise."

Jane stepped inside the pristine living room. A vase of pink hydrangea had been added to the side table since her last visit, but otherwise, everything was exactly the same. "I need to talk to you, Ellen. Could we sit down?"

"Of course. Can I take your coat?"

"I'll keep it on for a minute. I'm a bit chilly." In truth, the coat felt like protection against any arrows Ellen might choose to fling at her. Jane followed her into the kitchen, where a cereal bowl and a banana peel next to the sink were the only signs of disorder.

"Do you want something to drink?"

"Just water would be fine." Jane pulled out a chair at the table and sat.

"Well?" said Ellen, when she had delivered the water and sat down across from her. "What's the matter? Is it Leander?"

"No. I . . . I've come to ask your forgiveness, Ellen. I'm long overdue."

Silence.

She plowed ahead. "When I slept with Robert all those years ago, I did it with no thought for you. I only cared about what I wanted. I hurt you badly; I know that."

Ellen's face had gone white. She stared at the oak table-top, with her hands in her lap. For a long time, she did not speak. When she looked up at last, there was a softness in her face that Jane had never seen before. "I would have married him, you know." Her sister's voice was wistful. "We would have had a family together. It was what I always wanted: Big, noisy celebrations, like your family has. Kids going off to college and coming home for the holidays. A houseful of grandchildren. Instead, I have . . . this." She gestured around her at the kitchen. At the emptiness. "You didn't just hurt me, Jane. You ruined my life. And then you went on to have everything you ever wanted. Everything *I* ever wanted." She said it calmly, with no malice. A simple statement of fact.

You didn't have to let it ruin your whole life, Jane thought. But she could not say it aloud. That was not why she was here. Instead, she said, "Oh, Ellen, if you only knew how sorry I am."

"That doesn't change anything now."

Tears slipped down Jane's face. "Is there anything I can do or say to get you to forgive me?"

For a long moment, Ellen did not speak. At last, she shrugged, a resigned and hopeless gesture. "Go home, Jane. Just . . . go home to your family, and your happy life, and leave me alone."

Jane opened her mouth, but her sister looked away.

"Go on."

"Ellen—"

Ellen stood and strode into the living room, where she opened the front door and waited.

Jane felt an inch tall. Picking up her purse, she obeyed

the silent injunction. At the door, she stopped. "*Please*, can't we talk about this?"

"It's too late. Sometimes, it just is."

Jane could see, by the set of her sister's mouth, that this was her final word. She stepped out into the morning, and Ellen closed the door behind her.

The slant of sunlight had not changed. The begonias and marigolds still gleamed with dew. She pulled her coat tight around her. She had not even been there long enough to take it off.

❧

The first week in October, a gastroenterologist placed Leander's feeding tube. Jane had long dreaded this day. She was squeamish by nature, and the thought of a rubber tube implanted in the wall of her husband's abdomen was almost more than she could bear to think about. As well, it represented a certain point of no return, and everything in her wished that they could put it off for one more week. One more day, even. But his weight had dropped to a state of near emaciation, and there was no longer any denying the need for it.

It was accomplished in a morning, and the clinic nurse arranged for a home care agency to come out two days later and teach them how to use it. To Jane's surprise, David insisted on being there for the session. "Someone else in the family should know how to take care of Dad too," he said. "It doesn't all have to be on your shoulders."

The home care nurse was a rugged, garrulous young man named Blake. As he was setting out his equipment on a TV tray in the living room, they learned that he had already hiked the Pacific Crest Trail, kayaked the Allagash Wilderness Waterway, and spent three summers crabbing off the coast of Alaska before he decided to go to nursing school, "because I wanted to try something *really* interesting." He was a bit larger than life, perhaps, but Jane had no doubt they were in good hands.

He taught the three of them to clean and care for the tube and to use the pump that would administer Leander's feedings. "He should still eat whatever he can by mouth," Blake told them. "Calories and nutrients from real food are always preferable to manufactured stuff. But these are high-protein feedings, and they'll help him gain back a good bit of the weight he's lost." It was all much simpler than Jane had feared, and Blake did not leave until he was satisfied that both she and David could do it all successfully.

Later that night, when Leander was asleep, she slipped from the bed and made her way down to the living room. There, in the half-light from the streetlamp outside, she ran her fingers over all the equipment. The pump, the bags and tubing, the case of liquid feedings. The gauze and long Q-tips, and rolls of paper tape. The newest members of the family. Picking a can of formula out of the case, she hefted its cool, smooth weight in one hand, then sat in Leander's recliner, holding it, and let her mind wander.

Her thoughts were interrupted by the sound of the chair lift's motor. She turned to see Leander gliding down the stairs, looking ghostly in the half-light.

"I didn't mean to wake you up," she said.

"I don't think I was sleeping all that soundly." The chair stopped, and he reached for the walker that he kept at the foot of the stairs. He came to stand in front of her. "What are you doing?"

"Oh, just thinking."

"About formula?"

She smiled and set the can down on the TV tray. "About everything, I guess. All the changes."

They fell silent, cloaked in the intimacy of darkness.

"You know what we haven't done in a long time?" he said at last. "We haven't danced."

"Not since the night before Sephy's wedding."

"Shall we?"

She smiled. "I would love that."

He turned his walker and, crossing the room to the sound system on the bookcase, selected a CD. "Slow fox-trot?"

"I think so."

Acoustic guitar filled the air. She went to join him, and he set his walker to one side and took her in his arms. "You may have to lead a bit," he said. He draped both arms over her shoulders like a teenager at a high school dance. "And I'm afraid you'll have to prop me up."

"We'll make it work."

"Life's a dance, you learn as you go,
Sometimes you lead, sometimes you follow."

They stumbled. "Let's try it in half time." That worked better. He was heavy against her shoulders, but she adjusted her stance, and they danced on.

"Don't worry 'bout what you don't know,
Life's a dance, you learn as you go."

Halfway through the song, Jane could tell he'd had enough. They stopped and stood in one place, swaying with their arms around each other until the music ended.

Gently, Leander kissed her on the forehead. "Best dancing partners in the world," he said. "Some things never change." Leaving the walker where it stood, he leaned on her all the way to the stairs, and they went up to bed together.

❧

Jada and Hammer were seeing a therapist in Quahog once a week, and Ivy and Nick agreed, with a cautious loosening of anxiety, that they were beginning to see a calmness in their son that had been lacking before. He seemed more settled, less frenetic. Rarely now did he fly into a fury, and it was sometimes clear that he tried to think before he spoke. The school board had allowed him to stay in school, under certain provisions, and so far this year, he had shown no signs of making trouble.

Midmonth, Libby had an ultrasound, and David announced the news one Thursday night at family supper. "The Darling X chromosome continues to prevail: it's a girl!"

"Yes!" Jada jumped up and punched the air. "A girl cousin!"

Hammer said in disgust, "Man, that sucks."

Ivy was mortified. *"Hammer!"*

"Sorry," he muttered. Then, to his parents' astonishment, he added, "I mean, congratulations. I guess a girl would be pretty cool too."

❧

At first, Sephy read the e-mail with a sense of unreality, but the second time through, she felt a faint rustle of excitement.

Why not? To her right, the young local man who was waiting for the computer began to drum his fingers on the table. He looked distinctly cross.

"One more second," she told him with a smile. "I just need to print something; then I'm done."

He smiled back in a flash of white teeth, with an appreciative leer at her red hair and white skin. "No problem, beautiful." His English was strongly accented. "Hey, let me buy you a Coca-Cola."

"Oh, my husband'll be along any minute," she said firmly. "But thanks anyway." She hit *Print*, waited until she heard the answering rattle of the printer behind the counter, then logged out. "It's all yours." She felt his eyes on her, more curious than threatening, as she went to the register, where she paid thirteen Namibian dollars for her printout and a cold bottle of Coke. She took them to a corner table, out of the man's line of vision. Her Irish coloring always turned heads here. White people were common enough, but redheads were another story. It was certainly a different experience for a once-overweight girl who had spent most of her life feeling invisible. She no longer had the extra weight to hide behind, and after a year of living in Africa, she had finally learned to accept the idea that people were simply going to stare at her wherever she went.

Justice was at the post office, picking up veterinary supplies. She read the e-mail again while she waited for him. He came through the door at last, and all eyes turned his way as well: a bespectacled white man a head taller than anyone else in the café, and carrying a cardboard box under one arm. There was no hiding in a crowd for either one of them in this country.

He sat down and set the box under the table.

"Did you get everything you wanted?"

"Yep. It's all in the Land Rover except for this." He nodded at the box. "This is stuff I didn't want to leave out in the heat."

Sephy pushed the printout across the table. "Read this. It's from David."

Justice picked up the paper and adjusted his glasses. As he read, his eyebrows rose.

"What do you think?" she asked, when he was done.

"What do *you* think? Do you want to?"

"I'd love to. I could surprise everyone for New Year's and stay long enough to see my new niece or nephew born. Plus, I'd like to see Dad and reassure myself that he's okay. Who knows how many more times I'll get to see him? David says he'll pay for my ticket."

Her husband frowned and glanced across the table at her still-flat belly. "Are you sure you feel up to it?"

"I think so." Automatically, she put a hand to her stomach. "Mostly it's just being tired that bothers me, and I can sleep all I want back in Maine."

"It'd be good for you to get a full night's sleep for a change." He scrutinized the e-mail again. "But a full month? That's a long time to be apart."

"I know, but it's such an expensive and exhausting trip. It would hardly be worth it to stay less."

He sighed. "I'll miss you."

"I'll miss you too."

"Not as much as I'll miss you."

She understood. "It's always harder to be the one left behind."

He reached for her half-empty bottle and took a sip. "Can Dr. Marta and Glory get along without you for a month?"

"They'll manage. Glory can take care of the straight-forward births by herself, and she has her daughter to help her now."

He reached for her hand. "You'd better tell David to book your ticket then."

"I wish you could come with me." She put a hand to her stomach again and smiled. "With *us*, I mean."

෴

"Mom, let Amy and Libby and me cook Thanksgiving dinner this year," Ivy said during an early morning phone call. "It's our year to go to Nick's family on Thursday, but we could have everyone over here to celebrate on Friday."

"Your house isn't nearly big enough for all of us, Ivy."

"We manage for family supper nights well enough."

"Yes, but we have to sit on the couch and folding chairs to eat, with our plates balanced in our laps. That's no way to have Thanksgiving dinner."

Ivy was not about to give up so easily. "The table, if we put the leaves in, can fit eight. I have a card table to add to the end, and if you bring yours too, that's seating for twelve, right there."

"Counting Grammie Lydia, there are twelve of us, but what if Laura comes? Then we're thirteen."

"We can squeeze. Besides, when's the last time Laura showed up for Thanksgiving?"

"Hope springs eternal. But, Ivy, the tables would stretch all the way into your living room. No, it's a kind thought, my dear, but let's have Thanksgiving at number 14, like we always have."

"But it's so much work for you. You're already out straight with your piano students, practicing for whatever monster-size holiday production Amy has up her sleeve. And taking care of Dad—"

"A delightful state of affairs," Jane said firmly. "My piano students are a pure joy, as is anything I do for your father. As for the Holiday Extravaganza, I have the music well under way, thank you."

"Come on, Mom!" Ivy's tone was skeptical. "You're not worn out at all? Not even a little?"

"Well . . . ," she conceded. "Maybe a bit. But in the best way. I like being busy."

"I'll tell you what," her daughter said. "Why don't we eat at your house, but you let the rest of us do the cooking and cleanup? You can spend the day doing nothing. Sit in the family room with your feet up and watch the game if you want." Without rancor, she added, "Just like the men."

Jane no longer felt the need to protest as she might have done a year ago. "I think I would like that. Are you sure you girls wouldn't mind doing all the work?"

"Mind? I love making a mess in someone else's kitchen."

"You'll keep an eye on Amy? We don't want anything too outré for Thanksgiving dinner."

"Tempeh and farro casserole," said Ivy knowingly. "Or seitan with wheatgrass gravy."

Jane was alarmed. "She won't try to make all that?"

"Don't worry; we'll keep Amy on a short leash. It'll all be

very traditional, you'll see. You'll have nothing to do that day but enjoy yourself."

Jane had her doubts about this, but to her surprise on Thanksgiving Day, Ivy turned out to be right. At first, she had to fight the pull of the kitchen. She had no qualms about the quality of her girls' cookery, but it seemed necessary to be sure they were planning to serve the cranberry relish in the crystal bowls and were not putting the sterling in the dishwasher.

"I'm *not*, Mom!" was Amy's exasperated cry, the third time Jane mentioned it. "Chill *out* about the silverware."

Leander appeared in the doorway. "Come on, Janey, give us some music, and leave the girls to do the dirty work in here."

"Yes," said Amy. "*Do.* Go sing!"

"That would be so nice," added Libby, more kindly.

"Sing together, like you used to!" Ivy joined her voice to the hue and cry, and Jane could see she was outnumbered.

"Well . . ."

"Better yet, I'll get my guitar, and we'll dust off some of our old duets." Leander took her by the elbow with one hand and, with the other on his walker, steered her gently out of the kitchen.

"Do you think you can still play?" she asked him.

"I'll give it the old college try."

But he couldn't. "I just don't have the coordination," he said, before he had even finished tuning.

Jane had never been much of a guitarist herself. "The piano it is, then." They sat side by side on the bench. "How about this one?"

"Why do birds suddenly appear . . ."

"The Carpenters!" Amy's ecstatic voice rang from the kitchen.

Leander joined Jane on the next phrase. His voice lacked the old strength, but her husband could still harmonize like nobody's business.

She smiled at him through a great rush of tenderness. How many times had they sung together, over the years? She dropped out and let him take the next stanza. He had always claimed it as his to sing.

"On the day that you were born the angels got together
And decided to create a dream come true . . ."

As always, when there was music, Jada materialized, soon followed by David.

As the final chord died away, Jane looked at her son and granddaughter. "Any requests from the peanut gallery?"

"'Long Black Veil'!" said Jada promptly. David had introduced her to the song the summer before, and she was fascinated by it.

"It's not really a piano piece, sweetie."

"Uncle David can play it on the guitar!"

Jane raised her eyebrows at her son. "David, would you do the honors?"

"My pleasure." David picked up his father's guitar and gave an experimental strum. He adjusted a tuning peg or two and strummed again. "That's better."

"Ten years ago on a cold dark night,
Someone was killed 'neath the town hall light."

"No Johnny Cash!" cried Amy, from the kitchen.

"Ignore her!" Ivy called. They heard her say sternly, "You do not need to voice your opinion about *everything*, Amy."

Jane smiled.

David nodded at Jada, and she joined him with gusto.

"She walks these hills in a long black veil
She visits my grave when the night winds wail . . ."

They sang through three Frank Sinatras and a Stephen Sondheim and, at Jada's request, "Over the Rainbow." David and Jada gave a creditable rendition of "No Woman, No Cry," which was loudly applauded by Amy, who should have been mashing the potatoes.

Ivy came to stand in the doorway. "One more, then you can all come to the table."

"How about 'Leaving on a Jet Plane'?" Leander suggested.

Jane knew it well.

"All my bags are packed,
I'm ready to go.
I'm standing here outside your door . . ."

The tears that were always so close to the surface welled up and overflowed. Jane played on, but she could no longer sing.

Her husband and son carried on without her.

"So kiss me and smile for me.
Tell me that you'll wait for me.
Hold me like you'll never let me go."

Amy appeared behind them and slipped her arms around her father. From the corner of her eye, Jane saw that her daughter's face, too, was wet with tears.

"If two people love each other there can be no happy end to it." It was true. In the end, Jane thought, no matter how wonderful the experience, there was nothing like love for breaking your heart.

They were halfway through their pie when Jane heard the front door open and close. "Hello?" she called. The chatter around the table stopped. "Hello?" she said again. She pushed back her chair to go and see, but she was saved the trouble when their visitor appeared in the doorway.

"Laura!" she gasped.

The room erupted into a clamor of exclamations and questions. Through it, Jane watched her daughter in silence.

Laura was different. She had not, as yet, said a word, but it was as plain as day that something had changed. Didn't the Bible say, *"A person's wisdom brightens their face and changes its hard appearance"*?

Jane held her arms open.

For the first time in years, her daughter hugged her as though she meant it. Then Laura was laughing and crying at the same time. "It's good to be home," she said, and there was none of her old stiffness or hauteur in it. Just a kind of lightness that Jane had never heard from her before. It was joy, she realized. The kind that comes from being free of something malignant that has long had a hold on you. Laura pulled away and eyed the remains of Thanksgiving dinner on the table. "Although it looks like I'm a little late."

"You're never late if you're coming home," Jane said.

"WELL, MOM," SAID IVY, "I never thought I'd see the day when Jane Darling would serve take-out Chinese food at her New Year's Eve party." They were in the living room, setting up the folding chairs and tables from the church. "I feel a little at odds with no cooking to do."

"I thought I might let go of some of the work this year."

"Whatever will the neighbors say?" Amy waggled her eyebrows.

"Shut up, Amy." Ivy's tone meant business.

"I was just joking."

"Well, I think it's a great idea—Ow!" said Libby. She lowered herself carefully into a folding chair and rubbed her bulging belly. "Just Braxton-Hicks contractions," she said to Jada, whose face had momentarily lit up. "Your cousin won't be here for weeks yet. Anyway, it's not the food that's important, it's being together. That's what everyone really comes for."

"I wanted Butter Side Up to cater it; they do such a nice job. But they were already booked," Jane said. "And there will be other years to do it the way I like." Her throat ached just saying it, because of what it meant, but it was the truth. And if you believed God was good, then truth was not anything to be afraid of. Or rather, you might be afraid of it, but that didn't mean you couldn't face it with courage anyway.

The doorbell rang. "Jada, go get the door, would you, honey?" said Jane.

Jada looked at Ivy in alarm, and Jane saw Ivy give a fractional shake of her head. "I . . . I can't," said Jada, a bit desperately, Jane thought. "I . . . have to go to the bathroom!" She fled the room.

Jane frowned. "Ivy? What's going on?"

But Ivy had pulled out her phone and was staring at it with great concentration. "Hang on a second, Mom . . . text from Laura. It's a long one."

Amy seemed to be deeply engrossed in making sure the edges of a tablecloth hung evenly. Libby had put her feet up on another folding chair and was clearly going nowhere.

"What are you all up to?"

Nobody answered.

The doorbell rang again. Throwing up her hands, Jane went to answer it.

She saw the flash of red hair before the door was completely open, and her heart gave an answering flash. *"Sephy!"* Then she was in the arms of the daughter she had not seen in a year and a half and weeping tears of pure delight.

"You bad children!" she cried, laughing, as she came back into the living room with her arm around Sephy's waist. "You all knew about this and no one breathed a word." She caught sight of Jada, who was peering around the doorjamb, from the hallway. "The bathroom!"

Jada ran across the room and flung herself at her aunt. Ivy, Amy, and Libby piled into the mix, and then the Darling women, who had never learned the art of talking by turns, were all clamoring to be heard at once. At last Jada clapped her hands to her ears. "I can't understand a word anybody's saying!" she shouted

The clamor stopped.

"That's better," Jada said, a trifle sternly.

Sephy held Libby at arm's length and looked her up and down. "Look at you!" she said to the girl who had been her best friend since childhood. "You're so . . . *pregnant*!"

"That I am."

"Well," said Sephy, "you and I have something in common then."

Then they were off again, and nobody heard a word anyone else said for quite a long time.

When Libby had said that no one at the party would care what they ate, her words were more prophetic than she knew. To Jane's surprise, her friends and neighbors, for so many years accustomed to pâte à choux and caviar at her New Year's parties, did not bat an eyelash at finding egg rolls and chicken fingers from The Lucky Panda instead. DeShaun and Penelope had come through with a magnificent fruit display, though, and there was still champagne, as always, so in Amy's wry words, all was not lost.

It was after ten thirty when Leander came and put his arm around his wife. "There's someone at the door for you," he said in her ear.

"Well, bring them in!"

"She's not here for the party. She just wants to talk to you."

"Who is it?"

"Ellen."

Her heart began to race. "At the front door?"

"Yes. Better get your coat. She said she won't come in." He gave her a nudge in the right direction.

God, direct this conversation, Jane prayed, as she took her long wool coat from the closet and pulled it on.

Ellen stood on the sidewalk, in a down jacket and knitted hat, a very picture from the L.L.Bean catalog. "Hello, Jane."

"Ellen! Won't you come inside?"

"No, I'm not staying."

Jane waited.

"The cancer is back."

Grief and sorrow settled over her, as familiar by now as a well-worn blanket. Jane knew better, however, than to try to hug her sister. "I'm sorry to hear that. Is it . . . is it bad?"

"They found a spot on my liver, and two on my lung. Yesterday I had a PET scan. Yes, it's bad. It's everywhere."

"Oh, Ellen!" So much sadness, for so many different reasons. "Did they say how long?" The old Jane would never have asked such a question, but she had looked the worst squarely in the face this year, and there were no longer any answers to be afraid of.

Her sister's voice was matter-of-fact. "Six to nine months. They said I could have palliative chemotherapy, and it might give me an extra three months. I've decided not to do that."

It seemed there would be no end to tears in this new year either. Jane let them flow without apology; Ellen could sneer if she wanted.

But Ellen only said, "I wanted to bring you something." From her shoulder bag she pulled a business envelope and held it out. "It's the name and address of the people who adopted your son, back in 1972."

Jane stared. "But . . . but the records all burned. They told me that."

Ellen shook her head. "The records may have burned, but Aunt Sophie knew the family. They were from Lexington; it was a private adoption. I heard her and Mum talk about it more than once." She gave a shaky laugh, and Jane watched her breath puff out, white and explosive under the streetlight. "I sometimes wondered if maybe Mum knew I was listening and hoped that someday I'd tell you."

She felt sure she was in a dream.

"When Mum died, I found this among her papers." Ellen nudged the envelope toward Jane's hand.

Jane closed nerveless fingers around it. "Mum died eighteen years ago. Are you saying you've had it all this time?"

"Yes."

She looked at the unsealed envelope. In her mother's handwriting was her name, as she had seen it so precisely scripted a thousand times before. *Jane*. "I'm afraid to look inside."

"Don't you want to know?"

She nodded, unable to speak.

"Do you want me to tell you?"

She nodded again.

Ellen's voice was gentle. "His name is Arthur Bly. He's an oral surgeon in Delaware. He has a wife and two sons."

A wife and two sons. She was a grandmother again. Would she never run out of tears? "How do you know all that?" she managed.

"You can find anything on the Internet, if you have a place to start. And I had this." Ellen nodded at the envelope. "It's all written down in there."

Jane's throat was clogged and aching. She could not have said a word had her life depended on it.

"Happy New Year, Jane." Her sister touched her hand with one gloved fingertip, then turned and walked down the sidewalk to where her car was parked along the curb.

Jane watched her get in and pull away. *Thank You,* she breathed to God. *Thank You.*

She was suffused with a kind of quiet joy. With a certainty she could not explain, she knew that whatever the envelope held, it would lead her to something good, when the time was right. She tucked it into her coat pocket and gave it a pat. She would open it later tonight, when her guests had gone. And in the morning, she would tell Leander the whole story. He would help her decide what to do. Meanwhile, she had a houseful of family and friends waiting for her, and a party to get back to.

There was so much of life left, both to sorrow over and to celebrate. She was rich beyond measure.

Epilogue

THE BIRD CHOIR in the crab apple tree was putting on a particularly fine performance this morning. It was the kind of glorious June day when all of creation seems to sing its heart out, and from the white wicker chair on the screened porch, Jane savored every note of it. Her heart was both empty and full today, but that was no longer anything new. She had become accustomed to this, in the months since her husband had died. To the fact that sadness could coexist with joy, that the pain of loss could commingle with gratitude for all she still had. They were not contradictions: they were equal and opposite truths existing together like parallel railroad tracks running in the same direction.

Once he'd gotten the feeding tube, Leander had rallied, and they had him for five more years. Those years had been an unexpected gift. But the previous winter, he had caught a cold, which turned into pneumonia. A week later, he was simply gone, having slipped beyond the veil into the next world as quietly as he had lived in this one. On the day of his funeral, the church had been packed to standing room only, with the people who loved him. They said good-bye to him on a February day, when the earth was iron-hard with winter, but they left his burial until spring.

Today was the day.

Jane was halfway through her second cup of coffee when Laura appeared in the doorway to the kitchen. "You okay, Mom?" Her daughter's face, once perpetually hard and resentful, now radiated sweetness. As well, there was depth there: the kind that is only carved by patient perseverance through suffering.

Jane thought about her answer. "Mostly, I think. I'm mostly okay."

Laura came and sat down in the chair beside Jane's. "You know what I was remembering just now?"

"What?"

"The way Dad used to make us sing as a family in front of the church. I dreaded it so much: I just knew we'd mess up and humiliate ourselves. But we never did, and everyone loved it so much that I was always glad we'd done it in the end."

"That's right."

"Dad always pushed us beyond what we wanted to do toward what we were *capable* of doing instead, because he knew where the real reward lay. What a lesson for life that was."

Jane reached for her daughter's hand and gripped it, wordless.

After a moment, Laura said gently, "We should leave soon."

"All right." Jane carried her cup to the kitchen sink and gathered her sweater and purse. On the hall table glowed a large arrangement of yellow roses in a vase. She paused to touch one satin petal as she passed. Among them, a card read:

*Our thoughts and prayers are with you. Arthur, Kate, Caleb &
Ethan.* Her oldest—and newest—son and his family. How
kind it had been of them to remember the burial today. She
followed Laura to the car. Her daughter had flown in the day
before, leaving her husband back in Phoenix to tend his urology practice. Alistair and his twelve-year-old son had come
east with Laura in the winter, for the funeral, but this time
she was alone, and Jane was selfishly grateful to have her all
to herself for a week.

The burial plot was in a corner of the small cemetery,
bordered on one side by a pine wood and on another by a
quiet access road. As Laura pulled to one side of this road
and parked, Jane saw that most of the family was already
gathered. She got out of the car. Three small figures detached
themselves from the crowd and barreled toward her: David's
girls. Five-year-old Anna was in the lead, with three-year-old
Natalie and Nicole trying their best to keep up. Straight up
and over a grave they ran, while a hugely pregnant Libby
attempted a feeble, "Girls! Don't run in the cemetery!"

The girls either did not hear or did not pay attention. Tackling Jane and Laura around the legs, they cried,
"Grammie!" and "Aunt Laura!" Their joy seemed somehow fitting, and Jane was grateful for its leavening effect. It would not
do to be too gloomy today. Leander would not have liked it.

Sephy's children, who did not know Jane as well, hung
back. There were seven of them, all African children whom
Sephy and Justice had adopted from orphanages in the past
five years. In spite of their reticence, Jane kissed them each
in turn, from fifteen-year-old Sylvia down to two-year-old
Lazrus. Sadly, Sephy had never yet succeeded in carrying a

baby to term, but she and Justice were coming to grips with this. "God wanted us to have these children instead" was the view they chose to take.

"Ivy and company not here yet?" Jane asked.

"Late, as usual," said Amy. She and Mitch were still cheerfully childless, because Amy maintained that "the arts program is more than enough baby for me."

"Mom, the funeral director and burial crew want a word with you," said David. He took her elbow, but Jane hesitated.

"Bring Grammie Lydia, too, won't you, David? This is her son we're burying, after all."

David obligingly fetched his grandmother from the folding chair where she sat with Lazrus on her lap. She leaned on her grandson a good bit as she walked now. Leander's death had taken its toll on her, and although neither Lydia's health nor her mind were what they had been even a year before, her cheerful optimism had not faded one whit. She came slowly, her smile as sweet as summer rain. Together the three of them went to speak to the men beside the mound of dirt and the deep, rectangular vault they had placed that morning.

Jane had, until this moment, avoided looking at the casket, but it was time now. She turned her eyes to it without flinching. The children had chosen it well: a plain box of polished cherry, with iron handles. On the lid, over their father's heart, was engraved a simple treble clef. She stepped carefully onto the green turf carpet around the grave and touched the smooth, cool wood. *Hello again, my love.*

They had met her first year out of college, when she was teaching music in Portland and renting a room from a crazy old woman. One evening, Jane had answered the doorbell to find a shy, gangling young man with long hair and oversize glasses standing there. The old lady was his grandmother, and Leander had stopped by to check on her. His grandmother, enthralled by a television show, had all but ignored him. Taking pity, Jane invited him in for coffee.

Vaguely, she heard David, beside her, working out details with the funeral director.

They had talked for hours in the kitchen that first night, over cups of instant Sanka, and only when he left did Jane catch sight of herself in the window and realize, with horror, that her hair had been bound up in hideous pink rollers the whole time. But he kept coming back. Nine months later, he proposed to her, before he had so much as tried to kiss her. *"For better or worse, in sickness and in health, 'til death us do part,"* they had promised one another.

Now, more than forty-two years later, here they were.

"If two people love each other there can be no happy end to it."

Her son touched her on the elbow, and she realized that the mournful-looking funeral director, in his dark suit, had stepped discreetly back. Whatever had been discussed, it had been decided without her.

And here came the rest of them now, moving en masse toward the grave site. She saw that Ivy's family had arrived. Jada, twenty and home from college for the summer, broke away from the group and hurried ahead, carrying her violin and bow.

"Hello, beautiful girl," Jane called, holding out her hands to her granddaughter. "Are you playing something for us today?"

"I'd like to, if you wouldn't mind."

"Mind? Your grandfather would love it."

She watched the rest of them approach. Sixteen-year-old Hammer, every bit as tall as his uncle Justice, had his hands stuffed self-consciously in his pockets. She saw that DeShaun's tall, blue-eyed fiancée had come with him, and that Ivy carried a large sheaf of yellow daffodils in her arms.

"Ready to start?" said David.

"Here." Ivy began handing around daffodils. "To send Dad off with."

There would be no eulogy; that had all been said at the public service in February. Instead, they formed a half circle around the coffin. On Jane's right, Ivy reached out and took her hand. To her left, Jane looked down at her fragile, sorrowing mother-in-law, and took her hand as well.

Beyond the graveyard, the pine forest was alive with the bright warble and trill of sparrows. From somewhere, a hint of apple blossom drifted through on an unfelt breeze. The sun across Jane's shoulders was a benediction. In the silence that settled, Jada stepped back from the group and lifted her violin to her shoulder. The first notes of a familiar hymn flowed forth into the warm spring day as though eager to take their rightful place in the music of the spheres.

> *God be with you 'til we meet again,*
> *By His counsels guide, uphold you,*
> *With His sheep securely fold you;*
> *God be with you 'til we meet again.*

God be with you. It was the very origin of the word *goodbye*. And was that not the crux of the matter? If God was with you, then good-bye was not forever. *'Til we meet again.*

One by one, Jane's children and grandchildren stepped forward and laid their daffodils on the coffin.

'Til we meet, 'til we meet,
'Til we meet at Jesus' feet,
'Til we meet, 'til we meet—
God be with you 'til we meet again.

Jane was the last to lay her daffodil atop the rest of them. Such a big pile. *Look what's come from us, Leander! All this life, all this love.*

One of the workers stepped forward to turn a handle. The coffin lowered into the vault, and the music reached up, up, beyond the tips of the pines. *God be with you.*

As one, her family turned and walked toward the cars, their faces wet with tears and wide with smiles. Grief and joy: the bitter notes and the sweet.

'Til we meet again.

Meanwhile, there was a picnic waiting for them back home. The music of life beckoned, *Dance on! Dance on!*

DISCUSSION QUESTIONS

1. Jane believes God will heal her husband and that accommodating his disease shows a lack of faith. Leander and the Darling children believe they must accept the diagnosis and make plans and changes accordingly. Whose perspective did you agree with? In moments when there seems to be a tension between acting in faith and accepting reality, which direction do you lean?

2. At a crisis point in her faith, Jane thinks, "That same God, who was supposed to be able to heal all your diseases, in the same sentence claimed the ability to forgive all your sins. . . . Was everything she'd based her life on a lie? Had she invested her soul in a snake-oil God: attractive, promising, but ultimately powerless?" Have difficult circumstances or unanswered prayers ever led you to question God's power or goodness? How does Leander's analogy about simple math versus calculus speak to such doubts? (See chapter 7.)

3. Laura is a master at covering and rationalizing her drinking, yet there are still consequences—big and small—she can't prevent. And the person she could be, shown in her compassion to Milton or desire to help at the homeless shelter, gets buried by bad decisions. How did you feel watching Laura repeat her destructive patterns? If you or someone you love has wrestled with addiction, did this ring true to your experience?

4. Ivy and Nick confront light and heavy issues with two of their children, often lamenting that parenthood doesn't come with clearer guidelines. What did you think of their decisions about Jada's desire for cornrows and to have a middle-school boyfriend? About Hammer's demonstrations of anger? If you're a parent, can you relate to Ivy's doubts when she wonders, "What did she know about being a mother? The answer was as plain to her as it must be to the rest of the world: nothing"? When have you seen hope that, as Ivy prays, your "nothing" will be enough?

5. As her last child moves out, Jane reflects that "for thirty-four years, she had been a mother with children at home. Tomorrow, what would she be?" How does Jane's identity shift over the course of this story? Have you felt a similar loss of identity in the face of a major life change? How did you respond? How did it ultimately change you?

6. Jane and her sister, Ellen, have a distant relationship due to a decades-old hurt—one Jane knows is her fault.

But while she once made efforts to fix the relationship, Ellen's rejection "served only to rub the wound ever more raw," so they've fallen into a pattern of avoiding each other. What does Jane ultimately realize was missing from her attempts to make things right? Do you think it would have made a difference, years ago, in how Ellen responded to her?

7. While Laura wishes she could be "one of those people who effortlessly loved Jesus," she cherishes her autonomy and knows that "either God was in control of your life, or you were—never both at once." How easy is it for you to give God control over your life? Do you believe there are people who effortlessly love Him? Or is faith, to some degree, a struggle for everyone?

8. As Leander's disease progresses, the Darling children begin to step in and make decisions for their parents, which often means going around Jane. Are they right to do this? Were there any points where you felt they crossed the line?

9. Both Laura and Jane are keeping big secrets from the people in their lives. If each woman came to you with her secret, how would you advise her? Should both secrets be brought into the light? Why or why not?

10. Amy is an entrenched vegetarian, yet she makes steak for Mitch; Mitch has flatly refused to dance, yet he takes lessons from Joe. Think of a time when you catered to the interests of someone you love despite

your own preferences, or when someone did the same for you. What was the result?

11. After months of avoidance, Jane finally feels prompted to think the "what-if" of Leander's death through to its conclusion. Where does this lead her? In moments of fear, do you tend to run or to wrestle through your fears? Have you ever faced circumstances that meant your life wasn't going to turn out the way you'd expected? How did you respond?

12. Leander's mother, Lydia, tells her daughter-in-law, "There is no such thing as 'the good old days.' . . . The 'good old days' are always now, Jane." Is there a period in your life that you consider "the good old days"? What do you think of Lydia's assertion that "we make our own contentment wherever we are"?

13. Leander asks, "What is courage, after all, but being afraid of what's in front of you and doing it anyway?" How do you see this type of courage demonstrated by Leander? By Jane? By Laura? By the other Darling siblings?

14. The epilogue to this story takes us several years into the Darling family's future. What was as you expected? What surprised you?

TURN THE PAGE FOR
AN EXCERPT FROM

AVAILABLE IN BOOKSTORES AND ONLINE

TYNDALE
FICTION

www.tyndalefiction.com

CHAPTER

1

NICK WAS GOING TO HATE HIS BIRTHDAY GIFT. Even as she taped down the ribbon and set the wrapped package on the kitchen table, Ivy Darling was already sure of this. It was a book of Mark Strand's poetry, and although she had gotten her husband a book of poetry every birthday for the six years they had been married, he had yet to open the front cover of one of them. That did not stop her from hoping, nor from appropriating the books for her own collection after a decent waiting period. Gifts, she thought, sometimes said more about the giver than the receiver. When you gave something you loved and thought beautiful, you were inviting another person into your world. You were saying, *Here is something that brings me joy. I want to share that joy with you.* She couldn't help it if her husband had never been all that much into joy sharing.

To be fair, it was also important to give something the other person actually wanted. With this in mind, Ivy had bought Nick a year's membership to the Copper Cove Racquet and Fitness Club, which he would love, as well as a bathrobe, which he needed.

She would give him all three gifts when he got home from work, before they went to his parents' house for dinner. She did not want him to unwrap the things she had chosen in front of his mother, who would be hurt if her own gifts were upstaged. Nor did she want to give them in front of Nick's sisters, who would diminish them by being bored with everything.

She found the broom and swept up the scraps of wrapping paper, then emptied the dustpan into a plastic shopping bag and carried it to the back porch. The five o'clock sunlight flashed off the windows of the vacant house next door, making her squint. The place had been empty as long as she and Nick had lived here. It was a depressing sore on the pretty neighborhood: the house bleached and shabby in the summer sunshine; the grass growing high against the warped and splintered front steps, unstirred by human movement. A faded For Rent sign sagged in one window. She turned her back on it and went inside.

Ivy was sprinkling chopped nuts on top of the iced birthday cake when she heard Nick's car in the driveway. She met him at the door with the remains of the frosting and a kiss.

"What's this?" he said, frowning at the sticky bowl.

"It's your birthday icing. Did you have a good day?"

He stepped around her and set his briefcase under the hall table. "It was all right. What are you doing?"

"Making your cake. We're going to your parents' for dinner, remember?"

He ran a hand through his thick hair. "I forgot. I was hoping to go for a run. What time do we have to be there?"

"Six o'clock. I wanted you to open your presents here first."

He went through to the kitchen and began washing his hands, eyeing her over the top of his glasses. "You're not wearing that to my parents' house, are you?"

Ivy looked down at her T-shirt. It was yellow, with a picture of half a cup of coffee over the words *Half Full.* Below that, her faded cutoff shorts ended in ragged hems. "What's wrong with what I'm wearing?"

"You look like a slob."

She gave him a gritty smile. "You say the nicest things."

"I'm only saying it for your own sake. Don't you have anything with a little shape to it?"

"Yes, but it wouldn't be nearly as comfortable."

"Come on, Ivy."

"All *right*, I'll change before we go. But if we're going to be on time, you have to open your presents now."

He dried his hands and turned to survey the packages on the table. "What'd you get me?"

"A present you'll love, a present you need, and a present you'll learn to love."

"Hmmm . . . ," he said, pretending to think. "A Porsche, a Porsche, and a book of poetry."

"Close. Come on, you have to open them to find out."

She sat down across from him while he opened the packages. She had been right on all scores. He was indifferent to the poetry, satisfied with the bathrobe, and pleased with the gym membership.

"There's no excuse for me now," he said, pulling his wallet from his back pocket and tucking the envelope into it. "I'll be in shape before you know it." Nick, who was already in great shape, was the only person Ivy knew who thrilled to the prospect of more self-discipline.

"You look great just the way you are," she said, standing and kissing him on the top of his head. "But if you want to half kill yourself in the gym five days a week, knock yourself out. We should probably leave in fifteen minutes, unless we want to give your mother an ulcer."

"Okay. Just . . . don't forget to change your clothes."

Her smile felt grittier this time but she did as he said, reminding herself that he was only trying to protect her from his mother, who had a finely tuned radar for her daughter-in-law's every shortcoming, fashion or otherwise.

❧

Nick's parents lived across town, never a long drive even at the time of day considered rush hour in bigger cities. For three-quarters of the year, Copper Cove was small even by Maine standards so that now, in June, when the tourist season had filled the beach houses and hotels along the water, the town still did not feel crowded. Cars moved lazily along High Street, pulling in at Cumberland Farms for gas and at Blue Yew Pizza or Salt Flats Seafood for supper. Traffic, Ivy was sometimes surprised to realize, was just not something you ever thought about here.

At Nick's parents' house, his sister Tiffany met them at the door. "Oh, it's you."

"We thought we might show up," Ivy said. "You know, since it's Nick's birthday party and all."

"Happy birthday," Tiffany said grudgingly. "Everyone else is already here. The guys are watching the Red Sox game with Daddy." She aimed this bit of news at Nick. "And Mumma's in the kitchen," she added, a clear hint that Ivy should join her mother-in-law there and *not* join her sisters-in-law at whatever they were doing.

They followed Tiffany through to the kitchen, where Nick's mother, Ruby, was emptying fish market bags into the sink.

"Oh, wow, lobster," Ivy said. "Thanks for having a birthday, Nick."

"Nicholas!" cried his mother, turning from the sink and drying her hands on a towel. "Happy birthday, sweetheart. Thirty-two years old!" She tipped her cheek up for a kiss, smoothed down the sleeves of his shirt, and straightened his collar. Ivy had an image of a plump, pretty wasp buzzing around a pie at a picnic.

She set her cake carrier on the sideboard. "I brought the cake."

"Wonderful." Ruby brushed imaginary lint from Nick's shirtfront. "What kind is it?"

"Carrot cake with cream cheese frosting."

Ruby turned from Nick and eyed the cake as though Ivy had said it was made of sand and seaweed. "Oh . . . ," she faltered. "I *was* afraid one cake wouldn't be enough for all of us, so I *did* ask Jessica to make a cheesecake to go along with it." She smiled damply at her son. "You know how Nick loves cheesecake."

Ivy felt her nostrils flare. As a matter of fact, Nick did *not* love cheesecake. He preferred *carrot* cake. It had been one of life's long lessons, however, that objection was always futile with her mother-in-law. She felt her mouth twitch in a rictus grin. "Can I help with dinner?" she managed to choke out.

"You might set the table. We'll use the good china. The cloth is on the ironing board in the laundry room. You'll have to put the leaves in the table, but Nick can do that for you."

Nick trotted off to find the extra leaves and Ivy, having retrieved the tablecloth, began counting out forks and knives from the sideboard. The familiar task calmed her. "It's quiet around here," she observed as her mother-in-law added salt to two enormous canners full of hot water on the stove. "Where is everyone?"

"The men are watching television, and the girls are looking at Jessica's new scrapbook."

Nick had three sisters. His family, the Masons, and hers, the Darlings, had always belonged to the same church. In her growing-up years, none of Nick's sisters had seemed to object to Ivy as long as she had been just another girl in youth group. But from the moment Nick had brought her home as his girlfriend, Jessica, Angela, and Tiffany had circled like a pack of she-wolves guarding their kill. Together, they presented a solid, hostile wall designed to keep Ivy on the outside. They whispered with their heads together when she was in the house and stopped talking when she came into a room. They planned sisters' shopping trips in front of Ivy and did not invite her to come along. When Nick and Ivy were engaged and a family friend hinted that the groom's sisters might want to throw the bride a shower, they'd been offended and told Ivy so, with the greatest of umbrage.

Ivy liked people—all kinds of people—and in general, people liked her back. She was unused to having her friendliness met with such stubborn, protracted rejection, and at first she had been bewildered by Nick's sisters' antagonism. "They hate me for no reason," she had once wailed to her own twin sister, Laura. "I can't understand it. It's like being in eighth grade all over again." By the time she and Nick had been married a year, however, she was wiser. Nick's mother doted on him, and this was at the root of her daughters' treatment of Ivy. Nick's sisters were not horrible to her because of anything she personally had done; they simply resented Nick for being their mother's favorite and were punishing Ivy for being his wife. It was a situation Ivy had gotten used to.

More or less.

When the lobsters were ready, Ruby sent her to call the family to the table. She found Jessica, Angela, and Tiffany upstairs, in Angela's old bedroom, looking at what appeared to be paint chips from a hardware store. When they saw Ivy, they stopped talking.

"Yes?" said Angela, who was Nick's middle sister, tucking the paint chips under one leg.

"Your mother says come to the table." She would not give them the satisfaction of being asked what they were doing.

"Thank you, Ivy. Tell Mother we'll be there in a moment." Angela stared at her until she took the hint and went back downstairs to the kitchen.

Nick's father, Harry, had muttered a long, rambling grace and they were all cracking their lobster claws when Angela rapped her fork against her water goblet. "Everybody! Everybody," she called, half-rising from her chair. "Vincent and I have an announcement to make."

"Angela, that goblet is *crystal*," her mother protested.

"Well, it's an *important* announcement, Mother."

Some blessed instinct of self-preservation warned Ivy of what Angela was about to say and gave her a heartbeat of time to compose herself for it.

"Vincent and I—" Angela looked around the table in delight—"are *pregnant*!"

It was evident that Jessica and Tiffany already knew, but that to the rest of them, it was a complete surprise.

"And here's the best part," Angela said, looking at Vincent and gripping his hand atop the tablecloth. "We're having the baby at *Christmas*! My due date is the twenty-fourth, but the doctor says if I haven't had it by then, he'll induce me so the baby can be born on Christmas Day. Won't that be so much *fun*?"

ACKNOWLEDGMENTS

It takes a community to write a book. My deepest thanks to those who answered my questions, corrected my misconceptions, and generously shared their knowledge with me when I asked. I am an imperfect listener, and this is a work of fiction, so if the things I have written in this book do not accurately reflect reality, I plead artistic license and ask your forgiveness.

First and foremost, I am grateful to John and Linda Gregoire, who took the time to talk with me about their own journey with ALS. Your generosity, humor, and hope are an inspiration I will not soon forget. To find out how John and Linda are making a difference in the lives of other families affected by ALS, and to learn how you can get involved, visit www.hope-jg.org.

Thank you also to: Dan Austin, who taught me a thing or two about collectible Mustangs; Brennen and Rick Behimer, for answering questions about the arcane world of cattle fencing; Chef Geoffrey Boardman, director of the culinary arts program at Southern Maine Community College for showing me around and sharing his enthusiasm about the program; Ray Hepler, for sharing his firsthand knowledge about soup kitchens and homeless shelters; and Beth Taube, for bringing me up to date on the going rate for piano lessons. My husband, Sgt. Tim Gardner, deserves special thanks for answering my questions about the law and police procedure and just generally thinking I can do anything I set my mind to.

Finally, my thanks to the multitude of anonymous men and women who continue to light the path of recovery by sharing their experience, strength, and hope with others who have lost their way.

About the Author

CARRE ARMSTRONG GARDNER was raised in the Adirondack Mountains of New York—the most beautiful of all possible settings—where she spent countless hours rambling through woods and beside streams, making up stories with herself as the heroine. It wasn't until well into adulthood that she realized not everyone in the world sat at traffic lights or passed the time in doctors' waiting rooms creating plots and characters in their heads. It was that realization that first gave her permission to think of herself as a writer.

Carre's favorite stories have always been those about the ordinary lives of ordinary people. She believes every life is a fascinating drama, every person is the hero of his or her own story, and Carre's desire is to tell those kinds of stories in a way that makes readers love her characters.

As a teenager, she was a pianist, and a teacher encouraged her to attend conservatory as a performance major. But in a fit of altruism she decided to become a nurse instead—a career that had the double benefit of assuring a paycheck while allowing her to pursue music and writing in her spare time.

From 2007 to 2010, Carre lived and worked in Russia with her husband and children. Now she lives in Portland, Maine, where she works as a nurse at a local hospital. She has three teenagers and two rescue dogs, which is far too many. (Dogs, not teenagers.)

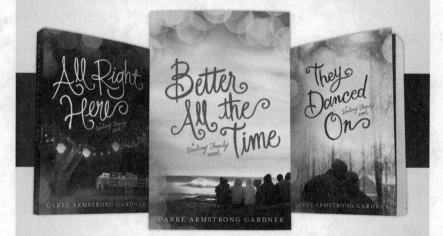

TYNDALE HOUSE PUBLISHERS IS CRAZY4FICTION!

Inspirational fiction that entertains and inspires

Get to know us! Become a member of the Crazy4Fiction community. Whether you follow our blog, like us on Facebook, follow us on Twitter, or read our e-newsletter, you're sure to get the latest news on the best in Christian fiction. You might even win something along the way!

JOIN IN THE FUN TODAY.

 www.crazy4fiction.com

 Crazy4Fiction

 @Crazy4Fiction